"Natalie Walters is a fabulous new voice in inspirational romantic suspense!"

**Susan May Warren,** *USA Today* bestselling author

"Natalie has crafted an addictive cast of characters dropped into a national security nightmare. Expect to keep turning the pages long into the night. I loved every minute."

**Lynette Eason,** award-winning, bestselling author
of the Danger Never Sleeps series

"Natalie Walters nails it with *Lights Out*—heart-pounding suspense and details so real you have to wonder who she's really working for."

**James R. Hannibal,** award-winning author of *The Paris Betrayal*

"*Lights Out* delivers on all the things I want to see in romantic suspense. The stakes are as high as they can be with an international terrorist threat that has the potential to kill thousands and impact millions. The simmering romance is complicated by past betrayal and present doubts. And the secondary characters—a diverse group with intriguing quirks and exceptional abilities—bring both humor and depth to this thrilling first installment of The SNAP Agency series from Natalie Walters. I can't wait to read more!"

**Lynn H. Blackburn,** award-winning author
of the Defend and Protect series

"Readers who pick up *Lights Out* should prepare for a book that will keep them turning pages long past their personal lights out. It is a compelling story of international intrigue and implications. It's also a story of second chances if the hero and heroine are willing to embrace them. Romantic suspense readers will fall in love with Brynn and Jack as they race against time and the terrorists to figure out who's killing Egyptian nationals and has painted a target on Brynn's back. A compelling must-read from one of my always reads, Natalie Walters."

**Cara Putman,** bestselling, award-winning author
of *Flight Risk* and *Lethal Intent*

# LIGHTS OUT

# Books by Natalie Walters

**HARBORED SECRETS SERIES**

*Living Lies*
*Deadly Deceit*
*Silent Shadows*

**THE SNAP AGENCY**

*Lights Out*

THE SNAP AGENCY

BOOK ONE

# LIGHTS OUT

## NATALIE WALTERS

Revell

a division of Baker Publishing Group
Grand Rapids, Michigan

© 2021 by Natalie Walters

Published by Revell
a division of Baker Publishing Group
PO Box 6287, Grand Rapids, MI 49516-6287
www.revellbooks.com

Printed in the United States of America

Library of Congress Cataloging-in-Publication Data
Names: Walters, Natalie, 1978– author.
Title: Lights out / Natalie Walters.
Description: Grand Rapids, Michigan : Revell, a division of Baker Publishing
    Group, [2021] | Series: The snap agency ; #1
Identifiers: LCCN 2021003893 | ISBN 9780800739782 (paperback) | ISBN
    9780800740610 (casebound) | ISBN 9781493432004 (ebook)
Subjects: GSAFD: Suspense fiction. | Mystery fiction.
Classification: LCC PS3623.A4487 L54 2021 | DDC 813/.6—dc23
LC record available at https://lccn.loc.gov/2021003893

Scripture quotations are from THE HOLY BIBLE, NEW INTERNATIONAL VERSION®, NIV® Copyright © 1973, 1978, 1984, 2011 by Biblica, Inc.® Used by permission. All rights reserved worldwide.

Baker Publishing Group publications use paper produced from sustainable forestry practices and post-consumer waste whenever possible.

21   22   23   24   25   26   27       7   6   5   4   3   2   1

They always say be careful what you say around an author because it could be used in a story. This book and series are dedicated to my friends in those three-letter agencies who were less than careful.

## 1

**Ma'adi, Suburb of Cairo, Egypt**
**3:17 PM Tuesday, January 13**

Seif El-Deeb watched the noisy trio of American boys cross the street away from Cairo American College. The international school had just let out for the afternoon, and the sound of privileged children laughing about their day mingled with the horns of waiting drivers and taxis trying to navigate the afternoon congestion.

"Seif, you will send your child to this school?"

The old man behind the wooden counter of the koshk laughed at his own question, causing the cigarette at his lips to bounce. Seif ignored the vendor as the man continued chuckling while he straightened the rows of chips and snacks.

Toying with the metal band around his finger, Seif shook his head. Mostly to himself. The vendor already knew the answer, which was why he was laughing. CAC was a private school with a tuition rate only the wealthiest Egyptians could afford. And foreigners. Especially Americans. Or the grandchildren of the former president.

Seif eyed the twelve-foot cement wall surrounding the school. Iron paling embedded at the top gave the impression of a fortress, as did the private security officers positioned at the front and rear entrances to monitor every student, parent, and visitor entering

9

or leaving. Their presence had doubled since the protests against President Talaat began more than a year ago. A promise by both the school and the president that these children would be kept safe at all costs.

A fortress of education and protection Seif's son or daughter would never know.

Lighting his own cigarette, Seif stepped aside as the three American boys walked up to the street kiosk and purchased candy. One of them, a blond, set the Egyptian bill on the worn and splintered counter just as a breeze came through, lifting the money into the air. The boys laughed as the old man scrambled for it, none of them helping as they took their candy and walked away.

Seif hurried, following the money as it floated in the air over the busy intersection. Ignoring the blaring horns and shouts, he stepped into the street and caught the bill before it flew farther away.

"Shukraan." The vendor thanked him before tucking the money into a box. "These kids do not know how fortunate they are. Allah has blessed them, and they forget it can be taken away."

Taking a long drag from his cigarette, Seif continued to watch the boys make their way to a large, white Toyota Sequoia. The heavy *thunk* of the door closing after they crawled in told Seif the vehicle was weighed down with armor.

*Allah has blessed them.* What about him? Or his wife, Heba? Or his child she was currently carrying? Where was Allah's blessing for them? He'd been good. Memorized the tenets of the Quran, fasted for Ramadan, never missed a call to prayer, and yet here he was working two jobs just to provide for his family.

A business card burned inside his pocket. Fishing it out, he rolled the curled edges back and studied it.

Mahmoud Farag
+20 010 1251 175

Just a name and a number. The card left on the seat of his work van three weeks ago. Seif assumed it was job related, someone wanting zabbato. A favor. Street deal. As a technician for Nile Telecom, Seif had discovered that while he did not possess the kind of education protected by a fortified wall, he possessed a job that gave him favor. Those zabbatos were what kept Heba happy, safe, and out of the squalor he grew up in.

He dropped the finished cigarette to the ground and smashed it with the toe of his shoe. "Mas salāma."

"En shallah," the old man responded.

*God willing.* Yes, that was the hope, but the funny thing about hope was that it seemed to be selective—blessing those with the wealth to afford it, the power to control it, or the will to fight for it.

Seif's mobile rang. The number matched that on the card. Did he have the will to fight for it? For himself, he'd grown up suffering. For Heba, she was not his first choice when it came to their arrangement, but he was slowly coming to love her. But for his child, the ever-present ache in his chest pulsed. For his child, he'd do whatever it took.

Spitting the taste of tobacco from his mouth, Seif answered. "Al salamo aalaykom."

"Wa aalaykom al salam," the male voice responded to the greeting. "White car, to your left. Pink dice in the mirror. Get in and say nothing."

The Arabic came out low and raspy, and Seif had to press his mobile phone to his ear to hear over the din of the growing traffic around him. "White car?"

"White car. On your left. Pink dice. Say nothing."

The clipped response sent a chill across Seif's shoulders despite the rare twenty-one-degree temps keeping the city balmy this early in the year. Searching to his left, Seif panicked. There were nearly a dozen white cars parked or moving in and around the school's barriers. Shading his eyes, he searched for pink dice, but the glare of the sun was too much, forcing him to cross into the chaotic traffic.

A black car screeched to a halt, nearly clipping him, and the driver stuck his head out of the car, cursing. Seif pressed the fingers of his right hand together, a gesture asking for the impatient driver to wait. The irate man inched forward, horn honking until Seif moved far enough over that he could steer around him, leaving a string of curses in his wake.

"You have one minute," the voice said.

"Wait. Please." Seif moved quicker, eyes scanning every car for pink dice. His heart pounded in his chest with each passing second. A ticking time bomb threatening to erase the hope he had allowed to enter his heart.

Seif thought he saw a flicker of something pink. He pushed aside a woman in a burka, no apology on his lips—only a prayer to Allah that this was it. In a near jog, Seif worked his way around a large SUV, ignoring the driver eyeing him with suspicion. He searched every white vehicle around him, until finally—he saw them. Pink dice.

He yanked the back door open and dropped inside, a breath of relief spoiled only by the thick cloud of cigarette smoke filling the vehicle.

"I am here." The words were meant for the man on the phone, but the phone remained silent against his ear. "Hallo? Hallo?" Seif pulled the phone away to look at the screen just as the driver jerked the car forward and into traffic.

*Say nothing.*

Leaning back in his seat, Seif replayed the instructions in his mind. He glanced at the rearview mirror and caught the driver eyeing him. Redirecting his attention out the window, Seif watched as the driver efficiently maneuvered around traffic, taking him out of Ma'adi.

Where was he going?

His mobile vibrated in his hand. Turning it over, he saw Heba's face smiling up at him. He brushed his thumb, fingernail dirty from his last job, across her cheek. He was doing this for her. For their child.

The car hit a pothole, hard, sending Seif bouncing in the back seat. He grabbed the overhead handle and braced himself as he monitored the changing scenery outside the car. They were no longer traveling in the city, crammed with high-rise apartments, shops, and markets. The landscape outside his window had shifted from overcrowded city to arid wilderness.

The wadi. He was being taken to the desert.

Fear sent his heart pounding in an erratic rhythm. He bit down on his lip, holding back the urge to ask questions, find out where he was being taken. The road turned rougher. Large ruts cut into the dirt road sent the car jostling so much that Seif feared he was going to be sick.

Thankfully, the car began to slow as another vehicle approached in a cloud of dirt. When it drew nearer, Seif saw that it was an old pickup truck. The road was narrow, and Seif expected his driver to pull to the side, but he continued going forward much faster than was necessary.

Bracing himself, Seif tightened his grip on the handle when the car lurched to a stop directly in front of the truck. Dust swirled around the vehicles, both drivers remaining where they were, but it was not an impasse.

A man jumped out of the back of the truck and started toward their car. The door at Seif's side was yanked open.

"Come," the man in the cream galabeya commanded. The turban on his head extended over part of his face, exposing only his dark eyes.

Seif got out of the car and wiped his sweaty palms down the back of his jeans. He noticed the man eyeing his choice of clothing with contempt. In the city, Seif blended in, but out here his modern appearance made him stand out. The white car reversed, turning around before barreling back in the direction they had come from.

"Come."

Seif looked around. The wadi stretched out before him, no sign of life or a way to cry for help should he need it. Heba's pregnant form filled his mind, and Seif quieted his nerves. This was for his child.

He followed the man and was directed to climb into the bed of the truck with him. Seif did as told and hung on for his life as the truck sped toward an unknown destination. He quickly realized why the man had his face covered as dirt and rocks flew into the air. Lifting the collar of his shirt over his nose and mouth, Seif prayed once again that he had not misplaced his hope.

Unsure how much time had passed, Seif saw a village dotting the landscape in front of him. The truck slowed to a stop and everyone got out, leaving him to follow. A herd of camels chewed their cud near the small, corrugated metal homes. A trio of stray dogs barked at him while kids played a game of fútbol.

"Seif El-Deeb?"

"Naam." Seif nodded at an older man with a long gray beard and a cane coming toward him. "Farag?"

He shook his head. "Your wife is pregnant? The baby is not well, yes?"

"Yes."

Heba hadn't been feeling well, and her mother took her to the hospital. The doctor did a sonogram and saw the deformity and suggested aborting the child. Heba was inconsolable. Seif promised her he would work harder to pay for the doctors. Whatever his child needed, he would provide . . . except. Except Seif was already working hard to afford the lifestyle Heba was accustomed to. How could he add more work? Her family would look down on him, convinced they had been right about him the entire time.

The man's eyes were cloudy, but the wrinkled skin around them seemed to sag in sadness as he reached into his robe and pulled out an envelope.

"It is good what you are doing for your child. Inshallah, all will be well."

Taking the envelope, Seif nodded. He let the contents fall into his hand, and his knees went wobbly. An Egyptian passport. A mobile phone. And an airline ticket to Washington, DC.

*I am going to America?*

Seif glanced up, trying to make sense of what was happening—what was being asked of him.

"I don't understand. Heba, my wife, will she not go with me?"

Another shake of the head. "You will travel to America. You will be contacted when you land"—a gnarled finger tapped the cell phone in Seif's hand—"by a man who will give you further instructions."

"La'a." Seif nearly shouted, the act drawing concerned glares from a pair of men standing nearby whom Seif hadn't noticed. Each carried an automatic rifle over his shoulder. "No." In a previous phone call with Mahmoud Farag, he promised he would get Heba the right doctors to help her, to help our child. He looked down at the airline ticket. "She should go to America with me. They have the best doc—"

The man held up a hand, silencing Seif. "Your wife and child will have the best doctors here in Egypt, but first you must do your part."

A car pulled around from the back of the village, exhaust darkening the air behind it.

"You want to help your family, yes?"

"Yes."

"Then go. Inshallah, all will be well."

The idling car's engine rumbled behind Seif like a sinister growl. Dropping the passport and phone back into the envelope, he climbed into the passenger seat. As the village grew smaller with every mile, Seif studied the airline ticket he held in his hand.

Passports, like the education at Cairo American College, were a privilege. Obtaining one took money, connections, and luck. But the ticket to America . . . that was a blessing. Was Allah blessing him? Finally?

Seif's eyes caught the date on the ticket. *Today!* He swiveled in his seat to look over his shoulder at the specks in the distance. In the back seat was a black backpack.

"The bag?"

The driver slid an unfriendly glance his direction. "Yours."

Seif pulled the backpack across the seat and opened it. Inside were a pair of jeans, a T-shirt, a map of Washington, DC, and a roll of American dollars. He zipped the bag and pushed it to the floor between his feet.

Seif had no idea why he was going to America or what his part was, but if this was Allah's blessing, he would accept it—and ignore the feeling he had made a deal with the devil.

## 2

*Homegrown Violent Extremists don't look like the stereotypical terrorist. HVEs can be anyone who subscribes to the grievances held by global jihadists against the United States of America. They can be your next-door neighbor, your child's teacher, or the teen who delivers your pizza. That's what makes them so dangerous— their ability to blend in and deceive you.*

Brynn Taylor exhaled, reading over her notes again. Leaning back, she rubbed her eyes. The glow of the computer screen was giving her a mild headache. Or was it the stress of the last week?

For the last seven days she'd been briefing intelligence officers from seven countries on the new look of terrorism, reminding them that homegrown cells posed the biggest threat to defending their homelands against terrorism. No one wanted to suspect their friendly neighbor might be building a bomb in their basement or plotting a mass shooting, but more and more, that was becoming the reality.

Brynn's cell phone chirped with a text message.

I'm heading to bed. Long day tomorrow.
Leftover pizza in fridge. Penny's asleep on your
bed. Sorry.

17

Sending a thank-you response, Brynn felt bad. Her friend Olivia Sinclair and Olivia's black lab, Penny, were in town for their annual training required as arson investigators. The perks of having her friend visiting for a few weeks meant fewer nights eating alone, talking with someone about anything other than work, and Penny—Olivia's arson detection dog who loved to snuggle when her work harness came off. Unfortunately, the timing of this year's visit had Brynn missing too many dinners with her friend and snuggles with Penny.

Laughter drew Brynn's attention to the baristas behind the counter. The bubbly sound felt loud and foreign in the coffee shop given the late hour. Brynn didn't think she'd find this many people willing to brave the freezing windchill to burn the midnight oil on a Tuesday night, but wasn't that the vibe in Washington, DC?

Her gaze drifted to a man half-perched on a stool. Male. Fifties. Overworked and underpaid given the wrinkled suit and loose tie at his neck. Lobbyist? Public defender? Whatever his job, the pale band of skin on his ring finger signaled the price it had demanded.

She scanned the other side of the coffee shop. Two college-aged girls sipped lattes with their hair in that messy-bun look that said "I don't care." However, the well-done highlights and designer purses showed they very much cared.

Next to her was another man. Middle Eastern, possibly Syrian given the dialect she'd overheard when he was on the phone earlier. Late thirties, maybe early forties. Dark hair, even darker eyes when they were opened. Right now, they were closed. His head moved in rhythm to whatever was coming through his wireless earbuds. Still buried in a thick coat, the Syrian tapped his thumb against the binding of holy text she recognized as the Quran sitting in his lap.

If the coffee shop were to explode right now and there were survivors, Brynn bet every single one of them would point to the man in the corner. And they'd likely be wrong.

As a targeting analyst for the CIA, she was to monitor and assess indicators leading to potential global threats that might cause the radicalization and mobilization of US-based violent extremists. She'd built her whole program around the premise that *anyone* could be radicalized and ready to commit violence abroad, or worse—at home.

From over her laptop, Brynn focused on a young man near the front of the coffee shop. Caucasian. Midtwenties, maybe. Hard to tell with the permanent scowl etched into his forehead. Unlike the college-aged girls, the guy wasn't wearing his school colors and didn't have a stack of textbooks spread across the table in front of him. And unlike the Syrian, who walked into the coffee shop twenty minutes earlier with his cell phone pressed to his ear arranging flight plans for his family, the young man hadn't picked up his phone once in the two hours since he dropped into the leather chair near the front of the shop.

A millennial not on their phone was like a bird without feathers, unnatural and suspi—

The door to the coffee shop swung open, and a burst of frigid air chased after the man wearing a wool overcoat who entered. Her suspect glanced up and smiled for the first time all night as he stood and embraced the man in a friendly hug. A quick survey revealed both men shared similar features, including the cleft in their chins.

Brynn pulled her scarf tighter around her neck. She needed to get a grip. Sinking a little lower in her chair, she reached for her cup of coffee and groaned. Cold. Served her right for trying to assess some poor guy waiting for his brother as the next Timothy McVeigh.

It wasn't that she suspected everyone. She just couldn't turn the suspicion off. It made her an excellent intelligence officer, but it also made her a dreadful friend. Daughter. Girlfriend.

Shaking the errant thought from her mind, Brynn turned her attention back to her work. Tomorrow she would wrap up the Diplomatic Intra-Agency Cooperation program, or DI-AC as they called it, in a pretty little bow and show Frank Peterson that she was ready to move forward in her career.

The consular position in Ankara, Turkey, had just opened and the timing was . . . perfect. Emotion warred within her. Three years ago, her career serving overseas came to an abrupt and painful halt. Putting aside the goals she'd set for her future, Brynn convinced herself that accepting the mundane and tedious assignments in DC was worth it to take care of her father. Now he was gone, leaving nothing to distract or keep her from pursuing the next step in preventing terrorism.

Brynn cleared her throat and the shadowy grief still claiming a space in her chest. The night before her father passed, he made her promise not to let her career consume her once he was gone. She promised, if only to give him peace of mind. But she had seen the look of doubt in his eyes, because he knew the truth—with him gone, there *was* no life outside the CIA. She straightened, a renewed energy wiping out the fatigue settling over her, and clicked her laptop back to life. If she wanted her family's sacrifices to mean something, then she needed to get back to work.

Another gust of icy January air swept into the coffee shop, and Brynn thought about ordering another drink to warm her fingers with when footsteps approached.

Glancing up, she met the tired eyes of Joel Riley. Except . . . they weren't just tired. His expression was tight. Brynn's stomach tensed. Seeing Riley outside the office was jarring enough, but his look sent fear down her spine.

"What is it?"

"We have a problem." Riley's eyes swept the place so quickly most wouldn't have noticed it unless they were trained. "You need to come with me."

Brynn was already gathering up her stuff but paused. "Where? What's happened?"

"In the car."

Without hesitation, she quickly finished collecting her things and followed Riley out of the café. Those three words sent a chill across her skin worse than the blustery weather forcing Brynn to shield her face behind her scarf. Riley led her to a black SUV idling outside. She was grateful the driver had the heater on full blast when she climbed inside.

"Did you walk?"

"Yes," Brynn answered, scooting across the seat for Riley to get in. The coffee shop was only a block from her apartment and on the east side of the Capitol Building, making it a prime location for employees of nearby businesses and the government as well as tourists looking for a reprieve from the weather, hot or cold. "Tell me what's going on."

He pulled out his phone and tapped a message into it, then set it on his knee and turned to her. "Remon Riad is missing."

Brynn blinked. "Remon Riad." She quickly placed the name to the Egyptian intelligence security officer from her DI-AC program. Shorter man maybe a couple inches taller than her, balding but kept his hair shorn close to his head, smiled a lot. "What do you mean he's missing?"

Riley gave the driver a nod, and they pulled away from the curb. "John Sosa went to the barracks at nine this evening for roll call, and Remon wasn't there. They went to his room, and he wasn't there either. They asked the others, and no one's seen him since this morning."

"Since this morning?" Her voice pitched, and she took a quick breath to regain control. "What about the afternoon roll call?"

"They missed him."

"*How* did they miss him? It's a head count." She recalled the weeks she'd spent at the Farm making sure she never missed roll call or risked getting kicked out. "What about his stuff?"

Riley exhaled, his hand fisting over his cell phone. "Gone."

*Gone.* Brynn's heart pumped heavy in her chest. This wasn't good. There had to be an explanation, but a sick feeling turned her blood cold. Not even three days ago Riad had remained after class to talk with her. She'd expected it to be about the program, but the second he mentioned something about a favor, Brynn quickly shut him down. The CIA doesn't do favors, and it was better not to indulge any idea she could offer anything—a fact she explained to Riad that day. But there had been something in his expression. A look of undeterred resolve as he apologized. He didn't bring it up again, and Brynn had forgotten all about it until now.

The SUV took a left, rumbling down the unusually empty streets that gave the large vehicle the room to accelerate in the direction of . . .

"Why aren't we headed to the barracks? We should search his room, talk with the others, and—"

"The barracks have been searched. Sosa has a team on-site questioning everyone."

Brynn's mind raced. "He's got to be somewhere. Did they check the hospital? Maybe he was sick—" She stopped. It was unlikely her suggestion held merit. The foreign security members were informed that in the event of illness or emergency, they were to contact her or Riley immediately.

Her thoughts paused when the SUV gained speed on the highway heading north. Awareness hit her square in the chest. She knew exactly where they were headed—Langley. "Peterson knows?"

It was a rhetorical question. Of course her boss knew, but Riley was kind enough to simply nod. Five years her senior in the agency, Joel Riley had started out in the CIA's Directorate of Operations as an operations officer. He served on several successful missions in Eastern Europe before returning stateside and requesting a transfer to the Directorate of Analysis. Some at the agency gave him a hard time about leaving such a prestigious division, but Riley said he had no regrets. A fact he affirmed every time he spoke about his wife and children, which was often.

"Brynn." He shifted, but it wasn't the movement that drew her eyes back to her colleague. It was his unsettling tone. "As soon as

Riad's disappearance was reported, Director Peterson had senior-level analysts go over his background."

She forced herself to breathe, trying to calm the sudden fear twisting her stomach into knots. An extensive background check had been done on all the visiting intelligence officers before they were even considered for the program. The security of the United States had been her top priority. There was no way—

"Remon has a third cousin on his mother's first husband's side of the family who has been associated with the Muslim Brother-hood."

What was left of the air in Brynn's chest whooshed out, and suddenly it didn't matter how high the heater was blasting, her blood turned ice cold. *It can't be.*

The DI-AC program was a first in the agency's history, and she had hinged the next step of her career on its success. While her father watched reruns of *Gunsmoke*, Brynn imagined the idea of countries finding commonality in the threat of terrorism and uniting in the fight against it. After spending countless hours re-fining the program, she submitted it, not expecting it to get any traction. But to her surprise, it was well received, and rumor had it that even the CIA director approved.

With the approval to move forward, Brynn was meticulous in the planning. She recruited the best team of analysts in their fields, and they double- and triple-checked their work. Each of the foreign intelligence officers was vetted extensively, because while their presence in the US was sanctioned, it was also unofficial. She couldn't just bring foreign spies to the US without jumping through a dozen hoops and then jumping through a dozen more.

A shudder coursed through her body, causing her stomach to clench with nausea. *A member of the Egyptian foreign intelligence . . . an operative . . . was missing.* On American soil. The implication of what that meant for her promotion and job paled in comparison to what it could mean for America.

After a right turn, the SUV stopped at a steel fence electrified with ten thousand volts and guarded by two men armed with automatic weapons. They passed their IDs to the guard, who scanned them and then handed them back before the gate slid open and they continued toward Langley.

Brynn's pulse hit peak speed when the surrounding parkland opened to the H-shaped superstructure. Bright landscape floodlights lit up the multistory building like a beacon of intimidation. She rubbed her gloved fingers over the laptop sitting on her lap as she thought about her brief. *What makes terrorists so dangerous is their ability to blend in and deceive you.*

How was she going to explain to her boss that an Egyptian operative with ties to a terror organization was missing somewhere in the United States, and she had missed it.

*Or worse—I've been deceived.*

# 3

McLean, VA
11:09 PM Tuesday, January 13

The awe of walking into the CIA headquarters for work on her first day had been daunting, and the feeling hadn't subsided in the ten years since. However, entering the epicenter of national intelligence in the middle of the night with a foreign liability on the loose—it was straight-up ominous.

Neither Brynn nor Riley spoke as they made their way to the Directorate of Analysis section on the north side of the complex. Normally, sunlight lit up the space through thirty-foot glass panels, but in the dead of night the hum of fluorescents overhead only added to the unnerving feeling she couldn't shake.

*The Muslim Brotherhood?*

How had she missed such a crucial piece of information? Riad's distant connection to one of Egypt's biggest terrorist organizations would have barred him from being considered for her program. Had his relation been overlooked or purposely omitted—hidden?

On the elevator, Brynn mentally flipped through the last two years. The Diplomatic Intra-Agency Cooperation program had been her brainchild. Leading a joint effort with America's allies to proactively prevent and defend against terrorism on a global level was the only way Brynn could see the hope of a future without fear of someone opening fire at a concert, church, or school.

This program was important to her, and she'd been extra thorough, knowing her boss, CIA Director of Analysis Frank Peterson, had gone the extra mile to make it happen. Some in the agency had doubts and didn't hesitate to express their concerns over her ability to coordinate and run such a program. It was unfortunate, but many still held old-fashioned opinions about equality in the workplace. Brynn was grateful Frank didn't subscribe to the antiquated bias. It also helped that he had three grown daughters, so he understood the challenges women faced. And that made this situation all the worse.

Brynn wanted to make him proud, but had she been so eager in her attempt to prove herself capable that she pushed her team to work too hard or too fast and they'd missed this? They'd been so focused, she'd been so foc—

Unease knotted the muscles in her shoulders. Brynn's focus *had* shifted when her father passed away eight months ago. Her mother's death had been unexpected. Her father's had left her unprepared. The sudden loss affected Brynn to her core. The CIA gave her leave to take care of the arrangements, but after her mother's heart attack, her father had made sure everything was in place so Brynn wouldn't need to worry. There wasn't to be any fanfare or memorial. Her father didn't want that. Most of Brynn's extended family lived in upstate New York and sent their regards while Brynn stood alone in the rain watching her father being buried.

She was all alone.

A fact she didn't need or want to dwell on, so she remained at work, turning her grief into purpose as she concentrated on her program. Had that adversely affected her work? Or was the oversight due to her desperation to put her career back on track?

Riley cleared his throat quietly next to her, and Brynn realized he was holding the elevator door open. They walked down the long hall, past empty workstations that would be buzzing with activity in just a few short hours. Stopping at the director's door,

Riley gave her a look she was sure he meant to be reassuring, but there was a measure of concern in his expression.

"Good luck."

"Thanks," she said before knocking softly on the office door. She took in a deep breath, preparing herself for what was coming and knowing full well she'd need more than luck on her side.

"Come in."

As she entered, the stale scent of burned coffee met her along with the sharp gaze of Director Peterson, who was standing in the middle of his office. For a man in his late sixties, Director Peterson was still in better shape than most men half his age. It was like he'd bullied his own body into submission, not allowing nature to turn it soft.

Rolling her shoulders back, she stepped farther into the office and paused when she caught sight of another man sitting in one of the chairs across from Peterson's desk. In a tailored charcoal-gray suit, the man didn't rise from his chair but simply gave her a cursory once-over. Brynn did the same. The man had to be about ten or fifteen years younger than Peterson, definitely fit given the cut of his suit. His graying hair was an inch or so longer on the top than the buzzed sides, giving him a stylish GQ look. Behind black square-framed glasses, blue eyes were still appraising her.

Brynn shifted, glancing down at her worn jeans peeking out from beneath her coat. Her fingers moved to the stray strands of blonde hair falling out of the knot she'd tied it into at the coffee shop. "Sir, I can wait outside until you're finished."

"No need, Taylor." Peterson walked around his desk and sat. He motioned for Brynn to take the second chair next to the man. "This is Thomas Walsh, director of SNAP."

SNAP?

"I'm sure Riley briefed you about Riad's connection to the Muslim Brotherhood—"

"Distant connection," Brynn said without thinking. Hard lines creased Peterson's forehead. "I'm sorry, sir, but I think it's an important distinction as we assess the situation."

"The situation"—Peterson's voice carried in the room—"is that we have an intelligence officer from a foreign country unaccounted for somewhere in our nation's capital. Which means we need to consider Riad a threat to our national security—"

"Sir, I ran extensive checks into the DI-AC candidates' backgrounds." Brynn's cheeks burned at her second outburst, but she continued. "Multiple ones. Each member of the program came here because they believe in order to defeat terrorism, our countries must be united and work together. I've had the opportunity to work closely with Remon Riad these last few weeks, and nothing about his personality or demeanor in class alerted me to him being a threat or disingenuous."

Except . . . Riad's favor echoed in her head like an alarm warning her she might be wrong.

Peterson sighed. "On any given day, this entire building is filled with people trained to appear genuine. It's our job to make someone believe what *we* want them to believe. You can call it diplomatic cooperation, but the *truth* is that we had fourteen spies from seven countries sitting in a conference room trained to do exactly what we do, except now one is missing and could be minutes away from executing the next 9/11."

Those final words sent a jab of pain slicing through her, and it must've shown on her face because the hardened edges of Peterson's face softened a fraction. Brynn's father had been a firefighter in New York on that fateful day. His station responded minutes before the first tower collapsed, raining down concrete, metal, and debris that pinned her father to the ground for hours. The terrorism that day ended her father's career and put her on the irrevocable path to never let it happen again.

"Which is exactly what my team will work to avoid," Director Walsh said, his voice level. Brynn turned to him. "Next week, President Allen will be flying to Cairo to open Wadi Basaela, the first American military installation in Egypt's history. The majority of the country understands our presence will continue to bring stability along with an improvement to the economy through jobs and the pledge of billions in aid. However, some are resistant to President Talaat's cooperation with President Allen and are becoming active in voicing their opposition. Riad's sudden disappearance is a liability to our national security."

Brynn processed the weight of this information. "With all due respect, Director Walsh, I've been analyzing and profiling terrorists for the last ten years, and my assessment of Riad as a well-respected Egyptian citizen who has selflessly served his country for the majority of his life does not fit the profile of someone plotting to destroy it."

"Ms. Taylor, your insight into Riad's behavior will be valuable to us in the coming days, but we cannot fail to assume the potential threat this poses under the circumstances."

"Us?"

"Starting tonight"—Peterson spoke on an exhale—"the investigation into Remon Riad's disappearance is being handed over to Director Walsh and his team."

The punch of his words sucked the breath right out of her lungs. She was being fired. Brynn fought to control her emotions. Ten years in the agency sacrificing everything to do her part and stop terrorism, and now it was over?

Director Walsh leaned across the space between them and held out a business card. "Tomorrow morning you'll be reporting here."

She read the card.

*Strategic Neutralization and Protection Agency*
*Floor 8 Acacia Bldg.*

"What?" Her question came out as a squeak. Clearing her throat, she looked at Peterson. "I don't understand. I'm not fired?"

"No." But there was an unmistakable warning in Peterson's

tone that said she was lucky that wasn't the case. At least not yet. "You're being assigned to assist SNAP in the apprehension of Remon Riad."

She was being assigned? To SNAP? "Sir, shouldn't I remain here? If the assumption is that Riad is a threat, then—"

"With cases of national security, *we* are to assume the worst-case scenario, Ms. Taylor." Director Walsh pushed his glasses up his nose. "Until proven otherwise." His attention cut to Peterson. "Who are you sending to Egypt?"

"Officer Joel Riley. His travel arrangements are being prepared as we speak." Peterson scooted closer to his desk and began typing at his keyboard. "He'll be on the first flight leaving tomorrow. 0700. Boots on the ground 1900 Egypt time. He'll check in with the station chief when he arrives, and until then we've already got a team on-site working intel."

Brynn blinked. They were sending Riley? "Excuse me, sir, but shouldn't I be the one going to Egypt?"

"Riley has worked Egypt before, and unfortunately, given the current climate there . . ." Peterson looked at her. "You're a Caucasian female with blue eyes and blonde hair. You'll stick out like a fly on a wedding cake."

Oh. He was right, of course. Riley was pretty much the opposite of her with his olive complexion and brown hair and eyes. He was also male, an important fact given Egypt's culture. But still, that didn't make the sting of being unable to do her job any less painful.

Turning to Director Walsh, she gathered her nerve. "So, I'll be running the investigation stateside?"

"As you know, the CIA is limited in its authority to operate within the US. Your role on my team will be that of CIA liaison, a position we identify as special missions manager."

*Liaison.* It didn't matter what fancy name they called it, Brynn knew exactly what it meant. She was being stripped of control. She'd rather be fired.

"Sir"—Brynn shifted in her chair and locked eyes with Peterson—"I won't rest until Riad is found and secured and we have answers." She held up the card. "But I don't need to work with some strategic agency to do that. I want to work here, with people I know and trust."

Peterson held her gaze for several long seconds before releasing a sigh. "You don't have a choice. This goes above my pay grade." His eyes bore into her. "And before you even ask, it's above the CIA director's pay grade as well."

"I'm sure you don't need to be reminded what's at stake here."

Her fingers curled around the edge of the business card. She was sure Director Walsh hadn't meant for it to come off as patronizing, but it had. Of course she knew what was at stake—and it wasn't just her career.

The safety of the American people—the security of America, herself—was at risk. If Riad was dirty . . . if he came here because of some plot, then any fallout would land squarely on her shoulders. Brynn's hands fisted as she thought back on the acts of terrorism committed on American soil and how the people demanded, rightfully so, answers to how agencies designed to protect America had missed the warnings. They wanted someone to blame. If she was wrong about Riad, her name would become synonymous with whatever disaster he was planning.

"No, sir." The muscles in her shoulders tightened as she straightened. "I'll be reporting to you?"

There was something, an uncertainty or concern, in Director Walsh's blue eyes that sent a wave of nervousness through Brynn. "I'll see you tomorrow morning."

Peterson gave her a quick dismissal and Brynn swiftly exited the office, closing the door behind her. Forcing breath back into her lungs, she took a moment, standing there in the hub of CIA intelligence, to figure out how in the matter of what—an hour?—her career was on the verge of crashing around her.

*"Ms. Taylor, may I ask a favor?"* Those words were going to haunt Brynn. The urgency of discovering what Riad needed and

how or if it was connected to his disappearance pushed her in the direction of her office instead of home. She sent a message to Riley letting him know she'd get a driver to take her back to her place and not to wait for her. It was going to be a long night, but if she'd missed something, she prayed she'd have the chance to figure it out before it was too late.

# 4

Jack Hudson took the steps two at a time, passing the stylized griffins guarding the entrance to the Acacia Building on Louisiana Avenue. It was barely after six in the morning, and business in Washington, DC, was already at full tilt. A wintry mix had pushed commuters onto the Metro, the increase causing delays that had forced Jack to grab an Uber.

Tucking his mother's casserole dish against his chest with his right hand, he used his left to open the glass door and step inside. His entire team would chase him out of town if he dropped his mother's famous lasagna. Shaking the dusting of snow flurries from his hair, he walked through the glass atrium to the elevators and scanned his card key before pressing the button for the eighth floor.

The 1930s private office building faced the Capitol and was the perfect location for the Strategic Neutralization and Protection Agency because it gave them quick access to specific people, businesses, and agencies integral to their assignments.

Shifting the covered dish in his hand, he checked the time. If Director Walsh was calling his team in before seven, it meant the assignment was serious. *"This assignment takes precedence."* Jack let out a breath, checking off a mental to-do list. Passports were

33

current. Rent and utilities prepaid. His fridge freshly stocked with his mother's cooking. Would he even get a chance to eat it? He glanced down at the lasagna. At least he had one meal covered.

The elevator door slid open, and Jack took another breath. He loved his job, but there were days when the long hours, travel, and constant state of alertness wore on him. Walking down the hallway, he passed the façade of doors leading to nonexistent companies before stopping at the last door on his left. A brass placard bearing the letters *S-N-A-P* was positioned next to the door above a black security panel. After he swiped his card, the red light turned green and he heard the mechanical sound of the lock shifting to allow him entry.

Jack shrugged out of his coat and hung it up in the closet. SNAP's office took up half of the eighth floor. The large front room was set up almost like a studio apartment. The sitting area to his left held a long gray couch positioned to take in the panoramic view of the Capitol, and a glass coffee table separated it from two black club chairs. On the right, a modern kitchenette with white cabinets, stainless steel appliances, and the Miele 6800 coffee maker Lyla had insisted on. Jack still wasn't sure how the expensive coffee maker fit into the budget, but then Lyla did have a way of getting what she wanted.

At the steel door at the corner of the room, he entered a code and scanned his thumbprint on the lock panel. Jack walked through the hallway and into an L-shaped space longer than it was narrow with twenty-foot ceilings. Like the front room, the wide windows spanning the length of the room gave their workspace, the inner sanctum of their office known as the fulcrum, a million-dollar view of Washington, DC.

This was where they did their everyday work and handled all the details before any assignment or operation. Home base, or for Jack, mostly just home.

Except someone had beat him there.

"How long you been here?"

Nic Garcia pulled a faded Red Sox cap off his head and ran a hand through his dark-brown hair, bringing it up an inch in every direction, before putting on the hat again. "What time is it?"

"After six."

"Then two hours." Garcia rose from his chair, stretching his six-foot frame before grabbing a file off his desk. "Got an alert about another shipment of fertilizer delivered to Guam."

"Should we be concerned?"

Garcia shrugged. "Not sure yet, but I want to stay ahead of it in case this new assignment requires more attention."

"Good call." Jack eyed a bouquet of balloons tied to a chair. "What's with the balloons?"

"They're for Lyla. Her birthday."

"Right. That's this weekend."

"Today's her birthday, but her party is Saturday."

Jack's gaze met Garcia's, and in the predawn light, he saw the look of a man who didn't miss much when it came to Lyla. "*The Princess Bride* movie party, I remember."

"She worked late last night." Garcia tugged his ball cap lower over his eyes. "The Sideris job."

Garcia joined SNAP five years ago, and within a few weeks Jack recognized Garcia's feelings for Lyla. Unfortunately, Lyla either remained oblivious or chose to remain oblivious to his feelings and had friend-zoned him. Fortunately for the team, that meant their focus remained on their assignments.

Jack checked his phone. "Lyla messaged me an hour ago and is on her way."

The beeping noise of the lock disengaging echoed down the hall, and Garcia looked momentarily relieved until an Everest-sized man appeared.

Kekoa Young's brown eyes landed on the casserole dish and a wide smile shone bright against the Hawaiian's dark skin. "Please tell me that's Mama Rosalie's raviolis."

"Sorry. Lasagna."

"Don't be sorry, brah." Kekoa looked at the dish and then between Jack and Garcia. "Unless either of you is expecting to eat it, because then *I'm sorry*." He chuckled.

"You realize it's freezing outside, right?"

Looking down at his feet, Kekoa wiggled his toes in his sandals, or slippahs as he called them, and then smiled up at Garcia. "You can take da boy outta da island, but you can't take da island outta da boy."

Kekoa slipped off a messenger bag and began unfastening his coat, which somehow managed to restrain the brute physical form of the man setting it aside. Unrestrained, Kekoa's body always seemed to grow right in front of his eyes. Jack was convinced the man bench-pressed refrigerators in his spare time.

Jack brought the lasagna to the fridge and put a sticky note on top warning Kekoa to leave it alone. He was halfway back to his desk when his phone vibrated in his pocket. He smiled, seeing Amy's name on the caller ID.

"Happy six-year anniversary, Jack."

Her voice tickled his ear. "Thank you." He paused in the hallway and leaned against the wall. "Are you in town? My mom made a ten-pound lasagna, and I'd be willing to fight Kekoa to save you some."

"I'd hate to be the reason you lose your life."

"I could hold my own . . . for like an hour. Probably."

"Well, you won't need to go to battle for me today. Production got delayed for a couple of days."

Jack ran a hand through his hair, not sure how to read his emotions on this. He'd met Amy Carmichael through Lyla, whose intention he was certain was to create an instant love connection. However, as a location scout for movies, Amy traveled the world for months at a time, which left them trying and failing more times than not to fit dates into their busy schedules.

"You're going to miss Lyla's birthday?"

"I know." A note of disappointment in her voice. "But—and

don't you dare tell her—I'm going to beg Ryan Reynolds to call her and tell her happy birthday."

Another beeping noise echoed, pulling Jack's attention to the front door just as Director Thomas Walsh walked in.

"Hey, I've got to go. The boss's in."

"Okay, I'll try to call later tonight. I've got to find the perfect safe house in Essex for a spy."

"Good luck with that."

Ending the call, Jack followed Director Walsh into the fulcrum.

"Sorry I'm late." He crossed the room, not removing his hat or coat, an urgency to his tone and movements. "Jack, let's talk."

Walsh started to step into his office, a square space separated by a floor-to-ceiling, steel-grid glass wall, when he paused and looked over his shoulder at Kekoa. "You have everything you need?"

"Shootz, boss. Just gotta wake up my babies."

"Get to it," Walsh said. "We'll need those babies up and screaming."

Kekoa's "babies" were state-of-the-art, high-tech computers nestled into an office space similar to Walsh's except it ran the width of the building. The glass-and-steel wall separating the space was designed to prevent radio or electrical signals from coming in or going out.

As Kekoa disappeared into his office, Jack continued after Walsh.

"I've spent the last two hours with CIA Director Peterson and the National Security Advisor, Doug Martin." Walsh set down his briefcase. "Sometime yesterday morning, an operative for the Egyptian Mukhabarat went missing."

"Mukhabarat?" Jack repeated, frowning. "There's an Egyptian spy missing here? In America?"

Walsh moved around his office, collecting folders and putting them into his briefcase. He handed one to Jack. "Remon Riad is a senior intelligence officer for Egypt and was here as part of a program called Diplomatic Intra-Agency Cooperation sponsored by the CIA. A week ago, Egypt, Saudi Arabia, France, the United Kingdom, Canada, Iraq, and Australia sent members of their intelligence communities here for a week-long conference. According to Frank, all the participants were vetted—"

"But they missed something," Jack interrupted, glancing quickly at the folder Walsh had handed him. It was Riad's dossier. "And they've asked us to get involved."

The sole mission of SNAP was incorporated into their name. *Strategic neutralization and protection.* They were a private agency contracted by the government to handle local, national, and international issues that could be a threat to US security and safety.

Because it was a private firm, the typical red tape preventing the military, CIA, FBI, and NSA from engaging didn't apply, giving Jack and his team the opportunity to strategically monitor threats and respond in a manner that went unnoticed by the public—a goal they measured their success by because Americans did not like deviations in their perceived status quo.

Walsh nodded. "Next week President Allen is flying to Egypt to dedicate Wadi Basaela, and needless to say, Riad's disappearance is problematic. If there's any malicious intent behind his purpose here in the US, then we need to figure it out, stop it, and make sure it has nothing to do with what's happening in Egypt. The last thing we need is the president of the United States walking into a trap."

"Agreed." As unsettling as that possibility was, Jack was troubled by the CIA's involvement. "Will I be working with Director Peterson?"

The hurried movement stopped, and Walsh locked eyes with Jack. "The director is sending over the officer who runs the program. She's an excellent officer—"

The hairs on the back of Jack's neck stood. No. There were hundreds of other CIA officers. It couldn't be her. It couldn't be—

"Officer Brynn Taylor will be acting special missions manager and cooperating with us until Riad is found."

Brynn. Jack's mouth went dry as he tried to regain the balance of the room spinning around him.

"Is this going to be a problem?"

Jack blinked, bringing his focus back to Walsh, who stared at him with concern. It made sense now why Walsh hadn't spoken to him about the assignment earlier. He was the only one who knew of Jack's past, giving the question he asked deeper meaning.

*Was this going to be a problem?*

Flexing his fingers a couple of times, Jack tried to work out the tension threading through every muscle in his body. It used to be a different kind of tension wrapping itself around his heart whenever he thought of Brynn. But now? Now he wasn't sure if it was anger or bitterness or hurt or fear causing his heart to race.

"There's no one else?"

Walsh removed his glasses and rubbed the bridge of his nose. "She's the officer in charge." He slid his glasses back on. "She was the one who invited Riad into the US."

A heaviness stole over Jack's shoulders. That meant *she* was the one at fault and the one who would bear the consequences of whatever Riad had planned. A familiar ache began pulsing in his chest.

"I can ask Garcia to take the lead if—"

"No." Jack returned his attention to Walsh. "I want the assignment. It's just—"

"You'll be working with the woman who broke your heart."

It sounded juvenile hearing Walsh speak his feelings aloud. Yet it was the truth. Brynn had not only broken his heart—she'd betrayed him.

A gentleness creased the edges of the skin near Walsh's blue eyes. "Jack, it's been eight years. People change. From what I could pull from Peterson, Taylor's made a name for herself within the agency. She's good at her job . . . very good."

Jack sighed. "I never doubted she would be."

Setting his glasses down, Walsh tapped the folder. "What's your fear here?"

His fear? In a flash Jack was back in the final days of training at the CIA facility, the Farm, in Williamsburg with Brynn. Each recruit had to lead a team through a simulated mission, adjusting to whatever the training officers threw at them. Moles, informants who defected, false leads resulting in the mission being uncovered by the enemy—an error leading to capture or death. After twelve intense weeks, it was the trainers' jobs to use this test as a filter to weed out the recruits by exposing their weaknesses. Brynn had been his weakness, but it was her betrayal that sealed their future.

"Sir, Riad's disappearance is critical enough to warrant our attention, and given what I know of Br—Officer Taylor, I'm concerned about whether or not . . . we can trust her."

Walsh studied him for a few minutes, and Jack resisted the urge to shift. If he was going to take on this assignment and lead his team, then Walsh needed to know what bothered him the most about working with Brynn—his fear. He'd trusted her once.

"Well"—Walsh leaned forward and flipped open the folder—"we don't have much choice in the matter, I'm afraid. We have to trust—"

"Sir, with all due respect, I'm willing to take the assignment. But I'm not willing to risk my team on someone who can't be trusted, and I don't trust *her*."

"Sir?"

Jack and Walsh twisted their focus to the door, where Garcia stood running a hand down the back of his neck. He glanced at Jack, his expression melting apologetically, and when Jack saw the blonde woman waiting next to him, he understood why.

Garcia gestured to her. "Sir, Brynn Taylor."

Heat blossomed in Jack's cheeks, and he stood stock-still as Walsh walked around his desk. Brynn's sharp blue gaze met Jack's, and he knew she'd heard him. But being the professional she was, she quickly averted her eyes to Walsh and pasted on a smile.

"Good to see you again, sir. It seems you're getting the extended version of my dossier from Mr. Hudson. I do hope he's told you that among my many bad qualities, I do have a few good ones."

Jack's shoulders knotted at her sarcastic tone because it contradicted the expression of surprise and hurt shadowing her blue eyes. He opened his mouth to say something, but the words dried up on his tongue.

Brynn pivoted to Jack. "It's been a long night and I understand working with your team is necessary, so I hope we can put aside any past biases and focus on the mission." She gave him a tired smile. "I'd like this to be over as quickly as possible."

# 5

Brynn stiffened her spine, refusing to look again at . . . *Jack Hudson*. How in the—

Director Walsh came around his desk and shook her hand. "Ms. Taylor, it's good to see you again."

Brynn wasn't sure she felt the same way. Careful to avoid Jack's gaze, she forced another smile. "Anxious to take care of this situation, sir."

*Do not panic. Do not panic. DO NOT PANIC.*

She fought to slow her adrenaline. In a city with at least a quarter million federal employees, it had to be Jack? He was the last person she wanted to work with again—a feeling she had no doubt was mutual given the lovely bio he was feeding Director Walsh when she walked in.

Jack didn't trust her. If the shock of seeing him after all these years wasn't enough to cut into her, the sting of his statement sent an unexpected sharp pain into her chest.

A cell phone on Director Walsh's desk rang, and he looked at the screen before looking back up at them. "Excuse me. I need to take this."

She turned to follow the man who had escorted her into the building, but Director Walsh waved a hand for her to stay before he and her escort stepped out, leaving her with Jack. *Well, this won't be awkward at all.* Brynn stared out over the interior of the high-tech hub that looked like a movie set from some spy thriller. All-black steel and technology, with the exception of some colorful balloons.

The stretch of silence between them annoyed her. Working with him would require they speak, and if he wasn't going to start, then she'd be the mature, professional one. "This is quite the setup."

Not her best first line, but at least she'd tried. Jack moved to her side and her breath caught. An unexpected and frustrating reaction.

"It's efficient." He crossed his arms in front of his chest. "I'm sure the war room at Langley is too."

*Is he baiting me?* Brynn narrowed her eyes on him. "It's not quite as glamorous as the movies make it appear, and"—she raised her hand, gesturing around her—"it looks nothing like this."

Refusing to look at her, Jack remained silent and rigid, his position giving her an advantage to study him. She peeked over, still not believing he was standing less than five feet away from her. The years had been good to him. His body had filled out in all the right places, and he'd allowed his dark-brown hair to grow longer than the military high and tight he'd worn while at the Farm. The stylish stubble covering the strong Italian jawline he'd inherited from his mother made him look . . . good. She was very grateful she'd made it home for a few hours to sleep, shower, and fix her hair before showing up. *Not that it mattered.*

Suddenly, those familiar chocolate-brown eyes settled on her, and instantly she was transported back eight years to their final day of CIA training at the Farm—when those same eyes looked on her with utter confusion. Betrayal.

Or so Jack had believed.

And she'd let him.

It was easier than trying to explain something not even she could quite understand in the moment . . . or it seemed, almost a decade later. Heat climbed up her neck, and she quickly averted her eyes, unwilling to let herself go back. He'd left without letting her explain, and whatever their past was—it was the past.

Brynn breathed a sigh of relief when Director Walsh stepped back into the office, his expression apologetic.

"I'm sorry about that, Ms. Taylor. I'm afraid I'm going to have to cut this meeting short, as I'm needed elsewhere." He arched an eyebrow at Jack and then back at her. "Jack, you've got the file on this assignment and will run lead."

"Yes, sir."

Brynn's momentary relief was replaced with anxiousness. Not only had her control over the assignment been taken, but she would be working with Jack—no, *for* Jack. Well, this couldn't get any worse.

"Do you have any concerns, Ms. Taylor?"

Only a hundred, but unfortunately, they had nothing to do with finding Riad and that's where her focus needed to be.

Clenching her jaw, Brynn smiled politely. Or at least she hoped it looked polite because it felt like a grimace. "No, sir."

Director Walsh gave a quick nod and then grabbed his briefcase and coat before pausing at the door. He smiled slightly and winked. "Now, you two play nice."

An unsettled feeling passed over Brynn as she watched Walsh leave. His departing words gave her the impression Jack had filled him in on more than her professional life.

"Is this going to be a problem for you?"

Brynn eyed Jack. "No. Is it going to be a problem for you?"

Jack's forehead creased. "Because I'm running this operation, and if it's going to be a problem for you, then you might want to ask your director to send someone else."

Was he being serious? He was the one who said he didn't trust her. "There's no one else, so I guess you're stuck with me. Can you handle that?"

Jack shrugged. "I can handle that."

"Good."

She hated that she sounded like an insolent child, but seriously. Did Jack not think she could do her job? That she was somehow still hung up on him all these years later? *Puh-lease.*

"We should get started." Jack crossed in front of her. "I'll introduce you to the team."

He didn't wait for her to respond and walked out of the office, expecting her to follow. She let out a sigh. If this mission ended soon, it still wouldn't be soon enough.

Taking a deep breath, Brynn forced herself to relax. Meeting Jack at the long conference table in the center of the room, she reminded herself why she was there. Find Riad. Not only did her job depend on it—the nation's security did too.

"Garcia." Jack grabbed a remote and pointed at several flat screens banking the wall opposite them. The televisions lit up with news stations from across the globe.

The man who'd checked her identity and led her into the office approached. He had a bit of military bearing in his walk, but the worn jeans, flannel shirt rolled at the sleeves over a Henley, and faded Red Sox ball cap gave off a more relaxed impression . . . except for his hazel eyes, which stood out against his olive complexion, kind but guarded.

He reached out his hand. "Nic Garcia, but everyone calls me Garcia."

"Brynn Taylor." She followed his lead as he sat and chose a seat across from him, which put an extra seat between her and where Jack remained standing. "Military?"

Garcia slid a sideways look to Jack, who nodded. "Yes, ma'am. Army EOD."

Explosives Ordnance Disposal? That piqued her interest. What exactly did SNAP need with a weapons and explosives specialist?

"Sorry I'm late."

A young woman with streaks of purple hair raced into the room and dropped an oversized Louis Vuitton bag on the floor. She shed her coat to reveal black leather leggings, break-your-neck

45

heels, and a sequined top completely out of season for the blustery January weather.

"My Uber driver forgot about the construction on—" She stopped talking and crossed over to one of four desks. Her fingers brushed against the bright latex balloons. "Are these for me?"

"Happy birthday."

The woman spun around to face Garcia. "Nicolás! Thank you for remembering." She walked back to the table and wrapped her arms around Garcia's neck, hugging him. "Oh, and I forgot to tell you my shooting instructor Randy said I'm ready for my first IDPA competition."

Brynn blinked, trying to imagine this stiletto-clad woman competing in the International Defensive Pistol Association shooting competition, and instantly reminded herself not to judge a book by its cover.

Garcia's face shifted into an expression of concern and amusement. "I hope you've stopped calling your gun Cupcake."

"Nope." She released his neck from her hug. "And I had some fun with the new guy at the range when I asked for some pew-pews instead of bullets." The woman giggled, even as Garcia rolled his eyes. She straightened and for the first time realized Brynn was there. "Oh. We have a guest."

"Lyla Fox, meet Brynn Taylor," Jack said, gesturing between them. "She's the special missions manager for our new assignment, and you're in time for our briefing."

With a raise of Lyla's pierced eyebrow, Brynn could feel herself being inspected by the woman's stunning blue-green eyes. "Brynn Taylor. That name seems familiar. Have we met before?"

"I don't think so."

"Who are you with?"

There was a touch of accusation in her tone that sent Brynn's nerves buzzing. "CIA."

A second passed before realization flashed across Lyla's face. "*You're* Brynn Taylor."

The way Lyla said it brought an unwelcome feeling. Brynn grew even more uncomfortable when she caught the shared glance between Lyla and Jack. Was there something between them? Lyla seemed a little young for him but was beautiful, and in the mere minutes since she walked into the space, the woman dominated everyone's attention. Maybe that was a trait Jack found attractive. *Why am I even thinking about this?*

"Kekoa," Jack called out over Brynn's head. "Time to get started."

Jack's abruptness cut into the anxiousness growing inside of Brynn. Twisting in her chair, Brynn looked over in time to see a giant man step out of an office similar to Walsh's. She might've taken a moment to appreciate the high-tech hardware filling the space, but she could not stop staring at the man walking toward them.

Black tribal tattoos covered both the man's muscled arms, and another stretched from above his T-shirt along his thick neck. Jack was six foot and this Jason Momoa doppelgänger towered over him by several inches.

"Howz it?" The man removed his black beanie cap, revealing a head of dark curls.

Brynn could've sworn she heard Lyla release a sigh.

"That never gets old," Lyla said under her breath, which got her an eye roll from Garcia.

"Kekoa Young handles our tech." Jack introduced the man who chose to sit next to her.

Brynn's hand was dwarfed in Kekoa's surprisingly gentle grip. "Computers, huh?"

He released her hand and then wiggled his fingers, which were basically the size of bratwursts, in the air. "Cryptology. Navy."

"You were in the Navy?" The skepticism in her tone caused her to scramble. "I, uh, mean. On a boat? You were on a boat?"

"A ship." Kekoa's correction was gentle. "*CVN 70* and the rest of my time at Fort Gordon."

"CVN 70?"

Kekoa nodded at Brynn. "USS *Carl Vinson.*"

Forget the computers, how in the world did someone the size of a minivan fit into a ship's berth? Brynn had taken a tour of the USS *Abraham Lincoln* and remembered how tight the quarters were for her. She couldn't imagine how Kekoa had made it work.

Her eyes found the Hawaiian flag—not the state one but the Kingdom of Hawaii's original design with the feathered kāhili and pointed paddles—inked on his bicep. "What island are you from?"

"Oahu, born and raised." Kekoa gave her a toothy smile and flexed the tattooed bicep. "You pretty smart for one haole."

Brynn grinned back at the familiar term used by island locals for visitors, especially Caucasian ones like she was. "I might be haole, but I eat like a local."

"Oh yeah? What do you like?"

"Loco moco."

Kekoa's dark-brown eyes lit up. "Loco moco? You ain't a haole, you a local girl! There's an ono place in—"

"Ahem," Lyla interrupted, shooting Kekoa a pointed look. The Hawaiian's animated expression sobered, but not before he shot Brynn a wink. "Shall we continue, Jack?"

Whatever tension Brynn had felt under Lyla's earlier scrutiny had doubled. *"You're Brynn Taylor."* The declaration implied Lyla knew something about Brynn. If she and Jack *were* an item, then it made sense that he might've told her about them. But what exactly? He didn't know the whole truth. Only his version.

"Lyla handles logistics and acquisitions for all our assignments."

Jack's words snapped Brynn's attention back to where it needed to be. "Acquisitions?"

"Lyla has an extensive network of resources at her disposal," he answered. "Anything we need for our mission, she'll acquire."

Huh. His choice of words made Brynn curious about the legality of said acquirements. Was she really supposed to rely on a bomb expert, a giant techie, a young woman dressed like she'd spent all night at a club, and an ex-boyfriend working for an agency she still didn't understand?

"Brynn Taylor," Jack continued, "is a targeting analyst for the CIA—"

"Targeting analyst?" Lyla swiveled in her chair. "I've never heard of it."

"In a nutshell, my division is responsible for identifying data critical to foreign intelligence in order to disrupt potential threats against the United States."

"Sounds like what we do," Garcia said, his voice low and measured even as Lyla sent him a sideways glance. He shrugged, leaning back in his chair.

"So, when the CIA trains you in betrayal, is the primary focus on enemies or friends?"

"Lyla."

The warning in Jack's rebuke forced Lyla's lips closed but did little to stop the heat burning Brynn's cheeks. The meaning behind the question was crystal clear—Director Walsh *wasn't* the only one who knew about her and Jack's past. *Awesome.*

"Kekoa, why don't you pull up the dossier on Riad, and Ms. Taylor can fill in what we don't know."

Kekoa rolled his chair backward and reached behind him to grab a silicon rectangle that Brynn noticed was a wireless keyboard. His fingers flew over the keys with deftness, removing any doubts she might've had about his ability to work on a computer.

A whirring noise sounded overhead, and Brynn watched three screens extend down from the ceiling. A few more keystrokes and Riad's passport photo popped up on the first screen, along with several other photos of the Egyptian. The number of photos was concerning because some seemed to have been taken without Riad's knowledge—like the ones the CIA grabbed through intel. *Why would a private firm like SNAP have them?*

Jack nodded at Brynn to begin. Straightening, she pasted on

a smile she doubted looked genuine but hoped it hid the anxiety coursing through her. Why was she so nervous? This was her job, and she was good at it. "Remon Riad, age forty-two, is an intelligence officer for the Mukhabarat, Egyptian Intel, or GID. He was here as part of an agency cooperation program to discuss joint counterterrorism options between allied forces—"

"Is he a double agent?"

Brynn was caught off guard by Lyla's immediate and brusque question. Or was it an accusation? "I have no reason to believe he is."

"But you don't know for sure?"

Annoyance and unease pulled tight the muscles in Brynn's neck. "What we *know* is Remon Riad is a decorated military officer and has an impeccable record as an intel officer. He came highly recommended by top officials within the Egyptian government. He's married with three grown sons and a daughter who's about to be married. There's no reason to suspect he came here with an agenda."

"Except you're here." Lyla's tone mocked. "Which means it's not that simple, is it?"

"Riad has a distant cousin related by marriage who has been connected to members of the Muslim Brotherhood."

The reality of her confession hung in the air for a second before Garcia glanced over to the wall of television screens and then back to Brynn. "However, we've seen a considerable decrease in MB activity since the ousting of Egypt's former president, but that could change with the US standing up a new military installation in Egypt."

"Wadi Basaela will be operational by the end of next week," Jack confirmed. "There's been open resistance to the US's presence in Egypt—especially in regard to the new base. The MB is of concern, but it's the National Liberation Jihad that's been most active. Kekoa's been monitoring any chatter having to do with NLJ or the MB in regard to the upcoming ceremony."

Brynn was surprised to hear Jack bring up the NLJ. They weren't a well-known organization but were well-connected to terror groups like ISIS and had come up on the CIA's radar in the last decade. Jack's knowledge of them and their threat potential was very telling of SNAP's involvement in national security.

Jack looked at Garcia. "I'd like you to keep your ear to the ground for any movement of weapons to the area. Until we find Riad, we're going to assume his disappearance and connection to MB pose a threat to our national security, international diplomacy with Egypt, and the physical security of President Allen when she arrives in country."

Lyla's eyes narrowed on Brynn. "Did you even do a background check on the spy before letting him into our country?"

"Of course I did," Brynn fired back at Lyla. "Every intelligence officer we brought into the country was fully and extensively processed. Their backgrounds, affiliations, family relations, everything scrutinized. Riad's connection to the Brotherhood is distant at best."

"And you'd bet your career on that?"

"Yes." Brynn met Lyla's stare. "I'd bet my career on it."

Because she had. And any future she'd hoped for in the agency.

"Well, you can bet your career"—Lyla held her stare—"but I'm not betting mine."

A beeping alarm echoed from Kekoa's computer hub and cut through the growing tension.

"Uh, can I—" Kekoa hooked his thumb over his shoulder toward his office. "I need to check on something."

A flicker of curiosity passed through Jack's eyes before he gave a nod of approval and Kekoa slipped away.

"The CIA will have an officer on the ground within a few hours to gather more information about Riad. It shouldn't take long for us to ascertain any potential threat and use it to help us find Riad." Brynn took a steadying breath, then her eyes flashed to Jack, who stood there with his gaze fixed on her. It was clear Lyla didn't trust that she'd done her job, but did Jack share the concern? His words from earlier rang through her head. *"I don't trust her."* The statement rattled her far more than Lyla's sarcastic interrogation. "I assure you, we followed protocol."

There was a softening in Jack's features—subtle but powerful, because Brynn's heart did a flip in her chest, awakening a fluttering of emotions she'd not felt in eight years.

"We're going to do our jobs like we always do. And if we do them right, then nobody's career should be on the line."

"I've got him."

Kekoa's announcement broke the trance as they all turned to find him standing in the doorway of his office, giving them a toothy smile.

"What?" Jack took a step toward him. "Who?"

"Riad. I've got his location."

Brynn's pulse pounded in her ears as relief and apprehension coursed through her. This was going to be over soon. A knot of tension corded in her stomach. She caught Jack looking at her, his face a mixture of emotion. Or maybe she was confusing her feelings for his relief?

*What feelings?*

Jack stood there . . . waiting. "Ready?"

She rose from her chair, grabbed her bag, and followed Jack out of the office, forcing herself to remember that the past was the past. She would not allow these flutterings to distract her. It'd been eight years and clearly—Brynn slid a glance at Lyla—he'd moved on. It meant nothing would stand in the way of her goal—find Riad and be out of each other's lives once more.

# 6

The vanilla-lavender scent was familiar and filled the Tahoe. Dangerous. At least for his heart, which had begun betraying him the second Brynn Taylor walked into Walsh's office—and back into his life.

Leaving Kekoa, Lyla, and Garcia back at the office to work on their assignments, Jack found himself second-guessing his decision not to bring one of them along. Except what would that say to Brynn? He could handle working with her. This was his assignment, and even though the shock of seeing Brynn after almost a decade was still messing with his head, he wouldn't let it keep him from focusing on the mission.

"Jack, the exit."

The GPS screen on the Tahoe's dash beeped. Snapping out of his thoughts, Jack quickly flipped his blinker on, taking the ramp off the Roosevelt Bridge and heading west. *So much for staying focused on the mission.*

Brynn shifted in the passenger seat. The tension from the office had carried over into the SUV, growing thicker with each passing second. Jack wasn't sure if it was due to them closing in on Riad's location or his foot-in-mouth moment from earlier. The flash of hurt in her eyes had affected him more than he cared to admit.

53

"I'm not sure hacking into VDOT is legal."

Jack couldn't help the chuckle that escaped his lips. He looked at her and found no trace of humor on her face. "It's not hacking if you have permission." He shrugged. "I think it was genius, actually."

He was duly impressed with Kekoa's method. As soon as the cryptologist had Remon Riad's photo, he used a facial recognition program to run it through the Virginia Department of Transportation. It took less than fifteen minutes before a highway camera captured his image and the license plate number of a rental car Kekoa tracked to a mom-and-pop rental car company in Arlington. The only problem was the last image taken was time-stamped an hour ago, leaving them blindly heading to the last location where cameras spotted Riad while they waited for an update.

What was taking Kekoa so long?

"Hmm, it was pretty genius. I might need to talk to recruitment about your little cryptologist."

"Little?"

She smirked, shaking her head. "I still can't imagine him on a ship."

"He spent a lot of time at Fort Gordon's Cyber Center, and there's no recruiting my team."

"We'll see." There was a tease in her voice and he felt the mood shift, reminding him how it used to be. "You've got quite a little team of Avengers."

"They're good people. Loyal and the very best at their jobs."

"Lyla seems especially loyal."

Through a side glance, Jack took in the curves of her face. A strand of blonde hair had come loose from the low bun at the base of her neck and now hung near her ear. Even in her profile, Jack could read the twist of her lips. Something was bothering her.

"Lyla is loyal and has a fierce protective streak, but she's also incredibly generous and kind once you get to know her."

Brynn released a laugh that lacked humor. "I'm pretty sure current girlfriends don't want to get to know ex-girlfriends."

Jack scrunched up his face as he digested her words before his jaw dropped, laughter spilling from his mouth. "You think Lyla and me—?" He laughed even harder, and Brynn pinned him with a look of confusion. "You think she's my girlfriend? Are you serious?"

"What?" Brynn folded her arms over her chest. "She was shooting daggers at me all morning like I was stepping all over her territory."

"She's like a little sister." Jack took a deep breath, trying to regain his composure. "Not to mention the same age *as* my sister."

"Love knows no age these days."

Jack quirked an eyebrow at her. "Is that so?"

"Whatever, Jack, shut up."

Another chuckle filled his chest, and from the corner of his eye he caught Brynn fighting her own smile. Hmm. Maybe this wouldn't be so bad.

The moment was interrupted by an incoming call. The name and number flashed on the screen—Amy Carmichael. Jack's thumb fumbled over the control panel until he hit the ignore button. He glanced over at Brynn, who was looking out the window. His conscience pricked with guilt, but he wasn't sure if it was because of Amy or Brynn.

Jack's gaze slid to her left hand. No ring. Didn't mean she wasn't in a relationship. He looked at his own ring finger. Bare. Not for lack of trying. His parents had always instilled in him to date intentionally. A difficult task given the dating world he lived in where singles liked their dates like they liked their food—fast and unfulfilling. Empty carbs. Or hearts.

Maybe that's why hanging out with Amy worked for him. Did a handful of dates in the last six months count as *dating*? Or was he trying to find a loophole to protect his heart?

He cleared his throat. "Any reason why Remon Riad would be in Northern Virginia?"

Brynn twisted in the passenger seat. "No . . ."

Her hesitation drew him to look over at her. Meeting those blue eyes of hers was a mistake. They'd always had an effect on him, and given the rush of feelings pumping through him, maybe they still did.

"Riad does not fit the profile of rogue agent. He's got a family, good job, retirement from his time in the military. Jack, the man has everything to lose. Why would he choose to give all of it up?"

Her question hung between them for a long second before she looked away. Jack returned his attention back to the road, forcing himself not to dwell on the similarities of a choice made eight years ago. Brynn's decision to put her career above all else still grated on him, but now was not the time to discuss it no matter how badly *he* wanted to know why.

"Jack, what you said to Walsh—"

The speakers in the vehicle rang again, the dash displaying an incoming call from Kekoa this time. *Not a second too soon, brother.* Jack's dismay at learning he would be working with Brynn had overruled his good sense when he told Walsh he didn't trust her. He'd never been good about keeping his emotions in check, and he felt guilty for his comment. Almost a decade later, thinking he was over it but sitting here with her, breathing in the fragrance that was so distinctly Brynn—the pain was still raw.

The last thing either of them needed was to bring up the past. It wouldn't change anything, so it was best to stay focused on the assignment and then get on with their lives.

Jack clicked the answer button. "Tell me you have an address."

"Brah, why you doubt my skills?"

Brynn covered a giggle, and it took a lot more control than it should've to remain focused on the road. If he thought her eyes had power over him, her smile almost always did him in.

"Kekoa, do you have the address?"

"Yeah, brah. The company tracks their rentals through OnStar. Sending you the location of one silver Toyota Corolla."

The GPS screen pinged and directions to an address in Fairfax,

Virginia, appeared. Jack hit the blinker and took the next exit. "Can you give me details on the location?"

"Already on it." Jack heard the sound of computer keys clicking. "It looks like a shopping center. There's a real estate office, bank, retail stores, Starbucks on two corners. Movie theater." More clicking. "A couple of restaurants. I don't see anything significant, but oh, wait a minute. I just got a readout from OnStar. Seems our guy has been taking advantage of the unlimited mileage on his rental."

"What do you mean?"

"Once Riad picked up the car, he traveled outside of Fairfax to Clifton, Virginia, for several hours before heading to Cherry Hill Park. It's a campground where I'm assuming he spent the night, because his car doesn't move again until six this morning when he returned to Clifton before driving to the Fairfax Towne Centre. He's been there for the last hour."

Brynn sat forward. "Anything significant about Clifton?"

"Uh . . ." The car went silent.

Jack frowned. "Kekoa?"

"Yeah, sorry, brah. I was running a search through the county property taxation page, and I'm not seeing anything stand out. A lot of farmland with a mixture of homes ranging in the low hundreds up to the millions."

"Brynn, you think Riad is looking to retire on a farm?"

Brynn gave him a side-eye, making it clear his suggestion wasn't funny. "Well, I'd assume the first time he might've been lost." She bit her lip. "But going to the same location a second time leads me to believe he was in Clifton for a reason."

"And we can't rule out a more nefarious purpose for his being there."

Brynn pressed her lips together as though she didn't want to admit he might be right. Jack couldn't imagine what kind of consequences she was facing at work. And no matter how hurt or angry he was about their past, he'd never wish failure on her.

He accelerated. A part of him hoped she might be right—that

Riad's actions had an innocent explanation—but if not, then he wanted to get to him as quickly as possible.

"Kekoa, contact Walsh and let him know where we are. Oh, and have the rental company report the car stolen so OnStar can disable the engine. We don't need Riad taking off."

"Got it, brah."

Jack ended the call and headed toward the shopping center where he hoped to find Riad's car, which he hoped led to finding Riad, which he hoped would prove Brynn correct. But doubt lingered. The last time he put so much hope into something, it landed him in a very dark place. One he hoped never to go back to.

Movement from the corner of his eye caught his attention. Brynn was drumming her thumb in a staccato beat against her legs, a nervous twitch Jack noticed the first time he met her on their first day at the Farm.

"Don't be nervous."

"I'm not nervous." She stilled her hands. "I'm frustrated. I've been working on the DI-AC program for two years. Two years analyzing and vetting every single detail. Meeting every curveball the agency threw at me to one, convince them to consider the program, but two, and likely the worst, taking every menial operational task handed to me regardless of qualification just to prove myself in a male-dominated environment."

A frustrated breath escaped her lips and Jack smirked.

Brynn turned on him. "Are you smirking? Does my misery delight you, Jack?"

"No." He tried to clear his expression, but it was hard given the fire lighting Brynn's blue eyes. A fire that at one time made his knees weak. He returned his focus to the drive. "I've never known you to grovel for anything."

"I don't grovel. Never have. Never will." She released a long sigh and turned so her attention was back on the road in front of them. "I go after what I want and will work twice as hard to get it if necess—" Brynn bit down on the rest of the word.

Jack's fingers tightened over the steering wheel. There was nothing about what she was saying that wasn't true. He'd seen it when they were training for clandestine operations and refused to believe it would be a problem for them, no matter how many signs pointed to the truth. His refusal to accept it had cost him his job and his heart—and he wasn't about to let that happen again.

# 7

*Grovel? No way.* She did not grovel. Her gaze slid to Jack, and Brynn could tell he regretted his words as soon as he said them. She felt bad for her own. Jack didn't need to be reminded what she was willing to do for her job. He had firsthand experience.

A deep pang resonated within her. She hadn't expected to fall in love with a fellow recruit. But Jack . . . he'd somehow managed to win her heart and ignite the unrealistic hope that a future with him might be possible even when everything the agency stood for said otherwise.

When it came down to it, they had made her choose.

If Jack thought it had been easy, he was wrong. Very wrong. The agency hadn't played fair, but nothing was fair when it came to stopping terrorism. If she wanted to do her job to the best of her ability, she had to put distractions in their place.

*Is that what my parents had been?*

On more than one occasion Brynn wondered if she would've made a different choice had she known her mother was going to die. She wanted to believe she would have, but stopping terrorism had become so ingrained in her head that she wasn't even sure anymore.

When she was flying back to the States, Brynn had had no idea her mother's death would upend not only her life but also her career. Hours after her mother's service and making sure her father's care was arranged, Brynn was already looking up flights to return to Somalia and get back to her job.

It wasn't that she didn't care about her mother's loss or the emptiness in her father's life, but she had a job to do. One that was personal to her and her family. The best way to honor her mother's memory and her father's sacrifice was to stop terrorism.

However, on the last day of her emergency family leave, Director Peterson called her into his office and informed her that her position in Somalia had been absorbed by another office in the State Department and she would be remaining in Washington, DC.

It felt like a punishment for abandoning post to attend her mother's funeral. Especially after all the menial tasks that had been passed on to her, but she didn't complain. Brynn gave it her all to the point that the food in her fridge spoiled, one of her neighbors thought she had died, and the last television show she remembered watching in real time was . . . well, she couldn't even remember.

And then there was her dad. He never complained about her infrequent and hasty visits. Or the way she'd zone out of a conversation because she was thinking about work. He never said anything. And Brynn convinced herself he was fine, but deep down she knew better.

There had been a longing in his gentle expression that had said he missed her and wanted more time with her—like he knew their time together was coming to an end.

"I'm sorry, Brynn. I shouldn't have said that."

Jack's apology pulled her gaze from the scenery outside and away from her melancholy thoughts.

"I'm sorry too. I didn't mean to *snap* at you." She smirked, her eyes cutting to Jack.

A smile played on his lips and, man, if her heart didn't give a tiny *thump-thumpity-thump-thump* at the sight of it.

"And I'm sorry your puns haven't improved."

"I'm sorry I implied you and Lyla were a thing."

Jack's eyes sharpened the same way they had when he abruptly declined the incoming call from someone named Amy. Was Amy important in Jack's life? An unwanted flicker of jealousy warmed Brynn's cheeks. She was just about to apologize for crossing a line when he looked over at her.

"Are you?"

Brynn began tapping her thumb against her phone and then stopped. A CIA instructor had pointed out her nervous gesture— a weakness. So she'd trained herself to control it, remove any outward cue that would expose her emotions. When it came to her training and the tests, she'd been successful. When it came to Jack—less so.

"Yes," she answered a little too enthusiastically. "I'm also sorry I'm going to have to recruit Kekoa to the CIA."

Jack's lips curled. "Don't even think about it, B."

Brynn's heart leapt inside her chest hearing Jack's nickname for her. A new kind of warmth filled her cheeks, spreading over her body and causing her to tug at the collar of her coat. She wasn't prepared for the familiar slip, and based on the pink coloring Jack's cheeks, he hadn't been either.

"We're here." He tipped his chin toward the windshield just as the shopping center came into view ahead of them.

She took in the length of the one-story structure spread over several acres as Jack pulled into the parking lot. This wasn't your typical strip mall. Fairfax Towne Centre was high-end, catering to a very specific shopper with luxury and designer stores. The dusting of snow edging the manicured landscape of evergreen shrubs almost looked picturesque against the modern design of the storefronts. Cobblestone walkways were punctuated with trees that, in the spring, offered shoppers ample shade but currently were barren except for the strands of twinkling lights still up from the Christmas season.

*Why would Riad be here?*

While Jack maneuvered through the lot, Brynn tapped her cell phone screen and pulled up the information Kekoa had sent her. "We're looking for a silver Corolla. License plate number RKA705."

After several passes between lanes, Brynn pointed to a car. "There."

Jack quickly found a parking spot a few spaces away, and they both climbed out of the Tahoe.

When Jack rounded the SUV and was at her side, Brynn reached for his arm, which caused him to stop and sent a zip of electricity up her arm. She let go. "Sorry, I'm not . . . well, we don't know what we're walking up to, and you know I don't carry."

Understanding filled his eyes. "I do." He patted the bulge at the side of his hip before unbuttoning his wool coat. "Stay to my left."

Jack's protective response immediately began messing with Brynn's heart. Which was ridiculous because he would've said the same thing to anyone. Most people assumed CIA officers carried weapons like James Bond or Jason Bourne, but the reality was that most were never issued a weapon. And, while she wasn't carrying a weapon, she had been trained to defend herself. Still, she wasn't foolish, and Jack being armed provided a level of security as they approached the car.

Brynn checked the license plate. RKA705. It was the right car . . . and it was empty.

She peered into the back windows and then the front ones. Nothing inside. Frustration curled around her shoulders. "He's not here."

Jack pulled out his cell phone and made a call. "Kekoa, I need a favor."

Those words sent guilt snaking through Brynn. *"Ms. Taylor, may I ask a favor?"* Her stomach twisted into a knot. She had chosen to keep Riad's request to herself because . . . because what did it even mean? She had no idea what he'd wanted, and mentioning it would only further fuel the idea that Riad was a threat.

She looked around. Nothing about the high-end shopping center stood out. Why here? What did it mean? Was Riad involved in something more nefarious, as Jack had suggested? Did this location have something to do with Riad's unspoken favor?

And did she tell Jack?

"Brynn, the door."

"What?" She spun around, startled. "I'm sorry, what?"

He pointed to the car. "Check the door."

She walked to the driver's-side door and reached for the handle. It opened. "It's unlocked."

"Thanks, Kekoa." Jack slid the phone back into his pocket. "Now pop the trunk."

Brynn did and then met him at the back of the car. "Let me guess, Kekoa hacked the car's system?"

"No." Jack lifted the trunk lid with a smile. "OnStar."

Shaking her head, Brynn peered into the trunk. A suitcase and laptop bag lay inside.

"I think this means Riad may still be around," Jack said, searching the parking lot. "Let's do a quick recon."

Jack's familiar tone of commitment sent a surge of adrenaline rushing through her, bringing with it memories of their time spent together working field exercises while training for clandestine operations. Jack's work ethic had been as steadfast as his loyalty, and Brynn had found it irresistible. A biting gust of wind cut through her coat, chilling her and bringing her back to the present.

Looking around again, she noticed the parking lot was growing busier with each passing minute. "Do you think we should leave the car? If Riad comes back and can't start his car, he might take off on foot."

Jack glanced over at the storefronts. "If we don't walk too far, we should still have a good line of sight down the center and be able to keep an eye on the car."

They walked across the parking lot, then stepped onto the busy sidewalk. Even though it was barely midmorning and blustery, post-holiday sales were bringing out the shoppers. Jack and Brynn hurried along the sidewalk, dodging oblivious shoppers while still maintaining a visual on Riad's rental car. Where was Riad?

"Do you think he ditched the car?"

Brynn glanced up at Jack. "And his suitcase and laptop?"

Jack turned in a circle, his brown eyes focused and serious as he scanned the area. "Something doesn't feel right about this." His gaze met hers. "You don't think he'd come here and . . ." He took a step closer and lowered his voice. "You know—" Jack balled his gloved hand and then opened his fingers wide like some sort of explosion.

Her eyes shot wide. "No." She gasped, quickly checking around them as if someone would've had a clue what they were talking about. "No, I don't think he would do that."

But was she sure?

Brynn scanned the faces around her when the squeal of a small child pulled her attention to a bakery where a little girl was dancing with a red balloon in her hand. A reflection in the window nearly choked her. She spun around and searched for the face she thought she'd just recognized. "Jack, I think I saw him."

Jack turned. "Where?"

Brynn walked toward a cluster of shoppers, eyeing the face of everyone around her. "I swear he was here, Jack."

"Did you see what he was wearing?"

She brushed a strand of hair out of her face. "Um, I think he had on a black coat. I didn't see his pants and . . . uh . . ." Brynn closed her eyes, recalling the glimpse of the man she thought was Riad. "A hat." She opened her eyes and touched her head. "He was wearing a knit beanie with 'USA' stitched on the front."

"You stay here by the bakery, keep an eye out for him and the car. I'll take a walk around and see if I can spot him."

Brynn nodded, still scanning the area for the distinctive hat. After a few minutes of looking, she let out a frustrated sigh, her breath forming a cloud against the cold air.

Jack walked back over. "No sign of him?"

"No, but maybe it wasn't him? Maybe I just wanted it to be."

Skepticism filled Jack's eyes. "Do you believe that?"

She hesitated before answering. "No. I know what I saw."

"Then let's go back to the—"

"Jack, there!" Brynn pointed through the crowd of people to a man wearing a black coat and khaki pants but no knit cap. Why did she think it was him? The walk. There was something distinct about the way Remon Riad walked—a confident stride—and yet this man . . .

"Is it him, Brynn?"

"I-I don't know." And then the man turned enough that she got a glimpse of his profile. "Yes! That's him."

Squealing brakes and the crunch of impact drew Brynn's attention to the parking lot, where a black car had T-boned an SUV. A woman jumped out of the SUV, panic etched in her face.

"My baby! My baby!"

Instinct urged Brynn toward the desperate mother even as shoppers began running to the SUV. The driver of the black car, a blond man, hadn't moved. Was he hurt? The entire right side of the SUV was crunched inward, making it impossible for the mom to open the door. She rounded back to the driver's side, desperation in her movements to get to her child.

"Brynn, where's Riad?"

Jack's touch at her back turned her to where Riad had been, only now he was gone. She swiveled her head in every direction, trying to spot him, but the area became congested with people coming to assist the mother and her child.

"He's gone, Jack. I've lost him."

# 8

Moustafa Ali tugged on the collar of his second button-down shirt. Sweat stains already discolored the light gray fabric. He took a breath and wiped the perspiration on his brow. He had one clean shirt left.

"Moustafa, yalla."

A heavy voice echoed off the cement walls, making him more nervous. He hurried to the closet and pulled a white button-down shirt out of the small duffel bag he was allowed to bring with him. The same one he wore for his sister's wedding a year ago. He lifted it to his nose and believed he could still smell the earthy scent of Arabian jasmine from her special day. Longing pierced his heart. He wanted to go home.

Pounding on the wall rattled a mirror, and Moustafa moved quickly to the ironing board and tried to press the wrinkles from his shirt. *This is for your future, habibi.*

Moustafa's parents and family had celebrated for an entire week when they received word of his scholarship to the American university in Virginia. Growing up, his papa would tell him stories of the freedoms in America. The riches he could make. And when Moustafa boarded his first plane, scared of everything, he kept only one thing in his mind—he would not let his family down.

He held up his shirt, the stubborn folds still there, but he was out of time. Checking his reflection in the mirror, he ran a hand through his thick black hair. Would his mama and papa be proud of him this day?

The door to his room swung open, and Hashem peeked his head in. "Hal 'ant jahiz?"

Hashem Mazdani was the first person Moustafa met when he walked out of the huge Texas airport two days ago. On the drive to the three-bedroom home, Hashem explained he had moved to Houston a year ago from Iran. His cousins, who lived in the home too, had arrived a few years earlier and also worked for Protech.

Afraid of what his parents would say, Moustafa decided it was best to wait to tell them about taking time away from his studies until after he had started the computer job. His papa told him dreams come true in America, and Moustafa's dream was to get a job, make a lot of money, and take care of his family.

Moustafa took a breath. "I think I am ready."

The traffic in Houston reminded him of home. Except the drivers here stayed in their lanes and there was less honking. Funny how he missed the noisy racket of his homeland.

An hour later, Moustafa got out of the car and slid his white shirt on and buttoned it up to his neck.

"Look at him." Hashem shook his head, laughing, his cousins joining in. He reached for Moustafa's collar and straightened it. "You do not have to be nervous."

Together they walked to a multistory building with very few windows. At the entrance a guard asked for their identifications. All Moustafa had was his passport and student ID card when he flew in, and Hashem had taken his passport to keep it safe. Embarrassment warmed Moustafa's cheeks when he passed over the student ID card, but the guard barely looked at it before waving them through.

"I will take you to Mr. Sokolov's office. You will fill out paperwork for"—Hashem rubbed his thumb against his fingers—"your money. Then you will begin work."

Moustafa swallowed, tugging at his collar. *S-ah-k-oh-l-ahv*. He rolled the funny sounds in his mind. Hashem helped him practice the hard name so he would not offend his new boss, but he was afraid his nerves would make him forget.

"Do not worry, my friend. This job is easy, and the best part?" He leaned close to Moustafa's ear to whisper. "They need us."

The atrium split into several different hallways. Hashem's cousins walked in one direction, and Hashem led Moustafa down another hall. They stopped halfway down beside a door, and Hashem clapped him on the shoulder.

"I will see you for lunch, then?"

"Yes, sure."

He watched Hashem disappear down the hallway before opening the door to a room that looked like a waiting area. A woman with dark curls sat at a desk behind a wall.

"Excuse me, I am here for Mr."—Moustafa took a breath—"Soo-ko-laf."

The woman gave him a tight smile. "What is your name?"

"Moustafa Ali. I am here for . . . interner . . . internash—" Moustafa fumbled over the word and the woman smiled again, sending a flame of heat up his cheeks.

"The internship." She picked up the phone. "Have a seat over there and wait."

Moustafa nodded and sat in the plastic seat. The television overhead was turned to the news, and his pulse pounded at the sight of the familiar Tahrir Square in Cairo where a reporter was talking. The sound was off, but the words at the bottom said, "New US military installation Wadi Basaela opening. President Omar Talaat optimistic."

He did not know this word, *optimistic*, but the president smiled, so he guessed it meant happy.

The scene changed from the traffic-heavy city center to a reporter standing in front of a walled fortress that seemed to blend into its desert surroundings. Next to the reporter was a man in a camouflage uniform, an American flag on his shoulder.

He wasn't sure how to feel about the Americans opening an Army base in Egypt. Should he be happy like the president? He'd asked his parents about it, and they shared his mixed feelings. On one hand, having the Americans there provided stability and jobs. Egypt needed that after the Arab Spring that pushed President Mubarak out of office, but what did having the American Army in Egypt mean? The camera angle changed and Moustafa had his answer.

A crowd of angry demonstrators held signs telling the Americans to get out. Leave Egypt. Some burned the American flag and the Egyptian flag, the faces of the American president and President Talaat drawn like ugly cartoons over them. Moustafa rubbed his hand over his knuckles. Would Egypt ever be at peace?

"Mr. Ali?"

Moustafa stood, turning to face a pale man in a brown suit waiting for him. "Yes, I am Moustafa."

"It is good to meet you." Right away Moustafa noticed the man had a thick accent. He held out a hand with a thick gold ring on one of the fingers. "I am Nestor Sokolov."

Mr. Sokolov led him into an office. "Please sit. Would you like some tea?"

"No thank you." Moustafa relaxed a bit at the offer. "I am so grateful for the opportunity to work here. I was nervous to take a semester away from school, but my professor said it would be good for my future."

Mr. Sokolov smiled. "Your professor is a smart teacher. The best way to grow as a man is to learn, and the best way to learn is to do, am I right?"

Moustafa frowned, trying to follow the meaning of his words. "I am only a second-year student. I hope I can do well for your company."

"You'll do fine, I'm sure." Mr. Sokolov began typing at his computer. He paused and sat back, scratching the top of his bald head. "Ah, you are a bright student. You like computers."

"Yes, sir." Moustafa sat forward. "My papa said the way of the future is computers, and I hope to one day work for my country's government or—"

Holding up a hand, Mr. Sokolov hushed Moustafa's enthusiasm. He reached for a piece of paper and slid it across the desk with a pen. "You will sign this."

Moustafa lifted the paper to read it, but Mr. Sokolov pressed it down and placed the pen over top.

"Do you know what a nondisclosure agreement is?"

"No, sir."

"It means you cannot discuss anything you do in this building with anyone. Not even the person working at the desk next to you."

"But are we not all doing the same job?"

"No." Mr. Sokolov tapped the paper. "Sign, or you do not work here."

Moustafa reached for the pen, ignoring the ball of worry in his stomach. He was probably just hungry. This was for his future. He quickly signed his name and slid the paper back to his new boss, who smiled.

"You like coding?"

"Yes, sir."

"Decoding?"

"Yes, sir."

"Good." Mr. Sokolov stood. "We're going to have you take some tests on the computer."

"Will I be graded?" Moustafa asked, following him to another room. Against the wall were two long tables with computers on them. They did not look like the ones at the university. "These are X300s."

"They are." He pointed to a chair in front of one and Moustafa sat. "There are no grades here, Moustafa, but if you do well, you get paid more."

Moustafa swiveled in the seat, his fingers pressing gently on the space bar to bring the computer to life. A buzz of electricity hummed as the system warmed up, and he could feel the same coursing through him. He loved computers. Loved being able to read a language many could not, and now he was going to be rewarded for it.

"Excuse me, Mister Sahk-oh-lahv." He faced his boss. "What if I get the highest score?"

"There are no high scores," he said, impatience in his tone. "You will do these tests, and then we will assign you a job. The better you do, the better your job."

"And more money?"

"Yes." Mr. Sokolov started for the door. "When you are done, I will come get you and take you to your new desk."

"Yes, sir." Moustafa couldn't help smiling. His new desk. Money. More if he did really well. Which he would because he was the best in his class. That's what his professor told him when he offered him this opportunity.

Moustafa would make him proud. His family too. Even if he could not tell anyone about his new job, he knew, on this day, he was changing his future forever.

# 9

*It couldn't be easy.*

Jack rubbed against the frustration working its way into his jaw. Remon Riad had managed to slip away from them, which meant his time with Brynn wasn't over. That reality toyed with his emotions and left him troubled.

Was it because he'd failed to grab Riad? Or did it have something to do with the sudden desire to make the worry etching its way into Brynn's delicate features go away?

*Beep, beep, beep.*

A tow truck loaded with Riad's car backed around the congested parking lot until it could navigate the ambulance and police officers still trying to take care of the earlier accident. Unable to locate Riad, Jack thought it best to tow the car in case the man decided to return, limiting his ability to flee. It would also allow them to do a thorough search of the vehicle.

As it pulled out, Brynn's pacing slowed. Her sharp blue eyes hadn't stopped scanning the area in the hopes Riad might show back up, but now they settled on him.

"We need to get back to DC. I'll take Riad's laptop to Langley. The analysts can look into—"

"Nothing."

The word hung suspended on a puff of breath in the cold air. Her expression stilled. "I'm sorry?"

"Riad's disappearance has been turned over to my team. The CIA doesn't have the authority—"

"I know what we're authorized to do, Jack."

The snap in her voice added to the burst of wintry air blasting their faces. A man and a woman, with shopping bags in their hands, cast a concerned glance their way.

"It's cold. Maybe we should get into the truck."

Brynn tugged her scarf around her neck and hurried past him to the Tahoe. He dug into his pocket and unlocked the vehicle, wishing he could take back his words . . . or did he? He wasn't trying to be difficult, but if she wasn't clear on who was in charge of the investigation, it was his job to let her know.

Once in the driver's seat, Jack was glad he'd used the remote engine starter to warm the Tahoe up earlier. Heat blasted from the vents, cutting the chill from his bones—but not the icy expression on Brynn's face.

"Kekoa's going to pull the surveillance footage of the shopping center. If we can spot Riad, then we might be able to track where and how he disappeared."

"This is your investigation, right?"

There was an edge to her tone, a challenge within the question. He nodded. "Yes, but you're—"

She held up a hand. "So, if *your* team discovers Riad is part of some terrorist plot, will it be you and *your* team taking responsibility when disaster strikes?"

He pressed his lips together.

"That's what I thought." She scoffed. "At the end of the day, you and your team get to walk away, leaving me and my career going down in flames."

Guilt washed through him. "Brynn, our job is to make sure we get to Riad before anything happens. You have my word on that."

She looked away, a soft sound escaping her lips. "I may not know

74

enough about your job, but you know about mine, and promises like that are arbitrary. There are no guarantees in this career."

Jack released a sigh. That was true, and Brynn's suspicions didn't surprise him. Most in the intelligence field considered skepticism an essential skill. Even he did. What did surprise him was the shift of suspicion.

"An hour ago you were convinced Riad didn't fit a profile and wasn't a threat. But I'm getting the feeling you might not believe that anymore. Why?"

Brynn adjusted the vents. She tugged off her gloves before pulling at her scarf. A second later she was moving the air vents again.

He frowned at her edginess. "I can turn down the heat."

"No, it's fine." She took a breath. "I'm sorry I snapped out there. It's just . . . I can't . . ." She pressed her lips together and glanced out the windshield as the ambulance drove away. "I'm trying to make sense of this whole thing." She faced him. "You read the file on Riad. Does he seem like the kind of person to behave like this?"

The question sounded like she wanted assurance. Jack considered his words before speaking. "Not on paper, no. But even the most steadfast human beings can shift under the right pressure."

Her blue eyes zeroed in on him, a flash of hurt passing across them before blinking it away. However, there was no hiding the suspicion he read in her face, and it made him uneasy. Back at the Farm, Brynn hadn't been one to waver in her conviction on anything unless there was evidence or a reason.

Jack frowned, his own suspicions rising to the surface. "Is there something else?"

"No." She looked away and settled back into her seat. "I want to get back and find out if there's anything on Riad's laptop."

The furrow in the skin between her eyes concerned him. His words to Walsh came rushing back. *I don't trust her.* Was there something fueling his mistrust of her, or were the memories of their past coloring his perspective? Would Brynn really hide something from him when her career hung in the balance?

Only one way to find out.

Jack backed out of the parking spot. "We need to eat."

"What?"

"I think better when I eat." He glanced at the time on the radio panel. "It's almost lunchtime."

"We need to get back to the office. Find out what's on the laptop."

He looked over his shoulder at Riad's suitcase and laptop bag. "They're not going anywhere."

"But Riad might be." Brynn's fingers began drumming again. Nervous. "Besides, I'm not hungry."

"Fine. Then you can watch me eat."

She shifted in her seat. "I, uh, I have lunch plans already. Just remembered."

"You do?"

Was she telling the truth? And why did his thoughts go straight to a faceless man? His fingers curled over the steering wheel as his thoughts circled back to an earlier one. Did Brynn have a boyfriend?

"Yes. And I can't back out of them."

The boldness in her voice was like a spur into his side. "Okay, well, invite . . . him . . . along?"

She glanced over, a defiant amusement lighting her eyes. "Her."

"Her?"

"My friend Olivia. I'm meeting *her* for lunch."

As he turned his attention back to the road, relief mixed with embarrassment warmed his cheeks. "Good. Invite her to lunch, because I'm starving. And food makes great company."

"Spoken like a true Italian."

The tilt to her lips did things to his chest, but he couldn't get past the idea that Brynn might be keeping something from him. And if it had to do with the mission, it didn't affect only him this time—it affected his whole team.

Several minutes into their drive, Brynn asked, "Want to tell me where we're going? I need to send Olivia the address."

"Mina's." He tapped the steering wheel, suddenly not so sure this was a great idea. "Is that okay?"

"Yeah, sure."

He kept himself from reading into her response as she quickly typed a text message to her friend. Mina's had been a favorite of theirs, and he hadn't thought twice about driving in that direction. It had been . . . instinct.

Nerves twisted into a knot in his stomach.

Jack found a spot on the street in front of the little restaurant and parked. If he focused on his hunger, maybe it would help him dwell less on the memories that would inevitably arise the second he walked into the little Middle Eastern café with Brynn.

The moment the bell tingled over the door, Jack's senses were hit with the familiar mixture of sharp spices, coffee, and stale cigarette smoke. Nothing inside the café had changed. Black-and-white tile, chipped and cracked, was barely walkable between the number of tables and chairs packed in. Posters of Egypt, Turkey, Jordan, Syria, and Morocco lined the walls, their edges torn, frayed, and curling. A glass display case holding baked goods with the cash register on top nearly blocked the entrance, making it almost impossible to move around if someone was paying or waiting to be seated.

A couple pressed past Brynn, leaving little room for him but to step out of the café to let them pass. "Still busy as ever," he said as he stepped back inside.

"Habibi, are my old eyes tricking me?"

The term of endearment cut through the café as customers glanced up to see Mina Samaan shuffling over, strands of gray hair peeking out from beneath her scarf, flour residue on the blue apron circling her round frame.

Reaching Brynn first, the sweet Syrian grandmother pinched both cheeks before kissing each side—left, right, then left again. "How are you, Mina?"

"Well, habibi, but"—she edged around Brynn and eyed Jack with hazy blue eyes—"tell me, is this my boy Jack now a man?"

"Al salamo aalaykom, Mina."

"Oh," she whispered, pressing a hand to her chest, eyes moist. "Wa aalaykom al salam. Come here, my boy."

Mina pulled Jack into an embrace, planting enough kisses on his cheeks that the customers seated around them started to laugh. "It's, uh, been a while."

"A while, pssh." Mina released him and used the hem of her apron to dab her eyes. "I thought we lost you." She turned to Brynn. "And you? How are you?"

There was meaning in Mina's question that turned Brynn's eyes glassy. "A little better every day."

Mina nodded, pressing a hand over her heart. "He was a good man. You make him proud."

Jack frowned. Who were they talking about?

"Mama, they are here to eat." Behind Mina, a woman with dark-brown hair tied up in a braid over her shoulder walked up. "Allo, Brynn."

"Hi, Asha!" Brynn greeted Mina's daughter with a hug and the traditional cheek kissing. "You remember Jack?"

Asha smiled at Jack. "Be still my heart, how could I forget?"

"It's good to see you, Asha." He blushed at the teasing. "How are you?"

She raised her left hand, fingers wiggling so he could see the gold band. "I'm married!"

"Congrats!" He grinned, but it didn't match the pride beaming in Mina's face.

"Now, she make me a teta."

"Mama, hush. I'm not ready to make you a grandmother yet." Asha's cheeks dimpled playfully. She gestured to a round metal table near the kitchen. "For two?"

"Actually, three," Brynn said. "My friend will be joining us."

Jack wasn't certain, but he thought he saw disappointment in Asha's expression as she led them to another table with four chairs. He took a seat, his chair tipping from an uneven leg.

"Do you need a menu?" Asha looked between them. "Or should I bring out your favorites?"

"Should we wait for your friend?"

Brynn shook her head at Jack. "No, let's order so it's ready when she gets here."

Jack smiled up at Asha. "Then our favorites it is."

Mina squeezed Jack's cheeks once more with a motherly sigh before shuffling back into the kitchen, Asha following with a curious glance at Brynn.

"She missed you."

Jack glanced over his shoulder and back to Brynn. "But not you." He thought about the emotional exchange between her and Mina. "You kept coming back?"

Brynn's gaze dipped to the table. "The food's good."

He could agree with her on that. For the next several minutes, Brynn filled him in on Mina's and Asha's lives, careful—it seemed to him—to include only one detail about Asha's traditional Syrian wedding. That it was beautiful. Was that on purpose? Was Brynn just being succinct, or was there another reason she avoided offering him the details? Before Jack could think on it further, Asha came over with a tray of food and set down plates of sliced lamb, falafel, dolmades, and fatayer.

Jack breathed in the tantalizing aroma. "This looks amazing."

"If you need anything else, let me know." Asha smiled. "Enjoy."

Placing his napkin on his lap, Jack looked up at Brynn. "I hope there's some left by the time your friend shows up."

Her eyes flashed to the door, an anxious anticipation in them. "She should be here soon."

Jack offered her a plate. "It'd break Mina's heart if we let this get cold."

Gaze back on him, Brynn accepted the plate with a nod and began filling it with food.

Waiting for her, he let his eyes trace the features of the face he once knew so well. The soft slope of her nose, the roundness of her cheeks and jawline that met the square shape of her chin—a feature Brynn grumbled was the worst trait inherited from her Scottish grandmother. But Jack disagreed. He loved the way it would jut out whenever Brynn's stubborn streak emerged.

Eight years ago, there had been a determined edge to her features. A woman in the CIA wasn't unusual anymore, but it didn't mean it was easy. Jack had watched Brynn work and train harder than any of their male counterparts. Her strength to face challenges head-on was one of the many things he found attractive about her. *One of a million things . . .*

"My dad always said I had perfect timing."

Jack's gaze swung to meet the light-brown eyes of a woman standing at their table with a black lab at her side.

Brynn stood and embraced the woman, whom Jack guessed was Olivia.

"It's snowing a little bit, and you'd think people would know how to drive in it over here. I mean, in New Mexico it's a desert, so of course it practically shuts down the state when a single flurry drops, but here it's—"

"This is my friend Olivia," Brynn cut in. "And Penny." Brynn pointed to the dog, who had quietly tucked herself beneath their table, dark-brown eyes watching everything happening around her. She wore a service harness, and on her collar was a silver badge that identified her as New Mexico Fire Rescue.

"And this is Jack Hudson."

Olivia sat, eyes fixed on him in a curious stare. "Jack Hudson?"

The way his name rolled off her lips twisted Jack's midsection. He glanced over to Brynn, her cheeks bright pink and her glare at Olivia—meaningful.

"It's nice to meet you and Penny."

"And to finally meet you— Ouch!" The table rocked, and Olivia winced before shooting an accusatory look at Brynn. "Thanks for letting me intrude on your lunch date."

"It's not a date," Jack and Brynn said at the same time.

Olivia smiled with a giggle before sliding out of her parka. The NMFR emblem with two fire axes intersecting was embroidered on the pocket of the long-sleeve navy thermal that matched her navy-colored tactical pants.

"It's a working lunch." Brynn tore off a piece of pita bread and looked at Jack. "Olivia and Penny are arson investigators."

"Really?" He tapped his chest. "I see you're from New Mexico. What brings you to DC?"

He'd caught her with a bite of food in her mouth, and she looked helplessly at Brynn. "They're here for the annual conference and training."

Finishing her bite, Olivia flashed a bright smile at Brynn. "And my sweet friend kindly allows me and Penny to invade her home for a few weeks every year. One of these days I'm going to repay the favor if I can ever get her out to the desert. It's not like she has a boyfriend holding her back."

"Olivia." Brynn's word lingered with warning. "Jack, why don't you tell Olivia what SNAP does."

"SNAP?"

"Strategic Neutralization and Protection Agency." Brynn answered Olivia's question, making her tone sound ominous. "They're, uh . . . a government agency . . . right?"

Jack ran a napkin over his lips to hide the smile. Knowing Brynn, she'd researched SNAP and been left unsatisfied with what she'd uncovered. But her less-than-subtle attempt to steer her friend's attention and gather information was an amusing tactic.

"No. We're not a government agency, but we do pick up government contracts. Really, we're just another boring contract company."

"Doesn't sound boring. I noticed SNAP operates not only domestically but internationally as well." Brynn sipped her water. "What do you do overseas?"

Olivia's eyes bounced between them. She kept quiet but also look entertained.

"Depends on the assignment."

"Fine, Hudson." She waved her hand, dismissing him. "I won't beg you for information."

"Wow. You gave up so easy."

"I'd like to know what your agency does." Olivia wrapped some lamb into a pita. "Sounds intriguing."

Finishing his bite of falafel, Jack dusted his fingers over his plate. "First, it's not my agency. Second, when our services are required, we *cooperate* with the government and federal agencies for the common good of America and her citizens."

"Wow," Brynn said mockingly. "How many lawyers came up with that sound bite?"

Jack held in a snicker and shrugged. "We get hired to take care of situations before they become situations."

Brynn tilted her head. "Like . . ."

He took a breath. "Like providing security for companies, intervening when situations arise—"

"Like?" Her eyebrow arched.

Jack wiggled his eyebrows. "If I told you, I'd have to—"

"Don't say it, Hudson!" Brynn pointed a finger at him. "That's our joke." Pink blossomed on her cheeks before she looked away. "I mean, my agency's joke."

"I think it's every agency's joke." Olivia rolled her eyes. "I've heard it at least three times this week from three different FBI agents." She took a bite of falafel and chewed, looking between Jack and Brynn. "Interesting you two never worked together before now."

Brynn's eyes grew round and Jack nearly choked on his dolmade. Swallowing his bite, he waited to see if Brynn would answer. When she didn't, he shrugged.

"I never really considered our paths would cross, I guess."

Brynn's eyebrows rose. "DC's not that big, Jack."

A rush of heat filled him as memories of their past floated dangerously close to the surface. Jack shoved them away. "I'm just saying I'm surprised you're here and not serving overseas. That was always your goal, right?"

Brynn finished chewing. "It still is." She wiped her lips. "But things changed, and I had to adjust."

Her tone was diplomatic, but it didn't match the quick glimpse of sadness clouding her blue eyes. What *things* possibly could have stood in the way of her goal? It didn't fit the woman Jack knew all those years ago. *Nothing* would've gotten in her way. And yet, here she was.

"Must've been pretty significant."

"My mother had a heart attack three years ago. I stayed in DC later to care for my father."

His heart dropped to his stomach. "Brynn, I'm so sorry."

She swallowed, a glimmer of emotion trying to break through the posture of strength hardening the softness in her face. "If you'll excuse me for a moment."

Jack watched Brynn stand and head to the small hallway leading to the restrooms. He closed his eyes, feeling like a jerk as he remembered the earlier exchange between Brynn and Mina. Opening his eyes, he found Olivia giving him a sympathetic look.

"I didn't know."

"It was unexpected." Olivia wiped her lips. "Brynn came home for the funeral and to help her dad get settled before she was supposed to return to Somalia, but her position over there was closed or something. She's been here ever since."

*I'm the worst person in the world.* "How's her father doing?"

Olivia's gaze moved over his shoulder, and her light-brown eyes turned apologetic. One look behind him and he understood why. Brynn had returned, eyes rimmed red, her jaw set.

She glanced down at Jack. "He died eight months ago."

The air whooshed from his chest, a painful ache filling its place. "Brynn—"

"It's fine." She cleared her throat and reached for her jacket and scarf. "He was in a lot of pain, and it was fast."

83

How fast? Jack had met Brynn's parents once, but he remembered the bond between her and her father. If he was honest, it had intimidated him—like an unspoken challenge to match up to the man Brynn admired with all her heart. Had eight months been enough time to mourn the absence of such an important—maybe the most important—person in her life?

The cell phone attached to Olivia's waistband rang out. She checked it and groaned. "I've got to go back to work. They need Penny for demonstrations."

"We should get back to work too." Brynn slid her scarf around her neck. She reached into her purse and pulled out some cash and dropped it on the table. "I'm going to talk to Asha. I'll meet you outside."

Jack grabbed his coat and added his own cash to the table, certain they were overpaying for lunch, but he didn't care. His bearings felt off-kilter. His heart was broken for Brynn's loss. He couldn't imagine how he'd handle losing either of his parents, but at least he'd have his sisters. Who did Brynn have to help her through the unimaginable? Saying goodbye to Olivia and Penny, Jack stepped out of the café, recognizing the concern wedging its way into his heart.

The last time that happened—it hadn't ended well for him.

# 10

If it wasn't for the near-arctic temperature, Brynn would've taken the Metro back to SNAP headquarters, if only to escape the pitiful glances Jack kept shooting her way. Her cell phone buzzed with another message from Olivia apologizing.

Brynn sighed as Jack pulled into the parking garage beneath the Acacia Building. She knew Olivia had meant well, but it didn't take away the feeling of vulnerability hollowing out her chest. Now Jack knew she was all alone.

Jack parked the car, and they climbed out and walked toward the elevator. He scanned his card key and hit the button for the eighth floor before his eyes slid to the white paper bag in her hand.

"Old CIA strategy?"

"What?"

The elevator arrived and they stepped in.

"Discover a weakness and use it to win favor. Good choice with Mina's baklava."

"Pssh." Brynn shook her head. "Mina wouldn't let me leave without bringing something back, and I know it's your fav—"

The rest of the word dried up in her throat at the smile cresting on Jack's face. A familiar flutter of attraction tried to work its

85

way into her chest, but she shoved it aside as the elevator doors slid open.

It was ridiculous. A simple lunch at Mina's—which she'd done whenever she could over the last eight years—and her mind was drifting to the past. Their past. One smile from him brought the past rocketing to the future like no time had passed. But it had. So much had happened since then, and it would serve her well to remember that. When put to the test . . . they both wanted different things.

Walking down the hall, Brynn shrugged. "I thought it'd be a nice gesture."

Jack keyed in his code to the SNAP office. "You don't have to win their affection."

"Don't act like you can read my mind, Hudson." She was teasing, but she hated that he'd been able to discern a nugget of truth to her intentions. She'd never admit that Lyla intimidated her a little bit.

The pungent aroma of oregano, tomato, and basil filled the kitchen of SNAP's office. A quick search and Brynn spotted the source. A glass dish sat on the counter, the tomato sauce and cheese baked on the edges the only evidence left of what might've been in there—but Brynn knew.

"Please don't tell me that was your mom's lasagna."

Jack removed his coat and hung it up. "It *was*." He held out a hand, and she passed over the order of baklava. He placed it on the counter while she took off her coat. "I forgot about it."

There was no way she was hungry, but her stomach gave a nudge of longing. "How could you forget about it?" Hanging up her coat, she reached for Riad's laptop bag. "We could've come straight here and had that for lunch while Kekoa worked on this."

"Worked on what?"

Brynn did a double take. The woman who'd walked in barely resembled the whirlwind of sass she'd met that morning. Gone was the purple hair, eyebrow piercing, stilettos . . . the edginess.

Instead, Lyla's light-brown hair was swept away from her face and into a bun. Without the makeup, her blue-green eyes appeared large and bright. And in a pair of black leggings and an oversized denim shirt knotted at the waist, she pulled off chic comfort in a way that made Brynn jealous.

"Riad's laptop."

"We need Kekoa to . . . hack into it." Brynn didn't know why she felt the need to whisper that last part, but it drew an amused look from both Lyla and Jack. She swallowed, her lunch feeling heavy in her stomach. "Uh, so I should take it back to—"

"Did someone bring food?" Kekoa walked in, nose in the air, sniffing. His dark-brown eyes locked on the white bag sitting on the counter. "I'm starving."

Garcia edged around Kekoa. "You just ate."

"Speaking of that—my lasagna?" Jack lifted the edge of the empty dish.

Lyla and Garcia exchanged quick glances before Garcia used his eyes to direct Jack's attention to Kekoa, who was already pulling out the foam container from the bag.

"What's this?"

"Syrian baklava," Brynn said. "We brought it back from lunch."

"To share," Jack added, taking the container from Kekoa. "Really, the whole lasagna?"

"Not all of it. I saved some." Kekoa tipped his head toward the fridge. "For you and my favorite wahine."

Kekoa winked at Brynn, a wide smile on his face. He was dressed in a short-sleeve T-shirt that wrapped tightly around his bulges of biceps, and she still couldn't fathom how he had made it work on a ship.

"Hey!" Lyla punched Kekoa's arm. "I thought I was your favorite?"

"When was the last time you brought me food?"

Lyla's lips pinched, her face scrunching in thought. "I brought you brownies last week."

"Bahahaha." The burst of laughter from Kekoa's lips was so loud and unexpected, Brynn startled. "You mean the hockey pucks?"

His laughter, a hearty noise that echoed around the room, resumed and soon Jack and Garcia joined in, leaving Lyla scowling. Brynn bit down hard on the inside of her lip to control her own giggle from escaping.

"I guess you're too busy laughing to eat this, huh?" Lyla swiped the piece of baklava Jack had plated.

Kekoa's laughter stopped, eyes wide, smile daring. "Two things." He held up two meaty fingers. "One, no slippahs in the house, and two, you don't get in the way of a man and ono grindz."

Lyla rolled her eyes, holding up her right index finger. "Reason number one why there's no lasagna left."

"All right, everyone, grab some dessert if you want and let's begin our debriefing." Jack led the way back into the Jason Bourne–like set of their office. He glanced over his shoulder at Brynn. "You can give that to Kekoa."

She looked down at Riad's laptop bag in her hand. Grip tight over the handle. Unease snaked through her. Jack was right. SNAP did have the authority to look into Riad's laptop—a fact she confirmed with a quick call to Peterson after excusing herself from the table at Mina's. Why was she so afraid to let it go?

"Kekoa knows to look for anything on there of value to our assignment." He nodded to Kekoa. "And only our assignment."

"Don't worry, sis." Kekoa reached for the laptop and Brynn released it. "I've got this."

There was no doubt in her mind the skilled cryptologist would find something—but what? Her nerves thrummed with anxiety. Even as her own beliefs about Riad wavered, if her assessment about the Egyptian spy was wrong—if she'd missed something or been misled—what did that say about her? If Riad was involved in something, she needed to stop him.

"Are we ready?"

Jack's question snapped Brynn's attention back to the room where everyone, including Kekoa, had taken seats around the conference table as they had that morning.

Kekoa reached for a plate, fork in hand, eyes glazing in anticipation of the bite of baklava he was about to eat when Jack spoke up.

"Let's start with the security footage from the shopping center. Were you able to get us that?"

"Brah." Kekoa quickly scooped a giant piece of the buttery, honey pastry into his mouth, chewed, and swallowed. "Too easy."

Wiping his mouth with a napkin, Kekoa grabbed his silicon keyboard and flexed his fingers like a pianist readying for his recital. He pointed over Brynn's shoulder to a large flat-screen television mounted on the wall with security footage streaming from different angles around the Acacia Building.

"It took some sweet-talking by yours truly, and Babs"—Kekoa's face went serious—"no joke, the woman's name is Babs, and she's fifty-two and breeds Chinese crested dogs, which are not pretty by the way. I had to look it up."

Lyla snorted, and Brynn was quickly becoming convinced Kekoa might be her favorite of the team. She kept her eyes from drifting to the only other person who may have claimed that spot by default once upon a time.

"Anyway, she sent me the video footage from the Fairfax Towne Centre's security cameras." A few keystrokes and the screens overhead filled with a dozen different angles of the shopping center. Kekoa enhanced one of the screens. "Over here"—the video angle changed—"you see Riad's car pull into the parking lot. Parks." Another camera shift. "Walks to the bakery but never goes inside."

Brynn's pulse ticked up. *What were you doing there, Riad?*

The camera angles switched again. "He walks around for a bit but never leaves the area around the bakery for twenty or so minutes. That's when you show up."

One of the angles enlarged, and a second later Brynn and Jack come into the shot.

"This is when you spot Riad."

Brynn watched herself turn, a surprised look on her face. *He was right there*. And she'd missed him. On the screen, Riad, wearing what she remembered, stands there for several moments before turning and seeing Brynn. Then there's a sudden jerk of his head, and his attention shifts as people begin rushing by him.

"The car accident."

"Right," Kekoa said. "If I go back to this camera."

Riad's reaction to the accident pushes him forward a step as though he wants to assist, and then something stops him, because he spins around. Brynn tried to read the expression on his face, but the angle was too high. He starts walking, the direction taking him out of that camera's viewpoint.

"Where does he go?"

Kekoa typed. "There."

Riad reappears in the corner of another shot, and it looks like he's talking to someone, his hands gesturing in the air, but the angle keeps his face and the person he's talking to hidden. A moment later, Riad begins moving again, briskly, shoulders hunched and head tipped forward.

Jack furrowed his brow. "Looks like he's bolting."

"No." Brynn frowned. "Something's wrong."

"What do you mean?"

"Riad's a proud man. He carries himself with confidence. It's one of the things I noticed about him, always walking with his shoulders back. Likely due to his service in the military, but it's also cultural."

Garcia nodded, eyes on the screens. "I can see it. His posture shifts when he sees you and Jack and then again after this conversation."

Jack pointed to the screen, where they watched Riad enter and exit different camera angles, Kekoa tracking him. "Is there a better view so we can see who Riad's talking to?"

Kekoa typed some more. "Nah, brah. Whoever it is stays close to the edge and out of sight. Even camera angles from across the way can't catch him."

"It's like he's using Riad as a shield," Lyla added.

"How do you know it's a he?" Jack asked.

Lyla looked at Jack and then at Brynn. "If she's right about Riad's posture, why would a proud Egyptian man cower to a woman?"

Brynn nodded. "Smart catch."

A moment passed between her and Lyla before she gave a single shoulder shrug. "Easy observation."

Except it wasn't. Only someone who understood Middle Eastern culture would make that connection. Lyla was definitely proving to be more than meets the eye.

"Wait, it looks like Riad rounds back to the bakery."

Jack's words turned her attention to the screen he was watching. A quick look at the other cameras, and Brynn caught her and Jack going in the opposite direction, looking for Riad.

"Is he going back to his car?"

"No," Kekoa answered Garcia. "Ugh. He's . . . wait . . ." Kekoa squinted at the screen, typing as the images overhead flashed through several camera angles. "He's gone."

Brynn stood, walking closer to the screens. "Can you back it up, Kekoa?"

He did, and Brynn watched Riad round the corner by a women's clothing store. He continues walking, but Lyla was right. The man makes sure to stay tucked in tight so he can't be seen.

Once again, tension riddled Brynn's body.

Keeping an eye on Riad's USA knit cap, she followed it until they got to the scene of the accident, where almost two dozen people were congregating to watch. A large man crosses in front of Riad and then Riad is gone.

"He couldn't have disappeared," Lyla said. "Unless Egypt's version of the CIA teaches tricks and tips from Houdini? Or was it David Copperfield who made the pyramids disappear?"

"An evasive tactic?" Jack said with a sigh. "If he's a good intelligence agent, he'd know cameras were watching him. Didn't want anyone to see where he was going so he couldn't be followed."

Brynn hadn't noticed he'd moved next to her, and his sudden nearness caused her insides to tighten, warning her of trouble. Or maybe it was his observation that unnerved her? She pointed up at the screen, using the gesture to put a few inches of space between them. Just enough so she could breathe. "Kekoa, if you go back a few seconds, there's something on the ground."

Again, Kekoa, without question, did as told even as Brynn's cheeks burned.

"Please," she added.

The Hawaiian gave her a lopsided grin with a wink. "What you lookin' for, sis?"

"Pause there, please." Brynn reached up, her fingertip tapping on the screen. "That right there."

Lyla wrinkled her nose. "The black blob on the ground?"

"Riad's cap," Jack said, confirming his theory. "He slipped it off so we couldn't follow him."

Brynn didn't like the way Jack said that. "He might've been coerced."

Jack faced her, and she could read the doubt in his eyes. "Which leaves us with one question—why was Riad there in the first place?"

"Most intelligence officers I know don't act without a purpose." Garcia's words grounded Brynn. "Riad's behavior suggests he went there for a purpose, and we have to consider he may have achieved his objective."

"*Achieved his objective*," Lyla mocked in a low tone with a flirtatious smile. She slid the plate of baklava to Garcia. "Eat some more sugar, Nicolás. You're too formal."

Garcia's jaw muscle flexed, the only movement in his otherwise controlled expression.

"If you won't eat yours, I'll take it." Kekoa reached across the table, hesitating only a second for Garcia's permission, which consisted of a tight nod.

Jack returned to his seat, and so did Brynn even though her nerves were on edge. Sitting was the last thing she wanted to do. However, pacing wouldn't exactly exude control, and she needed to hang on to any shred as she watched her profile on Riad crumble around her—likely taking her career down with it.

"Anything else pertaining to the assignment?" Jack asked, looking around the table. Garcia's hand wrapped around the brim of his Red Sox cap as he tipped it up a bit. "Garcia?"

"It's not relevant to the current assignment, but I got an email about an hour ago from Barksdale Air Force Base, and they noticed some of their systems have been glitchy. They recently updated their system with a defense contractor and wanted us to check into it."

"What's at Barksdale?"

"The Global Strike Command, which manages more than half of our nation's nuclear capabilities for combat readiness," Garcia answered Brynn. "It's where the Eighth Air Force is headquartered and the location of a squadron of B-52 bombers."

"The *Mighty Eighth*," Kekoa said around a bite of baklava. "'*Deterrence through strength, global strike on command.*'"

"Nuclear war and pastries. Yum."

And just like that, Lyla's sass returned.

"Nuclear *deterrence*." Garcia pushed up the sleeves of his flannel shirt, revealing muscled forearms that would make any girl swoon. "To prevent war."

A glitch in anything having to do with nuclear systems did not sound good to Brynn. She was learning something new about Jack's team and how deep their involvement stretched.

"Okay, check into it and keep me updated," Jack said before the trill of his cell phone sent it dancing across the table. He grabbed it but not before Brynn caught a glimpse of the caller.

Amy Carmichael.

Jack declined the call, his eyes flashing to her before he quickly tucked the phone into his back pocket.

An ugly feeling rushed into Brynn's chest, but she refused to allow it to take root. Jealousy never looked good on anyone, and she had no business worrying about who Amy Carmichael was or what she was to Jack.

*Eight years.* It had been long enough for both of them to move on, and while it appeared Jack likely had, it was a stinging reminder that after all this time she . . . hadn't.

## 11

Washington, DC
5:15 PM Wednesday, January 14

Sandpaper rubbing against his eyeballs couldn't hurt worse than hours spent staring at a computer screen. And for what? Either Riad was really good at hiding his true intentions or Brynn's original assessment was true—he did not fit the profile of a terrorist.

So why was he missing? And where was he?

Jack checked his watch. Quarter past five. A quick glance out the window and he could see the last of the DC traffic dwindling. Most of the city's employees were back on the road by three to fight the congestion of commuters on their way home.

"Let's close up shop, and we'll hit it again tomorrow."

Brynn's eyes flew from the laptop screen in front of her to meet his. "What?" She looked at Garcia and Lyla, who were both shutting down their computers and clearing their desks. "You're done?"

Determination in those fiery blue eyes invited Jack's heart back to the day at the Farm when another CIA officer dared Brynn in a physical fitness exercise. The man was at least a foot taller and forty pounds heavier by muscle alone, but it was ego that did him in. He didn't believe a CIA analyst—a paper pusher—could survive the obstacle course field operatives had to successfully maneuver. His first mistake was assuming. His second was underestimating Brynn's determination.

Not only did Brynn complete the course, she smoked the challenger's time by a full minute and waited for him to finish, legs swinging on the eight-foot wall she'd climbed back up to revel in her victory.

If he hadn't fallen for her before that moment, her toying smirk had sparked an attraction that apparently still flickered, given the way his pulse was dancing right now.

"For today, yes." He stood and stretched his arms and back, feeling the tightness of a long day in every muscle. "We've reached the end of what we can work on. Kekoa will continue to work on Riad's laptop."

"Don't worry, sistah"—Kekoa tucked a loose curl behind his ear before giving his laptop bag a pat—"my babies work all night long."

The look on Brynn's face said she would worry all night long. "It's not even six and—" Her brow pinched, and he read the challenge in her eyes. "You're seriously going to walk out with Riad out there somewhere in trouble or . . . worse?"

Lyla let out a stifled breath, eyes wide with expectation that seemed to say "Are you going to let her get away with that?"

Jack inhaled slowly as Brynn's question brought up his earlier concern. It was like she couldn't decide whether she believed Riad was who she thought he was or the growing proof that maybe he wasn't. It almost felt like her emotions were getting in the way, which was unusual. The Brynn he knew made her decisions with her head, not her emotions. What had changed?

"Unless you know something that'll lead us to him, we're done for the day."

"Ooh," Lyla cooed. "Gauntlet accepted and—"

"Lyla."

Garcia's voice was low, and Lyla scrunched up her face at him. "You're no fun."

Lyla's flair for the dramatic always reminded Jack of his sisters, which brought back to mind Brynn's question regarding a relationship between him and Lyla. While Lyla carried many amazing traits—pretty, generous, loyal, weird sense of humor—she wasn't his type. Amy popped into his head. Was *she* his type?

His gaze focused on Brynn. At one time he believed she was perfect for him.

Brynn's attention moved back to him, a ferocity in her eyes likely spurred on by Lyla. "You know everything I do. I just can't figure out how your agency gets anything accomplished working bankers' hours."

From the corner of his eye, Jack saw Lyla's mouth pop open, and it was all he could do not to become annoyed with her. But it would be misdirected, because it was Brynn who was challenging his leadership—again.

"My team, this agency, accomplishes plenty." His jaw ached with frustration. "In the last few years, my team and I have logged more hours in this office than in our homes. So when an opportunity arrives where we can step away and remember that life exists outside of this office, you can bet we're going to take advantage of it. Life's too short not to live it while we can."

Brynn's lips snapped shut, and a flicker of emotion passed through her eyes. Guilt pulled on his shoulders as he realized she of all people knew life was short, considering she'd lost both her parents, but he shrugged it off. All the more reason why she should understand. "See you tomorrow, Ms. Taylor."

\\\\\\\\\\\\

Jack stacked the last box into the back of the U-Haul and pulled the door down, securing it with a lock. Helping Kekoa move out of his rat-infested apartment was exactly the vigorous exertion his body needed after telling Brynn there was nothing more they could do until the following day.

The bewilderment in her question and eyes made him wonder how much of a life Brynn had outside of the CIA. And it only made him feel more guilty about what he'd said to her.

"I used to think camel spiders in Iraq were the creepiest things I'd ever encounter—until I came into this apartment, Kekoa."

Jack stepped into the mostly vacated apartment to find Garcia with his ball cap on backward, wielding a broom like a weapon.

"I swear these rats aren't scared of anything."

"I told you, brah."

Kekoa stepped around a green couch that looked like it might've been in style during the Nixon era. An orange pleather chair and Formica dining table would've added to the mod style if they weren't riddled with stains and cigarette burns.

"If I brought food home, they'd stare at me. I'm pretty sure they were plotting to eat me in my sleep." Kekoa gestured toward himself. "Look at me, I'm like rib eye to them."

Garcia backed toward Jack and leaned the broom against the wall. "Speaking of dinner, let's get out of here and grab some food."

"I'm for that." Kekoa flipped off the lights, and Jack swore he heard scurrying across the oak flooring. "See ya later, rats. May we never hui hou again."

The three of them hustled down the steps of the brownstone apartment complex and squeezed into the U-Haul's cab.

"You know I could've driven my truck," Garcia said, folding his long legs into the tight space.

Jack laughed. "What did you tell those rats back there?"

"That I never want to meet them again."

"I can assure you there is no rat problem at my place." Garcia adjusted his elbow so he could give Jack, who was lucky enough to be in the middle, more room. "My abuela was a fanatic about keeping her house clean, and my mom was same way. So"—he leaned forward so he could see around Jack to Kekoa, who was driving—"that means no eating on the couch, put away your dishes when you're done, and always hang up your towels."

"Hey, my berth was always tidy."

"You wouldn't know it from your apartment," Garcia mumbled.

"Against popular belief, freelance hacking doesn't pay consistently. That place was all I could afford when I left the Navy. DC is expensive, brah." Kekoa sent them a sideways glance. "Besides, my landlord may not spend a lot of money on keeping the rats out, but he has no problem paying his lawyers. If I broke my lease, I'd end up paying more than that place is worth."

"Lyla's working with Walsh to find you a new place." Jack shifted, his shoulders squeezed between Kekoa and Garcia, making it hard to imagine Kekoa sharing a berth—the size of a closet—with another person. "Affordable. And without rats."

A few blocks from Garcia's condo, they found a diamond in the rough—a parking space a few yards away from Burger on the Hill. Inside, they found a table near the back and quickly ordered. Voices echoed off the exposed brick interior and piping that gave the restaurant a trendy urban vibe. When their food arrived, Jack let the double bacon cheeseburger and greasy fries ease the tension in his shoulders.

"So"—Kekoa dredged three fries through ketchup—"you gonna spill the deets about your wahine?"

*His wahine?* Amy. Jack squeezed his eyes shut, remembering he hadn't called her back. And declined two of her calls. And missed a third when he was helping Kekoa move, but that was because he hadn't heard his phone ring.

"Amy and I are mostly just friends." Jack bit into his burger.

Kekoa smirked around the bite of fries. "Brah . . . I'm talking about Brynn."

The bite in Jack's mouth suddenly felt too big. He worked to swallow it and then chase it back with a sip of soda. He looked at Garcia, who shrugged.

"All day I'm catching some sort of vibes between you and Brynn. A history."

"Well, there's definitely that."

Kekoa waited for Jack to continue. "What happened?"

Jack picked a piece of bacon off his plate and ate it, considering how much he wanted to share. Garcia had become like a brother, but the only thing they'd ever shared about their past relationships with women was that they had them and that their careers made them difficult to maintain.

It was why Amy had been sort of perfect. Her career traveling all over made him feel less guilty. Of course, it also made it impossible to know if there was anything there besides a solid friendship. But that was a good start, wasn't it? And friends didn't kiss . . .

"I don't mean to intrude, brah. Just curious."

Jack could see Kekoa meant it. Garcia gave him a knowing look that said he understood, which Jack appreciated even while it caused him to worry. The last thing he'd want was for Garcia to end up like him.

"I met Brynn when she and I were training to become field operatives at Camp Peary—or the Farm as most know it. It was a mix of new recruits and current CIA officers hoping to transfer to the Directorate of Operations. She was already working as an analyst but wanted to work overseas."

In an instant Jack was transported back to the day he met her. In the library surrounded by a mountain of files. Brynn had spent so much time studying CIA history and the failure and success of missions, he joked that all that knowledge might make her a target. Brynn faced him, irritation in her eyes for only a second before she dissolved into laughter. She pointed out that she'd rather be targeted for her brain than the smear of chocolate icing clinging to his lip. Jack still couldn't eat a chocolate donut without thinking of her or that moment. He'd been certain—at least at the time—that the woman who reminded him of the smart girl from the Harry Potter movies his nieces loved so much had won his heart.

Kekoa cleared his throat and Jack shook his head, hoping to send the memory back into its corner.

"There was an exam at the end of training. A mock mission each candidate had to lead. The instructors would judge us on how we operated, the information we gathered, and the success. Brynn passed." He glanced between Kekoa and Garcia, feeling the warmth of embarrassment color his cheeks. "I did not. We went our separate ways after that."

"Oh, brah, that bites." Kekoa finished his second burger. "Just like that, no more?"

"Just like that."

"Well, you never know—"

"It was a long time ago." Jack cut Kekoa off, knowing where he was going. He couldn't count the number of times he'd thought it himself. What if he'd found her? Talked to her? Answered her calls? "You never know" was the possibility Jack allowed to toy with his heart even though his head already had the answer. He *did* know.

When it came time to make a decision, Brynn always used her brain.

Keeping his expression neutral, Jack raised his soda like he was giving a toast. "The past is best left there."

# 12

*Ms. Taylor.* Jack hadn't called her by her first name or even slipped up and called her by her nickname. He'd called her Ms. Taylor like it was a reminder that their relationship was professional and she had no right to call him out in front of his colleagues.

Brynn had tossed and turned all night, wondering if she should call him and apologize or send him a text. Then she realized she didn't actually *have* Jack's cell phone number. But her mind kept imagining the conversation anyway.

Stepping out of the elevator on the eighth floor of the Acacia Building, she shifted the bag of breakfast tacos in her hand. An offering she hoped would convey the apology she owed Jack and everyone else. And *maybe* she was trying to win the team over.

*Does that include Jack?*

Brynn sighed and pressed the call button on the security panel by the door of SNAP's office. It had only been twenty-four hours. One day. How had Jack gotten to her so fast?

The door swung open and Kekoa stood there, dark curls spilling over his shoulders, eyebrows wiggling to the same rhythm as his bouncing shoulders as he danced to . . . no music at all.

"Aloooooha!" He smiled.

Behind Kekoa's bebopping form, Brynn managed to get a glimpse of Lyla shaking her head and Garcia frowning.

"Uh, aloha." A flutter of nerves hit Brynn's middle. "I brought breakfast tacos."

Kekoa stepped aside and rolled his fists over one another, hips swaying as he backed farther into the room. "You see, Lyla. Feed the men in your life, and they'll make you a wife."

Garcia cringed as Lyla's eyes bulged.

"Excuse me?" She yanked her cell phone from the pocket of her frayed jeans and held it to her ear. "Uh, yes, 1950s, we found your Neanderthal."

"I'm joking." Kekoa stopped his spastic dancing and smiled. "You know I love me a hard-working wahine who can do it all. Like my mama."

Brynn stepped into the modern living room and kitchen that anywhere else in DC was nice enough to be in someone's home. Jack's words from the day before rushed back. Was this space designed with that in mind, the expectation being that the team would spend more hours here than in their own homes? She knew a thing or two about long hours, and Jack's comment about life outside the office had stung. Still stung.

Jack entered the kitchen. "Good morning."

"Morning." The twinge humming in Brynn's stomach all morning picked up, its beat almost as erratic as Kekoa's dance moves. She dropped her attention to the buttons on her coat in an attempt to buy her face some time to cool down. The downfall of being fair-skinned was the alert system her cheeks revealed.

"Brah, you really need to talk to Walsh about recruiting Brynn to our side."

She looked up at Kekoa, who was pouring salsa into his taco. He winked at her. Her gaze moved to Jack. He was watching her with those brown eyes that always seemed to read into her soul. She offered a timid smile, and when he returned it, it was like a kick start to her pulse.

"Coffee?" Jack asked Brynn as he started to walk around the island. "I can make you a latte or cap—"

"Stop right there, Jack." Lyla stepped in front of him, waving a finger in his face. "Don't you touch the machine."

Jack stepped back with his hands raised, a playful grin lighting his face, and Brynn's cheeks warmed again. She knew that look . . . at one time loved that look. At least when it was directed at her.

"Fine." He backed away. "I wasn't going to touch your precious machine anyway . . . unlike Garcia."

Lyla spun on her heels, her gaze zeroed in on Garcia, who seemed to shrink a little. "Nicolás Garcia, do I hop on to Kekoa's computers and check my social media?" Kekoa looked at Lyla, amusement mixed with alarm all over his face, which Lyla ignored. "Do I tell Jack how to do his job even if I have *concerns*?" Brynn stiffened. "Do you see me playing with bombs or weapons even though I've been begging you to take me to the shooting range?"

Kekoa made a face. "I really hope you don't want to play with bombs."

"All I'm saying is"—she walked over to the built-in coffee machine and ran her hand along the stainless-steel front, the black display lighting up at her touch—"I don't step into your world of expertise. Don't step into mine."

There was a touch of hurt in Garcia's eyes, but a shake of his head cleared it. "Whatever happened to a regular machine making a regular cup of joe?"

"You're not in the desert anymore, soldier." Lyla winked at Garcia. "You get the good stuff here. Now, what can I make you?"

"Coffee. Black."

Jack and Kekoa laughed. Lyla gave an exaggerated eye roll at Garcia, followed up with a wink that had him quickly averting his gaze. Brynn slipped out of her coat and set it on the couch with her purse. Taking the stool Garcia offered, she couldn't help but appreciate the camaraderie among the team. It wasn't only the comfort of the space that made this place feel like a home—it was the people standing around the kitchen island. Jack's team. It was so different from the CIA. Most officers at the agency preferred to keep their work life separate from their personal life.

Not that she minded, really. It kept her busy and focused and fulfilled. But glancing around the room, that last part didn't feel true anymore.

"I'll take an Americano. Brynn"—Jack glanced over at her—"vanilla latte?"

"Yes." She looked at Lyla. "Is that okay?"

Lyla pressed the touch screen and the sound of coffee beans grinding filled the room. She leaned a hip against the counter. "I can pretty much make anything."

It felt a little like a challenge, but Brynn wouldn't engage. "A vanilla latte would be great, thanks."

As Lyla turned and grabbed some mugs, Jack pulled out the stool on the other side of Brynn and reached for a wrapped break-fast taco.

"You don't have to keep bringing us food—"

"Eh." Kekoa arched a brow at Jack. "Speak for yourself, brah." He pointed a thumb at Garcia. "I'm living with Captain Turkey Burger, remember? His refrigerator is like that weird aisle at Whole Foods." Kekoa shuddered before glancing back at Lyla. "You'll be my favorite wahine if you find me a new place ASAP."

"Working on it."

Jack's cell phone rang, and he set down his taco and stepped away to answer the call.

Kekoa picked up his second taco and smiled at Brynn. "Mahalo."

"You're welcome. Any progress on Riad's laptop?"

Doubt crept across Kekoa's eyes for a second before a determined look settled into the roundness of his face. "Nope. Encryption is different than I'm used to, but I'll get it."

Jack walked back in. "Lyla, can you make our coffee to go, please?"

"We're leaving?" Brynn stood.

"No." Jack tilted his chin at Garcia. "We are."

Her shoulders fell, watching Garcia rise and grab his coat. No questions asked. Indignation filled her chest. "Where are you going?" Was Jack punishing her? "Does this have to do with Riad?"

"It doesn't have anything to do with Riad." Jack slipped on his coat. "Garcia and I are needed elsewhere."

"Oh." His tone wasn't harsh, but she couldn't help feeling embarrassed.

"You and Lyla can work together while Kekoa continues to work on the laptop."

"Oh." Her eyes flashed to Lyla, who stood watching, expression full of amused curiosity. *Great.* It probably sounded like she didn't trust Lyla, which wasn't the case. "That should be fine."

Lyla handed Garcia and Jack two to-go cups along with a look Brynn read as "Are you seriously leaving me with her?" Brynn worked to fight the exhale of frustration growing in her lungs. Why did it matter if she worked with Lyla instead of Jack? The fluttering in her stomach held her answer. She *wanted* to work with Jack today.

Jack and Garcia, with coats and coffees in hand, walked out. Lyla turned on her. "Looks like it's just the three of us."

Brynn's phone rang. She glanced down at the screen, expecting it to be Olivia, but the random digits triggered a quick response. She stepped away from the island and answered.

"This is Brynn Taylor."

"Brynn, it's Joel Riley." His voice echoed. "Can you talk?"

A nervous energy pulsed through her, and she glanced over at Lyla, who was working on their coffees, and Kekoa, who was working on his taco. Not knowing what Riley was going to share, she decided to step into the fulcrum. "Yes."

"I spoke to our assets here in Egypt, and there's nothing to indicate Riad had an agenda other than attending the DI-AC program. His relative . . . connected with the Brotherhood died eight months ago . . . there's no indication any communication . . . passed between him and Riad . . . over thirty years. However"— the lag in the call caused Brynn to pointlessly press the phone closer to her ear—"a friend of Riad contacted him a few months . . . wanted him to check on his son . . . America . . . a student . . . Moustafa . . ."

The phone went quiet, and Brynn quickly pulled it away from her ear to make sure the call hadn't disconnected. "Joel?"

"Sorry." His voice sounded a little clearer. "We're getting closer to Cairo. Moustafa Ali. He's a sophomore at George Mason University. His parents hadn't heard from him in a couple of weeks and wanted Riad to check on him."

Brynn chewed on her lower lip. If what Joel had learned was true, then it turned her suspicion back on its head. Riad checking on the son of a family friend sounded more in line with his character. Maybe that was the favor he'd needed?

"Do you have anything else?"

"May have . . . more . . . but . . ."

"Joel, you're breaking up again."

"I'll call . . . more . . . bye."

Brynn checked the phone and confirmed the call had ended. Frustration nipped at her nerves as she stepped back into the kitchen and met Lyla's suspicious stare.

"Everything okay?"

Under any other circumstances, Brynn would not be allowed to disclose details about CIA cases, but this was different. She couldn't pursue any leads stateside without SNAP, which meant she needed them to help her.

"That was my colleague Joel Riley. The one in Egypt. Riad was asked by a family friend to check on their son. Moustafa Ali. He's a student at George Mason."

"GMU is in Fairfax." The hissing of the milk frother nearly drowned out Lyla's comment. "Might be why Riad was at the shopping center."

"If he was meeting this Moustafa guy there," Kekoa said around the last bite of his breakfast taco, "he could be the other person in the video."

It made sense but didn't explain why Riad would take off and not explain the situation. Brynn reserved the pinch of hope that maybe they had a viable lead.

"Let's call George Mason and find out about him, shall we?" Lyla picked up her cell phone and tapped a few things before finally setting the phone on the island, a ringing noise echoing around them.

Brynn chewed her nail, anxious for something in this case to go the right way. Unfortunately, after two more rings a voice mail message told them the George Mason University offices were running on a holiday schedule and wouldn't be opening for another hour.

"We'll keep trying," Lyla offered before handing Brynn her coffee. "What do you want to do next?"

*Is Lyla asking me?* Lyla widened her blue-green eyes at Brynn expectantly. Biting the inside of her lip, Brynn thought over the new information. "If Riad was looking for Moustafa, then we have a couple of options. He could, like Kekoa suggested, have gone to the shopping center to meet up with him and that's the other person in the video."

"And if it's not?" Lyla sipped her coffee. "Riad is a foreign spy on the run. If he did find his friend's son, why would he take off? Seems a little suspicious to me."

Brynn didn't appreciate Lyla's accusatory tone, but she wasn't wrong and that was a troubling and irksome truth. She turned to Kekoa. "Can you send us the GPS location for the area Riad traveled to in Clifton?"

"Sure," Kekoa answered hesitantly. "Why?"

Turning to Lyla, Brynn asked, "You up for a field trip?"

## 13

Route 66
9:31 AM Thursday, January 15

Brynn's heart rate was having a hard time keeping pace with Lyla's driving. The Audi Q5 hugged the curves almost as snugly as the jeans and sweater Lyla wore.

"It won't help our mission if we die before we get there."

Lyla shot a quick glance at Brynn and smiled deviously. Thankfully, the congested morning commute slowed down Lyla's driving. "Nicolás is always complaining I drive too fast, among the other things he likes to nag me about. Typical older brother."

Brynn nearly snorted at Lyla's inaccurate assessment but thought better of it. From her vantage point, she studied the speed racer. Even with minimal makeup, Lyla exuded a confidence that was both beautiful and enviable. Especially for someone so young.

It made Brynn want to know her story. How did Lyla get involved with SNAP and Jack, and why in the world couldn't she see Garcia was totally into her?

Maybe she didn't want to see it? Maybe Lyla had her reasons like Brynn had when Jack unexpectedly showed up in her life.

Lyla's cell phone rang on the luxury vehicle's Bluetooth system. "Hey, Kekoa, what'd you find out?"

"Moustafa Ali was a registered student at GMU. I found the phone number for his dorm resident advisor, who actually answered,

109

and she said most students are still away for winter break but some are returning. She checked Moustafa's room and found it empty, which she also said wasn't unusual for some students, as they could be moving into apartments. She checked the spring semester's resident list and Moustafa's name wasn't on it."

Brynn frowned. "Wait, you said Moustafa *was* registered? Is he not registered any longer?"

"Nope. At least not for the spring semester, but it's weird because the records show he paid for a full class load. Even had scholarships."

"What did the school's registrar say about that?"

"Uh, I didn't talk to the school registrar. I did a little research since the offices weren't open yet."

The way he said the word *research* made Brynn hold her breath. *Do not ask what he means by that. Do not ask.*

"Okay, thanks for the update, Kekoa." Lyla hit her blinker to change lanes toward the upcoming on-ramp for 66. "I owe you one."

"Not brownies, I don't wan—"

Lyla ended the call with a huff. "One time. I don't like to bake, okay? Does that make me not wife material? Why does the wife need to be the one to cook anyway? I know plenty of men who cook, and they have very happy marriages."

The faster Lyla talked, the heavier her foot pressed the accelerator. Brynn wasn't sure if she should interrupt or hold on and pray.

"I'm not much of a cook either," she ventured. "It's takeout or sandwiches and soups. Sometimes my neighbor, Mr. Cooper, cooks for me."

"See?" Lyla elongated the word. "And I bet his wife is very happy."

"Well, she's dead, but I'm sure she was when she was alive."

Lyla looked at Brynn and then busted up laughing. "Sorry, I don't mean to laugh. It's not funny, it's just your face was so serious."

Brynn allowed herself to relax in the moment a little. A few seconds of silence spread between them before Lyla tapped her thumb against the steering wheel.

"So, tell me, Brynn Taylor. Why the CIA?"

The question caught Brynn by surprise, and she was unsure if it was less than innocent given Lyla's previous chilly reception. "I want to stop terrorism."

Lyla eyed her. "You sound like a post-9/11 recruitment commercial."

Brynn almost smiled at Lyla's astuteness. "My father was a NY firefighter for Engine 7. They lost five and two were badly injured, including my dad."

Lyla's shocked gaze swung to Brynn. "I'm so sorry. I didn't mean—"

"It's okay." Brynn sighed, still uncertain after all these years how to properly respond to someone's condolences. "He loved his job and was proud to serve." Pushing aside the heavy emotions, she asked, "What about you? Any family tragedy push you into your career?"

"Nothing like that." Lyla laughed. "Dad worked for the government. My mom stayed home to raise me. Grew up in NoVa."

"Said with all the emotion of someone who wants more out of life."

"Touché." Lyla smiled. "It's not lost on me how fortunate I am, but I will admit I've always been predisposed to life outside the country club."

For whatever reason, it didn't surprise Brynn to learn Lyla came from money or that she leaned toward a lifestyle opposite of her parents. In fact, it was almost textbook profiling.

"How long have you been with SNAP?"

"About five years. I joined right after Jack."

A memory returned from the night before. Jack had said he'd been working for SNAP for six years, but it had been eight years since their time together at the Farm. "Were you and Jack in law enforcement before joining?"

Lyla looked at her, a mixture of confusion and amusement on her face. "I was still in college—desperate to get out. And Jack had just finished treatment."

Brynn's stomach hollowed. "Treatment?"

This time when Lyla looked over, Brynn saw the fear creasing her smooth skin. She'd said something she wasn't supposed to, and her eyes were searching Brynn for a way to get out of it.

"What was Jack in treatment for?"

"Uh"—Lyla looked back to the road—"maybe you should talk to him about it. I wasn't thinking, and I spoke out of turn."

"Lyla, please." Brynn hoped her voice conveyed the genuine concern mounting inside of her. "What was Jack getting treatment for?"

Lyla's lips flattened and a bit of the edge had returned to her pretty features. "If you want to know, ask Jack."

Brynn sighed. It felt like the progress she'd made with Lyla had slipped away. She was hoping Lyla might become an ally, but it was clear that her loyalty belonged to Jack.

She glanced out the window, not even realizing how quickly they had traveled from congested city into the frosted terrain of farmland. They passed a sign for Clifton County. Large farmhouses sat in the middle of fields edged with tall spruce trees, making it hard to believe the busy suburb of Washington, DC, was only a few miles away.

"Hmm, I think I'm in the right area . . ." Lyla slowed her car down and looked left and right. "I don't see anything but trees and farmland."

Double-checking the GPS coordinates Kekoa sent them, Brynn searched the area. Maybe Riad really had gotten lost. "There's a road there you can turn around on."

Lyla pulled onto the rutted dirt road, her tires kicking up rocks, and looked for a place to turn around. Brynn spotted an opening where the barb-wired posts widened, giving the road more space. She was about to point it out when something caught her eye.

"What's that?"

"What?"

"Keep going, a little bit—there."

In front of them stood a small farmhouse, white clapboard splitting and rotted beneath a roof missing more than half its shingles. The windows were boarded up, and overgrown weeds and ivy were nearly overtaking the lopsided porch.

"It looks empty." Lyla stopped the car behind an old pickup truck with flat tires and a tarp over the back of it. "And creepy."

"Maybe this is the place Riad was looking for."

"You said the kid was going to George Mason. This is quite the drive to Fairfax."

"True, so what would bring Riad here?"

Lyla shrugged, cutting her engine. Pulling a cute pink knit cap over her cascade of chestnut hair, she glanced at Brynn. "Let's take a look."

"I'll send Kekoa a text and let him know where we're at." Because something in Brynn's gut said maybe they were onto something—or walking into the next story setting for a Stephen King novel. And someone should know where to look for their bodies.

Brynn climbed out of the car, her steps crunching against the frozen earth. Heart hammering the closer she got to the house. Passing the truck, she spotted a shed. "There's a—"

A loud snapping noise stopped her. Looking over her shoulder, she expected to see Lyla, but no one was there. She must've gone toward the porch, which was blocked by a pile of wood pallets. Great. They probably should've had a plan.

Holding her breath, Brynn searched the area when another noise twisted her around in time to catch a blur of black rushing toward her. Arms wrapped around her midsection, throwing her backward and crashing her hard against the ground.

"Get off!" she shouted before using her knee to incapacitate her assailant. A painful cry told her she'd hit gold, and she used it to her advantage. Swinging her foot behind the man's leg, she twisted herself out from beneath his weight before solidly striking him in the nose with the base of her palm.

He rolled backward, clutching his bloody nose, and Brynn pushed to her feet. The man growled and started for her again, but the second he rose up she struck the side of his knee with her foot, dropping him to the ground with another sharp cry of pain. She was ready to strike again when she noticed he was holding his hands up in surrender, fearful eyes pinned on something behind her.

Breathing hard, she turned to see Lyla aiming a gun at the man. "You okay?" Lyla asked.

Brynn looked down at herself, knees muddy, the back of her clothes wet from the snow. "Yeah, I think so."

"That was pretty impressive," Lyla said, her aim not wavering. "Why don't you bring your fella over here with the rest."

The rest? Before Brynn could ask, Lyla was using her gun to direct the man's movements. He rose slowly, hands still up, blood dripping over his beard. Without lowering his hands, he walked cautiously toward them, giving Brynn a chance to study her attacker.

His dark-brown hair was unkempt and dirty like the rest of his clothing. The brown sweater he wore was torn and had holes, too thin to keep him warm in this weather. His nails were filthy, and the smell . . . Brynn swallowed, fighting the urge to gag.

With her aim still trained on him, Lyla took a sidestep, giving Brynn space to walk around the stack of pallets. When she did, her eyes widened at the three men sitting on the porch, eyes hollowed but watching their every move. And like the man who attacked her, they were filthy, smelly, and afraid.

\\\\\\\\\\\

With Garcia hot on his heels, Jack pushed his way past the local deputies, showing his credentials to anyone trying to step in his way. The only thing slowing him down was the stench he walked into when he stepped inside the dilapidated farmhouse.

On a couch that made Kekoa's old one look luxurious, four men sat quietly, shoulders hunched as though they were trying to retreat into the cushions. Beneath dark, matted hair, their eyes tracked the movement happening around them even as they huddled beneath wool blankets. Jack saw Brynn standing near the fireplace, speaking with an older man in a heavy blue parka with "ICE" written in bright white letters on the back.

Her gaze lifted to his, and the chaotic pounding in his heart that had started the second Kekoa called him slowed. *She's okay.*

Jack heard Garcia release a relieved breath when Lyla entered the room and walked toward them. He looked her over. "Are you guys okay?"

"Yes." Lyla tilted her head at Brynn. "Girl knows how to hold her own." She peeked around Jack's shoulder at Garcia. "And I had Cupcake."

"Well, I can be glad for that, but it doesn't excuse you two being out here on your own." Jack fisted his hands. "A simple phone call, Lyla, and Garcia or I would've come with you."

"Hudson, don't even go there," Lyla warned. "You know we run tips all the time. Besides, there was no way to know we would stumble on this."

"Stumble on what, exactly?" Jack studied the men, his attention snagging on the bloody face of one of them. "Who got hurt?"

"Only him. I told you, Brynn took care of it."

That should've been reassuring, but it wasn't. Not only could Lyla have been hurt, but Brynn too. He tightened his jaw, not wanting his heart to go there.

"Jack, this is Agent Phillip Flores with ICE." Brynn crossed the tiny front room of the house with the man at her side. "The Clifton sheriff called him after they arrived."

"Ms. Taylor explained that she and Ms. Fox arrived here to follow up on an assignment for Director Walsh." He glanced over to Brynn. "And that's all she'd give me until I placed a call to Tom."

Jack appreciated that Brynn followed protocol by providing enough information without compromising their work, but he was stuck on the last part Agent Flores said. "You know Director Walsh?"

Agent Flores tugged his overcoat tighter. "Tom Walsh and I go way back. I'm happy to do him a favor, though I don't quite understand your involvement in what appears to be a trafficking case."

Trafficking case? "Would you excuse us for a moment?"

"Certainly." Agent Flores stepped aside as a female ICE agent entered the home with a duffel bag.

Jack started for the front door, Brynn, Lyla, and Garcia following. Outside, he rubbed his gloved hands together, noting there wasn't much temperature difference between inside the house and outside. He stopped in front of the Tahoe, and the back passenger window rolled down.

"Howz it?" Kekoa's voice carried a lightness his eyes did not share. "You two okay?"

"Kekoa, you would've been impressed by this one. She went kung fu on one of them." Lyla held out her fist to Brynn, who obligingly fist-bumped back with a sheepish look.

"Oh yeah?" Kekoa's hulking shoulders relaxed, and Jack understood why.

The man had been keeping an eye on both women and hadn't stopped worrying from the second he told Jack about the 911 call he'd monitored. He'd refused to stay at the office, and Garcia hadn't spoken the entire drive out. These two women, strong and trained as they were, had had the three of them terrified.

"We'll get you a medal when we get back to the office." Jack's gaze pinned Brynn. "But for now, please explain why you're here."

The skin between Brynn's brows pinched. "Riley called and said Riad was looking for a friend's son, Moustafa Ali, who's been studying here in the US. They haven't heard from him, so we asked Kekoa"—she flashed a look of apology at him—"if there was anything on the GPS to indicate where Riad might've been looking—"

"Or hiding," Lyla said.

Brynn nodded. "We drove here and found this place."

"And you called ICE?"

"No, we called the police and they called ICE." Lyla answered Jack, arms folding over her chest. He noticed she'd taken a decidedly purposeful step closer to Brynn. *Taking sides.*

"You heard Agent Flores. This is probably a trafficking case." Brynn gestured to the house. "The men are undocumented and have probably been in this dump for a while. They're hungry and in need of a hot shower."

Agent Flores walked over to Jack. "Would you mind joining us?"

"Lyla, you stay here with Garcia and Kekoa."

Ignoring Lyla's narrowed eyes, Jack turned on his heels and marched back toward the house with Brynn.

"Agent Angela Royce is a trained medic." Agent Flores gestured to the female agent Jack recognized from earlier. "She's been assessing and treating the men. I'll let her explain what she discovered."

Behind her, Jack noticed only two of the four men sitting on the couch with water bottles and granola bars and being watched by ICE agents.

"I've checked all the men. They're dehydrated and malnourished but are okay for the most part. During processing we take their photos, and that's what I wanted to show you." She picked up a camera from her duffel bag and gestured to the two men on the couch. "Por favor."

They put down their snacks, stood, and faced her.

"We have to take multiple photos of them for our records because oftentimes they don't give us their real names." She held up her camera. "Colgaté sonrisa."

Both men smiled. One timidly, the other a full one along with a chuckle as Agent Royce took the photo.

"Colgaté sonrisa?" Brynn asked.

"Colgate smile," Jack and Agent Royce answered at the same time.

Brynn looked between them. "Like the toothpaste?"

"Yes," Jack said. "Their commercials use the phrase *Colgaté sonrisa* to mean smile bright."

"Exactly," Agent Royce said. "I use it to sort of ease the stress of the situation."

Jack appreciated that the ICE agent was compassionate, but he was also confused. "What's the significance of this?"

"This way." Agent Royce led him, Brynn, and Agent Flores past what was supposed to be a kitchen but was more like an ugly jack-o'-lantern. The space was filled with holes and gaps where appliances should've been, and the floor was covered in trash at least a foot deep. The stench grew almost intolerable when they passed a bathroom before stopping at the end of the short hall.

Inside the postage stamp of a bedroom, two male agents stood sentry near the other two men, including the one who fought with Brynn. Blood still caked his nose, but it was the dark glower he sent Brynn's way that set Jack's nerves buzzing. Jack kept his gaze fixed on the bloodied man and put himself between him and Brynn.

Agent Royce held up the camera again, and both men barely looked up. "Colgaté sonrisa."

The men stood there. No change in their expression. No chuckle. No smile.

"Colgaté sonrisa."

At the repeat direction, the men shifted but neither of them smiled. Jack's pulse raced. He narrowed his eyes on them, studying their features. Cardboard and tinfoil had been used to cover the two windows, making it hard to see. Dark hair, dirty faces, dark eyes just like the other two guys, but . . .

"Aibtisama."

Both men's eyes flashed to Jack, sharing the same expression of panic, but neither smiled like he asked. Unless he counted the sneer of the bloody one.

"Min 'ayn 'ant?" Jack asked, demanding to know where they were from. The question caused the unbloodied one to tremble, and Jack wasn't sure if it was from the chill penetrating the dirty room or fear.

"One of the men from the front room has a record on file," Agent Flores whispered over Jack's shoulder. "He's from Mexico, and we're assuming the other one with him is as well."

Which meant the two standing in front of Jack were not.

"'Ant last fi mushkila." Brynn's Arabic had a softness to her tone that showed real concern for the hungry, dirty souls staring at them. "You're not in trouble. Where are you from?"

Jack grew antsy in the silence passing between them, when finally one of the men, the younger one, pointed to himself.

"We are from Egypt. I speak some English."

Brynn took a step forward. "Moustafa Ali?"

The man shook his head. "La'a. Tarek Gamal."

Jack saw Brynn's shoulders drop. The man was not the one Riad was looking for. He turned to the other man. "What is your name?"

The man pressed his lips together.

"Shoo ismák," Jack repeated in Arabic, his tone rough.

Irritation filled the man's eyes. "Seif El-Deeb."

"Do you speak English?"

Seif gave a tight nod. "British school."

There was smugness in Seif's tone that didn't match the fear hovering in his gaze. "Why are you here?"

"Work."

The simple answer felt anything but simple. It also aligned with Agent Flores's belief that this was likely a trafficking situation. But if it was true, why would Riad come here looking for his friend's son? Had Moustafa been trafficked to America? Human trafficking was a growing epidemic, but how did Riad fit into this? There were too many questions, and Jack's instincts were on high alert. None of this was a coincidence.

"We're going to take these two with us." He turned to Agent Flores. "Director Walsh will get whatever approval you need—"

"Now, wait a minute." Agent Flores held up his hand. "I can't allow you to take them with you. They need to be processed properly. If you want to question them in our facility, I can make that happen, but—"

"With all due respect, sir"—Jack turned so his back faced the two men and lowered his voice—"I can't give you details, but I can say it's a matter of national security." He took out his phone and pulled up Walsh's number. "A phone call will ensure your agency is protected."

## 14

Clifton, VA
2:49 PM Thursday, January 15

*What do four undocumented immigrants have to do with an Egyptian student and an Egyptian spy?* Brynn had hated word problems as a kid and despised them even more as an adult. Especially this one, which seemed to never end. New pieces were constantly being added, and she had no formula to figure it out.

Brynn rubbed her temples, hoping to ease the tension headache already throbbing. At least an aspirin would get rid of it. Was there a pill that would smother the flicker of tenderness growing inside of her for Jack?

She'd seen honest fear in his eyes when he entered the farmhouse and the relief when their gazes met. What did that mean? The question had flooded her thoughts immediately, and almost as quickly she'd tuned it out. He was concerned. Any decent person would be. After all, she saw the same worry in Garcia's and Kekoa's eyes.

Well, maybe not the exact same . . . Besides, it was probably just her spinning emotions from Lyla's revelation that Jack had been in some kind of treatment. What had it been for and was he okay?

The driver's-side door swung open, bringing a gust of cold air into the Tahoe. Jack slid into his seat and slammed the door closed with a grunt.

*How many phone calls does it take to satisfy an ICE agent and turn Jack's mood sour?* One. Jack's call to Director Walsh did not result in Jack getting his way and left him—

"Are you pouting?" She snickered.

His gaze swung to meet hers, and it was annoying that the aggravation lining his face gave him a rugged charm. "No."

Jack backed the Tahoe down the farmhouse driveway, frustration working the muscles in his jaw. He stopped and waited for Agent Flores, who was driving the sedan escorting Seif El-Deeb and Tarek Gamal to an ICE facility for questioning.

"It would've been a lot simpler if we were taking them."

"Just like that?" She snapped her fingers in the air mockingly. "This is likely going to become a federal investigation, Jack. You think you or Director Walsh have some ability to dictate how other agencies operate?"

He sent her a sideways glance that said he believed exactly that. With a huff, she asked, "So what are you guys, some kind of Blackwater?"

Jack gave a noncommittal shrug. "In a way, yes, but with less ego."

Brynn chewed on that. Blackwater was once a private military firm contracted by the government for their ability to provide high-level security services. They hired former members of the military's elite operators—Special Forces, Delta, Navy SEALs—offering a select set of skills to assist the US in the war against terrorism and provide security in foreign countries. They even protected government facilities stateside after Hurricane Katrina. Ego was likely a prerequisite of Blackwater's team members, but it also likely contributed to the string of incidents across the globe that resulted in numerous deaths of its own contractors as well as foreigners, which led to federal prosecution. Blackwater no longer existed—at least not under that name.

The implication that SNAP operated in a similar capacity . . . Brynn cast a glance at Jack, an old fear sprouting to life. He'd wanted to be a part of the CIA's Directorate of Operations, willingly accepting the risks of clandestine missions until—

She forced her attention to the scene beyond the windshield.

Jack steered the Tahoe behind Agent Flores's vehicle. Lyla pulled her Audi away with Garcia and Kekoa inside, heading back to the office to begin their own investigation into the two Middle Eastern men. How much clandestine work was SNAP involved with?

Snowflakes began to fall, and Jack turned on his windshield wipers. Agent Flores took a right at the stop sign and Jack did the same, following him down another narrow farm road. Brynn's phone chirped with a text message. She withdrew it from her pocket. Olivia.

> Hey friend, Penny and I are on our way back home. Time went by too fast. Plan a trip to NM this spring. It's beautiful and not fry-an-egg hot. We miss you. Oh, and say heyyyy to Jack. ;)

Heat inched into her cheeks, and she quickly typed a reply.

> Miss you already. If I'm in NM by spring, something didn't go right . . .

She deleted.

> Miss you. Will let you know about NM in spring. Stay safe.

Brynn settled into the leather seat and released a sigh that sent a sharp ache to her ribs. She unbuttoned her coat and slid her hand to her right side, her fingers playing along her rib cage. Tender but not broken.

"You okay?"

His question startled her. "Yeah, a little sore—"

Jack pressed his lips together, irritation in his eyes.

"What?"

He blew out a breath. "I'm frustrated, Brynn."

"I can see that."

His brown eyes locked on her. "Do you realize how lucky you and Lyla were that this"—he gestured to the vehicle ahead of them—"didn't end up worse?"

The earlier sentiment behind Jack's concern fizzled. She'd read it wrong. Brynn bit her lip, trying to calm her annoyance. "I received a tip and decided it was best not to waste time—"

"Following protocol and ensuring your safety"—his eyes flashed to her—"the safety of *my* team is not a waste of time."

Her cheeks stung. "We both went through the same training, Jack. I know what I'm doing. I handled the situation safely."

"This time, maybe, but you don't get to decide what or who is worth risking for the sake of the mission."

His words landed like a punch that hit so hard it took her eight years back. Jack was still holding a grudge for a decision she'd *had* to make. He wasn't being fair back then and he wasn't being fair now. "That's not what I did. Time is running out. If there's a chance to find Riad, I'm going to take it."

"Not without me."

"You were off doing something with Garcia."

"I was doing my job."

"So was I," Brynn countered, arms folding across her chest. "No one wants to find Riad more than I do, and no one has more to lose than I do."

"I'm not trying to stop you—"

Jack's words were muted by a horrific crunch as a black SUV rammed into Agent Flores's vehicle when it pulled into the intersection. The violent impact sent the sedan flipping several times until it landed upright near a ditch.

The SUV shot forward like it was aiming for the car again. Brynn noticed the steel push bar attached to the front, and a sick feeling filled her gut. "Jack . . ."

He gunned the engine, but a hard hit from behind sent their

bodies lurching forward against their seat belts. Her earlier injury seared with pain.

"Jack!"

The screeching noise of tires filled the air along with the ugly odor of burned rubber and smoke as Jack applied the brakes, but he couldn't keep the Tahoe from being pushed into the intersection.

Brynn whirled around to see who was behind them. "It's another black SUV. The windows are too dark. I can't see the driver."

"Hold on, Brynn."

She turned back in her seat just as Jack released the brake, unleashing the momentum and launching the Tahoe forward. Jack quickly steered their vehicle into a spin.

"What's happening?" Brynn screamed, bracing herself.

"They're taking them."

Through the windshield, she watched two men with black masks over their faces yank the immigrants out of the back of the car and shove them into the first SUV. The SUV that hit her and Jack was reversing to turn around.

Jack threw the Tahoe into park and unbuckled his seat belt. "Call Garcia."

Heart racing, Brynn watched Jack jump out of their vehicle, withdraw a gun from his waist holster, and aim it. With cautious urgency, he rounded the driver's-side door, but he was too late. The tires of the first SUV screeched against the pavement as it took off. And the other—already long gone.

She quickly dialed Garcia's number and told him what had happened. They were turning around, headed back their way. She could hear Kekoa in the background giving their location to 911 dispatch for fire and rescue. They assured her help was on the way.

Climbing out of the Tahoe, Brynn started for the crumpled sedan with the ICE agents still inside. Crossing the intersection, she stepped through broken glass and around pieces of the vehicle. Brynn looked in both directions for any oncoming vehicles—none.

In fact, it was eerily quiet.

"Brynn, be careful." Jack's words echoed in the cold air. His eyes scanned the horizon around them. No doubt he was concerned about another attack.

The vehicle's windshield was shattered but still partially in place. She moved toward the driver's side. The window was gone, and Agent Flores's head hung forward, blood dripping from a gash across his brow. He was unconscious . . . she hoped.

"Agent Flores!" She tried to yank the door open, but it wouldn't budge. Reaching through the empty space where the window should've been, Brynn checked his pulse. It was weak, but at least it was there. She tugged off her scarf and used it to compress the bleeding on his head, then looked over to see Jack checking the other agent. "How is he?"

"Airbags probably saved their lives, but it looks like his leg might be broken."

Brynn followed Jack's gaze to the bone she should not have been seeing. *Ew.* She looked away, forcing her stomach not to react. "Kekoa called 911. They should be here soon."

"Let's hope so." Jack glanced back at the Tahoe. "I've got a blanket in the back. We need to protect these guys from shock and hypothermia."

Less than a minute later, Jack returned with the blanket. He helped her spread it across the two agents.

"That's better than nothing." Jack sat back on his haunches, checked his watch, and surveyed the area around them. The soft sound of sirens echoed in the distance. "I'm growing to both love and hate that sound."

"Jack, you're bleeding." His eyes met hers with a frown. At the edge of his brow, a small gash was sending a stream of blood down the side of his temple. She started to reach for the wound but paused, hand in midair. "Above your left eye."

He reached up and felt for the wound, finding it with a cringe. "Must've hit against the steering wheel. What about you?" Jack looked her over, methodical in his search for signs of injury, but it didn't lessen the buzz vibrating her nerves. "Do you hurt anywhere?"

"Besides the soreness from earlier, I think I'm okay."

Brynn swallowed, forcing her focus back to Agent Flores. No matter how much her heart ached for Jack's concern to mean something more, she needed to remember he was only doing his job.

For someone trained to lie, Brynn was terrible at it. Or maybe he just knew how to read her. A skill that hadn't served him well eight years ago and one that wouldn't serve him well now if he allowed his heart to run away with it.

Two fire trucks and an ambulance had arrived and taken over. They pulled Agent Flores out of the car, and Jack was relieved to see him open his eyes and begin answering the EMT's questions. The other agent had a compound fracture and was being treated inside the ambulance. Lyla, Garcia, and Kekoa arrived at the same time as the county police, who were already several minutes into questioning Brynn.

"How's that?" A third EMT stepped back from Jack, inspecting his work on the cut over Jack's brow. "I don't think you'll need stitches, but keep it clean. And if you have any symptoms of a concussion, go to the ER."

"Got it." Jack glanced over at Brynn. "Would you mind checking her out as well?"

The EMT looked over his shoulder at Brynn, and Jack saw his eyes gleam with appreciation. "Sure."

Irritation grabbed hold of Jack, or maybe it was jealousy, but the growing chaos of the scene kept his focus on the very organized and efficient kidnapping of Seif El-Deeb and Tarek Gamal.

After answering questions from the police and ICE, Jack offered his business card to them in case they needed anything else and made his way over to his team. Garcia and Lyla were leaning against the Audi, eyes fixed on the chaotic scene. They both straightened when they saw him.

"Oh, your beautiful Italian face." Lyla's brows pinched, her lip puckered mockingly. "Tell me, will you be scarred?"

Garcia shook his head. "The correct question is"—he looked at Jack—"are you okay?"

"I'm joking, Nicolás." She bumped Garcia with her hand before meeting Jack's eyes. "I think scars are sexy."

"Ly—"

"I'm fine." Jack offered Garcia a sympathetic grin. Lyla took way too much pleasure in getting under his skin. Jack turned his attention on the troublemaker. "And it was a small cut, so no scar."

"Too bad." She responded with a one-shoulder shrug before glancing beyond Jack's shoulder. "What about Brynn?"

Looking back, Jack saw an EMT with Brynn, a stubborn look on her face. Obstinance looked cute on her. His pulse jumped, and Jack tempered the sudden reaction that was becoming all too frequent. *Amy.* Yes. That sobered him up. He needed to remember Amy. Or at least work out his feelings—whatever they were—for her.

Jack returned his attention back to the team. "She's getting checked out, but I'm sure she's fine too."

The Audi's dark tinted window slid down, revealing Kekoa. "Brah, it's too cold out there. I'm turning into frozen kalua pork pop." He held out a fist. "You good?"

"Yeah." Jack bumped his fist. "Brother, please tell me you've got something."

Kekoa's forehead crinkled, dashing Jack's hopes. "Black SUVs in the Metro area are like cousins at a local barbecue."

Garcia frowned. "What?"

"You never realize how many you got, and they keep showing up," Kekoa said, his attention focused on the laptop sitting across his legs. "If I had a make or model or—"

"How about a license plate?" Brynn's voice came from behind them. "Or at least a partial?"

"That would work, sis."

"7519." She looked to Jack. "That was the last four on the one that hit Agent Flores. I think it might've been a Toyota 4Runner."

"You take a hit and keep on ticking, don't you?"

Lyla's comment to Brynn drew a timid smile.

"I guess so." Brynn's blue eyes met his. "Your head okay?"

"Yeah."

"Except no scar," Lyla added. "That would've added a level of authenticity to your Dread Pirate Roberts."

Brynn looked at Lyla. "His what?"

"I've got a location!" Kekoa pumped his fist inside the Audi, causing it to rock.

"Heyyy." Lyla cradled the car. "You're going to break my car."

"Where?" Jack and Brynn asked at the same time, neither apparently concerned for the vehicle.

Kekoa stilled. "He's heading west on Yates Ford Road. About fifteen miles from here."

Only fifteen miles? "You're sure it's them?"

"Traffic cam shows them passing the intersection at Yates and Culpepper." He shot an anxious look at Brynn. "And I might have had some help from—"

"Doesn't matter," Jack said, ignoring the suspicious look Brynn shot him. "Send the location to my GPS and keep your eyes on them."

Jack and Brynn jogged over to the Tahoe. He checked the back, and aside from the smashed-in tailgate, the truck was still operable. They climbed in, and Jack whipped the Tahoe 180 degrees, grateful the damage wasn't bad. He pressed the gas and accelerated toward the location blinking on his GPS.

His adrenaline climbed with every passing mile. How could fifteen miles feel like a hundred? Agitation electrified every nerve when he hit a red light. He answered an incoming call from Kekoa. "Any movement?"

"The car isn't moving." Something in Kekoa's tone was unsettling. "There's a lag in the footage. I can't tell how long, maybe a few minutes, but the car hasn't moved. Hold on—"

The sound of typing filled the car. As soon as the light turned green, Jack hit the gas, pushing the truck over the speed limit.

"Why wouldn't it be moving?"

Brynn voiced the question racing through Jack's brain. He sped up, praying no one would get in his way. Jack grew anxious when they passed more mile markers.

"Where is it, Kekoa?"

"Should be just ahead," he answered.

"There." Brynn pointed at a black SUV pulled onto the shoulder.

Hitting his brakes, Jack felt his seat belt tighten against him. He pulled up behind the SUV, leaving plenty of room to maneuver. It looked like the same vehicle he watched El-Deeb and Gamal get tossed into. The windows were tinted black, making it difficult to tell if anyone was inside. No movement. Had they abandoned it?

Brynn's head swiveled around. "Where's the other car?"

"Kekoa, check the footage and see if anyone left the vehicle."

A few seconds passed. "Yeah, brah. One just like it pulled up. The driver got out and into that one before it took off."

"Just the driver?" Brynn was already unbuckling her seat belt.

"Yeah."

Jack put the truck in park and got out, Brynn right beside him. Pulling his weapon out again, he kept it aimed ahead of them, not willing to walk into a potential ambush. Taking a wide berth, he raised his weapon at the driver's side. Empty. Passenger side too. Cautiously, he checked the passenger-side door. It was unlocked.

When he opened it, Brynn gasped.

The two Egyptian men were crumpled in the back seat, their

bodies atop each other. Based on the amount of blood spatter, there was no doubt both were dead.

Brynn shook her head, looking at him with dazed eyes. "What is happening?"

"I wish I knew."

Jack surveyed the mess in the back seat while Brynn called the police for the third time. Nothing. He looked over the passenger seat, his eyes landing on a duffel bag on the floor. Strange.

The ICE agents allowed each of the men to collect whatever belongings they had at the farmhouse and put them into a . . . plastic bag.

"Brynn!"

Jack spun around and spotted Brynn halfway between the SUV and their vehicle. She faced him. Sprinting as fast as his legs would push him, he collided with her body as a fireball exploded behind them.

# 15

Did anyone love hospitals? Brynn sat against the cold plastic chair in the stark, sterilized room of Washington General. Ears still ringing, ribs aching, she glanced down at the palms of her hands, which bore angry red abrasions from being hurtled to the ground.

*A bomb.*

Brynn could hardly wrap her thoughts around that—or maybe her brain was still disoriented from the explosion. Or the weight of Jack's body covering hers as metal and glass from the destroyed SUV rained down on them. He'd protected her. Not that it surprised her. No, of course not. Jack was doing his job. *Doing his job. Doing. His. Job.* The pounding in her head ramped up, nearly folding Brynn over her knees. How in the world did soldiers handle this? She imagined Jack's head felt the same, or worse. Given that he'd used his body to shield hers, leaving him completely exposed to the brunt of the impact. Fear tore into her once she realized what had happened, unwilling to turn and find Jack's lifeless body over hers. She nearly cried when Jack began gently shaking her, asking if she was okay.

As a result of Jack doing his job, he was rewarded with bruises and cuts along the backs of his legs, the worst being a three-inch gash on the back of his thigh caused by a piece of metal.

A knock sounded at the door, and the noise reverberated like a gong in her head. "Ms. Taylor?" A male doctor walked in, her chart in his hands. "I'm Dr. Payne and—"

Brynn blinked to clear her thoughts, held up her hand. "Wait, I think my brain is a little fuzzy. I thought you said your name is Dr. Payne."

He smiled, a nice one that showed perfectly straight teeth. "I did. Ironic, huh?"

"Or frightening."

"Don't worry." Dr. Payne grabbed a rolling stool and swung a leg over it to sit. "I have access to all the fun meds. Now, I hear you've been playing with explosives."

His comment made Brynn think about Lyla's teasing remarks to Garcia from earlier . . . Had it really only been *that* morning? The day seemed to stretch into a hundred more unanswered questions, leaving her anxious to find the answers if she could get out of there.

"Do you know how much longer I have to stay?"

Dr. Payne set her chart aside with a chuckle and pulled a penlight from his pocket. "Not a fan of hospitals, huh?"

He flashed the light in both of her eyes.

"Is anyone?"

"Oof." He put his light away. "I keep telling the cafeteria they should bring in better food, make this place a bazaar of flavor, and then people would be dying to come here."

This close, Brynn had the best view of Dr. Payne's light-green eyes. A wave of sandy-brown hair fell across his forehead, which was furrowed in an expression of expectation for her to get his very bad joke.

"Does anyone appreciate that joke?"

He smiled, gave a shrug, and stood. "Not really, but we've got a running bet in the doctors' lounge how many patients we can get to laugh at it. I'm behind by six patients thanks to you, but I might get half a point if I mention you have a brain injury—"

"What?"

"You don't, which is good and maybe a little surprising considering what you went through. I'll have a nurse print out a sheet on concussion symptoms. If you get a headache worse than the one you probably already have or you begin vomiting or your words become slurred or your balance seems off—go directly to the ER. Do not pass go and do not collect two hundred dollars."

There was a purposeful pause, and Brynn gave in with a smile and a shake of her head. Good thing Dr. Payne had his looks going for him. He reminded Brynn of the doctors on the soap operas her mom used to watch. Brynn used to believe all doctors were dreamy and hunky until she arrived at the hospital after her father's injury. Waiting inside the chaotic New York hospital for news about her father, the only doctors she remembered were ones with panic-stricken and horrified faces. That day in September, terrorists turned the World Trade Center into a war zone and hospitals into something out of a horror movie.

"Will that work, Ms. Taylor?"

Dr. Payne's question shook her back to the present. The smooth skin around his eyes no longer crinkled in humor but worry. *Great, now he'll for sure think I have a brain injury.*

"Sorry. I was wondering about my, um . . . colleague. Jack Hudson. How's he doing?"

"I believe another doctor is checking him, but I can pass along a message if you'd like."

"Yes." Brynn clamped down her lips. "I mean, that's okay. I can go check on him when we're done here, right?"

Dr. Payne finished typing his notes into the computer. "Yes, but you'll have to wait your turn." He turned to her. "There's a limit on visitors."

Jack had visitors? Then it hit her—his team. Of course they'd be by his side. Nausea that had nothing to do with a head injury made her insides feel wobbly.

"The nurse will bring in your prescription with your discharge paperwork." Dr. Payne paused at the door. "Do you have someone to give you a ride home?"

"Yes." The lie came out on a whisper. She cleared her throat, fighting the unwelcome emotion balling there. "Thank you."

The second Dr. Payne left, Brynn swiped against the moisture in her eyes, angry. Exhaustion was taking its toll, bringing with it a wave of melancholy. And it was silly.

The sound of laughter pulled her attention to the door of her room, which Dr. Payne had left ajar. Brynn moved toward it, then peeked into the hallway. To her left, she spotted Kekoa, Garcia, and Lyla. A female nurse, a male nurse, and a female doctor were chatting with them, and Brynn took a step forward, concern rising in her chest. Was Jack okay?

*"Jack joined when he finished his treatment."* Lyla's comment was going to haunt her until she found out what Jack had needed treatment for. It was hard to imagine Jack as anything but healthy and strong. The latter she felt in the security of his grip over her body when the bomb exploded.

More laughter erupted and she paused. Certainly they wouldn't be laughing if Jack's injuries were serious? Another peek at the team and realization pushed her back into her room.

A heaviness stole over her. The events of the day flashed through her mind with enough speed it made her dizzy. A symptom of a concussion? Brynn sank into the hard plastic chair, taking in the emptiness around her. Or was it the haunting reality that after everything she'd been through, she was all alone?

No visitors. No one to drive her home. No one who would ask her how her day went or let her cry into their shoulder over the painful memories brought on by being back inside a hospital. Director Peterson hadn't even sent anyone to check on her. Did the CIA even know what went down? Or where she was?

Tightness grew in her chest and Brynn stood. No, she didn't have anyone to drive her home or to check on her, but that didn't mean her life was empty. She had a job that fulfilled her, the freedom to make choices without worrying about anyone else. At least she did now that her father had passed. Emotion rose to her throat as a deep ache settled in her middle.

She needed to get out of there.

A quick peek around the corner, and Brynn slipped out of her room and made her way to the nurses' station.

A woman in lavender scrubs looked up. "Can I help you?"

"Yes, my name is Brynn Taylor. I'm waiting for my discharge papers and a prescription for pain meds. I know you all are busy, so I thought if you could get me my paperwork, I'll grab my meds from the pharmacy myself."

The nurse shifted, revealing her name badge, Mallory Greene, and a smile of appreciation. "Let me check your chart really quickly." She typed on the computer. "Okay, sure. Dr. Payne is giving you a prescription for pain medication that you can pick up from the pharmacy." She moved to a printer and grabbed several sheets of paper. "Sign here, and this is the concussion paper."

Brynn quickly signed.

"If you have any—"

"I know." Brynn's eyes shifted to the group down the hall, the ache growing more painful with each passing second. "Go to the ER or call 911."

Nurse Greene eyed her for a second, looking like she was second-guessing her decision to release Brynn.

"The pharmacy is this way, right?" Brynn pointed to her right.

"Yes, do you—"

The phone on her desk rang, pulling Nurse Greene's attention away and giving Brynn the perfect opportunity to leave.

Without a second look back at the people who she'd inexplicably allowed to weave their way into her life, Brynn hurried down the hall. They weren't her friends. They weren't her team. They were a means to doing her job—find Riad and get out of Washington, DC.

*And as far away from Jack Hudson as possible.*

\\\\\\\\\

"She's gone."

Jack stared at Lyla. "What do you mean she's gone?"

"I went to her room, and she wasn't there. I asked Mallory, and she said Brynn signed her discharge paperwork about fifteen minutes ago." Lyla's blue-green eyes softened. "They wouldn't have released her if she wasn't okay."

He swallowed. "I know."

But he wanted to see for himself. To soothe the unease residing in his chest, which was proving to be more painful than the cut on the back of his leg.

Lyla walked over and put a gentle hand on his shoulder. "There's a woman in your life who's not going to run away from you, Jack. You deserve that at least."

Jack shifted, uncomfortable with Lyla's sincere but forward observation. Or maybe it was the fact that he was still wearing a thin hospital gown with his team only feet away. In the hallway, their presence imposed on the medical staff at Washington General, which should've gotten them all booted, but Lyla's friendship with his nurse, Mallory Greene, allowed them to stay.

"I mean it, Jack." Lyla stepped into his sight line. "Amy is pretty much the complete package, and I'm not just saying that because she's my friend. If you overlook the whole traveling part of your jobs, you guys are pretty much perfect for each other. And don't tell her I said this, but I think she might be ready to give hers up, you know, for the right reason."

Lyla lifted her left hand and wiggled her fingers, the gesture reminding Jack of his lunch with Brynn when Asha did the same thing. Marriage. There was only one person Jack had once considered marrying, but how could he marry someone he didn't trust? Marriage was a partnership and required trust, something Brynn severed a long time ago.

When Lyla lowered her hand, a heaviness pulled at her smile. "Jack, there's something I need to tell you."

His stomach, which was already a bit woozy, clenched. "What is it?"

"Don't be upset because I didn't say anything . . . really." She bit her lip. "But Brynn was asking me about when I joined SNAP and when you did, and I might've mentioned something about your treatment, but I didn't tell her why."

The rush of words spilling out of Lyla's mouth was disorienting, and it took Jack a few seconds to put them in order. He swallowed. "So she knows about my cancer?"

"No." Lyla shook her head, and he saw the remorse. "I told her if she wanted to know why you were in treatment, she'd have to ask you."

Nurse Greene entered the room, paperwork and a pair of scrub pants in her hands. Her interruption was perfectly timed. "You ready to get out of here?"

"Yes." Jack nearly jumped off the hospital bed and winced at the sharp pain in his leg.

She handed him the scrubs. "You can put these on. They're loose so they won't press on your wound." Pulling a curtain across the window, she paused by the door.

"Thanks."

"Come on, Lyla." Mallory pointed to the door. "Give the man some peace."

Lyla looked at him like she was waiting for a pardon for spilling the news to Brynn. He smiled. "It's fine, Lyla."

It was all the grace she needed. She smiled with a wink. "How about you introduce me to that cute doctor you were talking to earlier?"

Jack caught Garcia's raised eyebrows, clearly having overheard Lyla's flirty remark that he had no doubt she'd said loud enough to be overheard. He gave his friend an empathetic shake of the head before Nurse Greene closed the door on him.

Alone in his room, with only the hum of the fluorescent lights, Jack released a sigh. So Brynn knew something about his past.

Did it bother him if she knew about his cancer? What difference did it make now? *None.*

Then how come his head was swimming in confusion that had nothing to do with the impact of an explosive? What was he going to do about Brynn? About Amy? Lyla was right, Amy was wonderful and the complete package . . . but for him?

Jack shook the questions aside, anxious to get out of his peek-a-boo hospital gown and away from the emotions that were troubling him almost as much as a bomb nearly killing him and Brynn.

Carefully changing into the scrubs, he was grateful the cut on the back of his leg wasn't worse. He didn't need any stitches, but the skin around the cut burned like the anger he carried for the men responsible. When he was dressed, Jack grabbed the bag holding his belongings and met his team in the hallway.

"Yep, that's it." Lyla gave Jack a once-over before looking up and down the hallway. "A man in scrubs is hot. I need to find me a McDreamy."

"This isn't *Grey's Anatomy*, Lyla," Garcia said.

"Brah." Kekoa chuckled, punching Garcia in the shoulder playfully. "You're a fan of *Grey's* too?"

"No." Garcia's face held all the emotion of a man about to go in for a colonoscopy. He jutted his thumb at Lyla. "She made me binge an entire season. Worst twenty-one hours of my life, and I once spent twenty-three hours in a hole outside of Fort Benning with snakes, ants, and red bugs eating my flesh."

"Ew, Nicolás!" Lyla wrinkled her nose.

A doctor eyed them, and Jack knew it was time to get his crazy crew out of there. "I think we should head out."

Garcia turned to Jack. "I spent a few hours with the Virginia Fire and Explosives team. I'll work with them tomorrow at the scene and keep you posted." His lips pressed into a tight line for a second. "I've seen that kind of explosion before. I'm glad you and Brynn are okay."

"Thanks, brother." It didn't take the seriousness in Garcia's eyes to remind Jack how close it could've been for him and Brynn. A twinge of regret pinched at his conscience. He'd wanted to check on her, make sure she was okay, but the constant flow of doctors and nurses, the MRI—at Lyla's insistence—had distracted him.

"Me too, brah."

Kekoa started to come in for a hug, but Jack held up a hand, fearing what the crush of strength would do to his tender cuts and bruising. "A little sore, bro."

"Right." Kekoa held out a meaty fist for a bump and Jack obliged.

"Boys." Lyla called for their attention. "Jack needs to get home and get some rest." She eyed Garcia. "That means no shoptalk tonight." She turned to Jack. "Doc says you need someone to drive you home, and Garcia volunteered."

"And I'm going to see if Nurse Greene"—Kekoa smiled—"needs a date for Lyla's party on Saturday."

Lyla backed toward the nurses' station, shaking her head. "Get some rest, and remember what I said."

Jack's cell phone echoed from his coat pocket. He pulled it out and felt his cheeks flame with heat at the name on the caller ID. *Amy.*

Conflict filled his soul as he silenced the call. He'd only tried to call her back once and hated the sense of relief when she didn't pick up. What did that say about him? About them?

Was Amy a woman who wouldn't run from his side? He didn't know. Their careers kept them apart more than together, and they'd simply settled into a rhythm that felt more platonic than romantic. And if he were being honest with himself, Amy didn't spark the same flame of—*what?* The only thing Brynn sparked was confusion. And old feelings that he didn't need a map to know where they'd landed him. Heartbroken and unable to trust or commit to another woman.

# 16

The sky was a glorious blue belying the freezing temperatures that she considered perfect running weather—if she could run. The last twenty-four hours had taken its toll on her body, and the best she could do was a walk. A slow one that allowed the frigid weather to numb her cheeks and nose instantly. If only that numbing would stretch to the dull pain beating in her chest.

Brynn yanked out her earbud, annoyed. The ringing in her ears hadn't subsided since the explosion. Nor had her nerves. Or the mounting frustration since leaving the hospital. The painful awareness that she was all alone had followed her home, keeping her from sleep as she tried desperately to convince herself the void in her life wasn't that big of a deal.

Except that was a big fat lie.

Ignoring the aches in her body, she rounded the edge of the Tidal Basin in front of the Thomas Jefferson Memorial. Director Peterson had called first thing this morning to check on her, a gesture she appreciated until he followed it up with the directive to take today and tomorrow off to recover.

Two days off was the last thing she needed, but Peterson wouldn't hear it. It wasn't his call. And as if reading her next thoughts, he added that Director Walsh was the one who mentioned that mandatory time off was protocol for SNAP. Peterson also warned her that if he saw her step inside Langley, he'd force her to use every single day of her vacation even if he had to buy her an airline ticket himself.

Brynn had latched on to the humor almost as tightly as she had clung to the concern in Peterson's voice. He wasn't her father, but he cared about her, right? Man, she sounded desperate. After filling Peterson in on the events at the farmhouse, part of her wondered how much of his call was out of his growing frustration with her lack of movement on the case rather than his actual concern for her.

*She* was frustrated with herself. The assignment was becoming more and more complicated, with zero answers as to what was going on or why. With Riad still missing, there was no way the CIA would offer her a consulate position overseas. At this point she was working just to keep her job.

No. It wasn't about her job. It was about stopping the next 9/11. If Riad was part of some plot to bring terrorism to America, Brynn was going to do everything in her power to stop him.

And the last thing she needed was time off.

Peterson had mentioned Director Walsh's reassurance that the team would continue to work on the assignment, but no one on the team, not even Jack, was as invested in finding Riad as she was. Not that she didn't believe in the team. She was beginning to see glimpses of what they brought to the SNAP agency, but to them it was a job. For her it was personal.

Crossing beneath the barren cherry trees, Brynn slowed down as she entered the Roosevelt Memorial. Most visitors missed this secluded memorial on warm days, and on cold days like this one, Brynn had it all to herself.

Normally, a run or walk calmed her, but the struggle warring inside was only bringing more uncertainty to the surface. She needed a break. Walking to a bench across from the large blocks of granite that composed a lovely waterfall when the weather was warmer, Brynn took in Roosevelt's words etched into the stone.

*"I have seen war on land and sea. I have seen blood running from the wounded . . . I have seen the dead in the mud. I have seen cities destroyed . . . I have seen children starving. I have seen the agony of mothers and wives."*

She'd read those words dozens of times, but today they seemed to resonate deep within her. *I have seen war . . .* She had. Definitely not on a foreign battlefield like a soldier, but she'd witnessed the aftermath of 9/11, the suffering her father endured as his career was stolen, and then his health, and then his wife. So many battles and not a single victory.

Her gaze moved to the next quote. *"The structure of world peace cannot be the work of one man, or one party, or one nation . . . it must be a peace which rests on the cooperative effort of the whole world."*

Was that why she wanted her DI-AC program to work so badly? To bring together a coalition of intelligence specialists to wage a battle against terrorism that could only be won if they did it together? The last thing Brynn wanted to see—or hear—were the agonizing cries of those left behind to mop up the bloody aftermath of violent terrorists.

Not only had terrorism stolen the life she once knew inside of her home, it had stolen the life she had beyond it. Friends whose mothers and fathers had been killed were unable to look beyond their grief to understand why Brynn's father was still alive. They withdrew, leaving her unanchored in the chaos of what she, too, couldn't understand.

It became a question Brynn struggled with—why had her dad lived and others had not? When people heard the story, they would comment how lucky she was, but that was the last thing she felt. Yes, she was happy her dad was alive, but that came with overwhelming guilt.

Her guilt only increased with her time spent in Somalia. The devastation of warlords tearing the country and lives apart by the thousands pushed her to work harder than ever. The starving and battered faces of Somalians haunted her almost as much as those she saw on 9/11.

A sharp trill sliced through the peacefulness of the memorial. Brynn pulled her cell phone out, her pulse quickening when she saw the unknown number sequence that usually came when CIA operators dispatched calls . . . *Joel.*

"This is Brynn Taylor."

"Brynn, it's Joel." There was an echo after he spoke. "I've got an update."

And now her pulse was racing. "What is it?"

"It's possible Riad wasn't only looking for Moustafa Ali. His wife said he began going to a mosque in Heliopolis."

Brynn's breath clouded on the cold air. A memory played in her mind. "That can't be right, Joel. Riad's Coptic." Not only was that fact stated in his dossier, but Riad had a small black cross tattooed on the inside of his right wrist. A traditional and outward symbol of his faith.

"You're right, which is why his wife believed it had something to do with his job. I met with an asset who said the imam at the mosque has connections to wealthy members who are willing to invest in the propagation of Islam. If a member is in good standing, meets certain criteria, then they are provided with the means to travel to the West."

"Is that how Moustafa came to America?"

"I'm not sure, but we reached out to Moustafa's family, and the last time they spoke with him he mentioned attending a mosque in DC, Sidi Mosque. But—"

"Hold on." Brynn brought her phone in front of her. She quickly searched the Sidi Al-Rahman Mosque, but it wasn't in DC, it was in Fairfax. A surge of energy pulsed through Brynn, pushing her off the bench. Pressing the phone back to her ear, she controlled her voice. "The Sidi Al-Rahman Mosque is a block away from Fairfax Towne Centre, where we spotted Riad."

"Brynn, listen." Joel's tone was ominous. "The imam at the mosque is Joseph Ansari. He's an originating member of the mosque, a prominent figure within the American-Islamic community, and an informant for the FBI."

Almost three hours later, Brynn was perched inside a coffee shop a block away from the shopping center where she'd last seen Riad. In front of her was a red-brick building with a green metal sign over the awning that read "Sidi Al-Rahman Mosque." Friday services began at noon, and she'd made sure to arrive early enough to spot Joseph Ansari when he entered.

Playing with her piece of coffee cake, Brynn checked the time on her phone. An hour had passed. Enough time for her to learn that Ansari had been a professor of religious studies in Belgium before moving his wife and son to the United States to begin a teaching job at Georgetown. He had a son and two grandsons, all of whom lived together within walking distance of the mosque.

"Would you like anything else?" The same girl who'd taken her order was wiping down a table next to Brynn's.

The doors to the mosque opened, and men began exiting the building.

"No thank you," Brynn said, grabbing what was left of her pastry and tossing it into the trash on her way out.

Outside, she tugged her coat tighter, trying to cut out the chill seeping into her bones. January in DC was the worst, and on top of it, the beautiful blue skies from that morning had been overrun with gray clouds that came with an epic snowstorm predicted in the next few days.

Scanning the crowd, Brynn spotted Mr. Ansari chatting with another man. Hanging back, she waited until he was done and walking away from the mosque before approaching him.

"Mr. Ansari."

He stopped, turned, and looked her up and down. "Yes?"

"Do you have a moment to talk?"

There was no hiding the flash of suspicion in his eyes. "Do I know you?"

Brynn stepped closer to the man. "Um, no, but I wanted to ask you if you've seen a friend of mine. Remon Riad?"

She let the name-drop slip on a gust of wind, watching Mr. Ansari's reaction. His suspicion morphed into surprise and then fear as his eyes darted around them.

"Who are you?"

"A friend of Mr. Riad. Have you seen him?"

Mr. Ansari closed the distance between them, his eyes still searching the busy street around them. "If you are who I think you are, then you are wrong to have come to me."

Brynn's adrenaline spiked. Did he know she was with the CIA? Did that mean Riad had met with him? "Have you spoken with Riad?"

Something caught Mr. Ansari's attention behind Brynn. She glanced over her shoulder to see a woman pushing a stroller and a man walking into the coffee shop she had just left. Nothing out of the ordinary . . .

Mr. Ansari cleared his throat, pulling her attention back to him. He smiled politely and gestured ahead of him. "My son is expecting me home for lunch. Shall we walk?"

She forced a smile and began walking next to him. "Mr. Ansari—"

"I do not know who Remon Riad is."

Brynn looked at him, but Mr. Ansari stared straight ahead. "But you said . . ." Actually, she thought back on his response to her first question about Riad. Mr. Ansari had said nothing about him. Only commented on who she was. "Do you think I'm with the FBI?"

His eyes flickered to her for only a second. "Who else?"

She wouldn't answer that. "Remon Riad is looking for a family friend, Moustafa Ali."

Mr. Ansari's jaw tensed. "I cannot help you or Mr. Riad."

"You cannot or will not?" Brynn stopped walking, her toes and fingers painfully numb. "Mr. Ansari, I need your help, please."

He slowed to a stop, his shoulders rising with an inhale of air before turning and walking back to her. "I do not know this Remon Riad, but I remember Moustafa. He was a student of our teaching, but I have not seen him for several weeks."

"Do you know where I can find Moustafa?"

Mr. Ansari's eyes dimmed. "I do not."

Brynn wasn't sure he was being truthful but decided not to press. "What can you tell me about him? Moustafa. Did he ever appear to have . . ." She swallowed, unsure of how to word her question.

"Did he believe in Islamic extremism? Have the tendencies of a terrorist? Want to blow up a plane?" Mr. Ansari's directness shocked her. He smiled. "No, my dear. I did not perceive that to be the case with Moustafa. Although . . ."

Mr. Ansari's forehead furrowed in thought, and Brynn felt herself holding her breath.

"I remember him to be a bright young man, and last I saw him, he seemed very excited about an opportunity—"

"What opportunity?" Brynn interrupted, earning her that teacherly look of disappointment. "Sorry."

"I do not know, but I can assume that like most boys his age, whatever it was held the promise of bigger and better." Mr. Ansari shrugged on an exhale. "So many these days are looking for the next opportunity and missing the blessing that is often right in front of them."

Just as his words burrowed into her soul, a cutting gust of wind stole the breath out of her lungs and she shivered.

"I do not wish to keep you any longer." He tipped his chin down, a kind smile on his lips. "I wish you the best of luck finding your friend."

Before Brynn could respond, he turned and resumed his walk

home. Disappointed at the lack of information, she shoved her hands deeper into her coat pockets. Her fingers hit her cell phone, reminding her what Riley had said about the mosque in Egypt.

Turning her head, she saw Mr. Ansari approaching an intersection. He pressed the crosswalk button and waited. Brynn hurried toward him, momentarily cut off by a couple pushing a stroller. She stepped aside so they could pass and then met Mr. Ansari.

"Sir, I wanted to ask if you'd look at a couple of pho—"

"Ms.—" Mr. Ansari turned to her, his eyes wide. He clutched his chest. "My . . . chest."

"Mr. Ansari, what's wrong?"

The color drained from his face, his lips parting to gasp for air. "My chest. It . . . I cannot get breath."

He began to sway before his knees started to buckle. Brynn grabbed for him right before he collapsed. "Hold on, Mr. Ansari, hold on."

17

Washington, DC
4:45 PM Friday, January 16

Jack's anger pulsed hot. As he rounded the corner of the private medical facility, his gaze and his annoyance zeroed in on the woman pacing the hallway. Brynn turned, and surprise flashed in her eyes before he caught a momentary glimpse of relief, making her appear vulnerable.

He slowed. Was it an act? A conversation from their past rose to the surface. Brynn hated hospitals, and in the last forty-eight hours she'd been in them twice. The Brentwood Medical Spa, though, looked nothing like a typical hospital. Instead of hard linoleum, sterile walls, and shared rooms, this medical facility boasted oak flooring, warm taupe walls decorated with art, and private patient suites.

Still, the luxurious aesthetic could not erase the beeping noise of machines, the antiseptic smell, or the unease shadowing Brynn's blue eyes.

And yet, he had to steel himself not to give in to the desire to comfort her. She had disobeyed a direct order, and it was exactly why Jack had voiced his concerns to Walsh. Brynn could not be trusted.

"What were you thinking?"

At his harsh tone, Brynn's expression tightened. Her shoulders rolled back, spine stiffening as she faced him head-on. "My job."

He ground his molars. Her attitude had him stewing. "Your job is to follow orders. Going rogue will not work here. If I can't trust you to work with me—"

A half snort cut him off. "Work with you? In case you haven't noticed, I'm the one stuck on the sidelines watching you and your team work. I think the only reason I'm here is to take the hit as this continues to spiral downward."

Jack ran a hand through his hair in an attempt to curb his growing frustration. "I already told you the goal is not to let that happen. But finding you on your day off working an angle—"

"Wait." An awareness lit her eyes before accusation narrowed them on him. "How *did* you find me?"

He swallowed, expecting this question. "We know about Joseph Ansari."

She eyed him. "What do you mean you *know* about Joseph Ansari?"

"We have a contact at the FBI." He met her fiery gaze. "Mr. Ansari is pivotal to their Joint Terrorism Task Force. Sometimes our . . . interests cross."

"Did you know Riad was going to the mosque?"

Jack shook his head. "No, but when we saw its proximity to the shopping center and learned of Moustafa Ali" —he shrugged— "we made an educated guess."

"That still doesn't explain how you found me here."

"The JTTF is currently working a case. Your arrival outside the mosque today was unexpected."

Comprehension dawned and Brynn's posture softened a bit. Her soft, pale skin revealed exhaustion in the purple crescents beneath her eyes. She released a long breath, turned, and walked to a leather chair and sat.

"What was your conversation with Mr. Ansari?"

"Like you don't know." Her long blonde hair was pulled into a ponytail with loose pieces spraying out around her face, highlighting the worry lines creasing her porcelain skin. "I figured you'd have an audio recording of my conversation."

Jack sighed. He didn't know whether to feel aggravated by her obstinance or the way it unexplainably charmed him. "Brynn—"

"I'm sorry, Jack."

Jack's attention turned to Dr. Davey walking toward them. The surgeon was a friend of Lyla's family who the SNAP agency called on in situations like this.

Dr. Davey pulled his mask to his neck before turning to Brynn. "Ms. Taylor. We did everything we could."

Brynn inhaled sharply. "I don't understand. It was a heart attack. Mr. Ansari didn't seem unfit, was only sixty-eight. Were you able to contact his wife? Did she mention anything about a heart condition? Cholesterol? Blood press—"

"Sometimes hearts just give out." Dr. Davey pressed his lips together, gaze bouncing between Jack and Brynn. "We'll run some blood work—"

"We'd like to have our labs run it," Jack said. "Your labs don't need the extra work, and the timeliness of this case matters. If that's okay?"

Dr. Davey's expression tightened, but he understood Jack's request was more courtesy than permission. He sighed. "Fine."

"I'll have Lyla let you know where to send it." Jack reached for Dr. Davey's hand. "We appreciate everything you did."

"Of course." Dr. Davey's beeper went off. He grabbed it off the waist of his scrubs and gave it a quick look. "I have to go."

Brynn stood and stepped forward. "You're sure it was a heart attack?"

Dr. Davey swallowed, and Jack knew Brynn saw the same thing he did. Hesitation. "Unless the lab says otherwise, my thirty years of experience say it was just that."

"Remon Riad. Moustafa Ali." Brynn backed away, her eyes growing distant. "Tarek Gamal. Seif El-Deeb."

"We appreciate your help," Jack said to the doctor before directing his attention to Brynn. She'd taken a seat, her eyes closed as her lips repeated the names on a whisper.

"Riad. Ali. Gamal. El-Deeb."

It was a method he recognized from their time at the Farm. She'd memorize pieces of the mission in an attempt to figure out which were critical to the case. Like puzzle pieces scattered in her brain until they fit into a picture only she could see . . . or control.

"It doesn't make sense." Brynn looked up, a crinkle between her brows. "Riad. Ali. Gamal. El-Deeb. Joseph Ansari. The last three are dead after talking to me."

His jaw tensed. "What did you talk to Ansari about?"

"Riley called me and said Moustafa Ali was a member of the Sidi Al-Rahman Mosque. Like you said, the shopping center where we spotted Riad was nearby, and I thought maybe he'd gone there to talk to Mr. Ansari." She shook her head. "But he didn't know Riad. Though there was something . . ." She pressed her lips together for a second. "It seemed like he was nervous."

"He wasn't expecting you."

"Just like the FBI," Brynn added. "But was he expecting someone else? Do you think that whatever the FBI is working on has something to do with Moustafa Ali?"

"They're always working a case, but I'll reach out to my contact there and find out." Otherwise, whatever information Joseph Ansari might've had just died with him. "Did he mention anything about Moustafa?"

"Only that he . . ." Brynn's head rocked forward before she pressed her palms to her temples. "Um . . ."

Jack frowned. "Brynn, are you—" Her body crumpled, and he jolted forward to catch her in his arms. "Dr. Davey! Nurse! I need help!"

Brynn's head lolled to the side, the color in her face gone, causing the blue-green veins to stand out. Her lips were tinged blue. Jack reached for her pulse, but his fingers shook in a violent rhythm, making it hard for him to feel for the beat of life he was desperate to find.

"We've got her, Jack." Dr. Davey reached for Brynn, but Jack wouldn't release her. "Jack."

He let her go, watching in horror as Dr. Davey scooped her small frame into his arms, bypassing the wheelchair a nurse had rushed over. Gut-wrenching panic swept over him, and Jack dropped his face into his hands and prayed.

〰〰〰〰

The crying had always gotten to her.

Brynn had kept very still, her back pressing into the hard plastic chair someone had kindly offered her when she and her mother walked in. The hallways were crowded, smelled like campfire and an unfamiliar stench that made Brynn's knotted stomach swirl. She learned the unpleasant odor was burned flesh. And hair. And bone. Human.

That wasn't what gave her nightmares though. It was the crying. Or rather, wailing. Despair that began deep in the gut, shredding through the heart until it clawed its way out of someone's mouth in a skin-chilling sob.

Brynn sat there for hours, her skin covered in goose bumps, waiting for her mother to come back and tell her that her father was dead. And then her cries would join the ones echoing in the hallway of St. Vincent's Hospital with the other widows and orphans of 9/11.

Except, she didn't cry. Her father was okay. Injured but alive. Brynn had wanted to be happy—she had her daddy—but the cries wouldn't go away.

Laughter.

Brynn groaned and turned, trying to force herself awake. Or at least make the laughing stop. *Why would someone be laughing in the hospit—* Hospital!

Images flashed in her mind. Sidi Al-Rahman Mosque. Joseph

Ansari. Jack. Hospital. Her breathing . . . she couldn't catch a breath. She inhaled, and a vise cinched tighter around her lungs. She couldn't breathe. She couldn't breathe. She couldn't—

"Brynn, it's all right. You're all right."

A loud beeping noise competed with the soothing voice she thought she recognized, but . . .

Slowly, her eyes drifted open to find the source of the voice staring over her with familiar blue-green eyes. Lyla.

"A nurse is on her way."

"Nurse?" Brynn's voice rasped.

"Y'all know there's a limit on visitors."

Lyla stepped back as a nurse in pink scrubs entered the room, and Brynn was surprised to see Garcia and Kekoa. They played a weird game of Frogger, moving around so the nurse could get to the machine next to Brynn's hospital bed.

She glanced down at herself, realizing she was no longer wearing her clothes but a pale pink hospital gown made of the softest cotton with silk hemming. "What happened?"

The nurse took her vitals, her name badge identifying her as Rachel Allen. "Your heart decided to play a really bad joke."

Her heart?

The nurse placed a blood pressure cuff around her arm and pressed a button. She glanced over her shoulder to a bedside tray with a box on it. "Is that what I'm smelling?"

"Malasadas. Homemade." Kekoa beamed, his pride expanding the size of his body. "I made them for Brynn, but I can probably snag you a couple." He made his eyebrows dance before giving the nurse a wink.

She held up her left hand and wiggled her fingers, revealing the pink rubber ring. "Married, big boy. Army sniper."

Garcia chuckled.

"No worries." Kekoa raised his hands in defense. "I'll still share."

"I thought those were for her?" Lyla tipped her head to Brynn.

Before Kekoa could respond, Dr. Davey entered, glanced around, and let out a sigh with a shake of his head.

"All right, everyone out." He thumbed toward the door. "I need to check out my patient, and all of you are breaking visitation rules."

"I warned them." The nurse removed the blood pressure cuff from around Brynn's arm and did another awkward two-step with Kekoa's large frame. This caused him to snap a beat with his fingers, his head and shoulders moving in some kind of dance move.

"All that muscle and no rhythm—a shame."

Kekoa stopped dancing, and his jaw hung open with phony outrage. "I'm Hawaiian. I was born with hula sway in my hips." To prove his point, he jutted his hips side to side, nearly knocking into Dr. Davey, who huffed his disapproval.

Lyla, Garcia, Nurse Allen, *and* Brynn laughed.

"See, Doc." Kekoa smiled. "Laughter is the best medicine. Maybe I should be getting your pay—"

"Time to go," Dr. Davey announced. "Or I'll enforce a family-only policy."

Brynn's stomach sank.

"Doc"—Kekoa pressed a hand to Dr. Davey's shoulder—"we *are* ohana. And ohana means—"

"I have children, Kekoa. I've seen the movie."

"Come on, boys." Lyla ushered Kekoa out the door with both hands against his back, Garcia following behind her.

"It feels like the room doubled in size, doesn't it, Ms. Taylor?" Dr. Davey lifted the edge of the box on her bedside table, revealing rows of fried balls of dough. A sweet cinnamon scent filled the room. "Fried fat. Normally I'd warn you against eating one of these, but your cholesterol had nothing to do with your heart deciding to take a nap."

"My heart?" That was the second mention of it. What she could remember was being unable to breathe and passing out in front of Jack. "What happened? How long have I been out?"

"A few hours." Dr. Davey held up his stethoscope. "May I?"

She nodded, then jumped at the cold metal against her chest. Inhaled deeply and exhaled as directed until Dr. Davey stepped back.

"Sounds healthy." He typed something into a computer the nurse had rolled over before turning to her. "Ms. Taylor, I'd like to discuss what happened to you, but I think Jack needs to be here. I need your permission."

"I guess that's okay."

"Director Peterson is here and would like to sit in on the conversation as well."

At this, Brynn pushed herself up against the hospital bed and tugged a knitted blanket over her. "Uh, can I get dressed first?"

"Of course. Nurse Allen has your clothes."

The nurse went to an armoire built into the wall and pulled out Brynn's clothing. "Do you need any assistance?"

"No thanks."

Dr. Davey nodded. "I'll go get Jack and Director Peterson."

Once they left her room, closing the door behind them, Brynn slipped from the bed and quickly changed out of the hospital gown. She pressed a hand to her chest where her heart pounded beneath her rib cage. Nothing hurt. Why had Dr. Davey said her heart took a nap? What did that mean?

Her reflection in the mirror caused her to groan. Not even a lush sweatshirt could erase the bedraggled state of her hair or the smudge of mascara at the corners of her eyes. *Nice.* The whole team saw her like this.

The whole team.

Garcia, Kekoa, and even Lyla being there comforted her in a way she hadn't felt in a long time. Had Jack called them in? How long had they been there? She peeked over her shoulder at the box of Hawaiian donuts Kekoa had made for her. *Ohana.* Family. Emotions she hadn't been able to shake since her last visit to the hospital—was that only a day ago?—came rushing back.

A knock on her door startled her. She wiped beneath her eyes and quickly tucked the loose strands of her hair behind her ear before giving her head a quick shake. Wasn't going to look much better than this, but at least she wasn't greeting her ex and her boss in a nightgown.

"Come in."

The door opened, and Dr. Davey walked in, followed by Peterson and Jack, whose eyes widened in surprise when he saw her.

"Why are you dressed?" He cleared his throat, cheeks pinking. "I mean, you look like you're ready to leave."

"I am ready to leave."

Jack rounded on Dr. Davey. "You're not releasing her yet. She had a heart attack—"

"I had a what?" Brynn's heart quickened. She brought her hand to her chest again. "I had a heart attack?"

"An *episode*," Dr. Davey said. "But not because you're unhealthy, which is why"—he looked at Jack—"I'm allowing her to be discharged."

"Is someone going to explain what happened to my officer?" Peterson's grumble drew the attention of Jack and Dr. Davey.

Brynn glanced up at her boss, but his gaze remained focused on the doctor as he waited for an explanation. Had he just said "*my officer*"? Never once had she heard him speak possessively about anyone in their division, which gave his demand all the more power to find roots in her already emotionally fragile state.

Dr. Davey rolled over the stool and sat. "When Mr. Ansari came in earlier, he was presenting with the symptoms of a heart attack. But when we ran blood panels on him before surgery, the numbers weren't . . . right. I put a rush on it." Again he set his gaze on Jack, the message clear. "I may not have all *your* access, but I do get a few things done the traditional way."

Jack smirked.

"I contacted Mrs. Ansari, who gave me permission to disclose the information regarding her husband's health." Dr. Davey looked at Brynn. "When you asked me if I was sure it was a heart attack, something didn't sit right with me. According to his wife and confirmed with the medical file his primary doctor sent over a few minutes ago, Mr. Ansari was healthy. He had no history of heart disease, cholesterol, or any other underlying conditions. I was about to call the lab tech when they called me first. They asked if we wanted to run a drug test."

"A drug test?"

"Yes," Dr. Davey answered Jack. "It's common for labs to ask about toxicology panels when they see an irregularity in the blood work indicating drugs in the body. After Ms. Taylor's concern, I agreed. Not because I was questioning my initial belief of cardiac arrest but because of a symposium I recently attended by the AMA. With the rising opioid crisis, the American Medical Association is trying to—"

"Wait, are you saying Mr. Ansari had opioids in his system?"

Dr. Davey glanced over to Brynn. "No. But also, yes. Except not how you imagine."

Director Peterson blew out a frustrated breath, rolling on his heels. "Good grief, Doc, you know we're not paying you by the hour. Can we get on with it?"

Brynn had to bite her lip to keep from smiling. She was sure Peterson had zero idea the man he'd just chewed out likely made quadruple his salary. Dr. Davey wasn't amused but continued a bit quicker.

"Right before your episode, Ms. Taylor, I got the call about the drug panel, which reminded me of the symposium—" Peterson rocked faster on his heels, forcing Dr. Davey to speed up his words. "One of the doctors discussed fentanyl being inhaled and the dangers—"

"Mossad," Brynn cut in as her mind raced back to her time at the Farm. She looked at Jack. "Khaled Mashaal, remember the lecture?"

Jack nodded. "It was reported as a botched assassination attempt on the Hamas leader. They sprayed fentanyl into his ear, and he collapsed with respiratory distress that was—"

"Corrected with naloxone," Brynn finished before her attention turned back to Dr. Davey.

"Which is what I gave to you."

Brynn's gaze found Jack's, reading the tension pulling his features tight. Her thoughts swirled back to why *she* had been at the private medical facility in the first place. Ansari. Someone had poisoned Ansari and . . . her? "I don't understand. Why didn't I . . ."

Understanding filled Dr. Davey's eyes. "I believe most of the dose, if it was sprayed, was inhaled by Mr. Ansari. You must've breathed in the residual, which is why your reaction came later and why you're . . . still alive."

# 18

Washington, DC
10:28 AM Saturday, January 17

*"Still alive."* Two words had never haunted him more. Not even *"it's cancer"* had the punch Dr. Davey's words spoke about Brynn.

Jack ran his hand through his hair again, his muscles tight with stress as he stared out over the busy street outside the Acacia Building. The thick white clouds hovering low over the city hadn't followed through with their threat of snow despite the forecasters' insistent warnings. He moved away from the window, the wound on his leg a painful reminder that he needed to sit down. Rest.

He might've if he wasn't so worked up over the woman who was running—he checked his watch—twenty-eight minutes late. *Where are you, Brynn?*

Jack couldn't shake the anxiety growing in his chest. In less than a week, they had one man still missing, two shot dead, and another poisoned using a Cold War method. At the center of it all was Brynn. The woman he wanted to be angry with. The one he wanted to direct his frustration at. The one who'd scared the life out of him when she collapsed in his arms.

"You all right, man?" Garcia sat against the edge of his desk, arms folded over his chest.

"Yeah. I'm trying to figure out how an Egyptian spy, two dead

160

immigrants, an explosion, an FBI informant, and opioids fit together."

Garcia snorted. "That all?"

*No.* But Jack wouldn't let on that his feelings were slowly becoming part of the assignment. It wasn't professional, and it was getting more and more difficult to separate the job from the emotions rising every time he thought of Brynn.

"I can't tell if you're working out a physics equation in your mind"—Garcia squinted thoughtfully at Jack—"or if the buffalo wings from last night aren't sitting well with you."

"Neither." Jack laughed. He walked to his desk and pulled the large whiteboard toward the conference table. "Like I said, working out the details of this ever-changing assignment."

"Right," Garcia said, not sounding convinced. "How's Brynn?"

"Good enough. Dr. Davey released her from the hospital." A fact Jack wasn't in agreement with, but given Brynn's current track record for chasing leads without him, he figured it was better to let her come into the office for the debriefing. Director Peterson agreed. He checked his watch again. "She was supposed to be here a half hour ago."

"Seems that pretty little tornado is stirring up old feelings."

Jack speared Garcia with his eyes. "She's not."

"You sure?"

"I'm sure."

Lyla waltzed into the office. "Sure about what?"

"Nothing." Jack eyed Garcia, hoping his message to drop it was clear.

Garcia gave a half laugh. "So long as you're sure."

"How come I feel like I walked in on my two big brothers hiding a secret? Wait!" Lyla smiled, removing her coat. "Is it something for my birthday?"

Jack caught a glimpse of Garcia, frustration and hurt coloring his expression. Man, he ached for his friend. Not just friend-zoned but straight up brother-zoned. How Lyla remained oblivious to

Garcia's adoration was a mystery, but maybe it was for the better. Jack knew what it was like to give your heart to someone who didn't reciprocate those feelings. And the inevitable pain that followed. Maybe he'd talk to Garcia, help him avoid the same mistake he'd made with Brynn.

Then again, given what his heart was doing in his chest every time Brynn was around, maybe he wasn't the right person to say anything.

"What in the world?" Jack did a double take when he saw the tattoos inked on Lyla's arms. "What did you do?"

"Do you like it?" Lyla glanced down at her arms and looked up. "Kekoa helped me pick out the designs."

"It's temporary." Kekoa peeked his head out of his office. "Wipes off with soap."

"Lyla brought over the lease for Kekoa's new place." Garcia sat in a chair at the table, his tone sour. "Then turned my home gym into a tattoo studio."

"Temporary," Kekoa called out again. "And we cleaned up afterward."

"Aw, Nicolás." Lyla came up behind Garcia and wrapped her arms around his neck. "Did we bother you?"

Garcia tugged his ball cap lower. "No, but you did interrupt my workout schedule."

"Brah, you should've told me." Kekoa walked over flexing his muscles and winked at Garcia. "Now that we're roommates, I can give you some tips that'll bulk you right up."

Garcia's shoulders stiffened. At a little over six foot, he wasn't small or weak. In fact, the Special Forces EOD officer still maintained a rigorous physical fitness schedule that'd likely make up in agility where Kekoa had strength. But Garcia's tense posture had little to do with measuring who was stronger and everything to do with the newest member of the team getting more attention from Lyla in the last year than he'd received in the previous five.

"You keep eating those donuts"—Garcia patted his taut stomach—"and pretty soon those muscles are going to find their way to your gut."

"They're malasadas." Kekoa stretched his arms. "And don't act like you didn't eat one. You're going to miss me and my malasadas when I move out."

Garcia swung his gaze to Lyla. "And when is that going to be, Lyla?"

"I'm working on it."

A buzzer echoed, and all of them turned to the screen mounted on the wall. Jack's whole body relaxed seeing Brynn standing there.

"I'll let her in," Garcia said, shooting Jack a look with a clear message that said he knew better.

When Garcia disappeared down the hall, Lyla walked over, a message in her blue-green eyes too.

"Have you told her about Amy yet?"

"There's nothing to tell, Lyla." Jack caught Kekoa slipping back into his office. "Amy and I are friends. Brynn and I are . . ." Frustration knotted the muscles in his neck.

"Complicated?" Lyla supplied with an arched eyebrow.

"Sorry I'm late. I stopped and picked up bagels." Brynn stepped into the fulcrum, carrying only one bag while Garcia carried the other. She sent a nervous smile to Jack. "I hope that's okay?"

And just like that, her smile, those blue eyes searching for his assurance, it fed a need Amy simply couldn't meet. Which made it very complicated. A sharp jab to his ribs from Lyla, and Jack snapped out of his thoughts.

"Oh, yeah. I'm sure it'll be—"

"I smell—" Kekoa walked out of his office, nose in the air. His eyes landed on the bag Brynn was setting on the table. "Are those bagels from Lenny's?"

"Are there better bagels anywhere else?" Brynn winked and settled into a chair. "I also added a protein wrap for you, Garcia."

"Thanks." Garcia handed Lyla a plate as she handed him the wrap.

"You really don't have to keep bringing in food," Lyla said even as she grabbed an everything bagel and the tub of cream cheese.

"Speak for yourself, sistah," Kekoa said with a grin. "Food is the way to a man's heart, right, brah?"

The question was directed at Jack, and his cheeks warmed. He exchanged a quick glance with Brynn, who then busied herself with a blueberry bagel.

"I, uh, wanted to thank you guys for coming to the hospital. It was nice." Brynn cleared her throat and looked at Kekoa. "And those malasadas were amazing."

"Anytime, sis. You ohana now."

Brynn smiled and it reached her eyes, sending a desire through him to be the one who did that for her. If only that need wasn't warring with the warning that history often repeated itself.

"Right. I appreciate everyone coming in on a Saturday. Let's do a quick debrief." Jack looked to Garcia. "You have news from the Virginia Fire and Explosives Team? ATF?"

Garcia wiped his mouth, then balled his napkin and set it aside. "Well, it could've been a lot worse. It was a pressure-cooker bomb typical of the ones used in Boston and other attempted bombings."

"It could've been worse?"

Garcia nodded grimly at Brynn. "Yes. The amount of nitrate inside the pressure cooker was enough to cause the explosion, but the interior of the SUV and the bodies of El-Deeb and Gamal took the brunt of the impact, containing it in a way."

"How was it detonated?"

"ATF is working on that," Garcia answered Jack. "But most improvised explosive devices like this are detonated remotely."

Jack glanced over at Brynn and found her looking at him. The unspoken message between them was clear. *They were lucky to be alive.* That felt like a huge understatement—especially after yesterday.

It was like the Lord was watching over them.

He wouldn't deny that his faith had taken a nosedive into the

NATALIE WALTERS

shallow end of a pool filled with regret, anger, and fear when Brynn
betrayed him. He'd grown up knowing the Lord. His parents had
made sure of it, and it was easy to believe God was on his side
when things went the way he wanted. But Brynn's decision and
then his cancer diagnosis—it'd had him questioning everything.

In the midst of it, Jack couldn't see the steadfast faithfulness his
mother promised God was delivering. Instead, he second-guessed
his life, his choices, God's goodness. And then he met Director
Walsh, who, despite Jack's pity party, offered him an opportunity
to work for SNAP.

Studying Brynn now, he wondered if maybe her decision back
then was for the better. The overseas assignment she'd worked so
hard for had been cut short to be home with her father. It was a
worthy sacrifice, but it had to have been difficult. He thought about
his cancer and wondered how Brynn would have responded if they
had been together. Jack shook away the thought. He wouldn't put
her in that position.

"Which brings us to Seif El-Deeb and Tarek Gamal," Lyla said,
bringing Jack's focus back. "Kekoa?"

"Homeland Security is giving me a hard time." For the first time
since working with Kekoa, the Hawaiian looked a bit . . . humble.
"I can't find any passport information on either of them."

Jack looked at Lyla. "Can you take care of that?"

"Yep."

Lyla picked up her phone and began typing, and Jack caught
Brynn smirking at him. With an idea of what she was thinking, he
lifted up his fingers and snapped. She smiled with a roll of her eyes.

"What about Riad's laptop?" Brynn asked Kekoa. "Any luck?"

"Some. I've been able to breach a few layers of the system, but
it's only giving me access to surface information. There's another
level of security encryption that requires a chip similar to military
CAC cards. The Common Access Card, or smart card, would open
it up with a password that I could hack, but without one it's going
to take a bit more time."

165

Brynn's lips twisted, and Jack sensed her frustration. "Riad. Ali. El-Deeb. Gamal. Ansari."

Her recitation of names sent a shiver of fear down Jack's spine as he remembered her collapsing into his arms. "You were about to tell me what Ansari told you about Moustafa Ali, do you remember?"

Their eyes met, and she gave a slight nod. "Ansari remembered Moustafa but said he hadn't seen him for a while. He mentioned something about him being excited about some new opportunity."

Garcia frowned. "What opportunity?"

"He didn't know, but it had to have been one that would pull him away from a tuition-free semester at GMU. He came to America for an education, and something had to have enticed him to walk away." Brynn's chin dipped. "I can't help feeling Ansari's death is my fault."

"No way." Lyla set down her phone. "Joseph Ansari had been working with the FBI for years. It was only a matter of time before someone figured it out."

"While I don't think we can rule out that possibility"—Brynn gave Lyla an appreciative grin—"my gut tells me it's related to the murder of Seif El-Deeb and Tarek Gamal."

"Someone's trying to kill our investigation," Garcia said with zero emotion.

Jack sat forward, his heart rate beginning to climb. "If that's true, whoever is behind it has been one step ahead of us."

Lyla made a face. "Except how could they've known Brynn was going to meet with Ansari?"

"She was followed."

"Maybe." Brynn shrugged off Garcia's suggestion—an attempt to be dismissive—but there was a tightening in her voice that concerned Jack. "Or," she said, "someone is trying to clean up their mess."

"Ahem." Kekoa pointed to the screen above them. "If I could direct your attention, please." The screen came to life with a black-

and-white video of a DC street cam. "This is from a check-cashing place across from the intersection where Joseph Ansari got sick. You see him there walking up, tips his head to the couple with the baby, presses the button for the crosswalk. Brynn, you walk up, he grabs for his chest and—"

"He's already been poisoned at that point," Brynn said.

Jack looked to Brynn, her eyes fixed on the video. Was she reliving the moment?

Brynn looked back at him. "You remember the lecture on the Mossad's method. They sprayed the poison into his ear." She turned to Kekoa. "Can you rewind it, please?"

Kekoa did as asked, and they all watched it again.

"What am I missing?" Lyla asked.

"Ansari inhaled the poison, and the only people he had come into contact with were—"

"The couple," Jack finished Brynn's thought.

Lyla looked at him like he was crazy. "With the baby?"

"Go back again, please," Brynn asked. When Kekoa did, she pointed up. "Watch them. The woman crosses in front of me with the stroller blocking the line of sight on the man who—see there. He turns just a little bit. I think that's when he sprays Ansari with the fentanyl."

It all happened so quickly. Methodical. If Brynn had been any closer . . .

"Kekoa?" Brynn's voice interrupted his thoughts, and Jack watched Kekoa rewind the footage again. "Stop right there. Can you zoom in on the stroller?"

Kekoa did.

"It's empty," Lyla said with a gasp. "There's no baby."

"And no good shot of the couple's faces," Kekoa said, typing. "Only an odd angle of the guy's face."

"Caucasian and blond." Brynn's eyes narrowed on the screen. "Kekoa, can—"

"Actually." Lyla stood, checking her watch. "We all have a party

167

to get ready for in a few hours." She looked around the room until her eyes landed on Jack. "And you know the rule."

"Rule?" Brynn frowned.

"No work on birthdays unless—"

"Unless the world is ending," Lyla cut Jack off. "Or exploding." She cringed before looking at Brynn. "Too soon. Sorry."

Brynn glanced back at Jack with an "are you serious?" expression. He shrugged before standing. "We can pick this up tomorrow if anyone wants to come in on their Sunday."

Lyla clapped her hands. "Brynn, if you're free tonight, I'd love for you to come."

"Really?"

"Yes, but please don't bring any food." Lyla smiled. "The party is catered."

Jack read the hesitation in Brynn's eyes, but Garcia caught his attention.

"I wanted to give you an update. The port in Guam received another shipment of fertilizer. This time about ten bags, bringing the total from the first delivery to under fourteen hundred pounds."

"Timothy McVeigh used almost two thousand pounds in the Oklahoma City bombing," Brynn said matter-of-factly. "And the explosion in Beirut was caused by ammonium nitrate too."

Garcia's serious expression mirrored Jack's growing concern. If their resident explosives expert was bothered by this, then they needed to look into it.

"Who's it being delivered to?"

"Right now, nobody." Garcia removed his hat and scratched his head. "It gets delivered to the dock with a recipient's name, but no one claims it, and port authority can't get ahold of anyone. The shipments are just sitting there."

"Guam is reviving their agriculture," Lyla said, looking at her phone. "Many of the farmers lost their land post World War II and are working to reclaim land and develop it." She looked around at everyone in the room. "Maybe the fertilizer is for, you know, farming?"

Garcia looked skeptical, and Jack couldn't discount Lyla's comment. "Garcia, you continue to keep an eye on that shipment. See if you can look into where it was shipped from or purchased from. There's got to be a trail that'll tell us who it's for and why they need it."

"Got it."

Jack ran a hand through his hair, then rubbed the muscles growing tighter in his shoulders. With so many unanswered questions, sometimes the job felt never-ending. Brynn gathered her coat, and he reached for the sleeve to help her into it.

"Thanks."

Her familiar fragrance washed over him. "How are you feeling?"

"Good. Muscles are still a little stiff from the explosion, but I'm good." She looked into his eyes and must've read his concern. She smiled. "Really." Her eyes flashed to the cut above his forehead. "How's your head and leg?"

"Healing." He rocked on his heels. "I'm sure Lyla won't mind if you bring Olivia to her party tonight."

Brynn averted her gaze to her gloves. "Olivia and Penny are back in New Mexico."

Concern gripped him. "They left?"

Her expression was unreadable. "Yes, a few days ago."

A few days ago? That meant Brynn had gone home by herself the night of the explosion. Anxiousness mixed with guilt zipped through him. She was all alone. What if something had happened to her? If she'd had a concussion?

"I was thinking I'd stay home tonight and—"

"I know you're not planning on working tonight."

Brynn eyed him. "I need to find out how all this leads back to Riad so that I can report back to my boss and he can report back to the President of the United States. Who, in case you've forgotten, is scheduled to fly to Egypt next week."

"Ms. Taylor, don't make me pull you from this assignment."

She worked her jaw for a second like she was figuring out whether to call his bluff. It wasn't a bluff. If Jack thought Brynn would go rogue again, he trusted Walsh would allow him to make the call.

"*Ms. Taylor*, really, Jack?"

"Obstinance, really, Brynn?" Brynn looked away, but before she did he caught a hint of a smile.

"I'll pick you up at eight."

She waved him off. "I have a car."

"I'd like to pick you up."

"It's not necessary. I don't want you to go out of your way."

"Brynn," Jack said, exasperation coloring his tone, "you don't have to be so independent." He softened his words. "I'd like to pick you up and take you to Lyla's party."

"Fine." She rolled her eyes. "See you at eight."

Watching Kekoa escort Brynn out of their office, Jack tried to make sense of the feelings tormenting his heart. Brynn had not only swept into his life, but his heart was quickly making a space for her whether he wanted her to be there or not. Did he? And what about Amy? They weren't technically in a relationship, but there was that kiss.

Amy felt like the sure thing.

Brynn felt like the right thing.

Garcia came up beside him. "You're in trouble, brother."

Jack groaned. "I know."

## 19

Washington, DC
7:41 PM Saturday, January 17

"Let me get this straight. You go kung fu on someone, get rammed by a vehicle, Jack uses his body to shield you from a car explosion, and then you have a heart attack?" Olivia's voice was quickly approaching a level only Penny would hear. "From being poisoned? I had no idea my best friend was Jane Bond."

Brynn pulled the phone from her ear while also trying to slip into her favorite pair of boyfriend jeans with one hand. "I wasn't poisoned, and it was an episode."

"An episode of what? Jack Ryan? Ooh," Olivia squealed. "Yes! That's it. Jack Hudson, Jack Ryan? It totally fits!"

"Hold on." Brynn dropped her phone on the bed and used both hands to pull her jeans on. She chose a gray sweater with little pearls stitched across the front. Festive enough for a birthday but not so dressed up to look like she was trying too hard. Which she wasn't.

"Okay, I'm back." Brynn slid the phone between her ear and shoulder. "What were we talking about?"

"Nice try." Olivia giggled into the phone. "You know exactly who we're talking about."

"And I'd really like to stop talking about him."

Because the last thing Brynn needed was to bring up the very man she hadn't been able to avoid thinking about all day and who would soon be here to pick her up for Lyla's birthday party. Especially now that she knew Jack had gone through something that required treatment. And in a moment of weakness, she'd googled *treatment*, opening up thousands of hits for substance abuse and horrific diseases that turned her stomach and forced her to turn off the computer. Lyla was right. If Brynn wanted to know, she'd need to ask Jack, and she would if only to erase the images from her Google search out of her mind.

"Why? The man *shielded* you with his body."

"Yes, right after he chewed me out for going rogue." Brynn paused. "Can you believe that?"

"You do have an independent streak."

Brynn remembered Jack's earlier comment. "You say that like it's a flaw."

Walking into her living room, she grabbed her pair of cheetah-print flats. She was probably going to regret that decision in the subfreezing temps, but they were cute and tonight—hanging out with Lyla . . . and Jack—she wanted to be cute.

"It's not normally, but . . ."

"But . . ."

"It's not exactly a hunk magnet. Men appreciate being needed to some degree."

"Being needy is not attractive." Brynn frowned. "I'm not needy."

"I know that. And so does he, I'm sure. But what does it say to someone who wants to be part of your life? If you don't need them for anything, why would they stick around?"

Her stomach tightened. "Olivia, you know I need *you*, right?"

"I do." Brynn could hear the smile in her friend's voice, which caused the tightness to subside. "But I've known you your whole life. I've learned where I fit in."

And the tightness was back. Had she really made Olivia feel this way? After her father's injury, Brynn clung to her independence like an anchor. The uncertainty in her family swung them between doctor's appointments, her father losing his job, moving to the DC area so her mom could work, new friends, new schools, new life. She'd learned to be independent because the last thing she wanted to do was add another burden to her family's situation. It wasn't a flaw—it was practicality. What needed to be done.

"If I've made you feel like that, I'm so sorry."

Brynn's throat burned. Why was she so emotional lately? Maybe she should call Jack and tell him she needed to rest. He couldn't argue with his own directive, right?

"You don't need to apologize, girl. I love you the way you are, but you know I can't love you in the way, say, a handsome man who would protect you with his own—"

"I get it! I get it!" Brynn cut her friend off with a laugh. "Jack's a hero, but you better never tell him I said so."

She peeked out of her second-floor window to the street below, feeling suddenly self-conscious that Jack might be out there listening to this insane conversation.

"I promise to only bring it up at the wedding."

"Olivia!"

The earlier conversation's tension—gone. A thousand degrees of heat climbing her neck—check. And why, oh why did her thoughts go straight to Jack? In a suit? Looking all 007? Except Italian. Brynn's heart thunked—not thumped—but thunked wildly in her chest like a racehorse itching to get out of the starting stall. *Just let me runnnn.* Only her heart was saying, *Just let me loovvee.*

"Brynn?"

Snapping out of her odd racehorse daydream, Brynn squeezed her eyes shut. This was getting out of control. The doorbell to her apartment rang, and Brynn cringed again, praying Olivia hadn't—

"Was that your doorbell?" *Too late.* "It's eight o'clock on a Saturday night. Is that a hot date?"

"No." *Then why am I checking my reflection in the mirror?* "It's Lyla's birthday. She invited me, and Jack insisted on driving even though I took a Metro to and from his office today."

"Aw, see. He's protective."

*Or he's keeping an eye on me.* Brynn had half expected to find him or Garcia or Kekoa parked outside her apartment. Thankfully, they weren't, but that didn't mean Jack hadn't put someone there she didn't know or recognize. A simple snap of the fingers . . . She smiled, remembering how the teasing gesture had brought a spark to his eyes when she snapped her fingers outside the farmhouse in Clifton. Had she been teasing . . . or flirting? The heat of a blush warmed her cheeks.

Brynn schooled herself into keeping perspective. "I was thinking about canceling—"

"Don't you dare." Olivia's voice echoed loudly into the phone. Brynn heard the tinkling sound of Penny's collar, which meant her voice had startled her too. "You need this. Go have some fun."

Brynn pushed out an exaggerated sigh so Olivia could hear it. "Do I have to?"

"Yes! And I expect you to call me tomorrow with all the details of your date."

"It's not a—"

"Nighty-night." The phone clicked.

*Ugh.* Sliding the phone into the back pocket of her jeans, Brynn answered the door and almost had a heart attack.

"My name is Jack Hudson. You said yes to my invitation. Prepare to movie."

Jack stood at her door, one hand behind his back and the other pointing at her in a fencing stance, a black beanie on his head, and the ugliest fake mustache she'd ever seen above his upper lip.

Brynn burst out laughing. "You aren't serious, are you?"

"What?" Jack straightened. "It's *The Princess Bride*." He smoothed the mustache's edges. "It was my Inigo Montoya impression. Was my Spanish accent bad?"

"No, the accent was good, but that mustache is a little more Groucho Marx than Inigo Montoya."

"*Hey.* I paid extra for this. It's an authentic conquistador mustache." He zipped his right hand in the air as though wielding an invisible sword. "The lady said I looked handsome."

Aside from the dorky mustache, Jack, in his dark jeans and charcoal-gray peacoat, didn't have to try hard to look handsome. Even the slightly crooked bump in his nose gave his face just enough imperfection that it was charming.

"Can I get your coat?" Jack didn't wait for an answer, bypassing her to the coatrack. He took her jacket, a scarf, and a hat.

"Uh, I was going to call—"

"Lyla is the last person you want to cancel on," Jack said, but with the ridiculous mustache she couldn't tell if he was being serious or joking. He lifted a brow. "She once gave Garcia the silent treatment for three weeks because he left on an overseas assignment and forgot to check in when he landed. Never mind that any contact would've gotten the man killed."

"Where exactly was he?"

Jack tilted his head, a smile lifting the corners of the mustache. "Don't make me say it, B."

Brynn rolled her eyes before taking her coat from him and slipping it on. She reached for the scarf, but he stepped forward and wrapped it over her neck, his nearness bringing the spicy scent of his cologne. She swallowed, her eyes closing at the memories it brought back. Stepping back, Jack gently tugged her white beanie over her head, his fingers brushing against her forehead to tuck a loose strand of hair out of her eyes.

"You look great, by the way." He gave a gentle tug on the end of her braid. "A modern-day Buttercup."

A magnetic energy seemed to be vibrating between them. Or maybe it was Olivia's silly words coloring her perspective. Sure, it was possible a tiny bit of the attraction she'd once felt for Jack had returned, but that didn't mean it meant anything.

"Ready?"

She nodded. "Oh, wait." Brynn grabbed the shopping bag hanging on the coat-closet door handle. "For Lyla."

After a short drive into Alexandria, Jack walked Brynn into a renovated art-deco theater, its façade lit up with marquee lighting highlighting the evening's showing. But she'd have to be blind not to figure it out when she walked into the crowded lobby that looked like a casting call for *The Princess Bride*. Everywhere she turned, excited moviegoers were dressed up as their favorite characters. Dread Pirate Roberts, Buttercup, dozens of Inigo Montoyas with mustaches as disturbing as Jack's. There were even a few Vizzinis and Fezziks. It was a spectacle, but thankfully there were a few underdressed viewers like herself, so she didn't feel entirely out of place.

"You didn't tell me this was a costume party," Brynn said through a tight smile.

Jack looked at her like she was crazy. "You think I wanted to dress like this?"

"You made it! Yay!" Lyla stepped out of a crowd and walked toward them in a brown peasant dress that gathered around her figure in a way that made her look less farm girl and more damsel. Only, with the number of handsome young men watching her, Brynn doubted Lyla would ever be in distress.

Brynn held up the gift. "Happy birthday."

Lyla's eyes lit up. "You didn't have to get me anything."

"It's nothing special, but I heard you—"

The near ear-piercing squeal that erupted from Lyla drew the attention of those nearby. "Are you kidding me?" She pulled out the hot-pink leather, letting the bag drop to the ground.

"Is that a hot-pink gun holster?" Jack asked.

Lyla pressed it to her chest. "Yes!"

Brynn smiled. "I'm glad you like it."

"Like it?" She pulled Brynn into a quick hug that completely took her off guard. "I love it. Thank you so much." Lyla's attention snagged on something over Brynn's shoulder. "Nicolás, look what Brynn got me for Cupcake!"

Garcia walked toward them in a pair of very tight black pants and a black puffy shirt that opened at the neck to reveal the edge of a tattoo on his chest. Above his lip was a mustache he actually made look good. He smiled at Brynn and Jack, looking like the poor boy from *A Christmas Story* who was forced to wear the pink bunny suit. Kekoa, however, had chosen, like Brynn, to forgo costumes and stick with jeans, a T-shirt, and slippers.

The lights in the lobby of the theater dimmed a couple of times, and everyone cheered.

"Wait." Lyla popped up onto her tiptoes, looking around. "Before the movie starts, I wanted to introduce you to someone."

Brynn looked at Lyla. "Me?"

"Yes, you." There was a coy look in Lyla's eyes as she searched the room. "Wait right here."

Lyla dashed off, leaving Brynn frowning at Jack, who offered a confused shrug.

Garcia shifted, tugging at his pants. "How long do you think I have to wear this?"

Jack laughed. "How did you get out of a costume, Kekoa?"

Kekoa smiled at Jack. "Sometimes it pays to be part of the big and hefty club." He gave Garcia a teasing wink. "Costumes don't come in my size."

"I like your mustache," Brynn said.

"Thanks." Garcia rolled his eyes. "Lyla picked out my costume."

There was so much irritation in his voice, Brynn nearly laughed. He truly looked miserable—why couldn't Lyla see what this man was doing for her?

"Brah, let's go get snacks," Kekoa said to Garcia. "I'm starving."

"You literally ate an hour ago."

"So, I want to get something to eat before the movie starts."

"Fine," Garcia muttered, following Kekoa toward a popcorn station where guests were filling red-and-white-striped buckets with popcorn and their choice of candy and milk- or white-chocolate drizzles.

Jack turned to Brynn. "Would you like some popcorn?"

"Sure." The tantalizing aroma of buttered popcorn was hard to resist. "With Reese's Pieces, please."

Jack took a bow. "As you wish."

His smile, the bow, the tease in his eyes had Brynn's—

"Brynn Taylor, I'd like to introduce you to my friend Ari Blackman." Lyla stepped into Brynn's line of vision with a man at her side looking appropriately embarrassed. "He's in the Army." Lyla leaned in and whispered, "PSYOPS—but he doesn't play mind games with women, only the enemy." Lyla winked. "He's single and ready to—"

"Ahem." Ari's fake cough cut Lyla off. "I think that's good, Lyla."

"Nice to meet you." Brynn held out a hand, which she regretted the second she saw Jack walk over.

"Did you want butter on your popcorn?" Jack held up a bucket. He reached out his hand to Ari. "Good to see you again, man."

"You too. Staying busy?"

"Yeah, you?"

"Always."

The interaction between both men seemed genuinely friendly, but Brynn couldn't help noticing a slight bit of tension.

Ari looked at her. "How long have you been part of SNAP?"

"Oh, I'm not." Brynn shook her head. "We're working together on an assignment."

"Ah." Ari smiled. A nice one.

Lyla stepped up to Jack. "Weren't you getting some popcorn?"

"I *was*," Jack said, gaze hard on Lyla.

Brynn watched her lead Jack toward the concession stand even though everything in his expression said that was the last place he wanted to be. Was it jealousy? That shouldn't delight her as much as it did.

"I don't like butter," Brynn called after them.

"He's not happy I'm talking with you."

She faced Ari, who was tall enough that she had to look up a bit. He had a very suave style about him. Salt-and-pepper hair too mature for his young face made her curious how much was natural or done by a very good stylist. Facial hair was trimmed close, giving him that perfected five-o'clock shadow, and beneath dark wire-framed glasses, brown eyes peered down at her, assessing.

"Psychological operations, huh?"

Ari shrugged. "It comes in handy whenever a well-meaning friend tries to set me up."

Something told Brynn this handsome man probably didn't have trouble attracting the attention of women, which meant if he didn't date, it was likely due to his job. She was going to ask him about his connection to Jack when the lights dimmed again. Two ushers opened a pair of double doors, and the crowd cheered as they moved toward them.

"I should get going." Ari smiled. "Maybe I'll see you for the after-party?"

"Um . . ." Brynn swallowed. "Maybe?"

"I promise I won't get in his—" Ari's gaze drifted over her shoulder, and she turned to see Jack eyeing them. "Way."

Before she could respond, Ari tipped his chin, a knowing expression of amusement in his eyes, before joining the crowd entering the theater.

Jack walked over. "Are you smitten?"

"Smitten?" Brynn searched the rigid expression on his face. *Don't read into it.* "Over that guy?"

Garcia joined them, a bottle of water in his hand. "Lyla is."

"Brah, no, she's not." Kekoa carried a giant tub of popcorn. "He's too . . . intense for her. She likes laid-back, easygoing. Someone who's spontaneous."

There was intention in Kekoa's words that Garcia seemed to be ingesting, and Brynn couldn't help but wonder what was keeping

Garcia and Lyla apart when there was clearly something between them.

Inside the theater, they sat down as ushers passed out inflatable swords to everyone. A man at the front wearing a shirt with the theater's logo held a microphone to his lips.

"What's going on?" Brynn took the sword handed to her. "I thought we were watching a movie?"

"Ladies and gentlemen, mwovies is what bwings us togever today." The crowd went wild, swords swinging in the air at the man's impression of the priest from the movie. "Thank you for joining us this evening. Most of you should have your swords, and we'll be passing out another little treat. Any guesses?" A few people shouted out guesses, but the man shook his head. "Close, but what else would we serve you but peanut . . ."

The entire theater, including Lyla and Kekoa, shouted, "Buttercups!"

Garcia grumbled, and Jack laughed with Brynn.

"Are you ready for the movie?"

The crowd cheered.

"As you wish."

The man bowed, the crowd clapped, and the lights went dark as the screen in front of them lit up.

"What kind of movie is this?"

Jack leaned close to her ear, his breath tickling the hair at her neck. "It's interactive," he whispered. "Relax and have fun, B."

The light from the giant screen lit up his face, giving her a quick glimpse at the look in his eyes. It set her nerves dancing, which caused her gaze to skip to his lips. The movie scene shifted, pitching the theater dark and hiding the blush warming her cheeks. The last thing she needed to be thinking about was his lips.

Thankfully, the second Farm Boy and Princess Buttercup appeared onscreen, the entire audience began quoting the characters and challenging their neighbors to duels with their swords, Kekoa and Garcia the worst among them. Brynn didn't have to think about Jack's lips or the way Westley's devotion reminded her of Jack or how her pulse raced every time he shifted close to her, their arms accidentally touching on the armrest until finally neither of them moved away—no, she didn't have to think about that at all.

Except it was *all* she wanted to think about.

# 20

*"Love is many things, none of them logical."*

Jack remembered these words from his high school English class when they were asked to read *The Princess Bride* novel by William Goldman. Back then, he and his friends joked around at all the romantic references while the girls gushed over the fictional hero, lamenting how they wished Westley were real.

With Brynn at his side, laughing and waving her sword, Jack couldn't help but classify his growing feelings as illogical. It made zero sense to let his heart long for a romance that only existed in books or in the movies. He swallowed, annoyed by his cynicism.

He knew it wasn't true. His own parents had been happily married for almost forty years, and witnessing their love for one another made Jack think about romance differently. It wasn't only about the physical affection. Watching his mom and dad care for each other in small ways, him making her tea every morning, his mom making sure Dad's favorite chips were available during baseball season. It seemed minor, but it added up.

What wasn't adding up were the feelings reemerging for the woman who had left his heart fractured and was somehow now mending it together with her presence back in his life.

Brynn leaned over. "Hey, you okay?"

182

"I think I need a little air."

"Okay." Brynn grabbed her coat. "It's almost over anyway."

Jack started to tell her she could stay, but her immediate inclination to join him kept him quiet. But apparently not quite enough, because someone—he was pretty sure it was Kekoa—shushed them, causing Brynn to giggle. Jack and Brynn hunch-walked out of the theater so as not to block anyone's view of Westley's torture in the pit of despair. After they bundled up in their coats, he walked Brynn across the street to a row of restaurants, bars, and shops.

"Ooh, it's cold out here." Brynn's breath puffed in front of her face as she shuffled her feet.

He'd noticed her cute but completely impractical shoes earlier. "I'd give your toes about one minute in these temperatures before they turn black and fall off."

"Ew, Jack." She looked down at her feet, practically dancing to keep them warm. "I knew these were a bad choice."

"There's a Fieldman's over there. Come on."

"I'm not buying new boots, Jack."

"Come on," he insisted. "But first—" He pointed at a little coffee and hot chocolate kiosk designed to look like a log cabin, with a red-and-black buffalo-check moose logo. "Whipped cream?"

Brynn rubbed her gloved hands together. "Yes, please."

With their hot chocolates in hand, they hurried into the sporting goods store.

"Welcome." A teenage salesclerk behind the counter barely looked up. "We close in thirty minutes."

Jack escorted Brynn to the camping section at the back of the store. Tents, folding chairs, and a collapsible table complete with a propane grill circled a faux campfire.

"M'lady." Jack gestured to one of the camping chairs. After Brynn sat down, he smiled. "I'll be right back."

After a quick hunt for the right pair, two minutes later he returned to Brynn and held out a pair of fuzzy striped socks. "For you."

Brynn laughed. "I hope you paid for those."

"I did." Jack held out his receipt. "Now we can hang out by this delightful fire, and your toes will be toasty warm."

"Thank you, but you didn't have to," she said while reaching for the socks. She kicked off her shoes and pulled the socks on with a smile, closing her eyes. "These are soft."

"And warm?"

Her eyes opened. "Yes."

"Good." He let out a sigh and sat in the seat next to her. "We have exactly twenty-five minutes until the store closes, and I don't think that kid will let us stay even if I promise to buy this whole setup."

Brynn laughed softly before settling against her chair, and he couldn't help but stare. He wanted to see into her thoughts, her memories, discover what the last eight years had been like for her. His heart still ached for the tremendous loss of her parents. How was she coping?

"I can feel you staring at me."

Jack quickly averted his eyes to the cardboard flames. "No, I wasn't."

"Do you ever wonder what it would've been like if . . . things had been different?"

It was like she'd read his mind. He turned, their eyes meeting. How much did he confess? "In the beginning, yeah."

"And now?"

There was a vulnerability in her words, and he forced himself to censor his response. "Yeah. A little now too."

Her gaze shifted to the campfire, and she seemed lost in a memory, maybe.

"I still can't believe you're here." Embarrassment warmed his cheeks as a breath of nervous laughter left his lips. "I mean, after all these years we're working together."

"Probably not in the way you imagined."

Jack released a breath. "A lot of things didn't go the way I imagined."

She bit her lip, eyes searching his. "Jack, Lyla said something about you being in treatment, and I hate asking because I know it's private, but my mind and my Google search took me to places that are going to give me nightmares if you don't tell me. But if you really don't want to—"

"It's fine, Brynn. Lyla told me she let it slip."

Brynn's nose wrinkled. "So all this time you've let me worry about it on my own?"

She said it playfully, but Jack could see the genuine concern in her eyes and it warmed him. "Non-Hodgkin's lymphoma. I was diagnosed a few months after exiting the CIA program."

"And you're okay now?" She searched the length of his body before meeting his gaze again. "I mean, you look great." She pinched her lips together in a tight smile, embarrassed.

"I'm good, Brynn. Really." He repeated the words she'd offered him earlier. "In a way, I think it was a good thing I didn't get selected for clandestine services."

Brynn looked at her cup of hot chocolate. "Do you remember preparing for the final exercise? We studied every scenario. We researched decades of missions gone awry so we'd be ready."

Those long nights came back to him in a flash. Not only were they sleep-deprived and physically and mentally exhausted, but their instructors were skilled in torturing them psychologically. There were rumors the CIA instructors would place bets on which recruits would fail or pass, and like predators, they had no problem exploiting weakness.

He lost sleep imagining a thousand scenarios that had him trapped in some psychological exercise meant to mimic a real-life mission.

"It felt like I had been preparing my whole life for that moment, and the only thing standing between me and stopping terrorism was that test. Except that wasn't true. The one thing I hadn't been prepared for was you."

His heart stalled, and fear crashed over him. Did he want to relive this? A tear slipped down her cheek, and Jack's hand fisted to keep from reaching for her. The fear from a second ago shifted into a need. To understand. To hear. To know why.

"I didn't know they would use you against me."

Jack's fingers curled tighter around his cup. "What do you mean?"

"You were part of my mission." She swallowed. "I thought it was over. I had successfully obtained the objective, but then the mission changed. I don't know how they did it, but they showed me a photo of you tied up, beaten." She shook her head. "It was clearly a doctored photo, but they were making me choose. You or the mission."

Her lip trembled on those final words and Jack's heart, no matter how it harbored the hurt, couldn't take the waver in her voice. "You don't have to explain."

"But I do." Her thumb bounced against her cup. "Jack, the CIA discovered my weakness and used it to force me into a decision. They were making it clear that in this career, a choice must be made."

"You made the only decision you could." He tried for indifference, but he could hear the hurt in his words.

"Terrorists have no mercy. They're monsters, and I've experienced firsthand the devastation they cause. I couldn't give them you to use against me." She sniffled. "You know the agency is *mission first*. That final test . . . they were forcing us to understand what was at stake. The CIA knew about us, and they forced us to make a decision. For me, it was a lot easier choosing the mission when I knew it wasn't real, that you would be okay. Even if it broke my heart. Out there, in the real world, if it came down to the mission or you, not choosing you wouldn't just break my heart, Jack. It would break *me*. And that made you a liability. It made me a liability to the agency. That's why I did what I did—why we couldn't be together. I'm sorry I hurt you. It's something I've carried with me for eight years."

Jack twisted the cup of hot chocolate in his hand, trying to buy time and figure out the emotions beating wildly in his chest. News of Brynn's success had reached the barracks before she did. The details of her mission *and* her decision. He hadn't wanted to believe she'd give up on them so easily, but she had. He wasn't sure how to process the desire to take her back into his arms, and maybe his life, but also protect himself from the pain of her choice.

"We were young and in love and—"

Brynn moved to look up at him. "You loved me?"

*Ouch.* Jack kept his expression neutral even as his heart dropped into his stomach. An alarm seemed to echo through his brain, reminding him that *this* was why he didn't let himself become vulnerable.

"Of course I did, Brynn." He released a measured breath. "Like I said, maybe I was just young and naive. I thought you did—hoped you did too."

Brynn slid her hand into his, the warmth of her fingers sending a tingle up his arm and straight into the thumping organ in his chest. "I did."

The words felt like a life preserver tossed out too late.

Jack searched her face, expecting to see regret but instead simply saw the expectant look of someone who still owned his heart. He glanced down at their hands, unsure of how to react to his desire to not let go. Ever.

"If you would've told me what they did to you, I would've made it easy for you." He slid his thumb along her knuckles, letting the softness of her skin fan the flames of attraction dancing in his chest. "I would've walked away. Given it up for you."

"I would never ask that of you." Beneath long lashes, her eyes found his. "But I'm here now and—"

"Actually, you're not." An annoyed voice jerked their attention to the salesclerk. "You've got to go. We're closed."

Having icy snow shoved into their clothing wouldn't have been as jarring as the teenager's abrupt interruption. Jack and

Brynn looked at each other before they both began laughing. A much-needed release from the tension that felt like it was ready to explode . . . or lead to something Jack wasn't sure was a good idea.

Helping Brynn to her feet, he forced himself not to enjoy the touch of her skin against his again. They were escorted rather hurriedly to the glass front door, where the kid promptly locked it behind them, leaving Brynn giggling and holding her shoes in her hand.

"Someone should really talk to the manager about his sales technique. The least he could've done was try to sell me some boots."

Jack laughed, his hand falling to the small of Brynn's back, the move so routine it caught him off guard. Her eyes met his, and he could see the questions dancing in them.

"Jack?"

His gaze shifted to the brunette carrying a wrapped birthday gift in her hands, a curious look on her face. His hand fell to his side, his ears burning. He cast a sideways glance at Brynn, who was no longer smiling and had taken a step sideways, moving away from him.

He released a sigh. "Hey, Amy."

〰〰〰〰

An hour later, Jack couldn't get Brynn's devastated expression out of his head. After clumsily introducing her to Amy, he had to all but force Brynn to allow him to wait with her for her Uber. She wouldn't talk to him, wouldn't look at him. He'd hurt her, and that made him a fool.

A bigger fool, still, because he had also hurt the woman currently sitting across from him. After stopping by Lyla's party, Amy had suggested they grab something to eat and talk.

He picked up his water glass and took a sip, watching Amy scan the menu of a restaurant they frequented every time she was in town. It was one of the few that kept late hours, which made it perfect for their erratic work schedules. "Trying something new tonight?"

Amy set down the menu, her hazel eyes meeting his. He saw something tucked into the depths of them that heightened the anxiousness circling in his stomach. After Brynn had left in the Uber, Amy explained that the movie she was working on wrapped early and she caught the first flight to get back in time for Lyla's party. She wanted it to be a surprise for him too, but Jack noticed the edge of surprise in her expression when she found him with Brynn.

She gave a soft smile. "No. I'm just trying to figure out . . ." Swallowing, she bit her lip and reached for her glass. "I . . ." She let out a breath. "We're friends, right?"

Jack swallowed. "Yes, of course."

"Right, good." Amy searched his face, making his anxiousness rise. "Because I think after tonight, and no matter how much Lyla would *love* for us to be something more . . . it's not there. Right?"

He stifled the lungful of relief wanting to escape. "Are you asking me?"

She pressed her lips together in a mirthful grin. "No."

"Good." He released the breath.

"I'm not sure if I should be offended by your reaction," she said with a laugh. His face must've sobered because she quickly added, "Don't worry, Jack. I'm as relieved as you are. I just have better control over my response."

"Sorry." He wrinkled his nose.

Jack relaxed into his seat, the muscles in his body unwinding. He studied Amy, her dark-brown hair curling over her shoulders, the subtle slope of her nose that had a sprinkling of freckles across it and her cheeks. Amy was beautiful and kind and . . . not the one for him.

"When did you know?"

Amy gave him a teasing smile. "The night we kissed."

His eyes grew wide, heat filling his cheeks because one, he'd been caught looking at her lips, and two, Amy knew what he'd been thinking. "The night we kissed? Six months ago?"

"Exactly." Amy took a drink. "After getting to know each other for almost a year, we finally have a moment—"

"I'm not sure I'd call it that," he joked, knowing she'd agree. "That old lady was as stubborn as an ox. Who makes people prove they're a couple just to attend a couples' cooking class? It was ridiculous."

Amy laughed. "Isn't she your mother's aunt?"

"Yes." Jack rolled his eyes. "Stubborn as an ox."

"Well, it wasn't a great moment, and maybe that had something to do with the kiss being"—she lifted a shoulder—"meh."

Jack's jaw dropped open. "Meh?"

His reaction sent Amy into a fit of giggles, bringing moisture to her eyes. Her hysterics had him worried. Sure, he wasn't Casanova, but he had to be better than meh.

*Brynn seemed to enjoy it.*

The thought shot into his mind like a bullet piercing a piece of glass, shattering into a spiderweb of confusing cracks. Once upon a time, Brynn didn't mind his kisses, but would she feel the same now? His cheeks burned at the thought.

"You're thinking about her, aren't you?"

Amy's question brought another round of heat to his cheeks. "Are you sure you're not some sort of secret spy using the guise of movie and television production?"

She tipped her head to the side. "If I told you, I'd have to kill you."

He chuckled at the joke, reminded once again of Brynn. This was becoming a problem.

"Have you told her how you feel?"

Their waiter interrupted to take their orders, leaving Jack to consider her question. How did he feel in light of what Brynn had told him? It angered him to learn the CIA would go so far as to use him against her. It wasn't fair. Plenty of officers in the agency were married with families . . . and many were not. Brynn was right when she said they'd asked her to choose. Throughout their six months of training, the instructors made it clear—a choice would have to be made. A mission would require missed holidays, birthdays, even months of communication, and both the CIA officer and their family had to sacrifice.

When the waiter walked away, Amy looked over. "So?"

"I don't know what to say." He rubbed the back of his neck. *Am I really going to discuss my ex with my . . .* "This feels weird."

"Why?" Amy grabbed a breadstick. "If it wasn't established before"—she waggled her eyebrows—"I'll say it again. You and I are better as friends. It wasn't just the kiss—"

"I was under pressure," Jack cut in and gave the space around them a quick look before leaning in. "You're seriously going to hurt my chances at dating if you keep saying my kiss was less than stellar."

"Fine." She held up a hand in surrender. "We'll blame it on pressure."

Jack lifted an eyebrow at her. "Maybe it was who I was kissing? Ever think maybe your kiss was—"

Amy jabbed her breadstick in the air at him. "A gentleman never discusses a woman's kiss. Besides, you're deflecting. Let's say"—she eased back into her chair—"you're right. Maybe it was the woman." She took a bite of her breadstick, chewed, and swallowed, her eyes never leaving his. "Is Brynn the one?"

Jack tipped his chin up so his gaze went to the tin-tile ceiling of the steakhouse, thoughts of Brynn swirling in his mind. "I don't know."

"Are you afraid she'll hurt you again?"

He dropped his gaze to meet hers. "Truthfully, maybe."

She considered him for a second. "Is that going to keep you from loving her?"

"I didn't say I loved her." The words felt bitter as they left his lips, because that's exactly what he'd said. Less than an hour ago, he had admitted he loved her once, but did that mean he still did? "At one time I believed I did, but when she left, I think I got over her."

"Did you?" Amy looked at him like she didn't believe it. "I've heard the way you've talked about her. There was a look in your eye that . . . well, it's a look that seems reserved just for her."

Shame swept over him. "Amy, I'm sorry. I never meant to—"

She waved him silent. "I'm not saying this for pity, Jack. I'm saying this because even though I come from a broken marriage, I know the value of finding the kind of love that doesn't let go. If that's Brynn for you, then you'd be a fool to let her slip away a second time."

"She didn't *slip* away." Jack sighed. Except for Walsh and Brynn, he'd kept that day at the Farm, Brynn's decision, to himself. "When faced with the choice, Brynn didn't choose me. It's as simple and as complicated as that."

The waiter delivered Amy's meal and made sure they had everything they needed before he stepped away, leaving Amy still staring at Jack.

"Sounds far more complicated than simple."

"It is." Jack played with the silverware on the table. "Much like my kisses."

Amy groaned and then gave him a wink. "It wasn't that bad, but it felt a little too much like kissing my brother."

Jack made a face. "And on that appetizing thought, please eat before your steak gets cold and I ruin another beautiful lady's night."

# 21

Washington, DC
5:56 PM Sunday, January 18

Frustration nipped at Brynn's nerves. She looked at her notes spread across the conference table inside the SNAP fulcrum and then glanced up to the whiteboard filled with their theories about Riad's connection to the three men who had been killed in the last five days.

That fact was the only thing keeping her focused on the mission and not the awkward introduction to Jack's girlfriend the night before.

Her gaze moved to Director Walsh's office, where Jack and Garcia were taking a call from the director, who was who-knows-where in a meeting. On a Sunday evening. The only one not working today was Lyla, who Garcia mentioned spent Sundays with her family. At least someone had a life outside of work.

Brynn turned her attention back to the information they had been studying for the last several hours. Somewhere in front of her there had to be a clue. What was it?

"I think I found something." Kekoa crossed the room from his office. "And just in time."

Brynn turned to see Jack walk out of Walsh's office, Garcia behind him. "Sorry that took so long."

"It's fine," Brynn said, avoiding Jack's gaze. "Everything okay?"

193

Garcia went to his desk, grabbed something, and then tipped his fingers to the brim of his ball cap as he passed. "See you tomorrow."

Brynn's heart leapt in her chest. Tomorrow? She stared at her notes. They hadn't made any progress and Garcia was leaving for the day?

"Everything is fine." Jack sat in the chair next to her and looked to Kekoa. "Did I hear you say you found something?"

"Sure did." Kekoa unrolled his silicon keyboard with a flourish and began typing.

She forced herself to relax, grateful Jack was still ready to work.

"Lyla's favor came through on Tarek Gamal and Seif El-Deeb." A second later, the faces of both men appeared on the screen. "The reason I couldn't find anything on them is because they did not enter the US under their names." Kekoa typed, pulling up two passport photos. Both photos were of the men, but the names did not match. "Seif El-Deeb entered as Qasim Fadel and Tarek Gamal as Ammar Hammadi."

Brynn sat forward, a renewed energy pumping through her. "Any significance in those names?"

Kekoa hitched a brow at her. "Family names in the Middle East are passed on for generations. Like hundreds. Trying to narrow down who these names belonged to in order to specifically connect them to El-Deeb and Gamal . . . would take years."

"Oh." Brynn sat back. "Yeah, that would be hard."

"I'm going to assume you're not testing me." Kekoa gave her a sideways glance, a tease in his voice. "And I did find something interesting on El-Deeb."

A new image filled the screen. An older Arab man with gray hair in a long gray galabeya. Next to him were two women, one older and the other younger. Both were smiling and wearing the traditional Egyptian robe, but their galabeyas had ornate gold-and-pink threading that matched their head scarves.

"This is Ibrahim al-Hussan and his wife, Marwa, and their

daughter, Heba. Mr. al-Hussan runs a small grocery store in Giza. Their daughter is, or was"—Kekoa's voice lowered—"married to Seif El-Deeb."

Jack exhaled. "Is there any reason why Seif El-Deeb would be targeted? Does his family or his wife's family have any connection to terrorist organizations?"

"I can't find much on his family. Like I said, the name is very common. The only thing I found on his wife . . ." Kekoa pressed his lips together, looking guilty.

Brynn's concern grew, afraid not of what he found but *how* he did it. "What'd you find?"

"Egypt doesn't carry the same rules regarding health records, and it didn't take any fancy skills . . ." Kekoa raised his hands, eyes on Brynn. "Promise."

"Okay." Brynn nodded.

"Seif El-Deeb's wife, Heba, is pregnant and the baby's not healthy."

The three cups of coffee Brynn had earlier felt like sludge in her stomach. She stared at the photo of the younger woman. It was hard to tell how old she was, but the bright smile and light in her eyes radiated hope.

"Is the baby going to be okay?" Jack's concern pulled her gaze to him. He glanced over at her, a softness in his eyes, before looking back at Kekoa. "Will they have medical care for the child and mother?"

Kekoa shook his head and shrugged. "From what I can find, the family is not wealthy. Seif El-Deeb worked for Nile Telecom as a support analyst, which I think is like tech support. It seems like a pretty stable job, but he doesn't make much, and I don't think they cover insurance like our country does."

"They don't." Jack rubbed the back of his neck. "And culturally, it would be up to Seif to provide for his wife and child. I can't imagine the baby's care when it's born is going to be cheap."

"Which might mean Agent Flores was right," Brynn said, thinking about what the ICE agent said about trafficking. "What if Seif came here to earn money to send back to his wife? Got here and realized it was a scam?"

"He was trafficked," Jack said, eyes fixed on the photo of Seif El-Deeb. "He was willing to risk it all for his wife and child."

Brynn shifted, feeling like Jack's words held a deeper meaning meant only for her. She fought against the memories from the previous night trying to make their way back to her mind. It didn't matter that she'd almost allowed herself to consider what a future with Jack might look like, he had moved on. And finishing this assignment was what she needed to do to move on too.

"Seif El-Deeb might've come here to help his wife and child, but we can't dismiss that maybe he didn't." Brynn glanced between Kekoa and Jack. "Both men entered the US illegally. If they were smuggled here for work, it seems unlikely that whoever secured their fake passports and flights and got them to the house in Clifton suddenly decided to kill them. All of this appears . . . calculated."

Jack's eyebrows lowered. "You think they came here for another purpose?"

"If Seif El-Deeb's intention was to help his wife and child no matter the costs, we need to find out exactly what kind of work he was willing to do."

A heaviness filled the space, and Brynn watched Jack digest her words. His lips were parting to say something when his cell phone rang, the noise so jarring it caused her to flinch.

"I need to take this," Jack said, rising and walking into Walsh's empty office.

Brynn took in a long breath, the tension pulling at every muscle in her body. "I don't mean to sound like a broken record, but any luck on Riad's laptop?"

Kekoa's shoulders lowered. "It's weird. It's like Egypt doesn't want anyone hacking into their system and learning their secrets."

She grinned, appreciating his humor. "That *is* weird."

Jack stepped out of the office. "We need to go."

His dark expression worried her. "What is it?"

"A body has been discovered." Jack's gaze found hers. "They think it's Riad."

\\\\\\\\\

Inside the car, Jack explained that a jogger stumbled on a body assumed to be a homeless man in Rock Creek Park. When Metro police identified Riad, they called Special Agent in Charge Brett Samson, of the FBI's Joint Terrorism Task Force. He was the one who had phoned Jack and confirmed it was Riad and that he'd been shot.

*Shot.*

The news made her nauseous and numb, the latter having nothing to do with the frigid temperatures frosting the Tahoe's windshield. As heat blasted from the vents, her mind played through every interaction she had with Riad. Had he come to the US to find a friend? Was that the favor? Was it more? Was he connected to Seif El-Deeb and Tarek Gamal? Joseph Ansari? The whirling questions had her off-balance, a feeling she didn't like one little bit.

*What is happening?*

Her unspoken question lingered in the quiet of her mind as she stared out at the skeletal branches of the trees bowing and swaying in the wind. Longing filled her. What would it be like to be rooted and secured no matter the storm?

After her father was injured, Brynn lived in the insecurity of not knowing what would come next. Her parents told her she couldn't control the future, but Brynn wanted to be prepared. She poured all her energy and focus into her career, hoping it would allow her to reclaim the balance that had been stolen from her life.

The Tahoe took a left on K Street. Brynn sat forward, realizing they weren't heading in the direction of the park. "Where are we going?"

"After I spoke with Agent Samson, Walsh called. We're needed for a meeting."

"Right now?" Brynn's eyes flashed to the passing scenery outside the SUV. "What about Riad?"

"He'll be taken care of." Jack glanced over. "Everyone out there has a high-level security clearance, and their cooperation in the investigation is specific to the information I gave Agent Samson about the case. When they're finished, we'll get the report."

"And Walsh can't wait until that's done to meet? It's not like we're going to have anything to offer him."

"If it were just him, maybe." Jack pulled up in front of the White House. "But I don't think anyone here is going to wait."

# 22

"I'm standing in the White House."

Brynn cringed as her nervous whisper echoed loudly enough to earn her a snicker from the Secret Service agent checking their IDs.

"Actually, we're in the west entrance of the White House." Jack handed her ID back. "What's the matter?"

"Um." She gestured at her worn jeans and frayed JMU sweatshirt. "I'm not exactly dressed appropriately."

Her fingers moved to the stray strands falling out of the knot she'd tied her hair into, and she cringed again. She searched for a restroom and found Jack grinning at her.

"You look nice, B."

He was trying to assure her, but his compliment only made her more self-conscious. She gave his attire a once-over. Dark jeans, charcoal-gray sweater. Only thing out of place was the slightly disheveled hair caused by his beanie cap.

"Easy for you to say, you look like an Eddie Bauer ad." She placed her phone in a plastic bowl to go through the X-ray machine. "Have you ever been here before?"

"Yes." Jack walked through the metal detector. "A few times."

"So what? You frequent the West Wing for lunch?" She followed him through and then scooped up her cell phone before taking the visitor lanyard the Secret Service agent handed her. "Enjoy tea with the Secretary of State?"

"Only on Tuesdays," Jack teased, looping his lanyard over his head.

An aide quickly ushered them through the marbled hallways of the White House until they reached the West Wing. Deep-red carpet swallowed the cadence of their steps so the only sound echoing in her ears was the pounding of her heart inside her chest.

Their escort paused by a pair of walnut doors, then he opened the right one and stepped aside to allow Brynn and Jack to enter the Roosevelt Room.

Time slowed as Brynn took in the historical significance of the room. At its center was a large mahogany conference table, a fireplace mantel hung on the east side with a painting of Roosevelt astride a horse above it, and to her right a large Queen Anne–style armoire filled the wall. The flags of the armed forces flanked the American flag, and standing in front of them were three men— waiting. Brynn recognized Doug Martin, the National Security Advisor, Director Walsh, and Peterson, whose gaze held a thousand questions.

The dark-wood door to the right of the fireplace opened, and everyone stood as President Margaret Allen stepped into the room. Brynn's breath lodged in her chest. *I'm standing in the same room as the president of the United States.*

The woman was in her early sixties and had the charisma of Jackie Kennedy with the prowess of Anna Wintour. The media might've succumbed to comparing the first female candidate with the severe editor of *Vogue* if it weren't for Margaret Allen's decorated success in the US Air Force that preceded an equally successful appointment as director of Signals Intelligence Directorate for the National Security Agency. A role that led to the exposure and prosecution of Nigel Chapman, a British hacker, for impersonating a CIA chief intent on accessing sensitive information.

President Allen's opponents worked hard to label her ruthless, but the number of charity projects she'd worked on over the last three decades proved otherwise. She had the bearing of someone who didn't mess around or take garbage, likely the result of having to forge her way in a man's world. A sentiment Brynn knew well enough herself.

At this late hour, however, President Allen did not look ruthless. She tucked a strand of blonde hair behind her ear, and her blue eyes peered over the reading glasses on her nose as she took her seat at the center of the table, looking nothing but focused.

Everyone sat.

"Well, it looks like we've got ourselves a quandary." The soft southern drawl of the president's words spread between them. She glanced around the room, her eyes landing on Brynn. "Ms. Taylor, I don't think we've met."

"No, ma'am." Or was it *Madam President*? "It's a pleasure to meet you." Brynn fought back the cringe. *Pleasure?* "I mean, it is a pleasure, but I wish it weren't under these conditions."

President Allen smiled. "I think we can all agree on that." She looked at Jack, her smile growing with a fondness. "Hiya, Jack. Still turning up trouble, I see."

He returned her smile with a nod. "Just doing my job, Madam President."

Brynn controlled her expression, not sure what to think of the familiarity she sensed between the president and Jack.

"I'm sorry this didn't turn out the way you'd hoped, Ms. Taylor." Sympathy softened the president's features. "I've spoken with President Talaat, who has sworn his support to help us find the person responsible for Riad's death."

Brynn nodded. "That's good to hear, Madam President."

President Allen pressed her lips together. "What I'm about to share does not leave the walls of this office." Her gaze landed on each of them, pausing long enough to elicit verbal acknowledgment and acceptance. "President Talaat informed me the General Intelligence Directorate has been actively investigating members of the National Liberation Jihad and their involvement with ISIS. For the last several months, members of the NLJ have gone missing."

Brynn couldn't help looking at Jack from the corner of her eye. Was he wondering if Seif El-Deeb and Tarek Gamal were members of the NLJ?

President Allen continued. "Four months ago, Riad was look-ing for Wael Abdullah, a young man whose family reported him missing. He was a student at Ain Shams University but stopped attending classes and then disappeared. A month later, security footage in Central Tunis recorded Wael Abdullah walking into the Ministry of Interior's National Police Unit and detonating the bombs strapped to his chest."

"ISIS claimed responsibility." Brynn's lips snapped shut, and Peterson shot her a look. Had she really just interrupted the presi-dent of the United States? "I'm sorry, Madam President."

The corner of the president's mouth lifted. "You're correct, Ms. Taylor. However, Egypt's General Intelligence Directorate has linked Wael Abdullah and the other suicide bomber involved to the NLJ. The director of the GID suspects Riad's disappearance may have something to do with his continued investigation into the NLJ."

"I don't think he's wrong, ma'am." Brynn caught Jack giving her a tiny nod, and it bolstered her courage to continue. "I apolo-gize for interrupting, but at this point, I think it's safe to assume Riad might've come here to uncover a terrorist plot already in action."

"You're telling me Remon Riad knew about a terrorist plot already underway and failed to report it?"

Doug Martin's sharp tone reflected the troubled expression on Director Peterson's face. He frowned at Brynn, looked at Walsh and then to Jack before settling back on Brynn, awaiting her re-sponse like everyone else.

"I'm not suggesting that at all, Mr. Martin." The apples of Brynn's cheeks burned. "If Riad's investigation into the NLJ brought him to the US, then given recent events, we need to assume someone found out and killed him. We could be looking at a situation with terroristic implications *here* in America."

"This only solidifies my recommendation." Doug Martin turned to the president. "Ma'am, until we get this figured out, I think it's in your best interest and the interest of national security to either postpone the opening of Wadi Basaela or send someone else in your—"

"No, I don't think so." President Allen shook her head, steel in her voice. "This is exactly why I need to go. I've got less than a year left in this office." She tapped her finger against the table. "I will finish what I set out to do, which is bring stability to our allies in the Middle East."

"Remon Riad's death does not eliminate the potential threat to your personal safety and national security. HUMINT suggests growing hostility in Egypt."

President Allen released a sigh, slipped off her glasses, and settled back into her chair. "Jack, do you agree with Ms. Taylor?"

Brynn's head snapped to Jack. Had the president really deferred to him? Why?

"Madam President, Mr. Martin"—Jack sat forward—"Ms. Taylor's assessment is an accurate reflection of what might be an underlying threat. Every new lead we follow leaves us with more questions than answers."

"And a few scars to boot." President Allen eyed Jack with a bit of motherly affection. "I wasn't kidding when I said you're turning up trouble."

"Not my own, ma'am," Jack said. "The last several days it's felt like someone has been one step ahead, which suggests the NLJ may have footing here in the US."

"My entire program is designed around the premise that terrorism can and does happen all around us. We can't assume Riad was involved beyond what we know. We have to continue to follow the leads until—"

"There's not enough time for that, Ms. Taylor," Doug Martin said. "I cannot in good conscience allow a decision to be made on the whim of the very person who could've prevented this from the very beginning."

"Negative." Director Peterson spoke, his voice booming around them even though he hadn't shouted. "Officer Taylor was not negligent. She is one of my most thorough analysts. Her work is meticulous, and I have no problem challenging anyone who dares to say otherwise."

Brynn had to fight to school her reaction to Peterson's defense, which had left Doug Martin slack-jawed and looking to the president for support she didn't seem ready to offer.

"Mr. Martin, I'm not dismissing your assessment of the threat," Brynn said, wanting to bring deference back to the NSA. "What I'm saying is that unless we continue to try to figure out how all of this fits together—because I believe it does—the risk to President Allen and the United States will continue to escalate, leaving us at the mercy of the terrorists' timing."

President Allen was content to let Brynn's words settle among them, leaving her worried she might've overstepped.

"I would be irresponsible if I didn't agree that this unfortunate and untimely circumstance is worrisome."

"It's a bit more serious than that, Madam President," Mr. Martin nearly grumbled.

"And"—President Allen glanced at Mr. Martin, her expression kind but firm—"I'm taking my security advisor's concerns for my trip to Egypt this week very seriously. But midnight tonight I will be leaving for Cairo to meet with President Talaat, and I *will* be bringing with me the body of their decorated military leader and dedicated intelligence officer." She glanced between Brynn and Jack. "I refuse to accept that I won't be able to offer him an explanation and a promise that those responsible will be met with swift justice in whatever form necessary. We, at the very least, owe that to Remon Riad and his family."

"I believe I can speak for Director Peterson and myself," Walsh said. Brynn had nearly forgotten he was there. "Mr. Hudson and Ms. Taylor will continue to work diligently on this assignment while keeping Doug apprised of anything new they learn so adjustments to your schedule can be made."

Several seconds passed before President Allen tapped her fingers on the table with an inhale. "I think that'll work. Doug?"

The man shook his head, lifting his hand in a "would it matter if I didn't agree?" gesture.

"Doug?"

"Ma'am, at the very least I'd like to increase our security measures before your arrival and discuss the schedule with our counterpart in Egypt." He released a sigh. "But yes, ma'am, if you insist, we can proceed forward as planned."

"Good." President Allen pushed back from the table and stood, everyone in the room following suit. "I appreciate y'all coming in at the last minute and your willingness to pursue the mission for the good of our nation and the American people."

There was a collective response affirming President Allen's directive before she collected her binder and glasses and walked toward the inconspicuous door etched into the molding of the room. Brynn's lungs felt tight like she'd been holding her breath the whole time.

"Ms. Taylor?" The president turned. "Your father was a firefighter in New York on 9/11?"

"Yes, ma'am." Brynn shifted, her palms turning damp. "Fire House 7."

"Is that why you joined the CIA?"

Brynn swallowed. "Ma'am, that day will likely never stop being the worst moment of my life. For most Americans, their lives moved forward, but for me and others directly impacted that day, we can never forget. I joined the CIA because I never want another child or family to go through what ours did. The Diplomatic Intra-Agency Cooperation program is unique in that it brings together intelligence forces from around the globe under the expectation that the only way to combat terrorism is to do it collaboratively. America united is a nice sentiment, but to fight and win the war against terrorism, it's going to require a world united."

President Allen smiled appreciatively. "Ms. Taylor, your candor is refreshing. I'm sorry for what you and your family have been through, but I'm not at all sorry for what that means for our enemies." She tilted her head. "I'm counting on you and Jack. If there's something to be found—sooner is better."

# 23

Washington, DC
10:07 PM Sunday, January 18

"Are you sure you don't want to go home and get some rest?" Jack asked, entering SNAP's office and holding the door for Brynn. "You've been here all day, and we can start first thing tomorrow morning."

His thoughts went to the president's final words. The ceremony for Wadi Basaela was scheduled for Tuesday, which meant they had less than two days to find out what Riad was investigating and whoever was behind the growing body count. "Whatever form necessary" meant they had been given the authority to intervene at all costs.

"I'm fine." Brynn began to slip off her coat and then paused. "Unless . . ." Her eyes searched his face before moving to the couch. "If you're tired, the couch looks comfortable. I can stay up and—"

"I can't tell if your suggestion is genuine or a jab that I can't keep up?" Jack tugged off his knit cap and gave her a sideways glance. "And the couch *is* comfortable."

"Please tell me you have a regular coffee maker." Walking into the kitchen, she looked over her shoulder. "I just got on Lyla's good side and am not messing with her machine."

There was a glimmer of amusement dancing in her eyes, and it sent a zip of energy rushing through him that had nothing to do with the urgency of their mission.

Brynn waited for his answer.

"Under the island." Jack pulled a bag of Kona coffee from a cabinet next to the fridge. "Kekoa's mom sent this over. White chocolate macadamia. Is that okay?"

"Perfect." Brynn filled the coffeepot with water, and Jack heard her stomach grumble. She blushed. "Sorry."

Jack opened the fridge and spotted his mom's Tupperware container. He pulled it out and held it up for Brynn. "My mom's ravioli?"

"Yes, please." Brynn's eyes lit up, and she grabbed for it. "How did Kekoa miss this?"

He held up a sticky note with his handwriting on it. "I labeled it tofu ravioli. Apparently there are some things Kekoa won't eat."

Brynn's laughter mingled with the aroma of the brewing coffee and his mama's ravioli, and his mind wandered into risky territory. Imagining this moment ever so differently, the two of them working an assignment late into the evening with nothing but leftover Italian food and the current of attraction spreading between them . . .

"You ready?"

Jack blinked, his gaze focusing on Brynn standing in front of him, two plates in her hand. "Yeah."

Grabbing their cups of coffee she had poured while he'd been lost in his daydream, he followed her into the fulcrum.

"Do you want to eat first or . . ." She set their food on the conference table. "Eat and work?"

Brynn's unwavering focus on the assignment was the cold shower his thoughts needed. Jack might've been enjoying exploring his attraction to Brynn, but it was clear where her thoughts were. It would serve him, and his heart, well to do the same. Especially since not even a few hours ago, she'd barely look at him much less speak to him. He'd been hoping to explain about Amy, but the day hadn't gone at all as expected.

NATALIE WALTERS

"We can work while we eat." He set the cups down and moved to the whiteboard with their notes on it. He rolled it to the conference table, catching Brynn with a mouthful of ravioli.

"Sorry, I guess I was hungrier than I thought."

"Eat up." He smiled. "My mama would kiss you on both cheeks seeing you enjoy her food."

"She can cook for me anytime she wants," Brynn said around another bite. "Takeout and microwave dinners get old real fast."

Jack's mind threatened to go back to his imaginary scenario. Him. Brynn. Dinner. Late nights . . . He shook his head, reining in the squeeze of longing growing stronger. He looked over the board filled with their writing and notes taped up next to photos of Riad, the immigrants. Ansari. "I think we should start fresh."

"Good idea."

He pulled over a clean acrylic board and grabbed some markers. "Let's start from the beginning."

Brynn wiped her mouth and grabbed for the marker, but he stopped her.

"You eat, I'll write."

"But yours will get cold."

"We'll take turns."

"I won't argue with that." She smiled appreciatively and took another bite.

For the next hour or so, in between pausing to finish the last of their dinners and for Jack to refill their coffees, they laid out the facts of their assignment along with a list of unknowns. The latter being the longer of the two and the most troubling given President Allen's trip.

Jack respected the president's mission, but he couldn't help agreeing with the NSA. The worn lines of stress marking Doug Martin's face weren't there for nothing. The responsibility of protecting the nation and the American president from known threats was daunting, but having to predict, plan, and forecast unknown threats was unnerving.

209

There was no way to catch everything.

Brynn pulled her hair out of a bun, letting the long blonde strands fall over her shoulders. "Riley couldn't find a connection between Seif El-Deeb and Tarek Gamal. They lived in different cities in Egypt. They attended different mosques. There's nothing to indicate their paths would've crossed." She ran her fingers through her hair, the movement bringing the soft scent of her floral shampoo to his nose. "And the security footage Kekoa pulled from Dulles airport shows them entering customs on two different days."

"At some point, these two ended up at the farmhouse in Clifton." Jack searched through the paperwork. "Do we know who owns the house?"

"The home belonged to an elderly couple who died in the eighties. The children hung on to the property but recently sold it to an investment company, which appears to be a front."

Jack scratched the scruff on his chin. "The perfect place to hide illegal immigrants."

"Or traffic them." Her tired gaze met his.

"Maybe we should call it a night."

"No, I'm all right." She straightened in her chair. "You heard the president. We owe it to Riad to find out what's going on."

Jack studied the exhaustion tugging on Brynn's features. Was this what she did? Poured herself into every assignment? Except for the silent car ride to the White House, Brynn hadn't reacted to Riad's death. Was it her ability to separate herself emotionally that made her better suited for the CIA than him? Where was the balance?

On the days when chemo had ravaged his body, the last thing he'd wanted was people in his home, caring for him, but it was the very thing he'd needed. Who was taking care of Brynn?

"It still doesn't make sense." Brynn drained the last of her coffee. "Why would someone kill El-Deeb and Gamal and leave the other two alive?"

Jack released a sigh. Brynn was like the Energizer Bunny. "I don't know. And we still don't know what the connection is to Joseph Ansari, if there's one at all."

"Besides me." Brynn twisted her hair back into a bun but stopped, her eyes widening at something over his shoulder. "It's so pretty."

Jack followed her gaze to the panoramic windows on the south side of the building, facing the Capitol. Large, white flakes rushed past the windows, making it feel like they were in a snow globe.

Brynn walked to the window and pressed her palms to the glass, her expression awestruck and full of wonder—beautiful. Jack couldn't believe how quickly the old feelings he carried for her rushed back. But the truth, he was beginning to see, was that those feelings had never really left.

"Brynn, about last night."

"It's fine, Jack." She faced him. "It would be stupid to think our history wouldn't come back up, but you've got a girlfriend and we've got a job to do."

"Amy's not my girlfriend. Or isn't anymore. We sort of broke up."

"Sort of?" Brynn looked at him, nose wrinkled. "How do you sort of break up with someone?"

"We weren't technically going out. It's a long story, beginning with Lyla trying to set me up with the one person who loves her job as much as maybe you do." The space between Brynn's brows crinkled. "What I mean is, Amy and I never really became anything more than the other's plus-one for events or dinner companion when she was in town. Not a lot there to *break up*, ya know?"

"I'm sorry." Her words were tender and genuine. A twinge of anticipation hummed inside of his chest at the transparency in her blue eyes. Until they shifted to that familiar look of detachment. "So, should we look further into Joseph Ansari? His background? His connections at the mosque?"

The sudden jump back to work jarred him. A thousand memories crashed over him from their time at the Farm, bringing a flood of emotions ranging from bitterness to anger to confusion and twisting his heart like a dishrag, because even in the pain he couldn't stop loving her.

"Brynn—"

"Jack . . ." Brynn faced him, putting her inches away.

A bright light blinded Jack, startling him backward and away from Brynn. He blinked, but it took several seconds for his eyes to adjust to the fluorescent lights shining down on them and highlighting the blush on Brynn's cheeks.

"Brah, you said it was tofu ravi—" Kekoa walked into the fulcrum and then stopped. His wide eyes bounced between Brynn and Jack for several seconds before he realized he must've interrupted something. "I'm just gonna"—he took a few steps backward, hands in the air—"let you two get back—"

"We're just going over the case notes again." Brynn walked to their board and studied it. "Trying to figure out what we're missing."

"I thought you were done for the night?" Jack asked Kekoa. There was no disguising the frustration in his voice, but given Brynn's reaction earlier, the moment—his chance to explain or figure out where they stood with each other—was gone.

"I was." He lifted the laptop messenger bag slung across his chest. "But I think I figured out a program that might be able to hack Riad's laptop."

"You did?"

Brynn began walking toward Kekoa, renewed energy in her posture even as it left Jack feeling the distance he remembered from eight years ago. After their conversation last night, he'd allowed himself to believe maybe she had changed. That the attraction he'd been feeling for Brynn wasn't one-sided. Or was it?

Unfortunately, that question wasn't going to be answered tonight. Jack followed Brynn as Kekoa led them into his cybersanctuary. The hum of computers buzzed around them, and a cool blue light underlit the perimeter of the room, giving it a gamer vibe—except for the tens of thousands of dollars in technology.

Kekoa spun in the computer chair and faced a long workstation with several computers and screens on it. He plugged a wire into his laptop and connected it to another one, which Jack assumed was Riad's.

"Do we want to know what you're doing?"

Kekoa shrugged. "I doubt you'd understand anything I said even if I tried to explain it to you."

Brynn smiled, her amused gaze flashing to Jack's for a second.

"That's fair," Jack conceded. "But if you're about to hack into Egypt's intel server, an explanation will be required."

Kekoa twisted in his chair, stretched his arms in front of him, and popped his knuckles. Pride emanated from his grin. "If?"

"You did it?" Jack leaned forward, focusing on the random numbers filling the screen and not on Brynn's closeness as she also moved in. "What's it doing?"

"Coding," Brynn and Kekoa answered at the same time.

"Can you decode it?" Brynn asked

"Sistah, that's the easy part." Kekoa faced the computer again and began typing. "It's breaching the firewalls that are killah."

"Sounds like a long night." Jack turned to Brynn. "You should probably go home and get a few hours of rest."

"I'm not tired." But the exhaustion coloring the skin beneath her eyes and the yawn she couldn't stifle said otherwise. "I want to be here if he finds something."

"And unless she's got her snowshoes on, she's not going any-where." Kekoa shook his head. "Roads are packed. Metro's closed. It's Snowmageddon out there."

"Guess I'll get to test that couch of yours." Brynn yawned again. "Come get me immediately if you find something, Kekoa."

"Shootz, sis, I got you."

"Kekoa, make sure you don't bother us for the next few hours." He eyed Brynn. "We don't know what he'll find or when he'll find it, but we both need to be rested when he does." He pointed down the hall. "The couch turns into a sleeper. There are blankets and a pillow in the chest by the wall."

"Good night, boys." Passing him on the way to the front living space, Brynn gave him a glance he could not decipher—much like the feelings swimming in his chest.

"Good night, Brynn."

Kekoa looked over his shoulder in the direction Brynn had left and then up to Jack. "Brah, I'm sorry. I didn't mean to interrupt. I didn't know you and Brynn were—"

"We're not," Jack said, not even sure how to explain what Kekoa walked in on. "I'm going to rest my eyes on the couch in Walsh's office."

"Sure, boss."

Jack left Kekoa to his task but not before he heard the Hawaiian's abysmal attempt at whistling the theme song to *The Love Boat*.

# 24

*"The reason birds can fly and we can't is simply because they have perfect faith, for to have faith is to have wings."*

Chinara Okoye ran a hot iron against a pair of black pants. Steam puffed in front of her face, warming her nose. She tugged her worn sweater tighter over her uniform, fingers numb from the lack of heat in the damp basement she called home. *Just have faith.* No, perfect faith. That's what would give her the wings to fly away.

Footsteps overhead alerted Chinara to hurry. She quickly hung the pants on a hanger right as the door at the top of the stairs creaked open. Chinara paused long enough to discern the slow, weighted steps belonged to Miss Lee. Mister Lee stomped down the stairs, rushed. Others, if they ever came downstairs, had the hesitated steps of fear like she had on the day she arrived.

"Chinara, why is the window open?"

Miss Lee set down a basket of laundry next to the one Chinara was working her way through and started for the window. To get there, she had to push her round body through the stacks of boxes, overflowing black trash bags, and piles of paper covering the floor. She closed the window, silencing proof that life existed outside of the damp and dirty basement.

"We're not paying to heat the outside."

They weren't paying to heat anything. Chinara's fingers slipped to the tattered hem of her sweater. It was one size too small and showed the evidence of her haphazard sewing skills—an attempt to keep it from unraveling. At least it cut out some of the chill.

"Sorry, madam. I like to hear the birds."

"Birds." Miss Lee snorted with a shake of her head. She pointed to the laundry basket. "I've got one more load to bring down. And then you can have breakfast before Mister Lee takes you to work."

"Ma'am, may I have more books? To read?" Chinara pulled out a white shirt. There was a patch on the chest pocket. *Augusta*. That word she knew from listening to Miss Lee and her husband speak. She rolled the sounds of the next words on her tongue. *Elec . . . tric . . . coop . . . er . . . a . . . tive*. She frowned, not understanding. "I think knowing American words will help for school."

"You work hard." Miss Lee tapped the ironing board. "Work hard and good, and one day you might get what you want. But books? They will only fill your head with dreams that never come true."

Hope shattered within Chinara's chest. Fingers trembling over the iron, she swallowed several times against a rising sob. A single tear fell from her eye, darkening a spot on the next pair of pants. She pressed the iron over it, her sorrow singed with a hiss.

"You keep frowning like that and you're going to wrinkle your face, and then nobody will want to marry you."

"Yes, ma'am."

Chinara told herself to relax her face, but that only made it harder. She didn't want to get married. She wanted to go to school. Become a teacher and return to her homeland in Nigeria and teach young girls so they could be strong and independent.

A few weeks after arriving at the Lees' home, Chinara wanted to begin school, but she was told she must wait. Finally, after more than a month, she grew tired of waiting and packed her small bag. Mister Lee met her at the door, refusing to let her leave, and when Chinara dared ask why, he slapped her so hard it loosened a tooth in her mouth.

"*You are not an American.*" He spit in her face. "*I have your paperwork. One phone call to the police, and they will lock you up and you will never see your family again.*"

The memory made Chinara's stomach twist like she was going to throw up. Miss Lee had taken care of Chinara's bleeding mouth and brought soup down for her to eat for a week. She did not ask again about leaving until the day two girls with tanned skin and long black hair arrived at the house.

Chinara had tried to talk to them, but both girls remained huddled next to each other in the corner of the room, refusing, or maybe unable, to speak. The next morning both girls were gone. When she asked where they had gone, Miss Lee said they had found work. She asked Miss Lee if she would get to leave for work too.

"*You don't want that kind of work, Chinara. I'm protecting you. You wait, and we'll find the right home.*"

"*I do not want a new home. I want to go to school.*"

"*Maybe the family will allow you to go to school. But for now, you must do good work so a family will want you.*"

Her own family did not want her. They had given her to the man in a black car who promised she was lucky. She was going to America where dreams come true.

"Grab your coat, Chinara," Mister Lee called down. "We're already running late."

Chinara looked at Miss Lee, alarm fluttering in her chest like a caged bird.

Miss Lee grabbed the basket of clothes and hurried Chinara up the stairs. "She needs to eat."

"We're late." Mister Lee's stern tone caused fear to slide down Chinara's spine. He turned on her. "Get your coat."

Afraid of Mister Lee's quick temper, Chinara hurried to the rack by the door and grabbed the smelly coat that had once belonged to him. Miss Lee pushed a paper bag into her hand, and when Chinara peeked inside she found an apple, a peanut butter sandwich, and crackers. She smiled at Miss Lee, grateful for the simple kindness.

"Chinara!"

Hurrying to the car, she climbed into the passenger seat and buckled her seat belt, unsure of where or what was happening, only that her nerves were causing her fingers to twitch with nervousness.

*"The reason birds can fly and we can't is simply because they have perfect faith, for to have faith is to have wings."*

The words read to her out of a book by a missionary who dared to enter the filthy streets of El Ashiru were the first English words Chinara learned. Those words fed her need to both learn and discover, and she clung to the imagery of a faith so strong it could carry her away. As she began to understand what drove her mama and papa to flee their war-torn village in Nigeria and go to Egypt, the words felt as though they were spoken from the heavens to reassure her all would be well.

Chinara prayed for perfect faith, barely noticing the surroundings she rode by until Mister Lee pulled the car up in front of the biggest house she had ever seen. It was an estate like the ones royalty owned in her home country.

Mister Lee stopped the car at the end of the long drive and faced her. "You will help clean the home today." He looked around, and Chinara sensed her nervous energy inside Mister Lee too. He pulled out a photo and showed it to her. "Do you see the badge on the man's chest?"

She took the photo and studied it. A white man, old with no hair, stood with a white woman with dark, curly hair. On the man's chest, she saw a badge. "Yes, Mister."

He took the photo back and shoved it into his pocket. "What do you want more than anything, Chinara?"

Tightness wound in her chest, and she worried how she should answer. Was this a trick? Would he not allow her the freedom to clean this home for fear she would try to run away? She glanced around the neighborhood, winter's frost shimmering on wide lawns. Where would she run if she could?

"Chinara!"

Mister Lee's sharp tone jerked her gaze to meet his. "Mister?"

"You want to go to school, right?"

Swallowing, she nodded, fearing if she spoke the words of her dream, Mister Lee would find a way to steal it.

"If you want to go to school, you find that badge today and you bring it home, ya hear?"

Chinara frowned. "Y-you want for me to steal it?"

"Borrow." Mister Lee's funny accent scratched against her ears. "Do you know what that means? Borrow?"

She did not but her insides felt like jelly, so she nodded. "I will ask—"

"No!" Mister Lee growled. "You will go inside the home and clean it like you do for our house, ya hear? When you find the badge, you bring it to me tonight, and I will make sure you go to school. You don't speak to anyone or you'll be sorry. And bring me the badge. Do you understand?"

Chinara nodded quickly.

"Get out. I'll be back to pick you up later."

As she reached for the door handle, Chinara was yanked backward by the collar of her coat, Mister Lee's bony fingers holding tight. She peered into his dark, angry eyes.

"Don't mess up."

Chinara shook her head, unable to form words over the terror balling in her throat. Mister Lee released her, and she scrambled to get out of the car, nearly slipping on a patch of ice. Regaining her balance, she walked carefully but quickly up the drive toward the house that seemed to grow larger the closer she got.

At the door, Chinara peeked over her shoulder to find Mister Lee waiting in the car, watching her. She rang the bell and prayed God would help her find that badge or give her wings like a bird to escape the wrath of Mister Lee.

# 25

Brynn stretched, eyes closed, as she tried to hang on to the wonderful feeling of Jack's strong arms wrapped around her waist, his warm breath against her cheek just before his lips brushed against hers—

Her eyes flashed open.

"Oh, sorry, did I wake you?" Kekoa stood frozen like he'd been doing something he wasn't supposed to.

She glanced out the window where low-hanging clouds still covered the sky, giving off a pinkish hue as they continued to drop snow over the city. It took her a minute to gather her bearings. "What time is it?"

Kekoa looked at his watch. "Quarter past seven."

"Seven!" Brynn threw the knitted blanket off her lap and stood . . . a little too fast. The grogginess of exhaustion swept over her and pushed her back to the couch. "You let me sleep that long?"

"I lived on a ship. You don't wake bears when they sleep." He pointed to the espresso machine. "Coffee?"

Brynn folded the blanket. "Are you supposed to be messing with that?"

"I'm not scared of Lyla."

"You should be." Jack walked into the space, his gaze settling on Brynn. "How do you feel?"

Her hand went to her face, and she suddenly felt insecure. Did she have pillow lines? Smudged mascara? She ever so casually brushed her fingers around her mouth, praying she didn't have drool lines. "Why did you let me sleep so long?"

"You needed the rest." Jack smiled at her, opening a drawer. He riffled through several loose and crinkled pieces of paper before finding the one he needed and setting it on the island. "Kekoa, if you break that machine, not only will you be dealing with the wrath of Lyla, but you'll be paying for it. And I can assure you it is more than what we pay you."

Kekoa chuckled, stepping back, hands up in surrender. "I didn't want fancy coffee anyway."

Jack slid the paper across the island to him. "Call this place and you can have your fancy coffee plus the best huevos rancheros you'll ever taste. And they deliver."

Brynn peeked out the window. At least five inches of snow was on the ground, and it was growing by the minute. "Are you sure they're going to deliver?"

"The shop is around the corner, and I know the owner." He winked at her before heading down the hall toward the fulcrum.

Following, Brynn noticed his hair was slightly damp. He also wore a clean shirt and had the alluring scent of fresh soap. Had he gone home and showered while she slept?

Jack paused and pointed down the hallway where the bathroom was. "Across from the bathroom is a shower and locker room. Lyla keeps extra clothes there and has everything you need if you want to shower."

"I would love to." She bit her lip, heart still stumbling over her crazy dream. "Did Kekoa find anything?"

"Not yet." Jack paused, and her eyes moved to his lips. "Don't tell him I said that though. Man's got an ego to protect."

His closeness, the fresh scent of his skin, and the dream had

Brynn's breath catching in her throat. She swallowed. "I, uh"—
she pointed down the hall to the bathroom—"I won't be long."

Much like the rest of the SNAP office, the locker room was
more like a spa designed with modern elegance. Sapphire-blue
glass subway tiles in the shower contrasted beautifully with the
light-colored hardwood floors and cabinetry. But it was the high-
pressure shower pumping hot water over her body that impressed
her most. What she wouldn't give for this kind of water pressure
in her own shower.

Begrudgingly, she finished and rummaged as quickly as she
could through Lyla's locker, feeling like she was invading her pri-
vacy. She selected the largest sweater she could find to throw on
over the jeans she wore last night.

A woven basket on the marble countertops held brand-new
toothbrushes, toothpaste, face wash, and deodorant, leaving Brynn
grateful but also curious as to how many nights the team *lived* here
instead of at their own places.

Braiding her hair, she glanced at her reflection in the mirror. She
looked a hundred times better than she did when she walked in.
Lyla's dark-navy sweater hugged Brynn's body a little snugly, but
it would work until she got home. Her eyes went to her lips and
the dream of Jack nearly kissing her. Eight years, and she could
still remember what those kisses did to her. Her cheeks turned
red. What did this mean?

*That you love him. Still.*

She pressed her palms to her cheeks, her insides squeezing in
anxiousness and excitement—and worry. She loved Jack, but what
did that mean? She thought about the job in Turkey. If, and it was
a big if, she got the job, would she take it? Leave Jack? Could they
make it work long distance? Did she want to? Would Jack want
to? It hadn't seemed to work for him and Amy.

*Ugh.* Emotion filled her throat. Why would God do this to her?
*Now?* Why was it whenever her life seemed to be on track, it got
derailed?

Was she destined to be alone? She'd lost her parents long before their deaths. President Allen's question about why she'd joined the CIA . . . it was more than a choice. It felt like a calling. A responsibility. Her father had been a *lucky* one, and among that unfounded sentiment offered to her by strangers came the command to make her life count. That's what she was doing. Trying to do. All the long hours, all the sacrifices—they had to mean something. So why had God brought Jack back into her life? Was she destined to a life of loneliness?

The empty apartment. Nights worried about her job and the next threat shared over a microwave dinner for one. Career decisions that left her questioning what she wanted or where her life was going, growing burdens she had to carry on her own.

She'd had her father but not anymore. Now she was all alone. *"In life, you can be anchored to only one thing, Honey B."* Her father's words echoed from the past, his voice so audible it sounded like he was next to her. *"You put your trust in yourself, trying to control what was never meant to be yours to control, and you will get tossed by the waves of life until they sink you. And they will. You surrender that control, trust God, and no matter the size of the waves, you will be safe."*

Brynn had clung to those words in the uncertainty of life following that day in September. But how was she supposed to trust God to anchor her life when the world was in upheaval? For years, her life remained unpredictable and at the mercy of nineteen men who decided to use airplanes to destroy lives.

Brynn's grip on her father's words lessened as she grew up. She began relying on herself, believing the only way to avoid sinking was to control the waves. Keep the risks of pain, heartache, and loss at a minimum. Make choices to protect herself. Except in a moment of weakness, she'd confessed her feelings for Jack—a risk that had left her feeling exposed and vulnerable.

"No! No! No!"

Kekoa's frustrated shouts shook Brynn back to the present. She hurried out of the locker room and to his office, where she found Jack, hands threaded into his hair and concern furrowing his brow as he hunched over Kekoa's shoulder.

"Can you stop it?"

"I'm trying." Kekoa's fingers danced across his keyboard so fast Brynn had no idea how he was hitting the keys.

"What's happening?" Her adrenaline was spiking even though she had no idea what was going on.

"Riad's computer is being scrubbed."

Scrubbed? Brynn's stomach tightened with a nauseated feeling. The only reason someone's computer got scrubbed, at least in her profession, was because something classified had been released without authorization or proper security measures in place. The CIA's cyberteam would go in and wipe out entire computer systems using a virtual virus to erase the classified information. It was a pain and usually ended someone's career. Who would be doing that to Kekoa?

"Come on!" Kekoa growled, his fingers now stabbing at the keys. "Brah, you don't even know who you're up against."

Brynn might've found Kekoa's threats against his computer comical, but the tension radiating in the room sucked any bit of humor out of what was happening.

"I . . ." Kekoa shook his head. The digital numbers on the screen in front of him flickered. "I can't . . . it's going to . . . ugh." The screen flashed before it went black, sending Kekoa backward in his chair with a groan. He ran his hand through his curls and then to the back of his neck. "I'm sorry, brah. I tried."

Jack's hands dropped to his sides with an exhale before he brought one to Kekoa's shoulder. "That's okay, brother. You did what you could."

The sentiment behind Jack's encouraging gesture stirred the already growing admiration she carried for him. He truly cared about his team, and he didn't hesitate to show it—unlike her own boss.

"I messed up, brah. I should've been paying attention. I know better. You don't just hack into a secured government server and think they're not going to try to stop you."

"Wait." Brynn stepped forward. "Are you talking about Egypt? They scrubbed his computer?"

Kekoa glanced up at Brynn and mumbled an apology.

Her eyes flickered to Jack's for a second and saw remorse in them too. She took a breath. "It's okay," she said, hoping she came off as genuine as Jack.

Jack's cell phone chirped. He looked at it and then at Brynn and Kekoa. "I'll be right back."

Brynn couldn't stop her gaze from tracking Jack as he left Kekoa's office and walked toward Walsh's office, phone pressed to his ear. It looked like he was carrying the weight of the world on his shoulders, and the urge to take some of that on for him fired her up.

"Were you able to pull anything off of Riad's computer before it was wiped?"

Kekoa lifted up his index finger. "One word. *Dahry*."

"Dahry?" Brynn frowned, unsure of the Arabic word. She looked at Riad's laptop. "Is there anything you can do?"

"With Riad's laptop?" Kekoa pushed it with the tip of his fingers like it was contagious. "No. It's basically a paperweight now."

Her cell phone vibrated in her pocket. It was Joel Riley. *Good.* She glanced back at Kekoa, then gave the laptop a dirty look. Maybe Joel had something, because their connection to Riad's investigation was fried.

"Hey, Riley, please tell me you have something," Brynn said, stepping out of Kekoa's office.

"Two things." Riley's voice crackled across the line. "First, Seif El-Deeb's wife, Heba, found a business card for a man named Mahmoud Farag, and on the back was an address for a home in Virginia."

"The farmhouse in Clifton," Brynn said.

*Lights Out*

"No, in Annandale."

Jack walked out of Walsh's office, his eyes asking if everything was okay, to which she nodded.

"Brynn?"

"Sorry, poor connection," she lied, squeezing her eyes closed. This was exactly why she needed to proceed with caution when it came to Jack. He was occupying too much of her brain. "What'd you say?"

"It might be a rumor, but we're following up on it. If the National Liberation Jihad has someone inside President Talaat's circle—it could be bad."

Riley's revelation grounded Brynn's wandering mind and heart like . . . an anchor. "Someone in the Egyptian government is a member of the NLJ? Who?"

"The asset didn't know, and we're doing our best to find out."

"You have to, Riley. President Allen will be there in a few hours." Tension radiated in her voice. "Sorry. It's been a long night." Kekoa and Jack were talking. "Hey, do you know what *dahry* means?"

"Dahry?" Riley repeated. "I think it means back. Why?"

Back? She shook her head. "I don't know. Send me that address, and I'll go check it out."

"All right and stay safe, Taylor."

"You too, Riley."

Ending the call, Brynn walked into the middle of a conversation between Jack and Kekoa.

"Run a malware program through Precision Technologies," Jack said. "Their director of security said their software engineers have noticed some glitches in the system that appear to be interfering with their firewalls."

Brynn squinted at Jack, trying to remember. "Precision Technologies. Isn't that a military defense contractor?"

"Yes," Jack said. "They're a client of ours, and it seems Kekoa isn't the only one hacking into systems lately."

"You said glitches." Brynn tucked a piece of wet hair behind her

226

ear. "Like the ones Garcia mentioned a few days ago? At Barksdale Air Base?"

Kekoa's forehead wrinkled into a frown. "Yeah, but they're not exactly the same."

"Could they be connected?" She looked at Jack. "Seems a little too coincidental that a defense company and our nation's actual defense systems would be experiencing similar issues in their security systems."

"You're right." Jack scratched at his scruffy beard. "I'll give Garcia a call and see what he can find out from Barksdale."

"Call?" Brynn looked at the snow-covered cityscape outside. "Is Garcia not coming in because of the snow?"

"He and Lyla are on their way to Guam," Jack said.

"*Humph.* Enjoying tropical humidity while we suffer here," Kekoa added. "Next time, I get to fly with Lyla."

Brynn frowned at Jack, confused.

Jack smiled. "Lyla only flies first-class and usually in a private jet, which is how she and Garcia are traveling now."

"Private jets?"

"Don't look at me." He held his hands up in a defensive posture. "Private jets are not in our budget, but Lyla—"

"Has connections," Brynn said. "Well, I have some connections too. Riley sent me an address that Seif El-Deeb's wife found on a business card. It's in Annandale. You up for a drive in the snow?"

# 26

Annandale, VA
10:47 AM Monday, January 19

"Agnes Buchanan died five years ago in a retirement home in Arlington. The house went on the market shortly after but was then removed. She had one child, a son who died seven years ago in a boating accident in Florida. There's no record of anyone living there now."

Brynn read through the file notes on the property they were driving to, and Jack couldn't help but feel it was strategic on Brynn's part. If they focused on the case, they couldn't focus on what *almost* happened last night. A solid effort by her but a losing battle for him.

"Did Kekoa send you that information?"

"No." She held up her phone, her smile radiating mischievous spunk. "Virginia tax appraisal website, obituary, and the *Miami Herald* archives."

"Wow. Almost as talented as Kekoa."

Brynn's grin slipped, and she chewed on her lower lip. "You think his pride is going to be okay after losing to Egypt?"

Jack smirked. "He'll be fine. In case you haven't realized it by now, the genius needs a little humble pie every now and again."

"Just so you know, when we're done with this assignment, I'm giving Kekoa my business card in case."

"You're funny, B." *And making it hard to concentrate.* Her humor was one of many things that had attracted him to her in the first place, and now it was happening all over again.

His thoughts went back to the night in the store. They almost kissed. He almost kissed her. She wanted him to kiss her. Or at least he thought she did. He wasn't super familiar with kissy moments like that one, but he didn't think he'd misread the signals. Except yesterday she seemed distant. He glanced over at her. She didn't seem interested in talking about it last night, but the radio silence was making his mind run wild with . . . fear. Had he once again put his heart out there when he knew better?

"Jack, look out!"

Brynn's warning snapped his attention to a child in a bright-blue snowsuit barreling down a homemade snow hill and into the street ahead of them. Jack carefully tapped his brakes, slowing the Tahoe down without going into a skid. Snowplows and salt trucks were keeping the main thoroughfare streets clear of snow and ice, but they hadn't made it to the neighborhood streets yet.

A mom waved a gloved hand at them in apologetic thanks before nearly sliding down her walkway to get to her son. The boy was smiling like a kid who was living his best life . . . and then he saw his mom. The smile evaporated instantly as the little boy gestured to the hill, his lips moving a hundred miles an hour to explain. Jack chuckled.

"You think it's funny to almost run over a kid?"

Jack gave a friendly wave to the mother and a thumbs-up to the little boy, which warranted him a proud smile, before driving past them. "No, I'm just remembering when I was like that boy and doing all the dangerous things without a single care in the world."

"That kid slid into the street. If I hadn't seen him and warned you, he could've gotten hit and killed."

"Uh, have you looked around? We're the only ones driving in this snowy terrain."

"Okay, but still." Brynn settled back in her seat. "Sometimes the risk isn't worth the reward."

Jack gave her his best side-eye.

"What?"

"The CIA is all about risk." The snow began falling again, and Jack turned on the wipers. "And some rewards are always worth the risk."

Brynn's silence only amped up his concerns. Was she deciding if he was worth the risk this time around?

The GPS voice let them know they were approaching their destination, bringing Jack's attention to the road and mission. He surveyed the middle-class neighborhood. Most of the homes were ranch style with long driveways, all backing up to a thick wooded lot. Children, like the boy from the previous neighborhood, were taking advantage of the snowfall by building snowmen and sliding down hills that didn't lead to the street. There was even a father helping his three kids build a snow fort.

This was the kind of place that reminded him of his own childhood home, one where he could see himself raising kids someday. His eyes flashed to Brynn, who was pointing out the windshield, unaware of his thoughts—thankfully.

"The house is up ahead."

Jack spotted the one Brynn was referring to. White vinyl siding wrapped around the home, and it had a black shingle roof that matched the black shutters encasing dark windows. He pulled in front of the house and unbuckled his seat belt.

Outside the Tahoe, the cold nipped at Jack's ears, causing him to pull his knit cap farther down. Their boots crunched into the snow as they walked carefully up the sidewalk.

"Whoa." Brynn grabbed Jack's arm in a vise grip, her foot slipping beneath her. "Sorry. Ice."

Her breath curled into a cloud between them, and Jack couldn't resist letting his eyes find her lips. Brynn pressed her other hand against his chest and stepped back, putting some space between them, but not before he saw the look in her eyes. Desire. No misreading that. He smiled just like that little boy on the sled.

Brynn looked away and released his arm. She started to walk again when she stopped, looked at the driveway, and frowned. "Someone was here."

Jack blinked. "What?"

"Look at the snow on the driveway." Brynn pointed to the empty snow-covered driveway. "See how it's thicker along the edges, but the part in the middle is maybe only a quarter inch thick? That's fresh snow covering a spot left by a parked vehicle."

His eyes moved along the driveway, and he could barely make out the tread marks from where a vehicle had backed out. Jack looked at Brynn, his nerves ramping up over the unknown. The last thing he wanted to do was put her life in more danger, but that seemed to be exactly what they kept walking into. "You said no one lives here."

"I said there's no record," she said, correcting him with an edge to her tone. "Maybe they parked in the garage?"

Taking a breath, Jack followed her to the front door and nearly collided into the back of her when she stopped. "Wha—" His question fell silent when he saw the front door sitting ajar. Pulse jackhammering, he withdrew his weapon from its holster and knocked on the door. "Hello? Is anyone home?"

Silence met them, so Jack rang the bell and used the tip of his boot to edge the door open farther. "Hello? Is anyone home?"

"This is literally how every episode of *Dateline* starts, you know," Brynn whispered next to him. "Unsuspecting neighbors walk in on a grisly murder."

"Sheesh, Brynn. That's not at all promising given the trend following you lately."

She made a face. "Sorry. Didn't think about that. Should we go in?"

"Legally, no. But . . ." Jack looked over his shoulder at the houses nearby. No one was out or watching that he could tell.

He turned back to the house. "What? You've fallen? I can't hear you." He began shouting into the silent home. "My partner and I are going to come inside now."

Jack took a tentative step inside the home, weapon trained ahead of him as he surveyed the foyer, which opened to a living room, dining room, and kitchen. All empty.

Literally empty. No furniture. No people. No sign of life.

"Maybe Agnes really did just die and leave it," Brynn said.

Jack lowered his weapon but kept it at the ready. Something wasn't sitting right with him. He glanced up at the vent. "The heat's on, and up until a few minutes ago, someone was parked in the driveway."

"Hello?" Brynn called out before looking back at him. "We should check the house to make sure it's empty and no one"—her blue eyes searched the space around them, apprehension filling them—"got here before we did."

Jack didn't like the prick of foreboding that Brynn's instincts brought to his nerves. He wasn't being humorous when he mentioned the trend of death following her. Had it preceded them now?

"I want you next to me the whole time."

Brynn nodded. The two of them walked through the three-bedroom home and found most of the rooms empty of furniture and any signs of life. Back in the kitchen, Jack glanced out the window to the backyard. It was fenced, but overgrowth peeked through the snow.

"There's food."

Jack looked over to Brynn, who had the refrigerator door opened. She had pulled out a foam takeout container and opened it. She sniffed it and shrugged.

"You're braver than I am, B." He wrinkled his nose. "Is it spoiled?"

"No." She put it back inside, closed the fridge, and moved to another door. Opening it, she stepped back. "Basement."

"Behind me." Jack leveled his weapon ahead of them, forcing

himself to maintain focus despite Brynn's nearness at his back. "Hello? Anyone down here?"

No answer. He spotted a light switch, flipped it, and started down the wooden stairs. When he was a few steps from the bottom, he stopped, confused. The house was empty everywhere else but here.

Jack walked the rest of the way down and counted five folding tables in the unfinished basement, each with an assortment of items on them, including a computer and a printer. In the back was an old futon and a bathroom with some clothes and toiletries inside, indicating someone did live there.

"Is it a sweatshop?" Brynn picked up a white shirt from an ironing board before looking into a cardboard box on the ground. She lifted up a black polo shirt. "Starbucks? I'm pretty sure Starbucks doesn't get their uniforms from the basement of a house."

Jack read the patch on the breast pocket of the white shirt. VA Electric? He frowned and looked at another shirt. Same color, different patch. "Virginia Telecom."

He moved to another box, and his mood shifted from confused to disturbed. Sliding his gun into its holster, he lifted out the familiar gray polo sporting the embroidered logo of GoldTech Security.

GoldTech was one of their clients, and Jack knew without question they didn't get their uniforms from some basement in Annandale. He examined the patch closely. Something was off. The gold eagle logo was similar to the eagle on US currency. In its talons were arrows and an olive branch. He couldn't figure out what was different, so he set down the shirt, pulled out his wallet, and withdrew a dollar bill.

Picking the shirt back up, he instantly realized what it was. The eagle was transposed. Facing the opposite direction. It was a fake.

"Jack, you need to see this."

At the table with the computer and printer, Brynn stood with her hands on her hips, leaning over pages of paper that looked like blueprints. Next to them was a box full of plastic sleeves the size of business cards and what appeared to be a freshly printed ID card for Virginia Telecom with a photo of Seif El-Deeb on it.

"Don't touch anything," Jack said when he saw Brynn reach for it. "We need to call the FBI right now."

## 27

Annandale, VA
12:02 PM Monday, January 19

Brynn's nerves buzzed with adrenaline . . . or maybe it was the beginning stages of frostbite? She hustled over to where Jack and FBI
Agent Brett Samson were huddled, careful not to slip on the snow.

The discovery of the supplies to make the fake IDs and uniforms
were enough to warrant the FBI's interest, but it was the schematics
of electrical diagrams and the blueprints of buildings, including a
power grid outside Houston, that had their full attention.

"Anything?" Jack asked, holding out his hand to help her step
over a mound of snow.

"Nope." Brynn released Jack's hand, then rubbed her fingers
together to keep them warm and also minimize the effect of his
touch. "Neighbor, Peggy Miller, is a stay-at-home mom of four."
She tipped her head to the yard where three kids were tossing
snowballs at each other. "She recently had her fourth and didn't
pay much attention to her neighbor's house."

"I've got agents taking photos inside." A snowflake landed on
Agent Samson's cheek, the contrast nice against his ebony skin
before he wiped it away. "We've got a van on the way over, so when
they're done, we'll tag and collect the evidence."

"Wait." Brynn looked from the agent to Jack. "What if they

come back? Shouldn't we wait so we can take them into custody and find out what they're doing?"

Agent Samson shook his head as another agent stepped around them and headed toward the house. "No one's coming back."

Brynn could feel the frustration rising. She needed this lead. Needed to know how this was connected to Riad. "How do you know that?"

"One of my guys inside the house checked out some of the schematics you found. They're mechanical and electrical for circuit boards and power systems."

"And diagrams," Jack added, his breath fogging in front of him. "The power grid in Texas, right?"

"Yes, and another one for the Metcalf power station in Santa Clara, California."

Brynn's pulse jumped, recognizing the name. "Wait. There was an attack on a power station a few years ago."

"Yeah, in 2013. A group of snipers opened fire on the transformers." Agent Samson rubbed his hands together. "It was professional, planned out, and a wake-up call to how susceptible we are to domestic terrorism."

"Do you think someone is planning another attack? Is that what all those diagrams are for? The uniforms?" Her stomach churned. She looked between the two men, her thoughts swirling like the snowflakes falling around them. "Was that why Seif El-Deeb and Tarek Gamal were here? Maybe that's what brought Riad here."

"We're seeing an uptick in cases where terrorists are incorporating human trafficking into their plots." Agent Samson sighed. "The promises of education, money, and power can be alluring to those in dire circumstances."

Brynn's gaze locked on Jack's, and she could tell he was thinking the same thing. Seif El-Deeb's wife, Heba, had a high-risk pregnancy. He had exchanged his life for theirs, and where had it got him? Anger began to take root. "We need to find out who was living here. How they're connected to El-Deeb and Gamal."

Her eyes moved to Agent Samson. "Did you work with Joseph Ansari?"

Agent Samson tipped his chin. "Not directly."

Her eyes narrowed. "But someone was watching him the day I met with him."

"Mr. Ansari monitored the members of his mosque because he believed religions could coexist peacefully. If someone voiced radical ideas, he'd keep an eye on them and report their behavior if necessary." Agent Samson's eyebrows lifted. "We weren't watching him the day you showed up, but your 911 call triggered our system."

Brynn crossed her arms in front of her, trying to rub away the chill seeping into her bones. The squeals of Peggy's children next door had multiplied, and she noticed a few more kids had joined them. "So Mr. Ansari hadn't been worried about anyone recently?"

She understood the FBI often got the brunt of scrutiny when it came to their powers of investigation. They wouldn't infringe on any person's freedoms, but after 9/11 the lines sometimes became blurry. Two Middle Eastern men learning how to fly planes in Florida or a kid becoming enchanted by terrorist propaganda in an online chat room from his basement in Boston only became a problem after they committed their heinous acts of terrorism.

"As far as I know, no. But I'll make a few phone calls to be sure."

A rumbling noise of a car engine drew her attention down the street. A gray van was headed their way, its exhaust sending a smoke plume behind it. It was driving fast. Too fast for the slick conditions as she watched the front tires slide a bit before gaining traction again.

"Your guy needs to slow down," Brynn said, glancing over her shoulder at the kids playing. They had, like the boy earlier, taken advantage of the empty street and were using the slope of it to slide down on colorful discs.

Jack and Agent Samson looked over their shoulders at the vehicle still driving too fast.

"That's not my guy," Agent Samson said.

Brynn's heart lurched when she saw the van picking up speed and heading straight for the kids.

"Get him to stop!" Brynn turned on her heels and began yelling at the kids. "Get out of the street. Car! Get out of the street!"

But either the wind was carrying her voice in the opposite direction or the little earmuffs and hats covering the children's ears were muffling her warning shouts. Behind her, Brynn caught sight of Jack and Agent Samson running toward the van, arms waving in the air to get it to slow down. Brynn thought she heard the van's engine rev. Was this bozo going to hit these kids?

Her feet sank into the snow as she charged across the lawn. The door to the house swung open and Peggy stepped out, looking confused and then horrified when she realized what was happening. Her screams were muffled by Brynn's.

"Car!" Brynn kept shouting until one of the kids looked at her like she was nuts, and she pointed at the van. Thankfully, the kid responded by jumping to the sidewalk and then urging his friends to do the same.

Except for the kid about to take his turn sliding down the street. He sat on a sledding disc and rubbed his mittened hands together. He looked over his shoulder, only to realize no one was watching him. His eyes flashed behind him to the van, and his face crumpled in fear. Instead of getting up, he sat there like he was frozen to the spot.

Brynn was maybe five feet away from the boy when her foot hit an icy patch on the street, sending her legs slipping. She fought for her balance as she saw the van in her peripheral vision still coming toward them. Finding her footing, she made it to the boy in time to shove his shoulders hard, sending him careening out of the street and into a wooded drainage area, where he was smacked to a stop by a tree.

She turned, the headlights of the van all she could focus on before squeezing her eyes shut. The force of the impact surprised her, knocking the breath out of her lungs and landing her hard against the ground. There was a large cracking noise and a sharp pain shot through her left arm, causing her to cry out.

"Are you okay?"

It took Brynn a second to realize she hadn't been hit by the van but by—

She opened her eyes. Jack was lying across her, his face red, his breath warming her nose as he peered down at her. He shifted, and it felt like a knife had sliced through her arm.

"Ow!" She winced. "My arm."

"Hang on, we'll call for an ambulance." Jack rubbed his thumb over her cheek before sitting up, then used his hands to carefully cradle her head as he lowered it to the ground. He looked her over from head to toe and back up. "Anything else hurt? Your head?"

Brynn cringed as the pain in her arm increased. She'd never had a broken bone in her life, but if she had to guess what one felt like, it would be this. "No, I think it's just my arm. Might be broken."

A crowd of tiny faces soon surrounded them.

"Are you okay?"

"You saved her life, mister."

"Can you push me down the hill too?"

Brynn frowned at the little boy who'd made that last comment.

"An ambulance is on the way," Agent Samson said as he jogged over. "And the police. I've given them a description of the van."

"I have a photo on my cell phone," Peggy said, raising a hand clutching a baby monitor. She caught Agent Samson's confused look and then lifted her other hand, the one holding her cell phone. "My husband is always complaining about me being on my phone." She made a "that'll teach him" face.

"Ma'am, I'll get the photo from you in a minute," Agent Samson said. "But would you mind getting the kids out of the street, please?"

"Oh, sure." She blushed before her attention turned to the kids. "All right, everyone in my house for hot chocolate."

Sirens echoed in the distance, and Brynn heard some of the kids beg to stay and watch. But like a drill sergeant, Peggy ordered them into her house. Keeping her left arm tucked to her waist, Brynn tried to roll herself up to a seated position. Jack's hand stopped her.

"Don't move until the ambulance arrives. You might have internal injuries."

"I don't think I do." Her arm throbbed. "Just my arm."

"So stay still."

The snow was falling heavier now, big flakes landing on her face and eyelashes, which reminded Brynn of her mom's favorite movie, *The Sound of Music*. She blinked against the wet snow, deciding it was *not* one of her favorite things.

"I can sit up, Jack." She smiled at him. "Does Walsh pay you extra when you save people's lives?"

The worry lines on his face deepened as his soft gaze searched her face for a second before his lips thinned and his expression turned serious. "No."

Brynn wasn't sure why, but Jack's lack of appreciation for her humor and the look in his eyes made her feel like she had somehow done something wrong. Should she not have protected the kid?

"I c-can't believe that guy was going to hit those kids." Brynn's teeth chattered as big snowflakes landed on her face.

Jack glanced back at Agent Samson, and a message passed between them.

"What is it?"

"Brynn, I don't think the van was going to hit the kids," Jack said. "The van was aiming for you."

## 28

Washington, DC
5:23 PM Monday, January 19

"My first broken bone," Brynn said when Jack climbed into the driver's seat of the Tahoe. She glanced down at her wrapped arm and shook her head. "At least I have a good story."

Jack started the SUV and drove out of Washington General's parking lot at a snail's pace. After the ambulance had dropped her off at the hospital, she was grateful when he had arrived but noticed he was quiet and a little distant.

Brynn stared out the window. The weather had finally cooperated with the forecasts, and DC was sitting beneath almost six inches of snow, with more predicted to come overnight. A few brave souls were walking, or rather trudging, through the snow, not seeming to mind the cold temperature. A shiver ran down her arm, and she rubbed it away.

"I told the doctor I threw a kid into a ditch to save his life."

Jack barely smiled before he asked, "Do you have something to eat at home? We can run into a store or a restaurant and grab you some food before I drop you off."

"Drop me off?" Brynn frowned. "Aren't we going back to the office? We need to figure out—"

"You need to go home, B. Rest. Heal your arm." He cast a look

241

her way. "The team and I will continue to work on the case while you take some time off."

An ugly feeling coiled in her stomach. Her gaze dropped to her arm again. A broken elbow. After the doctor read her X-ray to her, she fought to control the tears of frustration. The last thing she needed was a broken bone. Another setback.

"I don't need any time off. The doctor said as long as I keep my arm in the sling and limit my activity . . ." She made a face, realizing that in the last week she'd been to the hospital three times. "It's only a hairline fracture, Jack. A broken bone is much better than the alternative."

"The alternative is all I can think about, Brynn." His gaze snapped to her. "You're in a cast because a van almost mowed you down in the middle of the street today. Last week you were almost killed in an explosion hours after fighting off someone who may or may not have come to America as part of some terrorist plot. Oh, and let's not forget about the poisoning that nearly stopped your heart."

"When you put it that way." Brynn wrinkled her nose at him, wanting to lighten the mood. "And to be accurate, *you* broke my arm."

"It's not a joke, Brynn."

"I know it's not." Instinct caused her to lift her left arm, and she winced at the sharp jolt of pain. *Oh, good gracious that hurt.* Through steady breaths, she managed to say, "Time is running out, and I still have a job to do."

"At what cost, Brynn?" Jack asked, his exasperation thick. "I've seen the lengths you'll go to for *your job*. It's not healthy, B."

"If you know the lengths I'll go for *my job*, then you'll know if you take me home, I'm just going to get an Uber back to the office. You'll save us both a lot of time if you just head to the office."

The muscle in Jack's jaw flexed a couple of times, the tight line of his lips revealing his frustration. After another minute, he finally shook his head and took the next left toward the office.

Brynn blew out a breath and shifted in her seat, accidentally bumping the middle console with her elbow. She bit down on her lip to keep from crying out, eyes watering from the pain.

"Does your arm hurt?"

"Yes," she snapped, angry at how her heart wanted to give in to his tender concern.

"Have you taken your pain medicine?"

"Yes," she said with force. "At the hospital. I told you, I can—"

"Take care of yourself. I know." He blew out a long breath, eyes still fixed on the road. "Brynn, I know you want a long career in the CIA. You've worked for that and deserve it more than anyone else I know, but I'm concerned about how much you're willing to sacrifice."

"I don't need you lecturing me on risk, Jack." Raw emotion balled in her throat. "What do you want from me?"

Jack pulled into the underground parking structure of the Acacia Building and parked the Tahoe before turning to her. "I want you to stop giving more of your life away to the terrorists who hurt your family. You've allowed yourself to become obsessed to the point of risking your life and everything in it. These last few days with you in the hospital . . . I'm afraid if I don't do something—"

"What do you mean?"

"Now that Riad's . . ." He looked at her for a second, swallowed, and then looked away. "The CIA's involvement in the case has shifted and—"

"What are you talking about?" She spoke over the dryness in her throat. "President Allen is landing or has landed in Egypt. There are still too many variables in this mission that require our involvement."

"In Egypt, yes," Jack said before swallowing. "But not here."

Brynn narrowed her eyes on him. "What are you saying?"

"I'm taking you off the case, Brynn."

"Taking me off—" Heat flamed her cheeks. Why would Jack do this? If he thought he was helping her, he was dead wrong. "You don't get to make that decision for me. This is my life. My career. And you had no right to interfere with it or me."

\\\\\\\\\

"Brynn, wait."

Jack hurried after her, carrying the coat she'd left behind in her rush to get out of the Tahoe or back to work or maybe just away from him. What had he done?

He met her at the elevator and scanned his security card. "Brynn, I'm sorry."

"No." She paced in front of him, cradling her arm. "Why would you do this?"

"Please stop, slow down. You're going to hurt yourse—"

"I don't need you to take care of me, Hudson." Her eyes grew watery. "I can take care of myself."

The elevator doors opened, and Brynn walked straight to the back and spun on her heels. Their eyes met, and the pain he saw in hers sent his heart spiraling. Her silent treatment followed them up to the eighth floor.

Jack followed her down the hall, desperately trying to figure out how to fix this when Brynn stopped short of the door to the office. She leaned against the wall, chin tucked, and when he saw her shoulders begin to shake, his heart dropped to his stomach.

He approached her with caution, trying to keep control of his desire to wrap his arms around her. "I know how important your job is to you, B. The last thing I want is for something to happen to you. Last time I checked, I think you need to be alive to serve overseas—if that's still what you want to do."

"Jack, I don't know what I want anymore." A tear slid down her cheek, and he was quicker than she was at wiping it away, his thumb lingering on the softness of her cheek. "When my dad was injured, all I wanted to do was stop the chaos in my life. Stop terrorists from destroying another family. But look where that's gotten me. I was so consumed with this calling that I didn't see my mom wasn't well. It literally took her dying to force me to spend time with my father. Now I go home to an empty apartment. I have one friend I only see when she's in town for training, and I might've given up the best thing to happen to me because I was afraid of having it ripped from my life."

Her voice cracked. "It's like I've been holding my breath"—she pressed her hands to her chest—"and I'm scared to release it for fear of what's coming next. And I'm exhausted. I can't keep up."

"No one is asking you to, B." His heart ached for her. She'd lost so much, and all Jack wanted to do was make it better. "There's going to be chaos and bad stuff happening in the world, and I believe we're called to take a stand against it. But when our trust lies in the control we *think* we have, we're saying we don't trust the One who is completely in control and completely good."

"I wish it were that simple." She blew out a breath. "My dad, when he was alive, told me I needed to anchor my trust in God, but that's a lot easier to do when everything is going right."

He understood her sentiment, especially in light of their careers. "But it's our faith in the hard times that keeps us anchored in the hope that God will restore order. It's a choice, Brynn. Choose fear or choose faith, but only one choice will bring peace."

"I'd really like to have some peace in my life."

Brynn looked so small and fragile standing next to him, which was the opposite of who she truly was. Strong, vibrant, fiercely independent. And he was in love with all those things, but this vulnerability . . .

He was done.

*And a fool.*

"I'm sorry. I want you to get everything you've worked for and you deserve so much more. I want you to have it all."

Brynn turned to him so that their bodies were close enough he could breathe in her vanilla fragrance. "What if that includes you?"

Scooting closer, Jack took her right hand into his. Her fingers weaved between his, and it was like an electrical jolt to his heart. "I mean, I'd probably be okay with that."

"Probably?" Her eyes opened wide, a smirk on her lips. "Way to woo me, Hudson."

"I never want to stand in the way of your dreams." He lifted her hand, bringing it to his lips. He kissed her knuckles softly, watching her look up at him beneath her long lashes. "But I'd love to be a part of them."

Brynn slipped her hand from his and brought it to his face, letting the tips of her fingers tickle the scruff on his chin. The touch, her presence, was intoxicating, and he couldn't resist the pull of desire drawing him toward her.

She moved in, her lips parting, and the exhilaration of anticipation left him feeling a little dizzy. Careful not to disturb her injured arm, he slid his hand around the back of her neck, bringing her close enough that their lips met, brushing—

## 29

Washington, DC
6:16 PM Monday, January 19

"Ahem."

Like a snowball had been shoved down his shirt, Jack jerked back to find Kekoa standing in the doorway, a sly smile on his tan face.

"Brother, you have impeccable timing."

Brynn giggled and moved back to put some space between them, but she didn't let go of Jack's hand.

"Sorry, brah, but something kind of important is happening." He raised his hands. "Not that what's happening *here* isn't important, but you know, maybe not as world-ending as what's going on inside here." He tossed a thumb over his shoulder at the inside of the SNAP office.

"What's wrong?" Jack asked as he followed Kekoa and Brynn inside and down the hall.

"You know how some of our clients have noticed attempts made against their security systems?" Kekoa led them into his office. "Well, the activity has picked up in the last forty-eight hours."

"Right." Jack moved a chair over for Brynn. "Did you figure out what it was?"

"A virus, I think. That's the reason I called you back here." Kekoa sat in his desk chair and rolled to his workstation. He began typing and talking. "I accessed Precision Technologies' firewall and began source tracing the attacks—"

247

"Attacks? As in multiple?"

"Dozens of our clients from all over the world," Jack answered Brynn, folding his arms over his chest. "Not only ours, but other security firms have noticed similar issues with their clients."

Brynn's forehead furrowed in concern. "You think it's a virus that's attacking their systems?"

Kekoa began typing again. "It is a virus, and it's attacking the security mainframe."

"Do you know where the attacks are coming from?"

"No," Kekoa said. "Director Walsh has called in reinforcements to field calls from our clients while *my* friends are doing the hard work. Remotely, of course. Which is why you need to see this."

Kekoa pointed at his screen, and all Jack could see was a skeleton of the earth with little lines pinging all over it. It reminded him of those airline commercials where the company shows all their destinations across the globe.

Brynn leaned in closer to the computer. "What is it?"

"Counterattacks."

Jack continued to watch the globe get covered with lines, starting from one part of the world and landing in another part over and over. "You're stopping them."

"We're slowing them down," Kekoa said with a sigh. "It's a good virus, if I can say that. Whoever created it knew how to defend against counterattacks. Once we go on the defensive, it ramps up the attack and actually . . . mutates."

"Like a real virus."

Kekoa nodded at Brynn. "Yep."

"How do we stop them?" Jack asked, feeling his tension rise. SNAP's clients, both in the government and in the private sector, were being attacked, and it was their job to stop it.

"We can't. Not completely. But I have an idea." Kekoa spun in his chair to face him. "My mom did a Bible study with her hula sistahs a while back, and she read something about the armor of Christ, particularly the shield of faith. Anyway, she said the kumu explained how the soldiers back in da day would use their shields to create a testudo."

Jack rubbed his forehead. "English, please."

Kekoa grinned. "*Kumu* is teacher and *testudo* is Latin for tortoise shell, or *honu* in Hawaiian."

"Go on," Jack said, catching Brynn covering her smile. "Do not encourage him."

"Anyway, the soldiers would make this tortoise-shell formation by bringing up their shields overhead and overlapping them so no javelins or spears would hit them."

"And how does this have anything to do with cyberattacks? We're not facing the Romans here."

"True, but I was thinking we could employ the same method. Go *shields up*." Kekoa got up and walked to a whiteboard. He drew a box and labeled it *computer*. Above it he drew thin rectangles, overlapping so that the computer was protected from edge to edge. And above that he drew arrows pointing down at the thin rectangles. "This"—he tapped the box—"represents the computer systems currently being attacked. These," he said, pointing to the rectangles, "represent a program we design to shield the systems from the attacks." He tapped the arrows. "Individually, we're not going to be able to install a program into every server, but if I work with the IT guys"—he looked at Brynn—"or wahines, we may be able to distract the enemy long enough to send in our own virus."

"Go all penicillin on them," Brynn said with a proud smile.

"Bahahahaha." Kekoa's laughter bellowed around them. "Good one."

Jack shook his head, then his cell phone rang. He glanced at the screen and saw Lyla's number. "Hello."

"Hey, Jack."

Hearing Garcia's voice answer jarred Jack. "What's wrong? Is Lyla okay?"

His words silenced the lingering laughter between Brynn and Kekoa.

"She's fine. Trying to find us a flight out of here, but the snow-storm in DC is making it hard for us to get back."

"And what about the fertilizer?"

"It's gone. Someone broke into the dock warehouse late last night. Dock employees didn't realize it was gone until this morning. Looks like someone came through an old access road, broke into the crates, and removed the fertilizer."

"No alarm was triggered? No security footage?"

"No. Seems the system went down last night conveniently."

Jack looked to Kekoa and then to his diagram, unease stretching through him. "Conveniently, huh?"

"Director Walsh put me in contact with some local security forces who are working the case now. We also spoke with the commander out at Andersen Air Force Base. We wanted to give him a heads-up, considering the base services the strategic bomber fleet."

"Did he mention receiving any threats recently?"

"No, but he said a squadron of B-52s arrived this morning as part of a training exercise, and there's some concern about the timing of all this."

"Two hundred and twelve miles!" Jack heard Lyla yell in the background.

"Lyla's miffed they can't find that much fertilizer hiding on an island this small," Garcia mumbled. "She wants permission to offer the local police force three brand-new squad cars if they work double time to find the fertilizer so she can fly home."

Jack rubbed his forehead. "Yeah, right. I need you both there to locate the fertilizer and whoever stole it." He looked through the office toward the window. Snow was falling again. "And unless Lyla can make the snow stop, she'd better grab some sunscreen and enjoy the warmth. Keep me posted."

"Sure thing, boss."

Ending the call, Jack updated Brynn and Kekoa on Garcia's news. He was about to suggest they order dinner when Brynn reached for a marker and went to the whiteboard. Drawing a line down the middle so as not to interrupt Kekoa's sketch, she wrote down *Texas*, *Guam*, *DC*, and *Egypt*.

Next to Texas she wrote *power grid*. Next to Guam, *fertilizer*, and in parentheses wrote *OKC*. Next to *DC*, *schematics* and *human trafficking/immigrants*, and next to *Egypt*, *illegal immigrants*.

"When I analyze data, I look for a common thread. For the last week I couldn't figure out what the connection was because I was looking at each event individually. But the missing fertilizer in Guam . . ." She looked at Jack and with a curl to her lip snapped her fingers. "It's like the missing piece."

Jack was never going to live the snap down, but watching Brynn in her element, seeing her work, it was alluring. "Go ahead."

"Unexpected shipments of fertilizer arrive in Guam, unclaimed and now missing. Enough fertilizer to blow up a federal building like Oklahoma." She pointed to the *OKC* on the board. "Tarek Gamal and Seif El-Deeb both arrive in DC undocumented and with fake passports. Before we can find out why, they're kidnapped and then killed. Along with Joseph Ansari, who had reported members of his own mosque for extremist behavior. Today we discovered fake IDs, uniforms, and the diagrams for electrical and mechanical equipment but also one for the power grid in Texas."

"Which reminded Agent Samson of the attack on the PG&E power grid in California."

"Right." Brynn nodded at Jack, but there was no delight in her eyes before she turned them on Kekoa. "Can you tell if the cyberattacks are coming from the same source? Same location?"

"No. A hacker this skilled would make sure to hide their trail."

She faced Jack. "Your clients, the ones being hit, are they all defense contractors like Precision Technologies?"

"Not all of them. Finance, banking, a few government offices, technolo—" He stopped talking, his blood running cold.

Brynn's gaze locked on his. "Jack, I think America is about to be attacked."

# 30

The van was packed. He checked his cell phone and made sure it was charged. Double-checked the bag to make sure he had the charger for his laptop. Keys?

He patted his pockets—empty. His frustration came out in a cloud against the cold air. He hustled back up the steps and into the home he shared with his mother and whatever boyfriend-of-the-month she brought home. At least this one helped pay the bills.

In his room, he found his keys on the desk next to the note he'd just written. Would his mom find it, or would he return in time to destroy it? He lifted the sheet of notebook paper, the edges frayed because he didn't care enough to tear it out nicely. Did it matter?

His eyes flicked to the television in his room. The first thing he'd bought when he got paid. It allowed him to hide out in his room and not have to listen to his mom fight or cry or complain about how life was unfair. Why did anyone assume life was supposed to be fair?

Grabbing his keys, he gave his room a final look. There were dirty clothes piled under the window, his textbooks spilling over his desk. Posters of his favorite heavy metal bands were tacked up on the wall, hiding the spaces he'd carved out to hide stuff. They were empty now.

Maybe he should've put the note in there. Then when he was gone, they would search the room and only if they were smart, or lucky, would they think to look in the walls. Or maybe they wouldn't. Maybe it would be years before his mom would have the courage to clean out his room and only then discover who he truly was. Would she be surprised?

He started to leave but then turned on his heels and grabbed the remote for his stereo and turned it on. His room filled with aggressive drumbeats, synthesized guitar notes, and a voice growling out words that resonated deep inside his chest.

Bouncing his head to the erratic rhythm, he gave his room a mock salute and shut the door behind him. The thumping music trailed behind him as he left his house, the music ingrained in his brain. He lifted his fists in the air and moved them up and down for the drum solo before his eyes caught the concerned stare of his neighbor, who was carrying a bag of groceries into her house.

Dropping his hands, he smiled and hurried over to her. "Let me help you."

"Thank you." The elderly neighbor handed over her bag. "My old bones don't like this cold weather. We're supposed to get more snow, you know, and I don't want my babies to starve."

When she opened the door, the harsh odor of cat urine stung his eyes. The mewing noise of her "babies" surrounded them like they knew dinner had just arrived.

He set her bag on the table inside her doorway and was turning to leave when she caught the edge of his coat. He whipped around, knocking her hand away in a move that nearly toppled her and left her gawking at him.

"That hurt, young man." She clutched her arm.

"I-I'm sorry." He straightened his coat, tugging it back in place and over the gun. If she'd seen it . . . if she got in the way . . . well, he had his orders. "You scared me." He glanced down at the cats purring and rubbing up against her leg. "Cats scare me."

"Oh, pshh, my darlings are harmless." She scooped one up and held it out to him. "This is Boris."

The ugly orange cat glared at him.

"I need to go," he said, backing out of the doorway and down the steps.

Inside the van, he turned the ignition and the rumbling noise of the engine fed the adrenaline pumping through him. Turning the radio up, he drummed his other hand against the steering wheel. He smiled.

Glancing over his shoulder, he double-checked *his* babies. Everything was ready. Finally. He threw the vehicle in gear and backed out of the driveway a little too fast and his wheels spun out. He laughed, enjoying the moment of chaos before the tires found purchase and he was able to maneuver the vehicle down the snow-packed road.

The drive took longer than he'd expected, but it couldn't be helped. His neighbor had been right about the weather prediction. More snow was falling, and it forced him to drive slower than he normally would. Another glance behind him and he was reminded that he needed to be mindful of his cargo. Too much was riding on their safe arrival.

*Riding.* He laughed at his pun. Was it a pun? He probably would've learned that in English class if he had paid attention. But his mind worked differently. At least that's what his mother told his teachers when they would call her in for a parent-teacher conference. Ha. If they could see him now.

He pulled into the parking lot, then waited until the lone figure appeared and walked over, his head swiveling as he checked the area around them. It wasn't necessary. Of the few who were brave enough to venture out to pick up last-minute groceries or fast-food dinners, he doubted any of them would be paying attention to them. And that's exactly how it was supposed to work.

For years he'd been the invisible one, and now it would pay off. He would make sure everyone saw him—finally.

# 31

Washington, DC
11:45 PM Monday, January 19

America, quite possibly, was on the verge of being attacked.

Brynn felt it in her gut, and when she and Jack made the call to Director Walsh, they expected President Allen would return home immediately. However, the president seemed bent on not giving whoever was behind the plot the satisfaction and passed along a message to Jack and Brynn that she was relying on them to figure it out. *So, you know, no pressure there.*

For the last several hours, Director Walsh had monitored a remote team working with SNAP's clients to warn them about a potential cyberattack while she and Jack were trying to "figure it out." Brynn didn't know if it was frustration or exhaustion or the throbbing ache in her elbow, but the facts were starting to blur together.

She used her thumb to pop the lid off a bottle of Tylenol, and her hand slipped, sending the little white pills skittering across Jack's desk.

"I've got it." Jack collected the pills. He pressed two of them into her hand and twisted the cap off a bottle of water. "You should rest."

She swallowed the medicine with a gulp of water and shook her head. "Do you really think I'm going to be able to sleep right

255

now? Besides"—she offered him a tired smile—"I'm trained for this."

"You're cute when you're ornery and tired."

"He isn't." Brynn tilted her head in the direction of Kekoa.

He was like a bulldog with a bone—unstoppable and focused as he and a remote cyberteam worked to create their testudo. Brynn didn't even see him get up for a snack.

Not that she was sure any of them could eat. At least she couldn't. Her stomach was tied in a tangle of knots as she tried to decipher the facts they had in time to prevent . . . what? Brynn still wasn't sure. What if all this was for nothing? How often did CIA intel suggest a threat, only to lead nowhere? Except for the facts they'd been staring at for hours surrounding Riad's death and the virus Kekoa discovered, was this whole thing just a big presumption?

"Let's go over this again." She rose and went to the acrylic board that was covered in their writing. "Riad begins investigating the National Liberation Jihad and their involvement in missing Egyptians. It leads him to come to the US in search of a family friend, Moustafa Ali, a student who hasn't been heard from since December when he finished his fall semester of classes."

"That leads you and Lyla to the farmhouse in Clifton, where Riad was looking for Moustafa, and you find Seif El-Deeb and Tarek Gamal." Jack tapped a pen against the table. "Both are kidnapped and then killed shortly afterward." He pressed his lips together. "And we still don't know who was involved or where they are."

"Right." Brynn yawned. "Riley lets me know about Joseph Ansari, who may have been the person Riad was trying to meet before he was taken. However, Ansari doesn't know Riad but does remember Moustafa, who he said was excited about an opportunity."

"An opportunity to what?"

Her thoughts went back to Agnes Buchanan's home. "It doesn't

256

make sense. If El-Deeb and Gamal were trafficked to work here in the US, how does Moustafa fit in?"

Jack's phone rang. He glanced down at it and then back up at her. "It's Agent Samson."

As Jack answered, she checked her watch—it was nearly midnight. A call this late never meant anything good.

"Sure, hold up. Brynn's here, and she'll want to hear this," Jack said before pulling the phone from his ear and setting it on the table between them. "I've got you on speaker, so go ahead."

"I have to be quick because it seems like we stepped into a massive hornet's nest here in Texas." Brynn exchanged a look with Jack. "After finding the schematic for the Texas power grid, the team and I flew to Houston. The agents here began pulling information on known characters of interest. They've been watching a fella by the name of Hashem Mazdani, an Iranian, who's been here for a few years. He works part-time driving for one of those ride-share companies and also for a data engineering firm."

Brynn made a face. "That's an unusual career path. Did he attend school here in the States?"

"No. As far as we can tell, he never attended anything beyond high-school level back in Iran. We don't believe he's an engineer, but he works for Protech, a Russian-owned data mining company that doesn't like to share their information without getting lawyers involved."

Brynn chewed on her thumbnail. Now the Russians? Stepping into a hornet's nest was starting to feel like a cakewalk at this point. "What is it about Hashem Mazdani that attracted the FBI's interest?"

"He's been known to spread NLJ propaganda at a few of the local mosques here in Houston."

Brynn glanced at their notes on the board, her pulse beginning to race. If the NLJ was involved, it escalated the threat.

"What kind of data are they mining?" Jack asked.

"We're working on finding that out thanks to your boy, Moustafa Ali."

"Moustafa Ali?" she nearly shouted. "You found him?"

"One of our informants noticed someone new living with Mazdani and working at Protech. The office here identified Moustafa Ali, but since he was in the US on a student visa and didn't have any records, they had no reason to be concerned until I contacted them. Last night we had one of our informants follow Ali to a café, and without too much difficulty, the kid began talking about his family in Egypt, going to school in Virginia, like you said."

"And you said he's working for Protech?"

"An internship." Agent Samson answered Brynn's question. "Apparently, his professor at GMU set up the program, but the kid is worried about missing school, failing his classes, and disappointing his parents. When the informant pressed further, Moustafa revealed the internship wasn't what he thought it was. Said it seemed illegal."

Brynn looked at Jack, his expression troubled.

"The informant convinced Moustafa to talk to agents at the FBI field office. He walked one of their tech guys through what he was doing for Protech, and it turns out he was hacking into the electrical service of customers here in Texas. We contacted the Electric Reliability Council of Texas, and they said they'd noticed a surge in outages but couldn't figure out where they were coming from or why."

Jack ran a hand through his hair. "So we're right. They were planning to attack the power grid just like the one in California."

"Not at all. They attacked the station in California with assault weapons. This is a more sophisticated plan."

Brynn heard the warning in Agent Samson's tone. "What's the name of the professor who set up the internship?"

There was some noise over the speakerphone before Agent Samson answered. "Dr. Abu Hamadi, teaches computer science."

*Of course he does.* Brynn's pulse sped up as pieces were beginning to come together. She grabbed her phone and started searching for information on Abu Hamadi. "According to the GMU faculty page, Hamadi is a tenured professor at GMU, where he's been teaching computer science for almost seventeen years. He's originally from Heliopolis, Egypt. Moved to the US in 1984 with his wife." Brynn read the last line of his bio, and her blood turned cold. "He's quoted here saying it's his privilege to teach students how they can use technology to change the world."

"Or attack it." Jack's voice was tight.

"We're waiting for warrants now to search the house where Moustafa and Hashem live, and we hope that'll lead to a warrant for Protech." Agent Samson's voice was muffled by more background noise before he continued. "If Hamadi was recruiting students to engage in cyberterrorism, then the agency is likely going to want to proceed with caution. Maybe even hold off on making arrests until we ascertain who all the players are. We can't afford to not cut this snake off at the head."

Brynn glanced up from her phone, her jaw slack. "Agent Samson, the president is in Egypt, and we've potentially uncovered a plot threatening America's infrastructure."

"I understand what you're saying, Ms. Taylor, and I'll do my best to communicate the urgency of the matter, but you know how bureaucracy is."

She did know. Protocol was there to protect, but it also slowed down the process, and that was something they couldn't afford to do when seconds counted. Kekoa walked over, signaling to them that he had something.

"We appreciate everything you're doing, Brett. Let us know if you need anything from our side." Jack ended the call with Agent Samson, both men promising to keep the other updated. He turned to Kekoa. "What've you got?"

"Brah, you ready for this?"

Brynn read the uncertainty in Jack's expression. "Go ahead."

"You've seen the movie *Independence Day* with Will Smith, right?"

"Yes," Jack answered, and then Kekoa turned to her and she nodded.

"Okay, so you remember when the only way they could defeat the alien mother ship was to go up inside of it and infect it with a virus so they could disable the defense system and the world could attack the ships destroying cities around the earth?"

"Yes."

"That's what this virus is doing. Or trying to do." Kekoa took a breath. "My team's been working hard to counter the attacks, but like I said before, the more we fight, the more their defense grows. So I thought, what happens if we let them in?"

Brynn's heart froze, and her eyes slid to Jack.

"Please don't tell me you allowed them to breach a client's system?"

"No way, brah." Kekoa chuckled. "We created an alternative. Set up the defense to direct their attacks, and then we allowed them to breach that one so we could see what would happen."

Brynn released a breath and then shifted in her seat, carefully moving her injured arm into a more comfortable position. "What happened?"

"It was so weird. It was like a spider—a million little baby viruses released and it froze the system. We couldn't get in or stop it or anything."

"What does that mean, Kekoa? Real world now," Jack asked.

"I think these viruses are an indicator of what the attack is going to do. The diagrams of the electrical and mechanical systems are only one part. I spoke with Colonel Green, the commander of US Cyber Command at Fort Meade. They've been monitoring an increase in activity surrounding military installations overseas. It's not unusual because there's always some local group of rebels or political protesters who don't want the military in their country, but these installations are also noticing attempts being made to breach their systems."

*"There's always some . . . who don't want the military in their*

*country.*" Like the National Liberation Jihad not wanting Wadi Basaela in Egypt. What were they willing to do to stop the US?

Brynn sat forward. "What installations have noticed this?"

"Forward Operating Base, Abu Ghraib, and Sykes in Iraq." Kekoa ticked them off on his fingers. "Aludeid Air Base in Qatar, Kunsan Air Base in Korea. Even Fort Gordon in Georgia."

"Wait." Jack frowned. "Isn't that where the Army Cyber Command is?"

"Yep. Spoke with them an hour ago. Their CAC system went down a few days ago without cause."

"That they know of." Alarm coursed down her spine, causing goose bumps to line her arms. "If the common access card system goes down, does that disable someone from using it to access their computer systems or enter the facility?"

"It's supposed to, but no program is infallible." Kekoa's voice lowered. "That's another reason why I wanted to talk to you. The team is working hard and not giving up, but I don't know if we're going to have the testudo up in time. The unknowns of a potential attack put us at a disadvantage. My plan was to go shields up before the attack happens, but we'd need to know—"

"When," Jack said with a sigh. "Will you be able to have anything up?"

"Trying, brah." There was defeat in Kekoa's tone, but then his mood shifted. "I do have something else for you." He looked at her. "A picture of the driver who tried to run you down, B."

Brynn tucked her chin, unable to avoid the smile playing on her lips or the way Kekoa's use of Jack's nickname for her wriggled its way into her chest. When she dared to look up, she caught Jack watching her, his tender smile sending a thrill all the way down to her toes.

Kekoa pointed a remote at one of the television screens on the wall. A black-and-white video from a gas station with the camera angled at the pumps started playing. Brynn checked the date stamp in the corner.

"This was afterward."

A van that looked like the one Brynn remembered—probably gray, though it was hard to tell in a black-and-white video—pulled up to a pump and a man got out. His head moved up and down like he was listening to music as he began putting gas into the van. It was odd. The man wasn't fidgety, didn't appear nervous, and there was nothing in his demeanor to suggest he had just used his vehicle as a weapon. Maybe he wasn't the right person?

"He looks young," Brynn said, squinting. "Early twenties? Can you clear up the video or zoom in?"

"I can do better."

The video switched, and now they were staring at the man from the inside of the gas station as he paid. Even though the man kept his chin tucked, hoodie over his head, there was a moment when his eyes flashed to the camera—like he knew.

And so did Brynn. "It's him."

"Who?" Jack looked back at her.

"The guy who poisoned Joseph Ansari. Kekoa, can you pull up the video from that day?"

"Sure."

Kekoa set the videos side by side. He paused the footage from the poisoning at the only point offering the smallest glimpse of the man's profile, a shock of blond hair peeking out from beneath his coat hood, but it was enough for Brynn.

"It's the same guy."

"It's hard to tell," Jack said. "There's a better shot of the man in the video from the gas station." He looked at Kekoa. "Is it enough for facial recognition?"

"I thought you'd never ask, brah." Kekoa flexed his fingers and pointed to the television next to the bank of ones reporting news from across the globe.

It was barely after midnight here in the States, but across the Atlantic the world was waking up. Brynn noticed Al Jazeera was already reporting about President Allen's trip to Egypt and the ceremony dedicating Wadi Basaela happening later that day.

"Chad Bowman." Kekoa's voice moved her attention to the screen, where a Virginia driver's license photo of a Caucasian man with blond hair and blue eyes stared back at them. "He's twenty-two and doesn't have a criminal record. Not even a parking or speeding ticket."

"I would have said he was just a distracted driver if he hadn't swerved toward Brynn," Jack growled. "What else do you know about him?"

"He's a student at George—"

"George Mason University?" Brynn and Jack said at the same time.

"Yeah, this is his final year."

"Please don't tell me he's a computer science major." Brynn closed her eyes, knowing the answer before Kekoa spoke it.

"Nope. Computer engineering."

Brynn groaned and opened her eyes. "Can you pull up Chad Bowman's transcript? Something tells me he was or is a student of Professor Hamadi."

"Yep, four semesters." Kekoa nodded and then frowned. "Hmm, this is interesting. There's an article about him in the *Army Times*. He's one of two students who received an internship at"—Kekoa glanced up, his eyes moving between her and Jack—"US Cyber Command at Fort Meade."

Brynn's pulse skyrocketed. She stared at the image of Chad. He looked like an all-American kid, but her own words haunted her. *"Homegrown Violent Extremists don't look like the stereotypical terrorist . . . they can be your next-door neighbor, your child's teacher, or the teen who delivers your pizza. That's what makes them so dangerous—their ability to blend in and deceive you."*

"Jack, we need to find Chad Bowman right now."

# 32

**Interstate 295**
**12:56 AM Tuesday, January 20**

Fort Meade, Maryland, was forty-five minutes away from DC on a good day. In the middle of the night when the roads were packed with snow and ice . . . Jack glared at the Tahoe's GPS. Fifty-seven minutes. *An hour.*

A lot could happen in an hour. Forty-seven minutes was all it took from takeoff to the time Flight 11 plowed into the first tower. Flight 77, fifty-five minutes before barreling into the Pentagon. Ten minutes for two brothers in Boston to kill three and injure hundreds.

Sixty minutes could go by in a flash or feel like an eternity.

Jack didn't know which to pray for.

"Whoa," Brynn said, her right arm bracing against the passenger-side door as the Tahoe's tires hit a patch of ice.

"Sorry." Safety. Jack prayed they would safely get to Fort Meade in one piece and in time. He glanced over at Brynn, only to see her covering another yawn before adjusting her injured arm and wincing. "You should've stayed back at the office with Kekoa. Rested your arm."

Brynn snorted. "You're not serious, right?"

His eyes met hers. "You're hurt."

"You can worry about me when we're not trying to find a terrorist." She offered him a smile. A tired one that still had the power to make his stomach flip. "I'm fine."

Jack knew Brynn wouldn't let a broken elbow stand in the way of doing her job, and that scared him.

Brynn's phone beeped, shutting down his thoughts.

"It's from the FBI." She read the message, then exhaled sharply. "They went to Abu Hamadi's home. No one was there. Chad Bowman's house was empty too, but a neighbor said she saw him leave sometime around five or six this evening." She paused. "Or I guess it was last night now. Agents picked up Chad's mother from work and are questioning her."

"You still think he's headed for Fort Meade?"

"It makes sense." Brynn turned to him. "Chad has access to Fort Meade. No one would question his presence there and—"

Her words were interrupted by ringing. Jack hit the call button. "Hello, sir."

"I've contacted General Paul Chen, the commander of the National Security Agency, and updated him on the situation," Director Walsh said. "He and Colonel Green are now operating under FPCON Charlie."

Force Protection Condition Charlie was the second-to-highest level of alert for military installations, and Jack was glad they were taking precautions. "Would they know if Bowman is on post? Doesn't he have to show his ID to the guards?"

"Yes, but if he used another form of identification—"

"The fake IDs at Agnes's house," Brynn said. "He could be using a fake ID."

"Very likely," Walsh agreed. "They've got a current photo of Chad Bowman and have patrols looking for him now. And the local authorities have a BOLO out for him."

"And Abu Hamadi?" Brynn asked Walsh.

"Yes, both men," Walsh confirmed. "Our friends at Langley helped us out. Abu Hamadi is actually Mohammed Abu Shahir Hamadi, a follower of the NLJ who actively publishes teachings on their website and others about restoring the central beliefs of the Sunnis. It doesn't outright promote violence, but the veil is thin enough to read between the lines, and in the last twenty-four hours there's been a four hundred–percent increase in the website's traffic."

"Four hundred percent?" Jack glanced over at Brynn, her jaw tight with apprehension. "It sounds like they're preparing."

"Yawm alhisab." Walsh's Arabic accent was perfect. "Day of Reckoning."

"What about President Allen, sir?" Brynn shifted in her seat, and Jack could see she was getting fidgety. "Has she been notified? Is she returning to the States?"

"No," Walsh said, the aggravation apparent in his tone. "She's decided to stay and make a statement."

Again, Jack's and Brynn's eyes met. "Is that a good idea, sir? We have no idea how this plot is going to go down."

"That point was made along with many others, but President Allen believes her sudden departure would demonstrate fear on her part and on our country's part that could fuel the current political agenda."

"Which is?" Jack's frustration level was rising.

"Egypt's economy is fragile. The election of President Talaat coming out of the Arab Spring has revealed a growing number of supporters who wish to oust him too. It appears the National Liberation Jihad is coordinating the efforts, but there's evidence they're being supported by ISIS."

Jack's fingers tightened around the steering wheel. "All the more reason to pull the president out of the country and postpone operations at Wadi Basaela."

"How do you see this playing out, Ms. Taylor?"

Walsh's question must have caught Brynn off guard, because she jumped a little and then turned to Jack as though she were asking permission to speak.

"Ms. Taylor?"

"Sir, my analysis of the situation says we're facing an imminent attack." Her dire words were the sobering Jack needed. He turned his focus on the road, listening to Brynn continue.

"Our discovery of the items at Agnes Buchanan's house leads me to believe this attack isn't going to be so overt as flying planes into a building or detonating a bomb in a public location, though I'm not saying it's not possible. This amount of forethought requires a lot of planning and preparation, likely years' worth. The situation in Texas tells me others outside the NLJ are involved. Individuals or countries with an agenda against the US. Protech is a Russian-owned data mining company. Until Agent Samson confirms what kind of data Protech was interested in, I can only guess it's more likely the company was involved in data snooping."

"Data snooping?" Jack interrupted. "Is that different from mining?"

"Not really." Brynn shook her head. "Just another name for it. Basically, they're using computer systems to find inconsistencies or uncover patterns in systems. It's something cyberanalysts use to uncover clandestine information, especially in the military."

"Which is General Chen and Colonel Green's concern," Walsh said before his voice became muffled like he was talking to someone else. He exhaled into the phone. "Kekoa let me know an individual, someone named Rodney Lee, was just arrested at Fort Gordon trying to use a contractor's ID to enter the base. The FBI is involved."

"I hate the feeling of being a step behind," Jack said. "Sir, I don't know if waiting for the Feds is the right course of action here. *Our* job is to neutralize the threat."

"Agent Samson mentioned the FBI wanting to hold off on making any arrests because they know this involves more than just a couple of Middle Eastern immigrants in Texas. Russia's potentially involved. Kekoa mentioned installations overseas having increased activity." She looked at Jack. "We can assume the fertilizer in Guam is connected, which means we could be looking at a massive bomb attack on Andersen."

Jack swallowed at the thought. Garcia and Lyla were there to assist the military and the local police force. He thought about the explosion in Beirut. An explosion like that in Guam would be beyond devastating.

"Abu Hamadi fits the profile of a teacher. Without reading his work, I'd guess he's probably charismatic and persuasive. After all, his teaching has led to the conversion of an American citizen who definitely does not fit the profile of a radical extremist." Brynn inhaled. "I don't think Hamadi is calling the shots here. Someone else has the power, the money, and the motive—and we can't neutralize the threat until we find that person."

"Unfortunately, I agree." Walsh's tone was resolute. "General Chen and Colonel Green are expecting you. Stay safe."

"Yes, sir," Jack responded before Walsh ended the call. He'd heard that rush in his boss's voice before, and it caused Jack's adrenaline to spike.

Jack exited the Baltimore-Washington Parkway, feeling the tug of the steering wheel as the tires tried to find purchase on the slick asphalt. It had taken fifty-three minutes, and he knew exactly what to pray for . . . *that they weren't too late.*

# 33

Fort Meade, MD
1:14 AM, Tuesday, January 20

Word problem of the day: Arguing with one man armed with an automatic rifle will bring how many more men armed with automatic rifles? The answer, Brynn learned, was seven. Nope, her eyes swung to the SUV that pulled up to the gate for Fort Meade. Two more MPs got out, bringing the answer to nine.

Due to the increased FPCON level, the military police at the gate wouldn't allow Jack or Brynn onto the installation without military IDs. *And* Jack's maybe too anxious explanation ending with him mentioning something about a terrorist . . . well, Brynn was here, shivering in the cold as she tried to explain to Sergeant Schafer what he meant while the sergeant's finger played dangerously close to the trigger.

"Sir, if you could please contact Colonel Green, he'll explain why we're here."

Sergeant Schafer held up a finger and walked over to the officer questioning Jack. They conferred on something and another MP took out his cell phone, which Brynn hoped was to do as she'd suggested.

Brynn checked her watch. She appreciated that they were doing their jobs, but it meant she and Jack were being kept from doing theirs.

"Ma'am." Another MP, a young man—if she could even call him that—gestured back to the Tahoe. He had to have been fresh out of high school, without even the hint of a five-o'clock shadow coloring his fresh face. "You can wait in there so you stay warm."

"Thank you." She started for the Tahoe when she heard Sergeant Schafer call out. Turning, she saw him hurrying toward her with Jack at his side.

Her heart thundered in her chest. *Are we too late?* "What happened?"

"I'm to escort you and Mr. Hudson to the ICC," Sergeant Schafer said, not slowing down. "General Chen will meet us there."

Brynn's boots crunched in the snow as she jogged to keep up. The jostling sent sharp bursts of pain up her arm, causing her to tuck it closer to her body. "The ICC?"

"Integrated Cyber Center," Sergeant Schafer answered, pointing to his military police vehicle. "You'll ride with me."

There was no arguing, not that either she or Jack would've wasted another minute. They climbed into Sergeant Schafer's SUV, and less than five minutes later they were pulling up in front of a steel and cement building known as the Integrated Cyber Center. Spotlights lit up the facility and highlighted the flat-metal-disc architecture feature at the top of the building. It looked like the spaceship from *Independence Day*, reminding Brynn of Kekoa's cinematic explanation. *Fitting.*

The next thing she noticed was the number of armed security personnel surrounding the building. A sharp bark pulled her eyes to a German shepherd being led by his handler around the perimeter.

"Follow me."

Brynn and Jack followed Sergeant Schafer into the ICC. She couldn't help but feel a zing of excitement zip through her when she stepped inside the facility. It had been built to provide US spies and cyberwarriors, like Kekoa, a central location where the

NSA and Cyber Command could operate in the new era of war—cyberwarfare.

She was unable to keep from gawking at the expansive interior as they followed Sergeant Schafer. They made their way toward the center of the building, a dome, her feet freezing at the threshold of the gray carpet.

"The watch floor," she said in barely a whisper.

Jack looked at her, a wrinkle in his forehead. "What?"

Brynn eyed him, shocked. "You don't know about this place?"

"I mean, I've heard about the ICC, but . . ." He shrugged.

"Jack, this is the watch floor. Think of it like the fulcrum, only . . ." She let her eyes roam. Copper partially covered the walls of the circular space built like an auditorium. Theater-style television screens curved to fit the walls, which were known as "knowledge walls" because they enabled those inside to watch intelligence reports in real time. "Incredible."

"Hey." Jack played offended. "The fulcrum is state-of-the-art."

"And this is next level."

"Mr. Hudson, Ms. Taylor."

Sergeant Schafer stepped aside, revealing an Asian man with salt-and-pepper hair, wearing an Army uniform. He held out his hand.

"General Chen," he said, introducing himself. "I apologize for the misunderstanding at the gate. We're taking every precaution."

"We understand, sir." Brynn knew Jack was working to keep the frustration out of his voice. "Have any of the guards at the gates seen Chad Bowman or Abu Hamadi?"

"No." General Chen shook his head. "Colonel Green has the MPs on patrol. Photos of both subjects have been put out, and they're searching the area." His brow furrowed. "What makes you think they'd come here?"

Brynn and Jack gave the NSA commander a brief rundown of the events that had led them there. When they were finished, she noticed the lines in the general's face had deepened considerably.

"I appreciate the information, but I'm finding it hard to believe a college professor and his student have the ability to hack our system."

"Sir, as you already know, our country has been under attack by foreign hackers for years. Those behind the keyboard are getting younger and savvier than ever." Brynn forced as much confidence into her words as she could. "You have all the information we have. I think we have to assume that if they've come this far, they may have the knowledge and ability to do just that."

General Chen pressed his lips together, thinking for a minute before he gestured for them to follow him out of the watch floor and to the left of the building. Long marbled hallways led them to a room that required the general to slide a card through a scanner, plus enter a code. The secured door beeped.

Cool air washed over them as they entered a dark room lit only by the glow of computer screens lined up on long workstations set up in multiple rows that faced a twenty-foot wall covered by giant screens like in the watch floor. It reminded Brynn of SNAP's setup—only grander in scale. And instead of one computer genius, Brynn guessed there were at least thirty of them there—men and women, some in military uniforms, the others in civilian clothing.

A man in a Navy uniform turned, his eyes widening on General Chen. He shot up out of his chair. "Attention."

Everyone stood, their posture stiff.

"At ease," General Chen said, and everyone returned to their seats, their attention back on the computer screens in front of them. The general looked at Brynn. "As you probably know"—he gave her a look that was part tease, part putting her in her place—"our job here in the Cyber Command Room is to disrupt the *enemy's* computer network—not the other way around. However, we've already been working with Petty Officer Young. We're coordinating with his efforts to create a testudo—quite a brilliant idea, actually."

It wasn't until he mentioned the testudo that Brynn realized General Chen was talking about Kekoa when he referenced Petty Officer Young. Even though his military career was over, Kekoa would always carry his rank, and Brynn appreciated that.

"We've been monitoring our system and our installation." General Chen looked at them. "No one is—"

Darkness swallowed them, along with the whining sound of machines shutting down. Brynn froze, her eyes searching the blackness around them. "Jack . . ." she whispered.

A chill cut Jack to the core, and he was about to reach for his weapon when the lights slowly came to life, casting the room and everyone in it in a dim and eerie atmosphere.

General Chen scanned the room, all eyes on him. "Explain."

"Sir, we're running on generator power," a soldier called out.

"Looks like the snow might've taken out a power grid," another voice spoke up.

Brynn looked at Jack, her expression saying the same thing he was thinking—*it wasn't the snow*.

"All our systems are back online, sir," a woman in a Navy uniform answered. "We're running checks now."

"We're prepared for this kind of situation." General Chen turned to him and Brynn. "If a power outage occurs, our systems lock down as part of our security protocol. All the data monitored here is divided and watched from various secure locations around the country."

"Like Fort Gordon?" Jack said, unable to keep the skepticism from his voice. "Sir, what would happen if your security networks were attacked?"

"It wouldn't happen," General Chen responded, his voice as controlled as the expression on his face.

"Sir, you've spoken to Kekoa." Jack appreciated the general's confidence, but he needed more. "You have to consider the worst-case scenario. If your system were to be infected with these cyberviruses, what could happen?"

General Chen inhaled sharply, lips pursed. Jack could see the stress his question posed on the man responsible for defending US national security and, in doing so, preventing an attack. He gestured toward the door, and Jack and Brynn followed him out of the room.

Once they were outside, he turned on his booted heels. "If a virus were to enter our system as Petty Officer Taylor suggests, it would cause a blackout."

"Like a power grid going down?" Brynn asked.

"Similar. But remember that when the power goes out at home, so does your security system. Now imagine a burglar sitting outside your house ready and prepared to enter your property because they know your defense system is down."

Jack lifted an eyebrow at General Chen. "Like what happened right now?"

"Mr. Hudson, we have a battalion of military police officers armed and trained to defend this installation. Most homes aren't barricaded like our fortress."

"Maybe not, but, sir, this isn't a war on land or sea—this is cyberwar," Jack said. "If a blackout occurs, what kind of information will be at risk?"

"It's not the access to information." General Chen rocked on his heels. "Like I said before, we have programs in place that will lock down our information." He looked between them. "The bigger threat comes from not being able to communicate with our installations or them with us."

Jack thought about the installations all over the world and the United States that Kekoa had mentioned. "Once the system goes down, it will leave them vulnerable to physical attack."

"It would be catastrophic," General Chen said. "And not only for the US. This type of offense, if successful, has the ability to destroy entire countries."

The door to the Cyber Command Room opened, and an aide walked over to General Chen and spoke to him quietly. The general nodded and looked at Jack and Brynn. "I'm needed back inside, but you're welcome to remain in the watch floor. I shouldn't be long."

Back inside the vast auditorium, Jack's gaze locked on the overhead screen televising President Allen's arrival in Egypt the day before. Speakers were mounted on both sides of the screen. President Talaat smiled proudly from behind a desk. Both the American and Egyptian flags flanked him, along with American General Wayne Ellis, American Ambassador Christine Delrico, and Egyptian Field Marshal Ahmed Abdel Kader. Several other members of both the Egyptian and American military stood nearby as President Talaat proclaimed his excitement for the upcoming ceremony dedicating Wadi Basaela.

Jack paused to listen to the televised speech. "It is my great honor to welcome American President Margaret Allen," President Talaat said in well-practiced English. "This moment in our country's history will be remembered as we unify our countries' strengths. I must thank the many members of my cabinet who have worked tirelessly to make this moment happen. General Kader howa dahry—"

The screen glitched, cutting off the rest of the Egyptian president's speech and bringing Jack's focus back to the mission. A glitch. Was that all it would take?

He pulled out his cell phone and dialed Kekoa. After the second ring, he picked up. "Hey, brother, I know you're busy, but we're at the ICC on Meade, and their system shut down a few minutes ago. They're blaming it on the weather, but—"

"I know. We saw it happen. I've got a team looking into it, but so far we're not seeing anything to indicate a breach."

"Do you think that's how it's going to happen?" Jack stepped closer to Brynn so she could hear Kekoa's answer. "Will they cause a blackout and send in the virus?"

"It doesn't have to be that extreme," Kekoa said. "It's sad to admit, but it could literally take someone accessing the internet server."

Brynn's eyes grew round. "The uniforms, Jack. There was one for Virginia Telecom."

"How would they access that server?"

"Like most homes that have cable and internet, there's usually a closet with cable lines. But the ICC would likely have a lot of their lines buried into the ground . . . except." Jack heard typing. "Okay, yeah, the secure lines would be buried in the ground, but the ones for basic cable for television or phone lines would still be housed in a closet or, for the ICC, a room."

Jack indicated to Brynn that she should follow him. They left the auditorium and began walking down the hall. "Kekoa, is it possible for you to pull up the schematics of the ICC?"

"Uh . . . I mean, I could, but, brah, this is the NSA—they're like cybergods. You don't want to make them mad by hacking them."

"We'll worry about that after we stop Abu and Chad from going *Independence Day* on America."

Kekoa chuckled, but it sounded forced. "Okay, brah." He inhaled. "There's a hallway at the northwest corner of the ICC. Exit the main doors, take a left."

Jack continued to follow Kekoa's directions, trying hard to be inconspicuous to the military police patrolling the doorways.

"Okay, we're at a dead end." Jack looked down the hallways on either side of him. "Left or right?"

"What are you doing down here?"

Jack and Brynn turned around and found an MP eyeing them suspiciously.

"General Chen asked us to check on the utility closet where the cable and internet lines connect."

The young soldier looked Jack over before his eyes moved to Brynn. Jack was sure they were going to be marched back to General Chen, but the MP turned to his left. "This way."

Relief poured through him. "We appreciate your help."

"No problem." The MP shrugged. "I'm anxious to get this over with."

"Us too," Brynn said with a warm smile. "I'm sure it's been a long night."

"Yep." The soldier stopped and reached into his pocket for his ID card, which he passed over the pad by the door marked "Utilities." The light went from red to green, and the soldier reached for the door but not before Jack got a glimpse of the photo on his ID. The soldier holding the door was White, but the soldier on the badge was Black.

They were walking into a trap.

# 34

"Brynn, watch out!"

She barely had time to register Jack's warning before two bodies collided with hers, shoving her into the ICC utility room. Using her good hand, she caught herself on the wall and turned to see Jack throw a punch at the soldier who had just escorted them.

"Jack, what are you—"

The grunt of impact when Jack's fist met the MP's jaw made her clench her teeth. The soldier's head flew back before his body collapsed to the ground. He didn't move, and Brynn looked up at Jack.

"What's going on?"

Jack reached into the soldier's pocket and pulled out his ID. He looked it over before holding it out to Brynn. "I don't think this is Specialist Carter."

When Brynn saw the photo of the Black soldier, she glanced down at the Caucasian one on the ground. She felt sick. "If he's here . . . where's Specialist Carter?"

Jack's head turned to the side. He pressed a finger to his lips while his other hand pulled out his weapon. Holding her breath, Brynn fought to listen over the racing heartbeat in her ears. Voices.

Jack moved in the direction of the voices, but Brynn stopped him. She pointed to the body on the ground.

"Is he dead?" she whispered.

"No, just knocked out." He looked down at the man and then back up at her. "You should go get some help."

"What if there are more like him?" She looked down at her arm, angry with her injury. There was no way she'd be able to defend herself, and she wasn't likely going to be much help to Jack, but she felt better with him by her side.

"Stay behind me." Jack raised his weapon, aiming ahead of him, and started down the hall.

The hallway was narrow, but after a few feet, the space opened to reveal a wall of wires coiled and labeled. In front of them were two men with their backs turned. Brynn recognized the profile of Abu Hamadi, but the man next to him had dark hair and . . .

"Put your hands up where I can see them and back away from the wires." Jack's command startled both men, who looked over their shoulders, shock in their eyes at seeing her and Jack standing there. "Hands up where I can see them."

The man with dark hair turned around. It was Chad Bowman. He'd colored his blond hair black and wore a navy-blue jacket with the Virginia Telecom patch on it. A badge clipped to it said his name was Paul Anderson—a man no one was looking for.

Abu Hamadi turned slowly, arms lifted, and Brynn noticed the white collared shirt. The patch on his pocket also read *Virginia Telecom*. His eyes moved to an opened laptop in the corner. Brynn took a step toward it, but Hamadi lunged at her, the glint of metal catching her attention just before Jack's body smashed into Hamadi, taking him to the ground.

Brynn cried out when the crack of a gunshot echoed around them.

Her gaze flew to Chad, who remained rooted to the spot, his eyes fixed on the tangled bodies of Abu and Jack. Neither man moved. Heart racing, she wanted to check on Jack, but her attention went to the laptop. She needed to get to it.

Keeping an eye on Chad, she only had one shot at this. Taking a careful step, she moved toward the computer and grabbed it.

"Give that to me," Chad growled.

"No." Brynn lifted the computer over her head and slammed it to the ground, making the screen go black.

"Nooo!" Chad fell to his knees and scooped up the pieces of the computer. "No. No. No."

Brynn searched the ground for Jack's gun or the knife she'd seen in Abu's hand, not wanting to think where it might be. She needed a weapon.

Chad's eyes narrowed on her. "You think you stopped anything? You didn't." He rose, his blue eyes crazed as they locked on her. "Allah's will won't be stopped."

"You're an American—"

"No! I swear my allegiance to the National Liberation Jihad."

"It's over now, Chad." Brynn swallowed, her throat dry. "The computer is broken."

Chad reached into his jacket and pulled out a gun and pointed it at her. With his other hand, he pulled his cell phone from his back pocket and held it up. "You didn't really think we didn't have a backup plan, did you?" He started for her, and she stepped back until her back hit the wall. He came in close. "Let's go."

Brynn stood her ground. She wasn't going to leave Jack. "Where? What are you going to do?"

He twisted his hand holding the phone so she could see the screen with a timer on it. Garcia's words slammed into her. The car explosion—it had been detonated by a cell phone. Brynn's heart shuddered.

Seeing her realization curled Chad's lips into a wicked smile. "Now you see me. Now you know I'm serious."

From the corner of her eye, she saw Jack's foot move. Or at least she thought she did. Was he alive? Tears burned the backs of her eyes, and she prayed it was true. If he was alive, the last thing she wanted to do was draw attention to him in case Chad noticed and decided to use the gun.

"Where's the bomb?"

"Which one?" Chad laughed. Taking a backward step, he moved to an unzipped bag and pulled the opening wide. Brynn recognized what looked like a pressure cooker—or rather the improvised explosive device that would detonate with a push of the button on Chad's cell phone.

"What are you going to do?"

Chad slipped the gun back into his jacket pocket. When he pulled his hand out, it held a zip drive. *The virus.*

"There's more than one computer in this building." His thumb hovered over the button on his cell phone, and he grabbed her arm. "Let's go."

Brynn searched her brain for a way out of this, for a way to stop him, but doing so would put the lives of everyone around her in immediate danger. If she could misdirect him somehow, there might be a chance she could talk him out of this.

"If you try anything, it only takes a single press of the button," Chad whispered next to her ear, sending chills over her. "I don't have anything to lose, but all these soldiers . . . they have families."

Bile climbed her throat. Brynn wouldn't allow Chad to terrorize a single family if she could help it, but how was she going to stop him? They walked out of the utility closet and headed toward the Cyber Command Room.

Armed MPs still monitored the hallways, but their attention was focused on an incoming threat, not the one behind them.

"Unless you have a security card," Brynn said through gritted teeth, "there's no way we're getting into the Cyber Command Room."

"Don't worry about that." Chad reached into his pocket and pulled out a card. "Professor Hamadi taught me well."

"Too bad you couldn't have used that knowledge for good."

Chad shoved her purposely, aiming for her broken elbow. The jolt of sharp pain radiated throughout her body and caused her eyes to tear.

"You don't get to say what's good for mankind." Chad swiped the card across the pad, and the light switched red to green. "The good of America comes at the price of everyone else."

They entered the CCR, and their presence immediately drew stares. A man in a blue uniform stood, and Chad waved him back.

"Stand down, soldier."

"He's in the Air Force," Brynn ground out.

The airman remained standing, his eyes bouncing between them, concern in his eyes. "Who are you?"

Another soldier spoke up. "You don't belong in here."

Chad quickly pulled out the gun and thumbed the hammer back.

"This gives me access to whatever I want. And before any of you decide to play hero"—Chad held up his cell phone—"a single press of the button and there will be nothing left of you for your families to identify."

Both the airman's and the soldier's eyes widened, the room dead silent at Chad's threat. The airman looked at Brynn for confirmation, and she nodded, which pushed him back a step.

Chad eyed a female in blue camouflage. "I need your computer." She didn't move. He lifted up the detonator and leaned in closer to her. "Wills. Is that your name?"

The woman licked her lips, shoulders pulling back with a fortitude Brynn admired. "Petty Officer Second Class Jasmine Wills." She gave him a wicked side-eye. "You're going to have to kill me before I give you access to my computer."

Chad looked taken aback by Jasmine Wills's abrasiveness, and Brynn would've put a hundred bucks on the sassy woman if she wasn't fighting a man with a bomb.

"Don't worry. No need to get physical. I can end this right now." He held up the cell phone, thumb over the call button. "You're ready to die for your country? So am I."

"No!" Brynn held up her hand. "Stop. No one is going to die today, Chad."

\\\\\\\\\\

Someone was going to die today, and if Jack had his way, it would be Chad Bowman.

He shoved Abu Hamadi's body off of him and rolled to his side. A sharp pain pinched at his side, and when he looked down, he saw blood spreading from his abdomen. He pulled up his shirt and, holding his breath, pressed his fingers around the knife wound. He winced. He didn't think Hamadi had hit any organs, but the amount of blood said it was a little more serious than a scrape.

Jack pushed himself up and then closed his eyes as the room swam before him. *Brynn.*

Opening his eyes, Jack forced himself to fight through the nausea. He needed to get to Brynn. And the bombs. He didn't know if Brynn had noticed his attempt to let her know he was listening, and it had taken every ounce of self-control not to jump up and end Chad's life right there. But with a gun on Brynn, Jack hadn't been willing to take the chance.

He slowly rose to his feet and made his way out of the utility room, pausing only long enough to use Specialist Carter's plastic cuffs on the fake and still-unconscious imposter. Gaining his bearings, Jack started to jog down the hallway, hand pressed to his side. Ahead of him a military police officer was patrolling. He was about to call out to him when he thought of Specialist Carter.

*What if there are more imposters?*

"Hey!" The MP narrowed his eyes on Jack and then reached for his weapon. "Stop where you are."

Jack did as told and raised his hands even though the movement caused his wound to protest in pain. "My name is Jack Hudson. Radio General Chen and tell him we found Abu Hamadi and Chad Bowman."

Weapon still trained on Jack, the MP grabbed his radio and

repeated Jack's request. In less than a minute, a swarm of military police officers had surrounded Jack, including two very angry German shepherds whose snarls and excited yips sent a shudder through him. General Chen walked between them, his eyes landing on the blood at Jack's waist.

"What happened?"

"We found Abu Hamadi and Chad Bowman in the utility closet." Jack used his head to indicate the direction behind him, unwilling to lower his hands lest the dogs take that as the signal to eat him for dinner. "Hamadi is dead. Another man is handcuffed. He was wearing the uniform for a Specialist Carter and had his ID. Bowman took off with—"

"Ms. Taylor," General Chen said. "I know. He's holding her and my CCR hostage—threatening to set off a bomb."

Jack's heart dropped along with his hands. "Bombs, sir."

"Pardon?"

"They've set up bombs. Multiple. You need to call in an explosives team and clear the building now."

General Chen cursed as he started down the hall, barking orders to the soldiers nearby.

"Sir, the virus." Jack hurried after him. "If Chad Bowman sends that out—more lives are at stake."

"I know that," General Chen snapped, pausing outside the auditorium. "This kid is a couple slices short of a loaf, if you know what I mean. He mentioned something to Ms. Taylor about the timing being perfect, but we don't know what that means or how much time we have left."

"I want in there," Jack growled.

"Not happening," General Chen said. They stepped inside the auditorium. "Last thing I'm going to do is give him another body."

The inside of the massive space had shifted so much, Jack wasn't sure he was in the same place. The screens overhead were filled with multiple videos of newscasts, maps, and video transmissions from across the globe that were changing every minute.

His gaze stopped on the video footage that had him dizzy. It was a livestream inside the CCR. Brynn was sitting next to a computer workstation with Chad Bowman. The others in the room were lined up on the ground at the front of the room.

"Sistah's buying us time."

Jack turned around, grateful to see Kekoa standing there with a smile that was completely inappropriate for the moment but also completely reassuring. "It's good to see you, brother. How'd you get here so fast?"

Kekoa's smile shifted into an expression of misery. "Lyla called in a favor to a friend who happens to own a H175 Airbus. Dude used to be a stunt pilot—it was the scariest ten minutes of my life, brah." His eyes drifted to Jack's abdomen. "Looks like I'm not the only one lucky to be alive. Have you seen a medic?"

"I've got one on the way," General Chen said.

"I'll be okay." Jack grimaced. Everything would be okay. He just needed to get Brynn out of the hands of an American terrorist.

# 35

The sound of machines powering down cut into Chad's tirade, turning his attention to the computers and the screens against the wall. All were dark.

Brynn watched his harsh glare land on Petty Officer Wills. "What did you do?"

"Nothing." The woman crossed her arms in front of her. "It's a security protocol. The system shuts down."

Brynn searched the perimeter of the room and spotted several cameras. They knew Chad was there. Did that mean they had found Jack? A horrible sickness washed over her as she thought of him on the ground. The gunshot . . . was he dead?

A sudden silence filled the room, and everyone's eyes turned to the wide vent that was no longer humming or sending cool air into the room.

Chad snorted. "Heh. They realize this isn't a movie, right? Do they think they're going to sweat me out?"

"The air-conditioning is only on to keep the computer systems cool." The airman from earlier eyed Chad with a derisive smirk. "No computer system"—he lifted a hand toward their blank screens—"no air conditioner."

"I didn't want to do this, but I guess I need to make it clear that

I'm serious." He aimed the gun at Wills's head. She flinched, her jaw tightening, and Brynn saw fear flash in her eyes.

The others stopped moving, their silence revealing a new level of alarm.

A phone at the back of the room rang, and maybe it was exhaustion or the growing pain in her elbow, but Brynn's thoughts went straight to every hostage scene in a movie. Was the negotiator calling?

Chad then took the gun off Wills and used the tip to push Brynn toward the phone. "Answer it."

Brynn walked over and lifted the receiver from the hook. "Hello?"

"Ms. Taylor, this is General Chen. How are you?"

She glanced over at Chad. "I've had better days, sir."

"We're working to—"

"Tell him I want the screens on," Chad shouted. "I want to see what's happening outside this room."

"Tell him we can do that," General Chen said, having heard the demand. "We also have someone working in the air vent and—"

"And I want to see what's happening in Egypt." Chad pressed the gun to Brynn's temple. "Or I begin shooting hostages."

"D-did you hear that?" Brynn asked.

"We're turning it on now." And like magic, two of the screens on the wall lit up. "Did you hear what I said, Ms. Taylor?"

"Ye—"

Chad yanked the phone out of her hand. "That's enough."

Brynn stared up at the two television screens on the wall coming to life. One was the live newscast from Cairo, Egypt, showing the arrival of President Allen and her entourage, which included National Security Advisor Doug Martin. The other was video from a security camera positioned outside the CCR showing a growing number of armed military and federal police officers.

How many people were going to die tonight and in the days to come if Hamadi's virus infected the nation's security system?

How many other groups like the one in Texas were prepared and ready to attack?

Brynn looked at the faces of the security specialists lined up on the floor. They were a diverse group in age, gender, and race. How many of them were married, had children? She guessed every one of them came to work expecting today to be just like any other day.

She looked at Chad, trying to figure out how this all-American kid with blond hair and deep-blue eyes full of hope and optimism had transformed into a terrorist as dark as the black dye he used on his hair. What would make someone angry enough to fall prey to the ideology of hate?

"What did they promise you, Chad?" Brynn's voice nearly wavered. "Power? Money? Your name forever remembered as a martyr?"

"You don't know what you're talking about." He sneered.

"Don't I?" Brynn adjusted her arm, the throbbing almost intolerable at this point. "I created a whole program about people like you."

"People like me?"

Brynn recognized the flicker of rage in Chad's eyes and knew she had to tread carefully. He was still holding a gun, and she didn't want to guess how many IEDs were set to explode with the press of a button. But if she could keep him talking, maybe it would buy General Chen some time.

"A pawn in *their* agenda." She pointed at the screen showing protests happening in Egypt. "Do you think the National Liberation Jihad even knows your name?"

A second of surprise registered in Chad's eyes before they turned dark. "They know my name. Respect me. Appreciate my skills." A wicked smile filled his face. "The money is good too."

Nausea lodged in her throat. In the past two years, Brynn had studied dozens of homegrown terrorists across the globe. They all had something in common. An emptiness tucked into the recesses of their eyes.

Brynn was no longer looking at the neighbor kid next door who had been bullied or let down by some entitlement they believed was owed to them. Chad had pled allegiance to a terrorist organization, and that made him a traitor.

Chad's eyes kept moving to the screen. President Talaat's motorcade had arrived at Wadi Basaela. He stepped out, smiling and waving at a crowd of Egyptians swinging the American flag overhead.

"It's almost time."

"You don't want to do this, Chad. Think about your mom."

Brynn's words drew a sharp glare from Chad. "Don't speak about my mother."

*Ahh*, so he did have some soul left. "You want people to know who you are, remember you? That's easy to say when you won't be around to face the judgment. Your mom will be the one people talk about. She will be the one to carry the burden of your crime. Is that what you want?"

Chad paced the floor near her, and Brynn caught the eye of the airman who had spoken before. She read the message in his expression, and with as much emphasis as she could muster with her eyes, subtly shook her head. Any attempt to attack Chad held a risk of the bomb going off. She needed to talk him down or hope someone was coming up with a plan.

"You." Chad pointed to Jasmine Wills, who had stood up to him earlier. "Get over here."

Petty Officer Wills hesitated for a second before standing to her feet and walking toward him—shoulders back, chin up, and a fiery expression etched into the features of her dark skin.

Chad must've sensed her pluckiness, because he took a step back, putting Brynn in front of him, and pressed the gun into her spine as he held up the cell phone. "Sit."

Wills did and then folded her arms over her chest like a petulant child being asked to do their homework.

"Put in your passcode."

289

"I can't," Wills said, defiance in every syllable.

Chad's lips curled as he pulled the hammer back on the gun. "You think I won't kill her?"

"No." Wills shook her head, looking genuinely scared. She moved her hand slowly toward the steel box at the bottom of the screen. "I can't put my passcode into the computer because they are shut down. I told you it requires a manual key."

Rage colored Chad's face a deep magenta, and Brynn started to close her eyes, preparing for the gunshot. Words she'd long forgotten filled her mind. *"We have this hope as an anchor for the soul, firm and secure."* It was a verse her father used to speak to her when he'd remind her to anchor herself in God. Firm and secure, that's what Brynn wanted—to be anchored in the hope God would deliver her.

A loud knock against the metal door startled her. Their attention flashed to the security video and Brynn gasped. It was Jack. He was alive. Tears turned her vision blurry.

"You need a key." Jack's voice filled the room. He held up a thick black key. "You can't operate the computer system without it."

What was he doing? She wanted to scream at him to leave. Get out of the building and take everyone with him.

The muscles in Chad's cheek pulsed with anger before he released a breath. "If you try anything, I will press this button and kill everyone here."

Jack held up his hands and turned to show he wasn't armed. The movement gave Brynn her first glimpse of the bloodstain on his side.

The door unlocked and opened, and Jack stepped inside and closed the door behind him. An unexpected peace washed over her. Meeting Jack's soft gaze zeroed in on her, Brynn felt like God was giving her an anchor in the chaos she couldn't control.

Walking slowly to the computer where Petty Officer Wills sat, Jack kept his hands in full view as he inserted the key and turned it. A few seconds later the computer buzzed with electricity.

Jack turned to Chad. "Go ahead. Do what you have to do, but let her and the others go."

"Open your operating system." Chad ignored Jack, his gun now pointed on him. "Go sit with the others."

Jack hesitated for a second and then obeyed. Chad continued to feed instructions to Wills and then smiled. "There. Now go."

Chad set the gun on the table, his thumb still too close to the detonator button for Brynn to consider even going for the gun. He pulled out the zip drive.

"You can't do this, Chad." Her voice wavered. "Are you really willing to kill innocent people? Yourself?"

"I am devout." His simple answer chilled Brynn to the core. He grabbed the gun and aimed it at her. "Sit."

Brynn did.

"All you have to do is hit enter." Chad smiled. "Then it won't be me who kills innocent people. It will be you."

Brynn's heart dropped to her stomach. "What? I'm not going to do it."

Chad's eyes narrowed on her, and he walked to where Jack was and pointed the gun at his head. "Do it now or I will kill him."

Tears slid down Brynn's cheeks. "Jack?"

"It's okay, Brynn."

No, it wasn't okay. She wasn't going to let Chad make her choose. There had to be another way. But what?

Jack snapped his fingers, bringing her focus back to him. "Brynn, you don't have a choice."

She frowned. "I can't, Jack. I can't let him kill all those people."

Chad laughed. "Even if you don't, I will after I kill him and then you." He pointed to the screen where President Talaat smiled as the camera panned to the military generals next to him. "Allah has provided dahry."

Brynn blinked, a memory fighting to find space in her head.

Jack snapped again. "Don't think about them." His voice was measured. "Think about me. About the team working in this room."

It didn't make sense. Was he really asking her to choose him over . . . *Trust.* The word popped into her head, and she saw Jack's lips shift into a subtle smile.

"Fine, I'll do it."

Chad walked back over to her and pressed the gun into her temple. With a trembling finger and a quick prayer, Brynn pressed enter and held her breath.

Nothing happened. Or at least nothing she noticed. The moment felt a little anticlimactic. The screens shut off, and she feared she'd done something wrong until slowly, one by one, the monitors turned fuzzy and then . . . a skull and crossbones appeared.

"What?" Chad started to lean over the computer when his head snapped back before the echo of the gunshot reached Brynn's ears.

# 36

Ahmed sipped his tea and enjoyed a simple meal of falafel and fresh fruit as he looked over the Nile. The echoes of chants being shouted carried to his location only a few blocks away.

News of the protests was running on every network, including the one on the television in front of him, but it did not stop the American president from showing up. Ahmed ground his molars, remembering President Talaat explaining his country's unrest as misunderstanding. Placating the Americans at the cost of making his countrymen sound ignorant.

The broadcast switched, and suddenly he found himself staring at the smiling face of President Talaat welcoming President Margaret Allen to Egypt. The screen changed to video footage of Wadi Basaela. The American military installation would be dedicated in an hour with all the pomp and circumstance worthy of a pharaoh. Reporters praised President Talaat for bringing stability back to the country. It made Ahmed nauseous. Angry. He moved through the channels, his blood beginning to boil. Every channel the same. No one dared go against the president.

*Until today.*

He pulled out his uniform and inspected it, making sure all his ribbons were straight. He spotted a speck of dirt and brushed it

293

away before turning to his shoes. Servants had made sure the dust from earlier had been polished away.

Today he would look his best.

Ahmed changed into his uniform and left his office, stepping into the courtyard of the Ministry of Defense. The air was dense with dust, but a breeze carried the fragrance of jasmine planted nearby. A whipping noise pulled his attention toward the sky, where the red, white, and blue colors of the American flag waved in the wind over his country.

*His* country.

The Americans were the ignorant ones. Their belief that Egypt remained locked in the Old Kingdom and unable to compete with their technology would be their downfall. *No*, he thought to himself, *it will be their pride that destroys them.*

Stalking toward the street, he saw the black sedan weaving its way through the throngs of people and traffic. It stopped in front of Ahmed. The driver moved with fluidity, getting out and opening the back door to allow him in, then closing it and returning to the driver's seat without a minute lost.

Ahmed gazed out at the city and smiled to himself. His plan had come together beautifully, and everyone was in place. He imagined the armored vehicles and soldiers preparing to line the streets in preparation for the week's festivities welcoming the Americans to their new home. He chuckled to himself, as there would be no preparing for what he had in store for the country that betrayed his family.

The day of reckoning was upon them at last.

A blast shook the streets of Cairo, sending thick black clouds rolling into the sky as Egyptians fled the scene, unwilling to check on the charred remains of Field Marshal Ahmed Abdel Kader.

# 37

"He's dead?"

Brynn's question jerked Jack's attention from his computer to where she was sitting on the couch, watching the news reports coming out of Egypt.

Her forehead wrinkled, skepticism playing in her eyes. "From a random car explosion?"

"Faulty wiring?" Jack shrugged. "Heard they're investigating the NLJ."

"Mm-hmm." She rolled her eyes at him and then bit her lip. "When I told you what Chad said about dahry, it was only a hunch."

"One that paid off, Ms. Taylor." Director Walsh stepped out of his office. "President Talaat suspected someone within his circle of sharing classified information. The term *dahry* literally means *back*. As in having someone's back or support. President Talaat and Field Marshal Ahmed Abdel Kader served together in the military. Talaat never suspected Kader to be the one trying to oust him, but the GID found evidence he was meeting regularly with members of the NLJ and receiving financial support from them."

Jack stared at the news report showing the burnt remains of Field Marshal Kader's vehicle. "He was planning another coup."

"A choice that didn't turn out well for Mr. Kader or those working with him. President Talaat has expressed his deepest gratitude to you, Ms. Taylor, for your keen intuition, which gave him and the GID time to respond to the field marshal's treason."

"Sir, if Kekoa hadn't pulled that word off of Riad's laptop, I never would've known. The credit belongs to him." Her gaze lowered to the floor. "Though I do feel responsible for Riad's death."

"Don't." Walsh's voice was kind but direct, and she looked up. "Riad knew what the risks were when he joined the Mukhabarat. He did his job honorably and with courage. President Talaat is posthumously presenting Riad with Egypt's highest award, the Order of the Nile, for his service to President Talaat and his country."

Jack could see Riad's death was going to linger with Brynn for a while. The death of Chad Bowman too, even though it was a necessary casualty of the war on terrorism. After a military police officer took the shot from his position in the shut-down air vent, an Explosives Ordnance Disposal Team came in and cleared the building, disarming seven explosive devices. He hoped Brynn knew how valuable her role was in the operation as well.

"And the virus?" Brynn scratched at the edge of the lime-green fiberglass cast that went from her left shoulder to her wrist. "Did Kekoa's testudo work?"

Walsh chuckled and shook his head. "Kekoa is never going to let us live that down. His testudo wasn't foolproof, but it did block quite a lot. Since we were ready for the attack, Kekoa and cryptologists and cryptanalysts were able to go on the offensive. For every viral attack, they countered with a tracer that's led to multiple cells here in the States and overseas."

"Like Texas and Guam." Jack folded his arms over his chest. "And Fort Gordon."

"We do have a bit of a happy ending there." Walsh unclipped his cell phone from his belt and tapped the screen. "They arrested Rodney Lee, the man who tried to enter the post illegally, and discovered he and his wife were part of a human trafficking ring.

They found a Nigerian girl there, Chinara Okoye, and evidence there were others smuggled into the country for forced labor. She's with a foster family right now until Child Protective Services and ICE work something out."

Brynn shook her head. "Poor girl."

"Hey." Jack reached for Brynn's hand. "At least she has a chance now. Hope."

"Ms. Taylor, your humility and compassion are admirable traits. Ones I look for in new team members." Walsh pushed up his glasses. "Have you made a decision?"

Jack's heart thumped in his chest. Director Walsh had spoken with him this morning about offering Brynn a position on the team. The last thing he wanted to do was put pressure on her, and he hated to admit that part of his heart still hadn't recovered from the last time she had to choose. But looking down at their intertwined fingers, Jack trusted God had brought her back into his life at the right time, and no matter what decision she made, they would figure it out. Together.

"I appreciate the offer, sir. As you know, I spoke with President Allen this morning and explained the details of the Diplomatic Intra-Agency Cooperation program. She's scheduling a meeting with CIA Director Thompson, Director Peterson, and National Security Advisor Doug Martin to go over the idea of making the DI-AC program permanent. President Talaat has even requested hosting the DI-AC program in Egypt next year."

"Sounds promising." Director Walsh raised his eyebrows. "So you'll be staying in the DC area?"

Brynn's gaze fastened on Jack's. "I think so."

"Good." Walsh clapped his hands together once. "I look forward to working with you in the future, Ms. Taylor." He twisted his wrist and checked the time. "You two should probably leave now if you hope to find any food left."

Jack laughed. "I'm not sure it's appropriate for the host to eat all the food before his guests."

"Does Kekoa know that?" Walsh grinned. "You two have fun and let me know how Kekoa likes his housewarming gift."

\\\\\\\\\\\

Brynn watched pedestrians taking advantage of the clear blue skies and the late-afternoon sun shining down on the snow, making it sparkle like a million tiny diamonds. People walking dogs, jogging, children enjoying the snow. All of them unaware of how close the US had come to another terrorist attack.

Jack reached over, his hand finding a spot on her shoulder knotted with stress. His fingers worked on the muscles. "You okay?"

She sighed. "Yeah. The last week has felt like a blur, almost like it wasn't real."

"But it was."

"Yeah, it's just . . . well, Field Marshal Kader and Chad Bowman are completely different. I've spent nearly a decade studying homegrown terrorism, yet the unpredictability is scary. What makes a person wake up in the morning and decide they're going to subscribe to a doctrine of hate? No matter what Chad Bowman went through in his life, it's hard to understand why he gave in."

"He made a choice, B. Chad Bowman decided to go after you because he'd allowed hate to fill him." Jack's knuckles brushed against the skin along her neck, the tickle raising goose bumps. "Look at everything you've gone through. If anyone has a reason to let hate rule their heart, it's you. But you made a choice to do good—to use your life to love others so much you're willing to lay down your life for them. You're a lot like your dad."

Emotion curled into a tight ball in her throat.

"He ran into the chaos to protect others." Jack's thumb caught a tear on her cheek. "Much to my displeasure, you do the same thing. You're brave and kind and fiercely independent, and I wouldn't change a single thing about you."

Brynn swiped at another tear. "You forgot to mention my stellar inflatable-sword skills."

"Oh, how could I forget, princess."

Jack's voice was husky as he brought her hand to his lips and kissed her fingers. Brynn longed to feel his arms around her and to kiss him. *When will I get to feel his lips on mine?* The last twenty-four hours had consisted of reports, debriefings, *sleep.* Brynn was ready for some alone time with Jack, but Kekoa insisted they celebrate a successful mission at his new place, and well, the giant Hawaiian teddy bear of a man was hard to say no to.

"Wow, maybe I should reconsider Walsh's offer." Brynn stared up at the glass-and-steel luxury apartment building in the middle of Arlington. She looked at Jack suspiciously. "You did this on purpose."

Jack held the door open for her, looking confused. "What?"

"You knew I'd try to recruit Kekoa, so you upped your game by giving him a ginormous raise for this apartment."

"You caught me," Jack joked, pressing the elevator button for the eleventh floor.

Brynn stepped into the elevator. "Seriously?"

"Lyla found him the apartment. She has—"

"Connections, I know," Brynn finished for him. "Maybe she'll hook me up with one of those amazing showerheads you have in your office."

When the elevator doors opened, Brynn and Jack stepped out and started down the hall, where the thumping beat of drums and tinny ukulele music echoed.

"B, before we go in there, we should probably talk about us." He paused, and she read the hesitancy in his eyes. He reached for her hand, their fingers intertwining. His eyes moved in the direction of the music. "They're kind of nosy."

Brynn couldn't help smiling. "What do you want to tell them?"

"You tell me." Jack narrowed his eyes on her playfully as he pulled her closer. Being careful of her cast, he moved his hands to her waist, sending a thrill of attraction zipping through her. "The choice is yours, princess."

"I don't know, Hudson." She slipped her hand around his neck, her fingers combing through his hair. Tipping her chin up so her lips barely brushed his chin, she smiled. "I've been known to make bad decisions."

"Okay, if this is going to be a thing—"

"Kekoa." Brynn closed her eyes with a groan that turned into a laugh. She looked back at the Hawaiian standing there holding a spatula in his hand and wearing the brightest aloha shirt she'd ever seen.

Jack ran a hand down his face. "Brother, this"—he gestured between them—"is never going to be a *thing* if you keep interrupting. And second, that is the loudest aloha shirt I have ever seen." Jack leaned forward, squinting. "Are those fish?"

Kekoa looked down at his shirt. "They're not fish. They're spam musubis."

"Spam what?" Jack asked.

"Very funny, brah." Kekoa started to wave them into his apartment when the door next to his opened. "Oh." He straightened. "Excuse me."

His neighbor, a woman with long brown hair and almond-shaped eyes, tried to step around Kekoa, but for every step she took, Kekoa awkwardly stepped in the same direction, essentially blocking her from getting around him.

"Sorry." He offered a bashful smile. "I'm Kekoa Young, your new neighbor, and I'm having a little wintertime luau. We got plenty of food if you want to come in."

The woman tucked a piece of hair behind her ear, dark chocolate eyes observing Jack and Brynn before looking back up at Kekoa. "Thanks, but I have plans tonight."

"Oh, okay." Kekoa's chin tipped downward for a second before his cheeks pulled back into that toothy smile. "Next time, yeah?"

"Uh, sure. Maybe." The woman slid around Kekoa and gave Jack and Brynn a tight smile.

"Um, neighbor," Kekoa called over their heads, and Brynn's eyes grew wide. "I didn't get your name."

The woman turned and offered the faintest smile. "Elinor."

"Elinor. Elinor." Kekoa repeated the name until Jack pushed him back inside his apartment.

"Ooh, I think Kekoa has a crush on his neighbor," Brynn whispered to Jack. "Extra points for Lyla."

Jack shook his head. "I hope not."

"I can't believe you got to eat breakfast with the president." Lyla carried two cups with orange liquid in them. She handed one to Brynn. "It's something called POG juice . . . nonalcoholic."

"Thank you." She took the glass. "When did you get back?"

"I have no idea." Lyla shook her head. "Don't even know what day it is."

"We got in this morning," Garcia said before fixing his attention on Kekoa. "Now can we eat?"

"Are you ready for some ono grindz?"

"If it's food and it's good, then yes," Jack answered Kekoa.

Brynn took in Kekoa's new place. Light oak floors contrasted with the sleek mahogany wood paneling that matched the modern cabinets. A stone fireplace was topped with a giant television facing a sectional. Mounted above it was a two-toned wood surfboard that Brynn would've complimented Lyla on if she wasn't staring at the *Independence Day* movie posters taped to the wall around it.

"Nice touch, huh?" Lyla smirked. "Couldn't resist."

"It's perfect." Brynn was about to put her purse down on the couch but jumped back when she saw something furry in the corner staring at her. "What is that?"

"That's Director Walsh's attempt at humor." Garcia picked up the stuffed rat. "Bought Kekoa this couch but wanted to make him feel at home."

"Not funny," Kekoa yelled over at them before his whole body shuddered. "Brah, I still have nightmares of tiny little feet running across the floor."

"I assure you, there are no rats in this place," Lyla said, lifting her glass. "Only the best for you, brahhhh."

Everyone laughed before Kekoa called them to eat. The kalbi ribs and shoyu chicken were *ono*. So delicious and Brynn ate way too much. When they were done eating, she slipped out onto the balcony and was delighted to see Lyla had thought of everything. A cushioned outdoor sectional was placed around an electric firepit that was already on.

Brynn sank into the cushions and grabbed a heavy knit blanket. Staring up at the stars, she could feel her body relax. Jack's words hadn't left her. Terrorists had irrevocably changed her life, and Brynn had used her obsession to stop them as a means to bring control back to her life. Stability. But the peace that she felt inside the Cyber Command Room hadn't left her, nor had her father's words about being anchored in the One who brings peace in the midst of the storm, and she was grateful. Grateful she could surrender control and relax in the hope only God could offer.

The sound of the sliding doors pulled her attention to Jack. "Can I join you?"

"Of course." She pulled the blanket to the side so he could snuggle in next to her before she rested her head in the crook of his shoulder. "Is Kekoa watching?"

"I think he's explaining the difference between Texas barbecue and Hawaiian barbecue to Garcia. It could be a while."

"Good." Brynn twisted around and looked into Jack's eyes. "We should take advantage of the distraction."

A slow smile spread over Jack's lips. Shifting just enough to bring Brynn close, he traced the edge of her jaw with his lips, sending a thousand delicious chills of delight marching over her skin. She ran her fingers over his beard, letting them slide through his hair until they found their place at the back of his neck.

His shoulder muscles bunched beneath her touch as he leaned in, the warmth of his breath hovering over her lips until finally—*finally*—they found hers. His kiss started tender and exploring, and Brynn could feel herself melting into it. Passion taking over as they made up for eight years.

When he finally pulled back, the smile on his lips, the desire in his eyes made her blush. "Let's not wait so long before we do that again."

Brynn matched his smile. "Kiss me, Hudson."

"As you wish."

Read On for a
Sneak Peek at the Next
**SNAP Agency Adventure**

"Death has no sting."

*Depends on how you kill someone.* He took a quick glance at the cedar beams crisscrossing the white plaster barrel ceiling, half expecting lightning to strike him dead. But if God was going to punish him for his blasphemy, it would've happened the second he'd walked into the church.

The hard wood of the pew dug into his back, a painful reminder of his childhood. Stained-glass windows lined the sides of the church just like in the one his mother used to drag him to when she'd pray for his soul. But no amount of begging had kept him from being swept into a life of power, money, and—his eyes landed on the simple wooden urn—death.

In the middle of two large vases of flowers and three floral wreaths was a photo of Arthur Conway. According to the small piece of cardstock in his hand, Arthur was "eighty-five, a loving grandfather, father, and husband to Michiko. A physicist from UC Berkeley, Arthur 'Artie' Conway played an integral role in the progress of science."

The *progress* of science.

He rubbed a hand over his mouth, covering the scoff before it could draw attention to him. An understatement if there ever was one. Arthur Conway did more than that, and as of a few weeks ago was healthy aside from the dementia that had overtaken his mind in the last six months. Or so it seemed.

The modest oak box didn't only hold the cremated remains of Arthur Conway. It held a piece of the puzzle in a decades-old game of power.

The pastor continued the eulogy, his words echoing off the gray stone walls of the Eighth Street Church and cushioned only by the occasional sniffle coming from the family sitting four rows in front of him.

Of the three people sitting there, only one truly interested him.

Elinor Mitchell. Twenty-nine. Her shoulder-length hair was twisted into an elegant knot at the base of her neck. Somewhere nearby an air-conditioning vent blew cool air, causing the loose pieces of her chocolate-brown hair to dance along her neckline. She'd chosen a charcoal-gray pencil skirt and a deep burgundy silk blouse instead of the traditional black attire. Smart choice. The jewel tone highlighted her creamy complexion and made her green eyes sparkle like emeralds. Or was that the tears?

"How long do these things last?"

The whispered question came from the woman sitting next to him. The strong scent of her perfume was more suited for a night on the town, but who was he to complain. He sent her a look that made her lips purse into a coy smile. Maybe he'd treat her to dinner—a small distraction in the plan wouldn't hurt.

He scanned those in attendance as the pastor continued to offer platitudes of comfort to the family. He was at least several decades younger than most, putting them as either neighbors or friends of Arthur, but there were a few who fueled his curiosity. He'd overheard two women sitting in the second row talking about returning to Jefferson Oaks, the assisted living facility where Arthur Conway had resided. Probably his nurses. There were two couples who spent several minutes chatting with Elinor's parents before the service started. Friends?

The pipe organ bellowed, and the people rose to their feet. He took the opportunity to shoot a quick glance behind him before he stood. His eyes stopped on a man across the aisle two rows back. He stood at the edge of the row, hands clasped in front of him as he sang. Besides the custom-tailored suit, nothing stood out to him and yet . . .

Picking up a white book from the back of the pew, he carelessly flipped it open. His eyes drifted to the domed fixture in the upper corner of the church ceiling. A camera. There was another across from it and a few, he'd noticed, at the entrance of the church. It wouldn't take much to hack into the system and download the footage. Find out who the man was and why it mattered.

At the moment, the only person he should be interested in was Elinor.

Her shoulders slumped just slightly as she dabbed a tissue to the corner of her eyes. When she had walked in with her parents, he sensed hesitation but didn't know what to read into it. Was it due to losing someone she loved . . . or was it something else?

The music slowed to a stop, bringing everyone back to their seats. He gave his watch a subtle glance. They would be waiting for his call.

As the pastor invited friends up to speak about the departed, he kept his ears attuned to anything that might be a clue. Unfortunately, when they were done, the only thing he learned was not to go fishing without a charged cell phone battery. Useless.

Agitation began to unfurl in his chest. Time was wasting and—

"Elinor" —the pastor's introduction interrupted his thoughts— "Arthur Conway's granddaughter, would like to say a few words on her family's behalf."

He sat up straighter, attention glued to the woman as she rose from her seat and walked to the podium next to the pastor. He gave her an encouraging nod before stepping aside.

Rolling back her shoulders, Elinor unfolded a piece of paper and looked out over the church. She seemed to be making eye contact with everyone, and he forced himself not to shrink back as her gaze moved past him. Or had it paused? Curious?

A trickle of sweat slipped down his spine just as she started to speak.

"On behalf of my family, we want to thank you all for coming today. My grandfather was a well-lived man. He always told me that. Said that when his time came, he'd be ready. I didn't realize I wouldn't be." She sniffled. "I spent many years in the care of my grandfather, and while my fifteen-year-old self didn't appreciate the many, many, *many* hours of nuclear theory stories, I did learn to appreciate his sense of humor, generous spirit, and faith. And oddly, I even learned to appreciate disco."

A few chuckles spread through the church. Even from this distance, her natural beauty stood out. Unlike the woman who'd edged closer to him in the last several minutes, bringing his gaze to her skirt that was hiked a little too high on her long legs. When would women realize the thrill was in the chase?

"I felt like he could explain almost anything to me. Almost. There were many times he'd start a story and I would get lost in the magnitude of his brilliance. But he never stopped trying to explain—" Her voice caught. She swallowed, pressing the curled edges of the paper flat. "He encouraged my curiosity, encouraged me to keep asking questions. So you can imagine how it felt to realize the very person I should've been asking questions of was my very own grandfather." She gave a half smile. "There was so much I didn't know about him, but it's like he's still encouraging me to learn."

The polished wood beneath him creaked, and he realized he'd begun leaning forward. Anxious to find out what Arthur Conway wanted his granddaughter to know about him.

"I took for granted the time I had with my grandfather, but I'm blessed to know that he gifted me a way to read his words. It gives me comfort that every time I open one of his notebooks, it feels like he's right there with me, sparking my curiosity and teaching me."

His attention snagged on Elinor's words. *Notebooks.* There were more? His agitation swiftly morphed into anxious energy. He pressed his palm to his knee to keep it from bouncing.

Constance and Peter Mitchell, Elinor's parents, shifted. Were they uncomfortable with Elinor's emotional words? What he knew of them, they spent very little time in the US and even less time with their only daughter. It made sense that any of Arthur's belongings would be passed to Elinor. He'd basically raised her.

And yet Arthur seemed to have kept some things from his granddaughter. She'd only recently learned he worked at Los Alamos National Labs, one of the most top-secret facilities in the US, when she'd found a photo stashed away in a notebook.

What else would she find in those notebooks? What had Arthur left behind for her to learn? The information he'd known . . . the role he'd played . . . he had to have known the danger it presented to himself and his loved ones. Did Arthur Conway knowingly put his granddaughter's life in jeopardy?

He would find out.

*Bzzt. Bzzt.*

His cell phone vibrated in his coat pocket, and he pulled it out. It was a message with a photo of a dark-skinned Middle Eastern man with thick black hair hanging low over his eyes. Four words were typed beneath it:

The ISA is here.

It didn't surprise him that Iran was now involved. It ticked him off. In Elinor's zealous excitement, she shared her discovery with the world. A deadly mistake?

It was for Ralph Bouchard.

A week ago, Ralph's body had been discovered, and an investigation was already underway. Elinor had unknowingly fired the gunshot that started the race. A deadly one. It wouldn't be long before they learned about Elinor.

She shared in Arthur Conway's brilliance. Graduating from Georgia Tech summa cum laude was enough to warrant the interest of major aerospace companies like Lockheed Martin and Raytheon, but in the end she chose Lepley Dynamics.

And in the last few years, her work had secured several multi-million-dollar contracts that made her very valuable to the company . . . but would that keep her alive?

He eyed his target. If she had the answers—maybe. Otherwise, Elinor was the one in danger of feeling death's sting next.

Elinor finished speaking and returned to her seat as the pastor offered a concluding prayer. Elinor and her parents stood as the fifty or so guests formed a line to offer their condolences. If he left now, it could elicit unwanted attention. He stood, swinging a quick glance over his shoulder. The man from earlier was gone. *Interesting.*

He took his place next to the woman, and leaning over her shoulder, he whispered, "They say death makes you take stock of what's most important in life."

She barely glanced back. "That's true."

Oh, now she was playing the game? He stepped closer to her, nearly choking on her perfume. "Do you know what's important to me?"

The shudder that raced down her body was almost imperceptible, but from this angle he caught the edge of her full lips pull into a smile for a second. They stepped forward with the line and were only a few feet away from Elinor and her family.

"Are you going to keep me waiting?"

He pressed his hand to the small of her back and leaned in. "Twenty-four ounces of melt-in-your-mouth beef at Ted's."

His phone vibrated in his pocket, and he pulled it out just enough to see the new message. He stared at Elinor's photo before his gaze slipped to the price beneath her name. Jaw clenching, he slid the phone back into his pocket.

"Are you asking me—"

"Another time."

He kept his voice low, eyes fixed on Elinor. He could see the shadow beneath her eyes. The brave attempt to smile and assure those talking with her about her grandfather that she would be okay. She had no idea she'd just become a pawn in the game of life.

They had started with five. Two were dead, but now . . . with Elinor . . . there were four, again.

Approaching her, he knew it wouldn't take much. A little pressure, a little discomfort, and people were quick to talk. Quick to reveal their deepest secrets. And if Elinor had one, he'd find out.

# ACKNOWLEDGMENTS

Thank you, Lord, for the gift and privilege to be able to write stories. You meet me every single day in my weakness and shine your gift through words that can hardly be attributed to me. May your Light shine through my stories always.

G.I. Joe, I wouldn't be able to do this without your support and love. Thanks for letting me bounce ideas off you even if it "could never happen." And to my kids, thanks for listening to me go on and on and on about my writing issues and waiting until I'm not looking to roll your eyes. And if you're reading this, then you'll know that I secretly like to go on and on and on about my stories just to see how long you'll let me. And because I don't think you'll read this far, if you do, I'll give you twenty dollars!

Tamela Hancock-Murray—I'm so grateful to be a Tamelite. You're the best agent!

Vicki Crumpton and the entire team at Revell—saying thank you doesn't feel adequate enough for all the ways you make me shine as an author. I'm blessed to be part of such an amazing publishing family.

Emilie and Christen—thank you for your constant encouragement and friendship. This writing journey wouldn't be the same without having best writing friends like you.

Shady—I owe you big-time for helping me keep this story authentic. Thank you for answering every question I had about names, language, and making sure I represented Egypt accurately.

It truly takes a tribe to support an author, and I have the very best. Crissy, Joy, and Amy—Charlie's Angels don't have anything on you. Diana—thank you for being quick to encourage me on the days when writing was hard.

And as always, to my Book Battalion and readers—I love what I do because of you. Thank you for being the very best part of this journey!

**Natalie Walters** is the author of *Living Lies*, *Deadly Deceit*, and *Silent Shadows*. A military wife of twenty-two years, she currently resides in Hawaii with her soldier husband and their three kids. She writes full-time and has been published in *Proverbs 31* magazine and has blogged for *Guideposts* online. In addition to balancing life as a military spouse, mom, and writer, she loves connecting on social media, sharing her love of books, cooking, and traveling. Natalie comes from a long line of military and law enforcement veterans and is passionate about supporting them through volunteer work, races, and writing stories that affirm no one is defined by their past. Learn more at www.nataliewalterswriter.com.

# Welcome to the little town of Walton, Georgia, where everybody knows your name— but no one knows your secret.

# Connect with
# NATALIE WALTERS

Find Natalie online at **NatalieWaltersWriter.com** to sign up for her newsletter and keep up to date on book releases and events.

Follow Natalie on social media at